C0-AWB-979

French Instrumental Music Between the Revolutions

(1789-1830)

March 26, 1906 — December 31, 1983

French
Instrumental Music
Between the
Revolutions
(1789-1830)

by
BORIS SCHWARZ

DA CAPO PRESS · NEW YORK · 1987

Library of Congress Cataloging in Publication Data

Schwarz, Boris, 1906-
  French instrumental music between the revolutions
1789-1830)

  (Da capo Press music series)
  Originally presented as the author's thesis (Ph. D.)—
Columbia University, 1950.
  Bibliography: p.
  Includes index.
  1. Instrumental music—France—19th century—History
and criticism. 2. Instrumental music—France—18th
century—History and criticism. I. Title.
ML497.S38   1987   780'.944   86-29354
ISBN 0-306-79545-0

This Da Capo Press edition of *French Instrumental Music Between the Revolutions (1789-1830)* was originally a Columbia University doctoral dissertation completed in 1950. It is published now by arrangement with the author, who edited, expanded, and updated the manuscript for the present edition.

Copyright © 1987 by Patricia Schwarz

Published by Da Capo Press, Inc.
A Subsidiary of Plenum Publishing Corporation
233 Spring Street, New York, N.Y. 10013

All Rights Reserved

Manufactured in the United States of America

LIBRARY
ALMA COLLEGE
ALMA, MICHIGAN

Publisher's Preface

This volume reflects the thinking and research of its author at two key points in his long career in music: at the start of his academic life in the late 1940s, as he was completing the doctorate in musicology at Columbia University while in the first of what would be three-and-a-half decades on the Queens College music faculty; and at the end, in the 1980s, during his last, amazingly productive years — nominally an emeritus professor and retired conductor/violinist but in fact a prodigious author and critic, much-in-demand juror in international competitions, always-on-call advisor and trouble-shooter for aspiring young performers, frequent lecturer and guest professor, distinguished participant at scholarly conferences . . . and more.

In these latter years Boris Schwarz found time to revise, expand, and update his Columbia dissertation — a landmark study of French instrumental music between 1789 and 1830 — into a manuscript ready for publication by Da Capo Press. But his untimely death on New Year's Eve 1983, a shocking loss to the international music community, interrupted work on the book in the final stages of its preparation. An accumulation of last-minute footnotes, end-notes, bibliography, and other scholarly addenda remained incomplete and uncollated in Boris's files at home, and the fate of *French Instrumental Music* seemed in doubt. Fortunately, Robert Schwarz, the author's son and a writer and music critic in his own right, jumped to the rescue, determined to bring this work into publishable form. It was Rob's energetic, wise, and diligent collaboration in pulling all the pieces together that, ultimately, made the book a reality.

The editorial and production staff at Da Capo wish to express our deep appreciation to Rob — and also to Patty Schwarz, who undertook the first painful foray into Boris's desk after his death. We take pride in offering this book as a tribute to the memory of a superb scholar and splendid human being.

— BEA FRIEDLAND

Contents

Introduction

This book deals with a rather neglected phase of French music. While there are numerous monographs on French instrumental music of the *Ancien Régime,* while there is abundant material on Hector Berlioz, we find hardly any serious discussion of French instrumental music composed during the intervening decades, between 1789 and 1830. The attention of historians dealing with that period seems to be entirely absorbed by the French opera, to the exclusion of almost all other fields of musical endeavor.

"Let us not speak of instrumental music: it did not exist in France at that time," is the verdict of Julien Tiersot,[1] and his confreres appear to corroborate this controversial statement by their almost complete silence on the subject. Yet nothing could be further from the truth. Certainly, the symphonies by Méhul, Cherubini, and Herold, the violin concertos by Rode, Kreutzer, and Baillot, the piano works by Méhul and Boieldieu, the chamber music of Cherubini, Reicha, and Onslow, and — last but not least — the numerous operatic overtures of that period deserve better than Tiersot's sweeping dismissal or the casual references to be found in music histories and encyclopedias. Perhaps one might object to the inclusion of operatic overtures which, strictly speaking, do not belong in the field of instrumental music; yet, they were widely performed as independent concert pieces and undoubtedly influenced the evolution of 19th-century orchestral music.

It must be admitted that none of these composers achieved universal greatness; nevertheless they occupy a position of historic significance, for they prepared the path for their younger contemporaries and successors. Beethoven and Schubert, Mendelssohn and Schumann, Weber and Wagner, Berlioz and Franck, Chopin and Liszt, are all indebted to the pioneering zeal of the "revolutionary romanticists," that generation of French musicians whose formative years were spent under the impact of the Revolution of 1789. In fact, the roots of French musical Romanticism reach back into the revolutionary decade of the 1790's and beyond. Berlioz is the spiritual descendant of Lesueur and the revolutionary *style énorme*. "1830 is the offspring of 1789," as Tiersot expresses it succinctly. It is this inner link between the Revolutions which lends French musical Romanticism its unique characteristic.

The emergence of musical Romanticism in non-German countries belongs, in the opinion of the German musicologist, Ernst Bücken,[2] to the "densest jungles of human knowledge." This is due, in part, to the comparative apathy of French, British, and Italian scholars toward this subject. On the other hand, Austrian and German musicologists have explored the contribution of their countries with such zeal and thoroughness that we have come to consider musical Romanticism an almost exclusive Austro-German possession. Especially the all-important French contribution has remained unrecognized for too long. Only in the last few decades have we gained a somewhat clearer picture of pre-Romantic traits in French music of the late 18th and early 19th centuries, but much remains to be done to complement and integrate the isolated research of French scholars into a full-scale presentation of musical Romanticism in France.

To contribute toward a clearer understanding of the French role within musical Romanticism is one of the main objectives of this exploration. The influence of the lyric drama of the 1790's — the "terror" and "rescue" operas of the revolutionary decade — upon instrumental music is stressed.

This influence, noticeable not only in France but throughout Europe, is particularly evident in some of the works by Beethoven and Weber who adapted the sceno-dramatic style of the French opera to the concert stage. Another significant contribution was the emergence of the French violin concerto which remained a model genre for several generations. While less creative in the fields of the symphony and piano music, the French role was by no means negligible, especially with regard to the new pianoforte style. The intimate art of chamber music was somewhat alien to the French musical concepts of the period, and its main cultivators were therefore foreign-born musicians residing in Paris, like Cherubini and Reicha.

The instrumental style of the period was conditioned, to a certain extent, by the prevailing musical taste of the public, and this taste is reflected unmistakably in the concert programs. It was, therefore, found desirable to preface the detailed discussion of the music proper by a general description of concert life in Paris during the Revolution, the Empire, and the Restoration. This subject has received somewhat casual treatment by French historians, especially if compared to Brenet's thorough study of concert life during the *Ancien Régime*[3] or the various monographs dealing with the *Société des Concerts du Conservatoire*,[4] founded in 1828. The intervening forty years, however, were by no means uneventful; in fact, this *Société des Concerts* was, to a certain extent, merely a resuscitation of the "public exercises" of the *Conservatoire* orchestra which were a pillar of French musical culture between 1800 and 1815. Here, symphonies by Beethoven were performed with exploratory zeal and youthful intrepidity as early as 1807, and some of the contemporary French comments show deeper understanding of his genius than certain disparaging reviews originating in Leipzig and Vienna. After the founding of the *Société des Concerts du Conservatoire*, no city in the world devoted itself more completely to the cult of Beethoven than Paris; but it is well to remember that the propellent spirit orginated in the early years of the century.

PART I

Musical Life in Paris

CHAPTER 1

Musical Life in Paris During the Revolution and the Napoleonic Regime

> From Paris the name and fame of a man of great talent resounds throughout the whole world. There the nobility treat men of genius with the greatest deference, esteem and courtesy; there you will see a refined manner of life, which forms an astonishing contrast to the coarseness of our German courtiers and their ladies . . .[1]

These words were written in 1778 by Leopold Mozart who rarely had anything favorable to say about French music and musicians. But the facts were undeniable. Paris was the musical capital of Europe, and its musical establishments were unrivaled. The venerable *Académie royale,* clinging to the Lully tradition, was rejuvenated by the appearance of Gluck in 1774 but also acclaimed his rival Piccinni. The *Opéra comique,* established in 1715 and devoted to the French dialogue opera, sparkled in works by Monsigny and Grétry, while the Italian repertoire was cultivated by visiting *buffa* troupes until it found a permanent home in the *Théâtre de Monsieur* (1788).

In the concert field,[2] Paris could point with pride to the famous *Concert spirituel,* established in 1725, which gave choral and instrumental concerts on religious holidays when the *Académie royale* was closed — altogether some thirty-five days each year. Successfully competing were the *Concerts de la Loge Olympique,* founded in 1781, after the *Con-*

3

certs des Amateurs (1769-81) had closed their doors. In these concerts, professionals and highly accomplished amateurs joined hands to perform symphonies and concertos; famous virtuosos were invited to appear as guest artists, and composers were commissioned to write special works, among them Haydn in 1785-86 (the "Paris" Symphonies, Nos. 82 to 87 in the Collected Works edition). About the same time, in 1786-87, the Notre-Dame cathedral attracted large crowds with the dramatized performances of religious music under a young and enterprising director, the composer Jean-Francois Lesueur.

During the last decade before the Revolution, music was everywhere — in the Royal Palace, in the salons of the aristocracy, in the modest homes of the bourgeoisie, in the cafés and the public gardens, on the boulevards and in the streets. "L'étendue de nos vues sur la musique est une suite de l'*espèce de fureur* avec laquelle on s'en occupe à présent," writes Chabanon in 1779.[3] The demand for new music was enormous and attracted numerous publishers who made Paris a center for music publication.[4] The manufacture of instruments flourished too; in the 1770's and 80's, young Sébastien Erard laid the groundwork for the improved construction of harps and pianofortes which would bring him European fame.[5]

Not only the quantity of music increased, but the quality of taste and appreciation improved. The rational approach to music, so dominant in France during most of the 18th century, yielded gradually to a more emotional concept. Music became a matter of sentiment and individual expression rather than intellect; instead of "painting" and "describing," it now strove to express vague sentiments: melancholy, revelry, yearning. Chabanon and Laborde,[6] condemning the old esthetic principle of "imitation of nature," placed stress on expression — significant in view of the approaching age of Romanticism.

> Music pleases independently of all imitation . . . Music appeals directly
> to our senses . . . Music is a natural and universal language . . .

are some of the characteristic thoughts of Chabanon. At the
same time, the attitude toward instrumental music changes;
the same Chabanon says that, if he had to choose between a
beautiful *cantabile* for voice and a good symphony, he would
unhesitatingly prefer the latter. Grétry, alluding to the famous
bon mot of Fontenelle, "Sonate, que me veux-tu?" says in
his *Mémoires:*

> Whatever Fontenelle has said, we know now what a good sonata, and
> especially a symphony by Haydn or Gossec mean.[7]

The emotional appeal began to be stressed also in the appreciation of virtuosos; while in earlier years, velocity, brilliance, and vitality were considered the prime requirements
for a successful performer, the emphasis now shifted to feeling
and *expression.* Yet, descriptive music never quite lost its
appeal to the French: Lesueur advocated the principle of
"imitation" for religious music (1787), and programmatic
compositions such as Gossec's *Symphonie de chasse* (1773-
74) and Méhul's Overture *La chasse du jeune Henri* (1797)
continued to fascinate the public. It is well to remember
that the impulse toward 19th-century program music came
from a Frenchman — Berlioz.

With the revolutionary events of 1789, the entire social
structure collapsed, and with it centuries of musical culture
and tradition.

> Controversy still rages round the subject of the Revolution. In history
> there is both a revolutionary and a counter-revolutionary legend. Even
> scholarly research does not quite escape from the influence of political
> bias.[8]

A similar partiality can be traced in the attitude of music
historians toward the Revolution. Some decry the interference
of the State in musical affairs, others praise the Government
as patron of the arts; some deplore the abolition of the church-
sponsored music schools (the *maîtrises*), others laud the separa-

tion of education and church; some denounce the rule of the mob, others welcome the abolition of the patronage system; some are repulsed by the vulgarization of music which others consider healthy popularization.

While the objective analyst will find some justification in each of these points, the fact is undeniable that throughout the revolutionary decade (1789-99), musical life in Paris continued to pulsate with undiminished intensity. Neither Revolution, nor terror, nor war could suppress the artistic needs of the people. In fact, as it often happens in times of stress, the artists seemed to intensify their efforts, while the public response was greater than ever before. With the proclamation of the *liberté des théâtres* in 1791, new theaters opened, including a rival *opéra-comique* in the Rue Feydeau. The public flocked to the theaters, but a different public it was — impassioned, despotic, often raucous. The spectators were apt to interrupt performances by demanding the singing of patriotic or revolutionary songs; such an attitude was actually legalized by a decree (Nov. 24, 1793) directing the theaters to perform the *Marseillaise* "every time the public would demand it."[9] In order to ward off anarchy in the theaters, a new decree (Jan. 8, 1796) ordered the playing of patriotic songs before every performance and during intermission; but not until 1798 was complete discipline and order restored in the theaters.

At first, the revolutionary events did not visibly affect the repertoire of the lyric theaters in Paris. During the year 1793, however, political pressure on the stage increased: Republican operas, historic scenes, and patriotic hymns adapted for the stage were introduced into the repertoire. The rising Terror produced tightened censorship; Republican indifference was considered as objectionable as antagonism:

> It is not enough that a work is not against us, it must be *for* us. The spirit of your opera is not republican: the word *liberty* is not uttered a single time.

With this explanation, the censor enforced a change in the libretto of Méhul's *Mélidore et Phrosine,* staged (with revisions) in 1794. This story is related, with undisguised irony, in the memoirs of Arnault,[10] the author of that particular libretto, who adds that a few dozen new verses with sufficient stress on "liberty" satisfied the censor. Often the mere inclusion of a Republican song proved sufficient; Grétry introduced the *Marseillaise* at the end of his opera *Guillaume Tell* (1791), Désaugiers interpolated the popular *Ça ira* into one of his comic operas. The height of patriotic fervor was reached in 1794 when no less than 701 new civic and patriotic hymns appeared, which were distributed through a monthly musical journal to the one hundred and fifty districts of the Republic for use at national festivals.[11]

After the fall of Robespierre, the revolutionary fervor began to ebb slowly, the mood of the people changed, and the inflammatory songs were replaced by refrains chastising the *buveurs de sang,* the "blood drinkers." Actors and musicians who were known to have belonged to the Jacobins were driven off the stage. Yet, the public did not permit trifling with Republian sentiments: in 1797, the opera *Le jeune Henri* by 'Méhul was hissed because of its royalist tendency. On the whole, however, the years of the *Directoire* were characterized by a return to normalcy.

In view of the turbulent conditions, it is surprising to see how many new and important operatic works were written and staged during the ten years of the Revolution; the number would put the operatic establishments of any modern capital to shame. Here is a list of the principal operas of the important Parisian composers which received their first performance between 1789 and 1799.

Cherubini:	*Lodoiska* (1791), *Elisa* (1794), *Médée* (1797) *L'hôtellerie portugaise* (1798), *Emma* (1799)
Méhul:	*Euphrosine* (1790), *Cora* (1791), *Stratonice* (1792), *Le jeune sage . . .* (1793), *Mélidore et Phrosine* (1794),

	Horatius Coclès (1794), *Doria, La caverne* (1795), *Jeune Henri* (1797), *Adrien, Ariodant* (1799).
Lesueur:	*La caverne* (1793), *Paul et Virginie* (1794), *Télémaque* (1796).
Kreutzer:	*Jeanne d'Arc à Orléans* (1790), *Paul et Virginie, Lodoiska* (1791), *Charlotte et Werther* (1792), *Imogène* (1796).
Grétry:	13 operatic works between 1790 and 1799, including *Guillaume Tell* (1791), *La rosière républicaine* (1793).
Gossec:	*L'offrande à la Liberté* (1792), *Le triomphe de la République* (1793).
Berton, Henri:	*Montano et Stephanie, Le délire* (1799).
Boieldieu:	*Les deux lettres* (1796), *La famille suisse* (1797).

Compared with the activity in the realm of opera, concerts played a subordinate role in the musical life of Paris. Being a subtler form of musical entertainment, they suffered more than the opera from the loss of their aristocratic clientele, and it took a number of years before a new concert audience was built, after the old *amateurs* were dispersed by the impact of the Revolution.

The established concert organizations did not survive for long; the *Concerts de la Loge Olympique* closed in December 1789, the *Concert spirituel* in 1790. Short-lived enterprises tried to fill the gap: in the fall of 1789, concerts at the *Cirque du Palais-Royal* were announced; in 1794, the *Concerts Feydeau* were organized which had only an "ephemeral duration."[12] Some instrumental music was performed by theater orchestras; we know that the young violinist Pierre Rode made his debut in 1790 at the *Théâtre de Monsieur,* playing the 13th Concerto of his teacher Viotti who was director of that theater; the following year, Rode gave the first performance of the 17th and 18th Concertos by Viotti at the same theater, renamed *Théâtre Feydeau.* It became customary to present instrumental music, both in solo and orchestral performances, during intermission time. Méhul's overture to *Le jeune Henri,* which was immensely

popular despite the failure of the opera proper, received almost weekly performances as intermission music.

Toward the end of the revolutionary decade, in the year
VII of the Republic (1798-99) the sporadic attempts at
organizing regular concerts led to the establishment of the
Concerts de la rue Cléry which were acclaimed for their
excellent performances.

One of the most far-sighted and enlightened acts of the
Republican Government was the establishment of the *Conservatoire de musique.* Based on the new democratic principle of free education for the qualified, its organization
remained a model of perspicacity and artistic integrity. Far
from being an accident, the establishment of such a music
school was the result of careful planning, artistic vision, and
astute political action. In order to understand fully the origin
and basic ideas which led to the Conservatoire, we must,
for a moment, digress into the field of musical education in
France before the Revolution.

Under the *ancien régime,* music instruction in France
was centered in the *maîtrises,* plain-chant schools attached
to every important cathedral, collegiate church, and abbey,
of which there were altogether some four hundred throughout the country.[13] Each had a small staff of musicians and
from twelve to twenty boy students who were entered by
their parents for a ten-year period, after which the young men
could enter a theological seminary or become organists or
singers. The curriculum included plain-chant, counterpoint,
some elements of composition, a little French, much Latin,
and some arithmetic. About four thousand students were
taught in these schools each year and were supported at the
expense of the church. However, the teaching was often poor,
the methods antiquated, instrumental music neglected,
dramatic music positively forbidden.

When Lully took over the *Académie royale* in 1672 he
realized immediately that his musicians were in need of spe-

cialized training such as the *maîtrises* were unable to provide. Thus, a new school, attached to the *Académie,* was authorized[14] the same year, later named *Ecole du Magazin* because it was located at the "magazin" where the operatic scenery was stored. Since girls were excluded from the *maîtrises,* they were given special attention at the *Ecole du Magazin.*

Instruction at this school was severely critized by Gossec who, in a memorandum written around 1780, charged that the students did not know their *solfeggio* and that the teaching accomplished nothing but to "spoil and break the voices and establish the worst possible principles of singing."[15] The indirect result of these criticisms was the establishment of a rival school; authorized by royal decree in 1784, the new *Ecole royale de chant et de déclamation* was opened the following year and Gossec was appointed director.[16] Naturally the original opera school, the *Ecole du Magazin,* vigorously opposed this new competitor, and a lively feud between the two schools ensued. The *Ecole du Magazin* survived until 1807 while Gossec's *Ecole de chant* was absorbed by the new *Conservatoire* in 1795.

Yet, this absorption played a very minor role in the history of the *Conservatoire,* for its true origin was embedded in the revolutionary events.

In September 1789, Bernard Sarrette, a twenty-three year old captain of the National Guard, assembled a military band of forty-five musicians who performed at all civic festivals and demonstrations. A year later, the City of Paris assumed the responsibility for the band, enlarged its membership to seventy, and provided it with a home. Here Sarrette worked ceaselessly to perfect the ensemble; old instruments were improved, new instruments designed and developed. Collaborating with him was Gossec as musical director and the seventeen-year old Catel, a student of Gossec, as assistant director. The duties of these two composers included the writing of special band music and the actual conducting of the band, while Sarrette's function was mainly administrative; yet it was primarily Sarrette's vision and perseverance which established the band as an important musical factor and laid the groundwork for the present-day excellence of French wind players.

Sarrette realized the need of adequate instruction on band instruments and obtained the establishment of a free municipal school, the *Ecole gratuite de Musique de la Garde Nationale Parisienne,* founded on June 9, 1792. Here, for the first time, France had a school for and by the people, controlled neither by the church, like the *maîtrise,* nor by the opera, like the *Ecole de chant.* One hundred and twenty students, age ten to twenty, all sons of Guard members, were admitted free of charge; their only obligation was to buy a Guard uniform, an instrument, and music paper. The teaching staff consisted of members of Sarrette's band and only wind instruments were taught. This limitation was deplored, as we read in a contemporary report:

> We need now establishments where the art of singing and the playing of string instruments could be equally perfected.[17]

Sarrette was well aware of these needs. His next aim was government recognition of his organization, and his position was strengthened by the excellent performances given by the band at the festivals of 1792 and 1793. He decided on a dramatic démarche: on November 8, 1793, Sarrette, accompanied by a municipal committee, brought his entire band, teachers as well as students, into the Constitutional Assembly. The rousing performance of the *Hymne à la liberté* and other popular selections greatly facilitated the adoption of a motion which read:

> Article 1: There shall be constituted, in the City of Paris, an *Institut national de musique.*
>
> Article 2: The Committee on Public Instruction will present to the Convention a plan for the organization of this establishment.

However, two more years elapsed until the law was promulgated establishing the *Conservatoire de musique* (August 3, 1795), and classes did not open until October 22, 1796.

Among the fifteen articles of the law pertaining to the organization and function of the *Conservatoire,* several points are noteworthy: the staff of 115 artists were to serve both as performers and teachers; 600 students of both sexes were to be chosen through competitive examinations; instruction was free.

At the end of the first school year, prizes were distributed to the best students, followed by a concert given by the prize-winners. The program reflects the musical taste of its time so well that we quote it fully, merely omitting the names of performers.[18]

   1. Overture to *Jeune Henri* . . . . .Méhul
                                             (played by professors)
   2. Air from *Corisandre.* . . . . .Langlé
   3. Clarinet Concerto . . . . Rosetti
   4. Air from *Alceste.* . . . . Gluck
   5. Piano Concerto . . . . .H. Jadin
   6. *Symphonie concertante for 2 cellos* . . . . Bréval
   7. Air from *Elisa* . . . . .Cherubini
   8. *Symphonie concertante for flute, horn,*
      bassoon . . . . .Catel
   9. *Duo italien.* . . . . Tritto
 10. Piano Sonata. . . . . Cramer
 11. *Symphonie concertante for 2 violins* . . . . Viotti
 12. Chorus from *Les Danaides* . . . . Salieri

Characteristically, this program offered only music by living composers (except Gluck who had died in 1787). This preference for contemporary music was typical of the attitude of listeners and performers during the 18th and early 19th centuries.

This first student concert of the new *Conservatoire* was a promise of greater things to come, for a few years later, in 1800, regular "public exercises" were established which soon acquired international reputation by the high excellence of performance and freshness of approach. These exercises, which continued regularly until 1815, contributed decisively to the development of French musical taste.

As we have seen, the primary impulse for the establishment of Sarrette's band and its official recognition was the desire of the authorities to secure the permanent services of a musical ensemble which was to perform at all civic and national festivals.

To evaluate these festivals properly, to see them in the right perspective, it is important to realize that they were born of a curious mixture of exalted idealism and political necessity, of public education and propagandist showmanship. Any attempt to stress one motive at the expense of the other will blur the picture. Hard pressed from without and within, the leaders of the Revolution faced the problem of welding the populace together, arousing the people's enthusiasm, replacing worn-out conceptions with new slogans, and keeping up the morale on the home front. It was mass propaganda on a hitherto unknown scale; Robespierre himself called the national festivals "an essential part of public education."[19] They were indispensable to hammer the new Republican tenets into the minds and hearts of millions. To achieve this basic aim, everyone was expected to do his share — and the artists, writers, poets, painters, and musicians heeded the call.

The revolutionary leaders understood the power of music and were determined to use it for their aims. Forgotten was the gentle and mundane art of the *ancien régime;* music now became a civic act, a social function, a moral force in the service of the fatherland and in the cult of glory and liberty.

The musicians, undoubtedly, were bewildered by this new concept of their art. Torn from the sheltered surroundings of the court, the chapels, the aristocratic salons, they were now confronted with an undisciplined, impassioned, largely uneducated cross-section of humanity. The concept of composer-artist was now replaced by that of the composer-citizen. His task was not to express individual emotion, but to speak the collective language of a people.

The new era called for a new musical style, built along clear lines, with strong rhythm, easy melody, simple harmony, brilliant orchestral color painted with broad brush strokes; in short, a fundamental simplification of musical forms, means, and expression. Music was needed that would exalt and unify, stir enthusiasm and strengthen determination, music of action, not of reflection. To find an adequate expression through music, this era needed not a Berton, but a Beethoven.

With very few exceptions, the composers of that period did not measure up to their task. Their adjustment to the new problems was superficial; they merely simplified their art without shaking off the conventionalism of a bygone period. They produced *Gebrauchs-Musik* which served its purpose without particular inspiration.

What was the reason for this failure of a whole phalanx of otherwise remarkable musicians? Could it be a lack of enthusiasm for the revolutionary cause, or a resentment against political pressure and constraint? Music does not flourish under decrees. We know that some of the musicians, for instance Grétry and Lesueur, were cool toward the new regime; others, like Gossec and Méhul, cooperated more enthusiastically, but most of them seemed eager to avoid the political arena.

The declaration of war on April 25, 1792, which involved the new regime in a life-and-death struggle with Austria, Prussia, and Russia, brought forth a wave of patriotic fervor, a mood of defiance, so irresistibly expressed in France's National Anthem, *La Marseillaise*. The author was an amateur musician and poet, Captain Rouget de Lisle, who was stationed in Strasbourg on the Western frontier; he jotted down words and music the night after the declaration of war. The song became immediately popular and spread rapidly. When the Republic was proclaimed, the hymn was sung at the *Opéra;* a few days later, on September 30, 1792, it was staged under the name *Offrande à la Liberté* and incorporated into the repertoire of the *Opéra.* Gossec's musical arrangement, for orchestra and voices, was in good taste but falsified the mood of the piece; it is interesting to compare this artful arrangement with the original song (published in Strasbourg in 1792)[20] and the present-day official version.

Characteristic of the martial and defiant mood of those days is a letter, written by the Secretary of War, Servan, to General Kellermann, on September 26, 1792:

> The fashion of the *Te Deum* is passed, one must substitute something more useful and more in keeping with the public spirit. I authorize you ... to have sung solemnly, and with the same pomp you would have accorded a *Te Deum,* the *Hymne des Marseillais* which I enclose ...[21]

The general answered by return courier that he would oblige.

Rivaling the *Marseillaise* in popularity was a song by Méhul, *Chant du Départ,*[22] written in a patriotic mood after the victory at Fleurus and first performed on July 4, 1794. Méhul's music is strong and perhaps somewhat more artful, but seems to lack the irresistible sweep of the *Marseillaise.* A few years later, in 1797, Méhul wrote a companion piece, *Chant du Retour,* in honor of peace.

Robespierre's plan of regular periodic national festivals did not die with him; the Constitutional Convention of 1795 established seven national festivals to be observed throughout the nation.

The better spacing of dates allowed for more thorough preparation which was reflected in a higher level of musical composition and performance. For these occasions, composers prepared special band music — marches, overtures, even symphonies. But the main part of the festivals remained reserved for vocal music — hymns, odes, and chants, for solo voices as well as for choirs. Yet, despite all efforts, the festivals did not take permanent root. Some of the reasons, as given by the Minister of Public Instruction in 1797, were the resistance of the clergy, insufficient funds, laxity of officials, and memories of the Terror.

***

The end of the *Directoire* in 1799 marked the end of the Revolution. On November 9, Napoleon Bonaparte seized power. The years of the *Consulat* (1799-1804) were essentially a period of political and spiritual preparation for the Empire. The trend toward normalization, begun under the *Directoire,* was accelerated during the first years of Bonaparte's regime. With the return of order and security, the old comfortable habits and customs reappeared. The salons — dispersed during the Revolution, tolerated during the *Directoire* — now quickly regained their old splendor. After years of privation, the so-called elite of society enjoyed life anew in an atmosphere of luxury. Musical conditions, too, acquired a new luster:

> Perhaps never before in Paris has music been so much appreciated and performed as now. Never has there been such a number of excellent composers and virtuosos from all the world. The political horizon is clearing up, the wounds which vandalism inflicted upon our civilization are beginning to heal; the arts influence the people of France once again . . .[23]

It was only natural that the celebration of revolutionary festivals was discontinued; the new ruler of France had no particular interest in commemorating revolutionary events. Only two dates were singled out temporarily: the anniversaries of the Taking of the Bastille (July 14) and the Proclamation of the Republic (September 22). But their celebrations differed from the popular festivals of former days, for they were commemorated indoors for a select and limited public. On the other hand, Bonaparte knew too well the propaganda value of festive demonstrations to abolish them altogether, but he preferred military displays and parades accompanied by the strains of martial music which was provided by the band of the consular guard.

Some of the most impressive commemorations of the early Napoleonic regime were staged in the spacious architecture of the *Église des Invalides* which was particularly suited for the use of divided choirs. In this setting, Lesueur's funeral music for Marshal Turenne, presented on September 18, 1800, impressed the audience deeply, according to a contemporary report:

> ... Hardly ever has one heard more beautiful music and a more perfect execution. Everything contributed to this perfection — a double orchestra, numerous choirs, the magnificent building with its sonorous vaults, and the enthusiasm of the musicians ... Le Sueur, placed between the two orchestras, conducted the whole; Cherubini and Kreutzer headed each orchestra and directed it. All the artists of the various theaters, many of the most highly respected professors of the Conservatoire, and the students of this institute, participated in this performance so that the orchestras numbered 500 musicians and singers. In short, there was nothing left to be desired except the freedom to applaud.[24]

No less impressive were the two secular oratorios given that same year (1800) at the *Église des Invalides* in the presence of Bonaparte and many high dignitaries to commemorate the Bastille Day and the proclamation of the Republic. For the first occasion, Méhul composed his *Chant du 14 juillet,* using three choirs and orchestras. The coordination of these widely separated ensembles was achieved by employing one chief conductor aided by several sub-conductors. While directing his composition, Méhul is reported to have tied a white handkerchief around his right arm to make his beat more visible to the three hundred performers.[25]

A work of even larger proportions was Lesueur's *Chant du premier vendémiaire,* composed for the anniversary of the Republic and given on September 22, 1800. Employing solos, vocal ensembles, as well as four choirs and orchestras with organ, it consisted of ten separate movements, eight of them with chorus. Undoubtedly, this monumental concept, utilizing the grandiose architecture for musical effects, served as inspiration for Berlioz — a student of Lesueur — when he composed his *Requiem,* with multiple divided choirs, which was given its premiere in that same *Église des Invalides* in 1837. There is an inner link, a spiritual kinship between

Berlioz and the revolutionary generation of 1789, between the "colossal" musical concepts of the 1790's and the similar endeavors of Berlioz, the "maestro festivalesque."

In discussing Lesueur's oratorio, Tiersot[26] ventures to compare, with certain reservations, the stirring opening of Lesueur's *Chant* with the beginning of Bach's *Saint Matthew Passion*. As for the performance, we find the following contemporary report:

> The execution was perfect and the ensemble astonishing, despite the innumerable difficulties of conducting four orchestras composed of such large numbers of musicians and placed so far apart. If one did not know to what point of perfection the Conservatoire had brought its performances, one could be surprised by that of yesterday, but one would have to repeat what has been said several times before.[27]

For the last time, we see the *Conservatoire* mentioned in its original role as official performing organization at a national celebration; soon its personnel was to be reduced and limited to mere teaching.

A memorable event, celebrated with all the flair for the grandiose which formerly characterized the important events of the Revolution, was the Festival of Peace. The occasion was twofold: the recently signed Concordat and the peace treaties with Britain and Austria. On Easter Sunday (April 17), 1802, a specially composed *Te Deum* by Paisiello was heard at the Cathedral of Notre-Dame; the two choirs, each consisting of about 150 musicians, were directed by Cherubini and Méhul. This Festival of Peace appears like a link between the past and the present, between the revolutionary tradition and the resurging religious spirit.

At the time of the Concordat with the Pope (1801), Bonaparte — always eager to imitate monarchic traditions — decided to revive the chapel services. Every Sunday at noon, mass was sung at the Tuileries, in the hall of the Council of State, since the old chapel was destroyed.[28] The service took hardly a half hour and used music by composers like Paisiello, Zingarelli, Haydn, Lesueur, and Martini. Since the time was limited, only fragments of a mass could be performed to which

Bonaparte listened in a military attitude, immobile, standing, with his arms crossed. His musical director was Paisiello, brought from Naples to Paris in 1802, who had eight singers and twenty-seven instrumentalists at his disposal.[29]

Paisiello's stay in Paris was short and none too happy. Soon he became the center of a feud between two musical factions — the pro-Italian and pro-French. To make matters worse, his only French opera, *Proserpine* (1803), was unsuccessful. Before returning to Italy in 1804, he is said to have recommended Lesueur as his successor.

Lesueur had undergone various vicissitudes during 1801-02 which culminated in his dismissal from the staff of the *Conservatoire* in September 1802. In appointing him, Bonaparte not only chose an eminently qualified musician, but also rewarded a man who had been loyal and devoted to the "premier consul" from the very beginning. It is curious to note that Lesueur proceeded to rewrite his music composed for the revolutionary festivals into Latin motets, thus abjuring his youthful "aberrations."

On May 18, 1804, Napoleon was proclaimed Emperor. The *Opéra,* renamed *Académie impériale,* chose as its first premiere on July 10, 1804 Lesueur's *Ossian ou les bardes.* Napoleon attended the second performance, on July 13, and the composer was asked to acknowledge the enthusiastic applause of the audience from the Emperor's box.

Napoleon was by no means the musical illiterate that he is often pictured. His interest in music was sincere, although his taste was limited and one-sided. In his preference for Italian music, Napoleon shared the musical taste of most reigning monarchs of the 18th and early 19th centuries. On the other hand, two of the important French composers of the day, Méhul and Lesueur, were among his protégés. As for his dislike of Cherubini, it was more a personal than a musical matter; both men had strong and uncompromising personalities.

The *style Empire* has been praised and vilified by historians; some consider it empty and superficial, others extol its pomp and splendor. Much, of course, depends on the political views of the writer. The brothers Escudier, who published a volume of causeries in 1856, reveal themselves as ardent "Bonapartistes" when they describe this era as

> one of the most marvellous in our history. Hand in hand with the greatness of events, with the éclat of military glory, went the prestige of the Arts ... Imposing spectacle of a nation arrived at the apex of its splendor ... Music during the Empire! was there ever a more interesting, a more significant subject? was there ever a more glorious period than the time of such composers as Grétry, Méhul, Spontini, Cherubini, Lesueur, Paer, Zingarelli, Berton, Monsigny, Dalayrac, Boieldieu ... ?[30]

The Escudiers could have easily added a few more names — Catel, Kreutzer, Rode, Baillot, Lafont, Paisiello.

On the other hand, we have the sober judgment of a present-day writer with strong Republican leaning, Combarieu, who says:

> The *Empire* pretended to continue the Revolution; but both *Empire* and *Restoration* failed to open to Art the beautiful sources of inspiration, as had done the men of the revolutionary period. Both these régimes favored ... the taste for the emphatic which had been the fault of the previous period, yet without counterbalancing it with those great patriotic and social ideas which may excuse the pompous rhetoric of the musical language ... [31]

True, the *Empire* produced the glittering pomp of Spontini's *Fernand Cortez*, but it also produced the quietly unpretentious *Joseph* by Méhul. It is a dangerous procedure to draw too close a parallel between social and political history on one side and artistic expression on the other. Only the lesser artist reacts immediately to environment and outside conditions, while the truly creative genius follows his own independent laws.

More than ever, the musical center of gravity was the opera, for it satisfied the general desire for pomp and display, as well as light entertainment. The theater boxes were filled by the new elite, mostly army contractors, purchasers of the national lands, or successful soldiers, displaying their new wealth and fresh nobility, and finding culture harder to acquire than riches and titles.

Napoleon's personal interest in opera was obvious: he attended important premières, supported an excellent operatic troupe at the Tuileries, and had prizes awarded to important works. These prizes, announced in the decree of September 11, 1804, were part of a larger plan: twenty-two prizes were to be awarded every ten years to the greatest accomplishments in the various fields of the sciences, literature, and the arts. Originally, music was to have only one prize (of 10,000 francs) for the best serious opera; a 5,000 francs prize was later added for the best *opéra comique*. The first distribution of prizes was planned for 1809, but delayed for a year; at the same time, the total of prizes was increased from twenty-two to thirty-five.

The verdict of the music jury* is quite interesting. The first prize in the opera class was awarded to Spontini for *La vestale,* pointing out its "incontestable merits and superiority of success." An honorable mention was given to Catel's *Semiramis.* In the category of *opéra comique,* the prize went to Méhul's *Joseph,* with two honorable mentions — Cherubini's *Les deux journées* and Catel's *L'auberge de bagnères.* The verdict was followed by vivid polemics; actually, the prizes were never paid to the recipients.

***

After a period of comparative inactivity during the revolutionary decade, concert life in Paris began to reestablish itself with the return of more stable conditions. We mentioned already briefly the *Concerts Rue Cléry,* organized in the year VII (1798-99), which filled a real need, for since the closing of the *Concert spirituel* in 1790, Paris had been

*On the jury were, among others, Gossec, Grétry, and Méhul.

without a regular concert organization. The response of the public was enthusiastic, and a foreign visitor, Reichardt, reported such crowded conditions that one could hardly step inside the hall.[32] Admission was only by subscription which created a "select" atmosphere; however, subscribers were permitted to transfer their admission cards to others.

The establishment of the *Concerts Cléry* grew out of the resurgence of social and artistic life at the end of the 18th century. A contemporary report furnishes the following description:

> Never was our musical sky more brilliant than during this last winter season (1799-1800). The works of the most prominent Italian, German, and French composers were performed by exquisite artists and excellent orchestras. The music-loving public listened with enthusiasm to symphonies by Haydn and Mozart, given with such perfection and precision at the *Concerts Cléry* that they seemed inspired by the spirit of the masters themselves . . .[33]

A "German connoisseur" described the concerts as follows (Dec. 1800):

> . . . With all the interest in music, it is surprising that Paris should have so few public concerts . . . At present there is only one organization, the *Concerts Rue Cléry*. The orchestra, although not very strong, consists of select musicians. The Haydn Symphonies are being played with a precision which surpasses everything. . .[34]

Soon, the *Concerts Cléry* are already called "famous"; "it is to be expected that they will become the best in the world."[35]

The *Cléry* orchestra numbered eighty players which can be considered a large ensemble compared to the fifty-seven instrumentalists of the *Concert spirituel* in 1789 or the seventy-men orchestra at the *Opéra* in 1790. Actually, the orchestra was too large for the narrow hall, and a contemporary observer, Reichardt, complained about the "intolerably loud" effect of the Haydn Symphony with the "Turkish music."

Beginning in 1804, the prosperity of these concerts began to decline; the immense luxury of various festivities, so we hear from a reporter, kept the wealthy public from attending concerts. "The old famous *Concerts Cléry,* known as the world's best in instrumental music and the finest in France as to vocal performance, has not as yet reopened this winter for lack of subscribers."[36] The reporter ascribed it to the fact that wealth has changed hands; formerly, when wealth was owned by "good society," concerts were considered indispensable enjoyment; now that the wealthy were "supposedly" part of the elite, nobody seemed to miss the concerts.

Aside from the inertia of their patrons, the *Concerts Cléry* was also faced with competition. In 1803, thirteen "capable local musicians" founded the *Concerts Rue Grenelle,* with the idea of establishing a true musical "academy."[37] The ambitious plan called for two three-hour meetings each week set aside for the performances by men, professionals as well as amateurs. Two other days were reserved for the performing ladies, and admission was limited to their families "in order to avoid embarrassment"; obviously the founders had little confidence in the musical abilities of the fair sex. One of the principal aims of this enterprise was apparently to offer music teachers an opportunity to present their students before an audience; however, professional concerts and student-amateur performances were to be kept apart. Another valuable part of this project was to put the orchestra at the disposal of composers who wished to hear their works performed before presenting them to a large audience.

In reality, the *Concerts Grenelle* proved to be highly professional when they first opened in the fall of 1803; the orchestra was praised as "unexcelled" and the success of the new enterprise imperiled the opening of the *Concerts Cléry* which was delayed for several months. For a time, both societies competed for the public's favor; two seasons later however, in March 1805, it was conceded that the *Concerts Grenelles* were but a weaker imitation of the *Concerts Cléry* which remained unrivaled in excellence.

In reporting on concert life in Paris early in 1805, a correspondent had the following to say:

> The three concert societies *(Grenelle, Cléry, Conservatoire)* are now going again, but because of the continuous festive activities they are not

> well patronized . . . At the bigger concerts one assembles in elaborate elegance, one gossips, and listens to music as something superfluous; the true friend of art, however, will derive more pleasure from the student concerts of the Conservatoire where one meets only those who understand and love music and enjoy it wholeheartedly . . . Here one finds truly great attentiveness, fair judgment, and sincere encouragement . . . [38]

These concerts, given by students and alumni of the *Conservatoire,* were known modestly as *exercises publics;* and their influence on French musical taste and performance standards were decisive.

During the winter of 1800-1801, three concerts (or *exercises*) were given, in November, January, and April. The critic of the *Décade Philosophique* was highly laudatory:

> . . . A numerous orchestra, consisting entirely of young people, performed with unity, precision, and firmness, using intelligence and discretion in the accompaniments which is even more difficult . . .[39]

The student soloists, the pianist Kalkbrenner and the horn player Dauprat, were praised, as well as the performance of a choral work, the *Litanies* by Durante.

However, the drastic reduction of the *Conservatoire* budget in 1801-02 threatened the continuation of these *exercises.* Encouraged by their teachers and by public opinion, the students organized an independent concert society, the *Concerts français,* and gave twelve successful concerts between November 1801, and May 1802. The *Courrier des spectacles* has the following to say:

> The happy idea which originated the establishment of the *Concerts français* is crowned by the most brilliant success. The artists, numbering sixty, all students of the Conservatoire and almost all recipients of awards in the competitions of this learned school, . . . have formed an association . . . to procure genuine enjoyment to the true lovers of music.[40]

The programs of these concerts were well planned and of great variety. At the beginning stood usually a symphony — invariably one by Haydn, except at the concert of January 30, 1802, when a *Symphonie en ut* by Méhul was performed. Also included on every program were an overture, usually by

Cherubini or Méhul; one or two solo concertos for various instruments, often a *symphonie concertante.* Interspersed between these instrumental works were vocal compositions, solo arias as well as ensembles.

Despite the brilliant success of these twelve *Concerts français,* the association was hardly able to cover the expenses. The students had no choice but to give up their independent organization and solicit a renewed affiliation of the concerts with the *Conservatoire.*

As soon as this support was secured, a new series of twelve concerts was announced for the winter season of 1802-03, to be given at the *Conservatoire.* The hall was small, seating only about three hundred persons, and the concerts were usually crowded, especially since the ticket prices were very moderate. In order to find accommodations, one had to arrive early, long before the hour set for the beginning — one o'clock on Sundays.

In 1806, the construction of a new concert hall was authorized by imperial decree but it took five years to build. The new auditorium, inaugurated in 1811 and still in use today, has a seating capacity of 1078 and is acoustically perfect, although somewhat too small for orchestral performance.

The indifference of the public toward concerts in general was scorned by contemporary reporters; so we read in the *Correspondance des professeurs et amateurs de musique* on May 21, 1803:

> Musicians in Paris are probably the most pampered but also the worst paid in the world ... There are only two concert societies in Paris — that of the established masters, under the name of the *Concerts Cléry,* and that of the students of the Conservatoire. Both give annually 24 concerts, and both hardly covered their expenses. What is the conclusion? That, generally speaking, music is little appreciated in Paris, and that the most distinguished virtuosi are forced into frequent emigrations...[41]

Indeed, many of the prominent French artists were concertizing abroad, and readily accepted lucrative posts in foreign countries, especially Russia.

As the years went on, however, the student concerts of the Conservatoire became firmly established in the public's favor and were eagerly attended not only by the connoisseurs but also by the "high society," *le très beau monde,* as a contemporary called it. The competition of these youthful and vigorous performances was too strong for the *Concerts Cléry* and *Grenelle,* which folded up quietly, leaving the field entirely to the *Conservatoire.*

Indeed, there must have been a peculiar fascination about the playing of the young *Conservatoire* ensemble, led by equally young conductors. For the actual conducting was in the hands of three fellow-students, all in their early twenties, who alternated as violinist-leaders — Marcel Duret, François Habeneck, and Ferdinand Gasse. While Duret is rarely mentioned, we find many laudatory comments about Gasse's spirited leadership. Habeneck, who assumed sole responsibility for the direction from about 1807 on (although he graduated in 1804), developed eventually into one of the outstanding conductors of his time. The performances were directed with violin and bow in hand, as was often the custom before the advent of the "baton" conductor. In fact, Habeneck preserved the habit of conducting with the bow from a first violin part, long after other conductors, like Spohr, Berlioz, and Mendelssohn, had changed to the baton and used a full score.

The performance standards of the *Conservatoire* orchestra must have been very high, for we find constant praise in the French and foreign press. The *Journal de Paris* (February 16, 1808) strikes a note of national pride:

> ... Foreign visitors admit that few orchestras in Europe combine so much warmth of expression with an equally perfect observance of *forte* and *piano*. These students, who would have been masters twenty years ago, perform with a clearness and a tonal finesse which is admirable.

The *Tablettes de Polymnie* (April, 1810) explain the rare unity of the string players in the following words:

> Formerly, the string players of an orchestra were individually accomplished players, but everyone had a different method of bowing ... The

result was a totally different method of attacking the string and thus an inevitable lack of finish and perfection in execution. Today these drawbacks are erased: Messrs. Rode, Kreutzer, and Baillot, who are the principal professors at the Conservatoire, have certainly each an individual method of bowing; but as a whole their methods resemble greatly that of their great master, the famous Viotti . . . The students of these three masters all have a broad and energetic approach; the result is such a unity of execution in the symphonies that, from far away, one could think that there were only one violin to each part.

The *Journal de Paris* (April 12, 1814) stresses the youthful spirit of the performances:

The glory of this establishment is based primarily on instrumental music . . . The more one hears the orchestra of the Conservatoire, the more one becomes convinced that it does not resemble any other orchesta. I admit . . . that one can hear elsewhere as much precision, purity, and unity; but where else can one find such warmth of young blood, such youthful verve? They . . . are radiant with fervor; their love for their art is a cult; and one knows how vibrant, ardent, enthusiastic youth's devotion can be.[42]

Less adulation can be found in the *Allgemeine musikalische Zeitung* which published regular reports from Paris. Criticism centered repeatedly on the tempo in *Allegro* movements of Haydn and Mozart which were found much too fast; especially in Mozart's works a great many details were lost. "As a rule, German music should not be played with French tempos."[43] Another correspondent still remembered Mozart's and Haydn's own interpretations in Vienna: the first *Allegros,* so he said, were never played as quickly as in Paris and lately in Germany; while both masters took their minuets fast, they differed in the treatment of finales where Haydn took a faster tempo than Mozart. This difference, so the correspondent thought, was inherent in texture and character, but was all too rarely observed by conductors.[44]

An interesting letter was published in August 1809.[45] At the *Conservatoire* concerts, so we read, one always discovers new talents. Méhul and Cherubini, inspectors of the *Conservatoire,* supervise rehearsals and choice of program, while the performance is conducted by a student chosen from the best violinists. The ensemble and the vigor of this orchestra is unbelievable; it is the first flame, the quick surge of youth, yet unaware of danger, disregarding all difficulties. The greatest talents are among the violinists and wind players, while the cellists are not as well developed for lack of a good teacher. The art of singing is neglected, for there is no method of voice instruction in France. On the whole, so the correspondent concludes, the French do not appreciate truly fine music; good taste is on the decline, and in all the whirl and swirl, only the most extravagant events arouse interest.

A similar complaint appeared a few years later:[46] the Parisian public does not know its own mind; if music is light, the professionals decry its platitude and poverty; if it is more elaborate, the laymen condemn it as too learned. At the same time, the correspondent compares modern music to a person afflicted with asthenic nervous disease — full of over-tension and convulsions. (Could he, perchance, mean Beethoven?)

Less choleric is the letter of a German observer in Paris, published in 1811.[47] He points out that Paris does not have the domination of the pianoforte, as is the case in Germany; the French prefer violin, flute, cello, and harp. Educated amateurs own full scores much more frequently than in Germany; scores of symphonies and operas by Gluck, Cherubini, Haydn, and Mozart find many more buyers in Paris than in Germany (whether also more friends, is another question, he adds). Piano reductions of operas are not liked; anyone who wishes to become acquainted with the music buys a full score.

***

The student *exercises* of the *Conservatoire* continued without interruption from 1800 until 1815, or, in other words, throughout the Napoleonic period. The concert season was comparatively short, starting in January or February and ending in May. The number of concerts pre-

sented each season varied from as few as three in 1815 (due
to the political upheaval) to a maximum of fourteen in 1812.
Altogether, a total of 144 concerts were given during the
sixteen-year period from 1800 to 1815, to which should be
added the two pension fund performances of Mozart's
Requiem presented jointly by faculty and students. This
uninterrupted record is all the more remarkable, since France
was in an almost continuous state of war during the years of
the Empire.

The programs presented at these concerts show careful
planning but are limited in scope. Almost all music of the
past was excluded; aside from occasional revivals of older
choral favorites by Pergolesi, Durante, or Jommelli, no music
more than one generation removed was performed.

Leading all other composers in frequency of performances is Haydn, whose symphonies and symphonic fragments
were played 119 times within the 144 programs of the *Conservatoire*. Mozart rose very slowly in the favor of performers
and listeners though the reason was probably inertia rather
than strangeness of musical idiom:

> As to symphonies, we hear always Haydn; and those by Mozart which were
> promised have not as yet made their appearance. The gentlemen (i.e.,
> musicians) are too highborn and easy-going to rehearse much; they know
> their Haydn well while Mozart would need study . . .[48]

And so, Mozart was "often and respectfully mentioned, rarely
played, and even more rarely understood."[49]

Vocal excerpts from some of his operas (*Magic Flute,
Figaro, Don Giovanni*) were given at the *Conservatoire* in
1803 and 1804, followed by two performances of the *Requiem*
in 1804 and 1805 under Cherubini's devoted leadership. Yet,
not until 1807 were Mozart's symphonies included in the
regular repertoire. That spring, the devotees of the *Conservatoire* were treated with a wealth of Mozart works: six performances of symphonies, including four of the Symphony
in C (probably the *Jupiter*), and one each of the Symphonies
in G minor and in D, as well as one unidentified symphonic

fragment. Also played were the overtures to *La Clemenza di Tito, Magic Flute,* and *Cosi fan tutte,* as well as vocal excerpts from the *Requiem* and *Figaro.* The following season brought repeat performances of most of these works, to which the Symphony in E flat was added as a novelty. From then on, Mozart became firmly established in the admiration and affection of the French who, to this day, consider him almost their own.

The same season witnessed also the first performance of a symphony by Beethoven in Paris. On February 22, 1807, the First Symphony was played at the *Conservatoire* under the direction of Habeneck. We may assume that the initiative came from him, for we know that he began the study of Beethoven scores in 1802, while still a student at the *Conservatoire.*

The response of critics and public was decidedly favorable; so we read in the *Décade philosophique:*

> This symphony ... belongs to a totally different genre, and it is a good work which is all the more meritorious. Its style is clear, brilliant, and rapid. It was performed by the orchestra with the usual perfection and pleased a great deal.[50]

Other performances followed slowly and were discussed with interest and understanding. Here is one excerpt from a review written in March 1811, probably inspired by the hearing of an (unidentified) symphonic movement at the *Conservatoire:*

> This author (Beethoven), often bizarre and baroque, sparkles at times with extraordinary beauty. Now he takes the majestic flight of the eagle, now he crawls along rocky paths. After penetrating the soul with sweet melancholy, he tears it immediately by a mass of barbaric chords. He appears to harbor together doves and crocodiles.[51]

Shorn of its florid language, this paragraph expresses the first, somewhat startled, impression made by the sudden contrasts and unprepared outbreaks to be found in Beethoven's music.

More penetrating is a review written after the premiere of the *Eroica* given at the *Conservatoire* on May 5, 1811; it appeared in the *Courrier de l'Europe et des spectacles:*

Beethoven, gifted with a gigantic genius, burning verve, and picturesque imagination . . . took the audacious flight of the eagle and impetuously passed over anything that opposed his rapid march. He believed himself great enough to create, for himself, a School which was particularly his own. Whatever the danger, to which his young followers expose themselves by adopting this school with enthusiasm boarding on frenzy, I must admit that most of Beethoven's works bear a grandiose, original imprint which deeply moves the soul of the listeners. The Symphony in E flat, played at the 10th concert, is the most beautiful of all he has composed, aside from a few somewhat harsh Germanisms which he used by force of habit. All the rest offers a sensible and correct plan, though filled with vehemence; graceful episodes are artfully connected with the principal ideas, and his singing phrases have a freshness of coloring quite their own.[52]

This French review shows more understanding than many of the acrimonious German criticisms which appeared in connection with the *Eroica,* despite the passing reference to the harsh "Germanisms" which shocked the French concept of balanced beauty.

Surveying the early performances of Beethoven's orchestral works by the student orchestra of the Paris *Conservatoire,* we find the following dates:

1807 (Feb. 22)	Symphony No. 1
(May 10)	Symphony (probably No. 1)
1808 (April 10)	Symphony in C (probably No. 1)*
1810 (March 25)	Symphony (possibly No. 2)
1811 (March 10)	Part of a Symphony (possibly No. 2)
(May 5)	Symphony No. 3 (*Eroica*)
1813 (May 2)	Symphony (unidentified, No. 1 or No. 2)
1814 (July 21)	Symphony (unidentified, No. 1 or No. 2)
(July 28)	*Prometheus* Overture
1819 (March 21)	Symphony No. 1
(Dec. 2)	Symphony No. 1
1824 (April 25)	*Nouvelle Ouverture, Fidelio*

All these performances at the *Conservatoire* preceded the historic date of March 9, 1828, when the newly-founded *Société des Concerts du Conservatoire,* under François

*Pierre (*op. cit.,* p. 486) lists the "Symphony in c minor" (No. 5) as having been performed on that date. However, this must be an error: the premiere of the Fifth Symphony did not take place until eight months later, on Dec. 22, 1808, in Vienna. The work was published the following year.

Habeneck, opened its concerts with the primary purpose of furthering a better understanding of Beethoven.*

Turning to the Italian repertoire at the *Conservatoire exercises,* we find that — in the field of instrumental music — the violin concertos by Viotti received a total of thirty-one performances, more than all other concerto composers combined. As to overtures, the uncontested leader was Cherubini whose overtures were played thirty-four times, more often than those of any other composer. The record is as follows:

Anacréon	10 performances
Hôtellerie portugaise	8
Faniska	5
Médée	5
Elisa	2
Lodoiska, Deux journées,	
Prisonnière,	
Unidentified	1 performance each

The Paris performances of the *Faniska* overture were especially significant, for this opera, written for Vienna in 1806, was never given on a Parisian stage.

Among French composers, the most popular and most frequently performed was Méhul. A skeptical observer might point out that Méhul and Cherubini were both members of the program committee, but actually there was no other French composer who could rival Méhul between 1800 and 1810. It is not surprising, therefore, to find his name again and again on the programs of each season, except for an unexplained interruption in 1806 and 1807. Most popular are his overtures, as can be seen from the following chart:

Jeune Henri	9 performances
Stratonice	5
Adrien	4
Euphrosine	3
Timoléon	3
Irato	2

*A few additional Beethoven performances, given in the 1820's at the *Concerts spirituels* of the Opera, will be discussed in the next chapter.

| Not identified | 2 |
| *Gabrielle d'Estrée* | 1 |

Total: 29 Performances

Charming, colorful, and effective as these overtures are, Méhul aimed higher and surprised the musical world with four symphonies performed in 1809 and 1810.

Other French overtures in the repertoire were *Semiramis* by Catel (four performances), *Montano et Stephanie* by Berton, and *Jean de Paris* by Boieldieu.

Equally important was a group of French violinist-composers who are barely mentioned in standard music histories: Rode, Kreutzer, Baillot, Lafont, Habeneck, and Mazas. Now that their works have been relegated to the status of instruction pieces, it is difficult to realize that their concertos and *airs variés* were the principal musical fare of violinists between 1790 and 1820, much preferred to the works by Nardini and Tartini, Mozart and Beethoven. The influence of men like Rode, Kreutzer, Baillot, and Lafont reached far beyond the French frontiers; their style and technique was spread through their compositions and appearances abroad; even a Beethoven found it useful to study their style before writing his own violin compositions.[54]

As a matter of course, the program policy of the *Conservatoire* was subjected to criticism from various quarters. There were chauvinistic attacks complaining of an excess of German music and Italian singing; there were writers criticizing the preponderance of instrumental music and the "miserable" vocal standards. The *Conservatoire* made efforts to improve the vocal department: in 1806, a *pensionnat* was established for eighteen vocal students, and the number of vocal works on the programs increased noticeably. After the dramatic department (for the training of actors) was established in 1812, we find some of the public *exercises* devoted to "lyric and dramatic" art, i.e., excerpts from operas and plays were given, interspersed with some instrumental music.

There was obvious concern to prepare the students of the *Conservatoire* as efficiently as possible for their future careers, and the public performances were considered part of the curriculum. It must be remembered that the *Conservatoire* concerts retained stubbornly the title *exercises publics;* their first responsibility was actually not to Music, nor to the Public, but to the student and his progress. This may explain, in part, the frequent repetition, year after year, of certain standard works: the personnel of chorus and orchestra was changing periodically (although quite a few students are known to have played in the concerts long after their graduation) and a certain repetition of repertoire was considered educationally desirable. Viewed from every possible angle, there is no doubt that the sixteen-year record of the *Conservatoire exercises* was an outstanding accomplishment.

***

CHAPTER 2

Musical Life During the Restoration (1815-30)

Napoleon's reign ended as dramatically as it had begun. The historic events followed each other in rapid succession: the military defeats of the French army between 1812 and 1814 which led to Napoleon's first abdication on April 11, 1814, and his exile to the Isle of Elba; the restoration of the Bourbon dynasty to the throne of France; Napoleon's triumphant return to Paris on March 20, 1815, his "Hundred Days" of reign, of renewed war and final defeat at Waterloo on June 18, 1815; and, a few days later, Napoleon's second abdication and the return to Paris of Louis XVIII. All this happened within the short span of thirteen months.

The Napoleonic debacle left France at the brink of material and spiritual exhaustion, and the folly of the "Hundred Days" only aggravated the situation. Yet, the recovery was amazingly rapid; within a few years, France was able to pay the war indemnity, rid herself of the occupation armies, and take back her rightful place in the family of nations.

After twenty-five years of strife, tension, and wars, the Restoration brought back peace and prosperity for which every Frenchman was craving. What did it matter that it also brought back the reactionary rule of nobles and clergy, the abrogation of liberties, the reestablishment of feudal privileges?

Only when the screws were tightened too much, especially after the ascension of Charles X in 1824, the people revolted again and deposed the Bourbons who were "incapable of learning anything or forgetting anything."

In the meantime, the good King Louis XVIII, plagued by the gout and the memories of the *ancien régime*, held court in the French capital which, more than ever before, was the artistic and cultural center of the world. France had lost a war, but she vanquished the conquerors in a more subtle and decisive way. European artists flocked to Paris either to study or to receive the stamp of approval. Among the visiting foreign musicians were Spohr and Moscheles in 1820, Mendelssohn in 1816, 1825, and 1831, Rossini and Liszt in 1823, Weber and Meyerbeer in 1826, Paganini and Chopin in 1831, Thalberg in 1835, Wagner in 1839. Some came for a few days, others arrived as visitors and stayed for many years; some were critical of Paris and its public, others were bitterly disappointed; but no one could escape the fascination of the French capital. Their letters and diaries, articles and memoirs constitute valuable source material concerning conditions in Paris during the 1820's and 30's.

Especially some of the German musicians — Spohr, Mendelssohn, and Wagner — did not feel happy in the Parisian atmosphere. Young, ambitious, sure of their talent, they expected to conquer and were disappointed when the sophisticated metropolis did not receive them with open arms. Young Mozart underwent a similar experience in 1778. They all vented their feelings in bitter comments and letters, expressing contempt for French music and French taste, and often blaming the alleged jealousy of their French colleagues for their failures. It must be remembered, however, that Mozart, Mendelssohn, and Wagner came to Paris as musical fledglings and did not present themselves with works indicative of their future greatness. Besides, in order to succeed in Paris, mere talent was not sufficient: diplomacy, influential friends, important connections, a certain *savoir vivre* were necessary. By a peculiar coincidence the more successful among the foreign visitors, like Liszt, Rossini, and Meyerbeer, had no particular complaints to offer.

When Louis Spohr arrived in Paris in December, 1820, he was already well known throughout Europe as violinist, composer, and conductor. A man of high intelligence and keen powers of observation, a musician of uncompromising standards, he was familiar with the current works of French composers and the taste of the Parisian public which was diametrically opposite to his. Yet, he was eager to make himself known in Paris, to perform and present his works. His French colleagues received him with great kindness, especially Cherubini and Baillot.

Spohr's opinion about the musical taste of the Parisian salons is unfavorable:

> It is very singular how all here, young and old, strive only to shine by mechanical execution . . . Everyone produces his own showpiece: you hear nothing but *airs variés, rondos favoris, nocturnes* . . . and from the singers romances and little duets . . . Poor in such pretty trifles, with my earnest German music I an ill at ease in such musical parties . . .[1]

However, the French musicians seemed well able to cope with his "German music," for they sight-read his difficult Nonet to the delight of the composer.

In general, Spohr had high praise for individual artists; he admired the great precision of the opera orchestra directed by Habeneck, and analyzed carefully the playing of his fellow-violinists.[2]

In his opinion, Charles Lafont was the most accomplished French violinist, lacking merely depth of feeling to be perfect. Spohr found Baillot technically almost as accomplished and having, in addition, a much larger repertoire of classical and modern works. With the "most perfect purity," Baillot played a string quintet by Boccherini, a quartet by Haydn, and three of his own compositions, though there was a certain mannerism of expression. Then Spohr added:

> That the quintets by Boccherini are being enjoyed as much as a quintet
> by Mozart, is another proof that Parisians cannot distinguish the good from
> the bad and are at least half a century behind in art.

After having spent some time in Paris during which he
made himself known in private soirées, Spohr ventured a
public concert at the *Opéra* in January 1821. The reviews
were not altogether favorable, which Spohr ascribed to the
corruptness of the Parisian press and to French vanity in
general:

> They all begin by extolling their own artists and their own artistic
> culture; they think that a country which produced Messrs. Baillot, Lafont,
> and Habeneck, need envy no other its violinists; and whenever the playing
> of a foreigner has been received here with enthusiasm, it is nothing more
> than a proof of the great hospitality which the French in particular show
> toward foreigners.[3]

Though Spohr's pride may have been hurt, he quotes the
following comment in the *Courrier des spectacles:*

> Mr. Spohr, as a performer, is a man of merit; he has two rare and valuable
> qualities — purity and accuracy; if he would remain in Paris for some time
> he could perfect his taste and then return to mold that of the good Germans.

Acidly, Sphr comments:

> If the good man only knew what the 'good Germans' think of the musical
> taste of the French?![4]

Spohr's young compatriot and friend, the pianist Ignaz
Moscheles, has the following comment to offer:

> Why does Spohr fail to awaken general enthusiasm here? Will the French,
> from a feeling of national pride, acknowledge none but their own violin
> school? Or is Spohr too little communicative, too retiring for the fashionable
> Paris world? Enough that today he has been obliged to give up his in-
> tended evening concert [i.e., his planned second appearance] from want
> of public interest. This really pains me . . .[5]

No such disappointment awaited Moscheles, for his
pliable nature adjusted itself more easily to Parisian conditions. He made a "great sensation with his extremely brilliant
playing"[6] and was welcomed in the salons of ambassadors,
aristocrats, and financiers.

Moscheles and Spohr were often invited together, and Moscheles liked to play the piano part in Spohr's quintet, originally written for Frau Spohr who was a professional harpist and pianist. When Baillot gave a reception in honor of Spohr and Moscheles, the list of guests included everyone prominent in the musical field: Cherubini, Auber, Herold, Adam, Lesueur, Pacini, Paer, Blangini, Lafont, Habeneck, Plantade, Viotti, Pleyel, Erard, Boieldieu, Garcia, and many others. Moscheles, like Spohr, praised the hospitality and kindness shown him by his French colleagues; but above all he loved Paris, the city, from the first moment:

> The impression as I drove through the crowded streets, and watched the brilliant shops filled with purchasers, will never be effaced from my memory.[7]

While Spohr and Moscheles spent only a few months in Paris, the two visitors of 1823 — Rossini and Liszt — were to find in France their second homeland.

Rossini's arrival in Paris coincided with the publication of the *Vie de Rossini* by Stendhal, a book which reveals as much about the author as it does about the subject.[8] But Rossini needed no help from the literati: a European celebrity at the age of thirty-one, he found Paris at his feet. Although his operas had been in the repertoire of the *Théâtre Italien* from 1817 on (*L'Italiana in Algeri* was the first to be shown), it was his personal presence which brought his popularity to its peak. Named director of the *Théâtre Italien* in 1824, he soon transformed it into the musical center of the capital. After his contract expired, Rossini was honored by the title of *"Premier compositeur du Roi"* and *"Inspecteur Général du Chant en France."* At the same time, the *Odéon,* directed by Castil-Blaze, began to present Rossini's operas in French translations (*Barber of Seville* and *La Gazza Ladra* in 1824, *Otello* in 1825, *Tancredi* in 1827, etc.); and finally, the *Opéra* performed *Moise* (1827) and *Guillaume Tell* (1829), after which Rossini — then only thirty-seven — abruptly decided to end his career as an opera composer.

That such unprecedented success should provoke bitterness and criticism among French composers cannot surprise us; indeed, we see a revival of the perennial French versus Italian tension in the musical world of Paris. It is curious to note that young Berlioz, the anti-academic firebrand who was just beginning his literary career, joined the "old podagrics" of the *Conservatoire* and the Academy in order to combat the Italian maestro; others who raise a dissenting voice were the composer Berton[9] and the critic d'Ortigue.[10] However, Rossini handled the situation diplomatically by treating the gentlemen of the *Conservatoire* — Cherubini, Lesueur, Reicha — with great respect; he also made friends with Habeneck whom he joined in the study of Beethoven's scores.

Another visitor who took Paris by storm, although in a different way, was *"le petit Litz."* Young François was only thirteen when he arrived in Paris in 1823, accompanied by his father. He hoped to complete his musical education at the *Conservatoire;* however, the bylaws of that institution made foreigners ineligible for admission. The rude manner in which Cherubini, the director, insisted on enforcing this rule, his lack of sensitiveness and consideration are reported vividly in one of Franz Liszt's essays.[11]

For more than ten years, until 1835, Paris was to become Liszt's home. He studied composition with Paer and counterpoint with Reicha; he became the *enfant gâté* of the salons and appeared side by side with the most famous artists of his time. After a semi-retirement of several years, he emerged in 1830 as a full-grown artist, aligning himself with the young Romantic firebrands, *Jeune France.*

About the same time, in 1825, another young musician, the sixteen-year old Felix Mendelssohn, arrived in Paris for a short stay. Educated in Berlin under the conservative guidance of Zelter, brought up in the tradition of Bach, Handel, Mozart, and Beethoven, he was appalled at the "superficiality" of the French musical taste:

> ... These people do not know a single note of *Fidelio* and believe Bach to be nothing but an old-fashioned wig stuffed with learning. I played Onslow

the Overture to *Fidelio*...and he was beyond himself, scratched his head, added the orchestration in his mind, at last sang with me; in short went quite mad in his delight. The other day, at the request of Kalkbrenner, I played the Organ Preludes in E minor and A minor. My audience pronounced them both "wonderfully pretty," and someone remarked that the beginning of the Prelude in A minor was very much like a favorite duet in an opera by Monsigny. Everything went green and blue before my eyes.

Obviously his family, to whom this letter was addressed, reproached him for being prejudiced, for he answered rather angrily in a letter to his sister:

... You talk of prejudice and bias, of grumbling and scoffing, and about the "land flowing with milk and honey" as you call this city... Is Rode prejudiced when he says to me: "c'est ici une dégringolade musicale?" Is Neukomm prejudiced who told me: "ce n'est pas ici le pays des orchestres." Is Herz prejudiced when he says: "here the public can only understand and enjoy variations." And are ten thousand others prejudiced who abuse Paris? ... What else is performed in the Italian Opera besides Rossini? ... What is published, what is sold, but romances and potpourris? ...[12]

Young Felix met all the leading musicians in town, and they often assembled for private chamber music sessions, especially at Baillot's home. During one of these musicales they tried Mendelssohn's Piano Quartet in B minor which went fast and furiously, especially the Scherzo which Baillot wanted to repeat. At the end, Baillot embraced Felix twice "as if he wanted to strangle me." Baillot was fifty-four years old at that time, Mendelssohn only sixteen ... but the following year the *Midsummer Night's Dream Overture* was written.

Mendelssohn returned to Paris six years later, and his comments became more mature and balanced, though hardly more complimentary for Paris.

More generous in his opinions was Carl Maria von Weber who interrupted his journey to London in 1826 to spend five days in Paris (February 25 to March 2).[13] He dreaded this visit, for his *Freischütz* and *Euryanthe* were being given in mutilated versions at the *Odéon,* despite his angry protests to the director, Castil-Blaze. Once in Paris, however, Weber seemed to have forgotten the purpose of his visit, namely to force a settlement with Castil-Blaze. Obviously he did not even see him, nor did he go to the *Odéon*. Instead, Weber rented a carriage and visited many of his famous colleagues — Paer, Catel, Auber, Cherubini, Lesueur, even Rossini for whom he never had any liking. He also attended the *Opéra comique* and was charmed by Boieldieu's *La dame blanche* which he considered the best comic opera written since Mozart's *Figaro*. A visit to the *Opéra*, where a revival of Spontini's *Olympie* was given, pleased him less; yet Weber was impressed by the quality of the *Opéra* orchestra under Habeneck which played with "a force and a fire like I have never heard before."[14] Weber found even time to visit the *Conservatoire,* where he attended a composition class of Fétis, and engaged the learned professor in a spirited discussion. Everywhere he was received with respect, admiration, and affection which touched him very deeply. It was one of his last joys, for a few months later, on June 5, 1826, he died in London, shortly after the premiere of his *Oberon.*

When Weber visited Paris, he was a European celebrity. *Der Freischütz,* first given in Berlin in 1821, swept the European opera houses; "no other German opera had ever been so successful and conquered so many and even the smallest stages in so short a time."[15] Yet, when the work was presented in Paris on December 7, 1824, it proved a failure. Hurriedly, Castil-Blaze, the shrewd director of the *Odéon,* withdrew the opera after the first performance and set out to "adapt" it to the Parisian taste. Completely altered, it was given again a week later, on December 16. Castil-Blaze invited a number of young enthusiasts to force a success, if necessary. The young generation of French artists, conscious of common ideals and beliefs, acclaimed Weber's work with enthusiasm, and gradually the public began to like it. Among those "overwhelmed with surprise and delight at Weber's music" was Berlioz, then barely twenty-one and still a student.

> I was positively intoxicated by its delicious freshness and its wild, subtle fragrance . . . I soon knew the *Freischütz* by heart.[16]

But just as the memory of that first impression had remained fresh in Berlioz' mind for many years, so his fury at the "adaptation" of Castil-Blaze remained unabated. He called him a "veterinary surgeon of music" and compared him to "that profane idiot, Lachnith," who had made the "adaptation" of Mozart's *Magic Flute,* transformed into *Les mystères d'Isis* and satirized by some as *"Les malheurs d'ici."* Berlioz lashed out furiously at all adapters and arrangers who dare to take liberties with masterworks:

> Detestable idiot! you have committed an atrocious crime, the most odious, the most enormous of crimes — an assault on that combination of man's highest faculties that is called *Genius.* Curses on you! *Despair and die!!*[17]

This indictment rings as true today as it did one hundred years ago.

The opinions of foreign visitors quoted thus far have given us a vivid, but one-sided picture of Paris. Since most of the articulate comments come from the pen of German musicians, one notices immediately that perennial tension between Germanic and Gallic conceptions of art and music. What the German calls "serious" or "deep," the French considers heavy-handed and labored; what the French calls *charmant,* the German ridicules as superficial. True, the musical taste of the Parisian salons during the 1820's was shallow, but so was that of the German burgher. In fact, all Europe experienced a "trivialization" of music as shown in brilliant or sentimental "salon pieces," mostly for piano; and, curiously, two of the most popular "composers" were actually Germans, namely Hünten and Herz.

What the foreign visitors did not realize sufficiently was the fact that, just as Hünten did not represent German music, Monpou — that popular composer of sentimental romances — did not represent the French. Actually, there lived and worked in Paris, during the 1820's, a number of musicians whose seriousness and erudition was comparable to any capital of Europe. Suffice it to mention the composers Cherubini, Catel, Lesueur, and Berton, the theorists Reicha, Fétis, and Choron, or the violinist-conductors Baillot and Habeneck. We may call this the "academic circle," for they all considered teaching an important part of their life work.

The profession of teaching, far from being the last resort of a stranded virtuoso, was taken very seriously by the "superficial" French; it is indeed remarkable how devoted these famous men were to their students and their teaching task. In the words of Méhul:

> To perpetuate oneself through numerous students of distinguished merit means to crown with dignity a long and honorable career; it means to discharge the indebtedness of the talent toward his country.[18]

It is primarily the merit of the *Conservatoire* to have elevated the teaching profession to a position of unprecedented dignity and importance; the *professeur de musique,* formerly a call boy for the nobles, became a pillar of musical culture and tradition.

Nevertheless, these meritorious musicians, active in the fields of instrumental and church music, teaching and theory, history and research, occupied only the periphery of musical life in Paris, while the center of interest was reserved for the operatic stage. Untouched by the turmoil of revolutions and wars, the taste of the Parisian public remained unchanged; it still preferred the lyric stage to instrumental music and even to the spoken theater.

The number of musical stages, substantially reduced by the Napoleonic decrees of 1807 and 1811 abrogating the *liberté des théâtres* of the Revolution, increased again during the Restoration. An important addition was the already mentioned *Odéon,* directed by that "musical veterinary"

Castil-Blaze, where notable premieres by Rossini and Weber were presented. The venerable *Opéra* continued to rely mainly on a repertoire of Gluck, Salieri, Spontini, and Méhul, and generally offered a picture of stagnation during most of the 1820's. There was more life at the *Opéra comique,* with Boieldieu, Auber, and Herold as favorite composers; most successful was Boieldieu's *La dame blanche,* first performed in 1825. The *Théâtre Italien* was dominated by Rossini's personality and works; during his directorship, a significant premiere took place — *Il Crociato* (1825) by Meyerbeer, the first of his operas to be heard in Paris. The last years of the 1820's brought the amazing revitalization of the *Opéra: La muette de Portici* (1828) by Auber, *Guillaume Tell* (1829) by Rossini, and *Robert le diable* (1831) by Meyerbeer ushered in the most successful period in the history of that institution.

***

Politically and artistically, the 1820's were a tense period in the history of France. It was a decade of mounting political repression through muzzling of the press, abrogation of academic freedom, discriminatory electoral laws, and other reactionary chicaneries which finally led to the July Revolution of 1830. It also brought the climax of a long-delayed artistic revolution — the French Romantic movement emerged victorious after years of struggle with classicistic concepts.

In the forefront of every artistic battle was Hector Berlioz. He had come to Paris in November 1821, barely eighteen years old, with the purpose of studying medicine. However, most of his time was spent in the music library of the *Conservatoire,* at the opera houses, and in company of young, progressive artists. Encouraged by Lesueur, whose private pupil he became in 1823, Berlioz decided to become a composer, against the determined wishes of his parents. In 1826 Berlioz entered the *Conservatoire,* where he studied counterpoint and fugue with Reicha, while continuing the study of composition in the class of Lesueur.

But even before having mastered the craft of composition, Berlioz began to compose; an oratorio, a cantata, a mass, and vocal fragments were written before 1826. With the supreme arrogance of youth and inexperience, he set out to have his music performed. In 1824, he approached Chateaubriand to lend him 1200 francs for a concert, a request which was refused politely. The influential Kreutzer, whom he asked to perform one of his works at the *Concerts spirituels,* answered cynically:

> My dear fellow, we cannot perform any new compositions at these concerts; we don't have the time to rehearse them and Lesueur knows it well.

And to Lesueur, who reproached him with this attitude, Kreutzer added:

> Good heavens! what would become of us if we were to help on the young fellows like that?[19]

By paying the expenses with borrowed money, Berlioz finally obtained a performance of his Mass at St. Roch in July 1825.   Two years later the work was repeated at St. Eustache, this time under the composer's personal direction, which marked Berlioz' debut as conductor, an art in which he was to excel later in life:

> I got through it pretty well, in spite of some blunders caused by my excitement. But how little I then possessed of the qualities necessary to make a good conductor![20]

In the meantime, Berlioz established himself more firmly in Paris. He was shrewd, charming, diplomatic, and ready to flatter, if need be, and he had influential friends among the aristocracy. He also cultivated the gentlemen of the press, being one of them since 1823 when, at the age of 19, he began to contribute regularly to *Le corsaire,* a boulevard paper of doubtful standing. But, above all, he had friends among the young generation of Parisian artists, that Romantic vanguard, *Jeune-France.* Writers, poets, painters, sculptors, musicians, most of them in their twenties, they were as yet unknown but yearning for success and recognition. Striving toward the same goal, fighting for the same ideals, they formed a strong brotherhood, united and determined to proclaim and defend the common cause. The Romantic revolt was never a "popular" movement; rather it was the decisive effort of a minority elite to impose its taste and its creed, *"liberté dans l'art!"*[21] Far from being dreamers, those young Romanticists were eminently practical; they made extensive plans to conquer the public by dominating the theaters, concert halls, expositions, and by gaining influence in the press.

Never before in the history of modern civilization had there been closer ties between the sister arts than during the Romantic era of the early 19th century. We see literature, painting, and music in an interchange of ideas and expressions, borrowing each other's media and transmuting them into their own language. There was a deep-felt awareness of the affinity between word, sound, and color.

Literature, of course, was the concern of everyone, for traditionally the written word "plays a far larger part in the cultural and national consciousness of France than it does of any other nation." Only a Frenchman could have made that characteristic statement, "literature is civilization."[22] Now, during the Romantic era, we find that the men of letters reciprocate this interest; especially noteworthy is their intense awareness of the power and potentialities of music. Of course, their tastes and degree of understanding vary: some, like Hugo and Mérimée, were less receptive than, say, Musset, Vigny, and Lamartine, whose sensitive nerves were attuned to music, while Balzac, Stendhal, and Gautier made a special effort to acquire a knowledge of music. No less receptive to music was the painter Delacroix, as his diaries prove so eloquently.

Painting, in France, was the earliest of the arts to break away from classicistic formalism: Théodore Géricault painted his *Chasseur à cheval* as early as 1812, and his famous *Raft of the Medusa* was completed in 1819. After Géricault's death at the age of thirty-three (in 1824), his friend and admirer Eugène Delacroix took over the helm; his early *Dante and Virgil Crossing the Acheron* of 1822, and the deeply moving *Massacre of Chios,* exhibited at the Salon of 1824, are masterpieces of Romantic painting.

In the meantime, Stendhal published his controversial *Racine et Shakespeare,* with the subtitle *Etude sur le Romantisme* (1823/25). In this earliest of the literary "manifestoes," the author expressed the opinion that all truly great writers of the past were "Romantic" in their time; in this sense he considered Sophocles and Euripides, Racine, Shakespeare, and Molière eminently "Romantic," while rejecting the "German galimatias which many people today call Romantic," among them Schiller. Lord Byron, in his opinion "the author of . . . many mortally boring tragedies," is not at all the chief of the Romantic school; the Romantic poet par excellence is Dante! In the Romantic play, Stendhal wants more truth, more naturalness, more realism; he advocates "un genre clair, vif, simple," going straight to the core. "One needs courage to be Romantic, for one must take chances!"[23]

About the same time (1823), an informal literary circle was formed, the so-called first *cénacle,* which its sponsor Charles Nodier called jokingly the "frenetic school"; among those belonging to the group were Hugo, the brothers Deschamps, Musset, and Vigny. Stressing hyper-sensitivity, frailty, and hypochondria became fashionable among young poets, so much that one spoke of the *"école poitrinaire"* or "consumptive school." With obvious contempt, the vigorous Dumas described his confrères in the following words:

> In 1823 and 1824 it was all the fashion to suffer from the lungs; everybody was consumptive, poets especially; it was good form to spit blood after each emotion that was at all inclined to be sensational, and to die before reaching the age of thirty.[24]

On the other hand we have the beautifully sensitive words of Musset, describing his generation in *La confession d'un enfant du siècle:*

> During the wars of the Empire, when their husbands and brothers were in Germany, the restless mothers gave birth to an ardent, pale, and nervous generation. Conceived between two battles, raised in schools to the roll of drums, thousands of children looked about them with a somber eye. From time to time, their fathers, stained with blood, appeared, raised their children to their bespangled breasts, then put them down to ride off again . . .

Musset speaks of the uneasy young generation finding itself in a world in ruins, in disillusionment and despair:

> . . . The exalted, the suffering minds, all those unrestrained souls in need of the infinite, bent their heads in tears; they wrapped themselves into feverish dreams, and nothing is seen but a few frail reeds on an ocean of bitterness . . .[25]

Thus a sensitive artist describes the disenchantment, the *mal du siècle* which gripped a whole generation.

But there were more positive, more virile and realistic aspects of the Romantic movement. In 1824, the cause of Romanticism, and especially of Romantic literature, received powerful support in a newly-founded journal of opinion, the *Globe,* which stood for all that was liberal and progressive, in politics as well as in the arts. Addressing himself to French youth, Jouffroy proclaimed in its pages:

> A new generation is growing up. It has listened and it has understood, and already these youths have passed their elders and seen the emptiness of their doctrines.[26]

We spoke already of the determined action of young Parisian enthusiasts who helped to establish the success of the *Freischütz* in 1824. Thus, Carl Maria von Weber became the first truly Romantic composer to be heard and appreciated in Paris, and — to quote Berlioz — "the effect was intoxicating."

But there were other and even greater influences that struck Berlioz, and with him the entire young generation of artists, like thunderbolts — Shakespeare, Goethe, and Beethoven.

The close affinity which the young Romanticists felt with Goethe and Beethoven was, strangely enough, not reciprocated; both disavowed their "unclassically sentimental contemporaries." "Classic is that which is healthy, Romantic is that which is diseased," was Goethe's verdict.[27] Formless, effeminate, sentimental, eccentric, affected — these were attributes which both Goethe and Beethoven despised and held in contempt. Nevertheless, they were looked upon as leaders of an artistic movement which, paradoxically, they both rejected. There can be no doubt that the Romantic musicians considered Beethoven their own; the following words of E. T. A. Hoffmann, the Romantic poet-musician, are characteristic:

> Beethoven's music moves the levers of fear, chill, terror, pain, and awakens that infinite longing which is the character of Romanticism. Therefore, Beethoven is a purely Romantic composer.[28]

While Beethoven's contemporaries admired particularly the works of his impassioned middle period, the "Neuromantiker" of the 1840's and 1850's considered the compositions of his last period their beacon.[29]

Shakespeare was brought to Paris by a group of English actors who staged *Hamlet* and *Romeo and Juliet* in 1827. Five years earlier, a similar enterprise was hissed; now the time was ripe. The young enthusiasts who filled the hall read and admired Thomas Moore, Walter Scott, Lord Byron, and Shakespeare in new translations; now they were confronted with Shakespeare on the stage — a mysterious, liberating force, breaking the barriers of stilted, frozen traditonalism. It was greeted as a revelation.

That same year, 1827, witnessed the publication of Victor Hugo's preface to his drama *Cromwell,* the manifesto of the Romantic theater, as well as Nerval's translation of Goethe's *Faust.* The young artists were deeply stirred; Delacroix began work on his lithographs to *Faust,* Berlioz set out to write the *Eight Scenes from Faust,* later published as Opus 1. He sent the score to Goethe who resided in Olympian grandeur in Weimar; but since Zelter, Goethe's musical "advisor," had an uncomplimentary opinion about Berlioz, the young composer was never honored with an answer. Almost twenty years later, in 1846, Berlioz incorporated his early *Faust* into *La damnation de Faust* for solo, chorus, and orchestra. To a young musician of Berlioz' generation, these extra-musical experiences were overshadowed by the contact with a musical genius hitherto almost unknown in France — Beethoven. The year 1828 saw the birth of a new orchestral organization, the *Société des Concerts du Conservatoire*, which, under the vigorous leadership of Habeneck, considered the propagation of Beethoven's orchestral works its primary task. It was a step of vital necessity and far-reaching consequence, for Paris had been without a regular symphony orchestra since 1816 when the famous orchestral *exercises* of the *Conservatoire* were curtailed by the Bourbon regime. Thus, a whole young generation of musicians and listeners was growing up without adequate knowledge of the symphonic repertoire; the occasional student concerts of the *École royale de musique* (successor to the *Conservatoire*) or the few *Concerts spirituels* were wholly inadequate to fill the need. In fact, as early as 1805 feeble attempts were made to revive the tradition of the *Concert spirituel*, terminated in 1790. The concerts acquired more stature in 1818 when Habeneck was put in charge; they were offered during Holy Week at the *Académie royale* (the *Opéra*). After 1821, Baillot and Kreutzer shared the direction. The programs list Beethoven's name half a dozen times during the 1820's, but the performances were perfunctory, even "worse than mediocre." Berlioz describes the shocking behavior of Kreutzer during a rehearsal of Beethoven's Second Symphony:

> At the first hearing of the passages marked with red pencil Kreutzer fled, holding his ears, and it took much courage for him to return and listen to what was left of the Symphony . . .[30]

It became customary to replace the slow movement of the Second Symphony with the Andante of the Seventh Symphony. This version was much applauded during the 1820's at the *Opéra* concerts. As for Kreutzer, Berlioz adds with sarcasm:

This was the man ... to whom Beethoven dedicated one of his most sublime sonatas for violin and piano; one must admit that the homage was well placed ...*

Characteristic is the comment of Berlioz who admits that, until the *Société des Concerts* began to function in 1828, he

never paid much attention to purely instrumental music. The symphonies by Haydn and Mozart ... played by a feeble orchestra on far too large a stage, and with very bad acoustic arrangements ... sounded confused, poor, meagre. I had read through two of Beethoven's symphonies and had heard an Andante played which made me feel dimly that he was a great luminary.[31]

At the *Concerts spirituels,* the programs were restricted to older selections because of inadequate rehearsal time; so we hear from Fétis:

... there was only one rehearsal devoted to the vocal and solo numbers. Since there was no time to try new symphonies, one was obliged to have recourse to the old repertoire which everyone knew by heart ...[32]

The Bourbon regime wasted no time in eliminating all vestiges of the revolutionary past. The *Conservatoire de musique* — conceived and created during the ardent early years of the Revolution — was singled out for particularly harsh treatment. It began in 1815 with the dismissal of its founder-director, Bernard Sarrette. To the reactionary forces in the new government, Sarrette was a symbol of what the *Conservatoire* represented — Republican origins, democratic procedures, freedom of art. His dismissal was the beginning of a well-laid plan to abolish the *Conservatoire* altogether.

The plan of action was as simple as it was clever: back in 1795, the *Conservatoire* had absorbed the *École royale de chant;* now, in 1816, the procedure would be reversed and a reconstituted *École royale* was to absorb the *Conservatoire.*[33] By March 15, 1816, the process was completed. The whole maneuver was an administrative plot or, to use Cherubini's

---

*Beethoven's Sonata Op. 47 was published in 1805 with a dedication to Kreutzer who never played it; he declared the work to be "utterly unintelligible."

stronger words, "a perfidious conspiracy of the Department of the Interior."

Many of the most respected teachers were dismissed "with regrets," among them the eighty-two year old Gossec who, paradoxically, had been the first director of the prerevolutionary *École royale*. Another was Catel; according to some biographers, he resigned in protest of the treatment accorded to Sarrette and refused all offers to rejoin the faculty in later years.[34] Cherubini and Méhul, although retained as teachers of composition, were deprived of their title of "inspectors of instruction." Many others who remained on the faculty (among them Kreutzer, Baillot, Habeneck, and Adam) were subjected to salary reductions. The whole school was reduced in scope; at times, the strained budget did not even permit heating the building sufficiently. Once again, the emphasis in instruction was shifted to the vocal department, favoring operatic preparation at the expense of instrumental teaching.

The immediate result of this reorganization, indeed a damaging blow to French musical culture, was the curtailment of the orchestral concerts which had contributed so immeasurably to the musical life of Paris. In a memorandum of 1816, François Perne, the new director, said that it was impossible, for the present, to resume the *exercises*, for, in order to continue, too many outside artists would have to participate which would falsify the character of "student" performances. Perne also implied that, for the past fifteen years, students had continued to participate in the *Conservatoire* concerts long after they had graduated and entered the professional field.[35]

To replace the concerts, Perne planned to present mixed programs — fragments of serious and comic operas, spoken tragedies and comedies, interspersed with instrumental music — in other words, a revival of the "lyric and dramatic" *exercises*. The educational value of the *exercises* was never questioned, for they were a "powerful means to make the students work." But instead of the regular *exercises* to be given every second Sunday, as planned, Perne succeeded in presenting only one in 1817, one in 1818, two in 1819, and none in 1820. There was more activity in 1821 when six programs were given, and an official decree (1822) reestablished six annual concerts under the old name of *exercices publics.* However, a month later Perne resigned as director, and Cherubini was named his successor on April 20, 1822 — a post which he was to occupy for twenty years. Due to these changes, no concerts were offered during that year. Obviously, Cherubini was interested in continuing and even expanding the student concerts, for a decree, dated January 29, 1823, increased the number of concerts from six to twelve and permitted the participation of alumni of the *École royale,* meaning students who had graduated since 1816. But very little became of these plans: six concerts were presented in 1823, and only three in 1824, after which the student *exercises* were dropped completely. Altogether there were only nineteen such performances during the Restoration (1815-30) as compared to one hundred forty-four during the preceding sixteen-year period (1800-15). More harmful than the mere drop in numbers, however, was the fact that Paris had lost the focal point, the nerve center of instrumental music. This, in turn, discouraged French composers from attempting works in the symphonic medium, for there was no organization, no forum, to present them.

The final discontinuance of the *exercices publics* in 1824 made some independent action almost inevitable and led to the foundation of the *Société des Concerts du Conservatoire.* Membership in this orchestra was open exclusively to alumni of the old *Conservatoire* and its successor, the *École royale de musique,* though members of the faculty and qualified students were also permitted to participate. The number of *sociétaires,* i.e. performing orchestra members, was fixed at one hundred. At first, foreign artists were rigidly excluded; the bylaws modified this ban somewhat by saying that, should the performance of a foreign artist be considered necessary, the entire active membership was to vote on that issue. Six concerts were to be given each year, to begin not later than the first Sunday in March, at intervals of two weeks.

The driving force of this new association was François Habeneck, a man who was thoroughly familiar with the traditions of the old *Conservatoire* concerts, having conducted them since his student days in the early 1800's. Prior to the official founding of the *Société,* he had assembled a number of musicians, mostly members of the *Opéra* orchestra and alumni of the *Conservatoire,* and aroused their interest by informally rehearsing Beethoven's *Eroica.* [36] These meetings continued informally throughout the years 1826 and 1827 until the time was ripe for the official establishment of the association.

The application to the authorities, however, came from Cherubini, director of the *École royale de musique,* who was anxious — so the authorizing decree stated —

> to restore to this school the reputation which it had acquired through the perfection of its public exercises and who assured us that these concerts are a powerful means of emulation for the students and even for the professors.

Thus, the *Société des Concerts du Conservatoire,* though in fact independent, was officially a continuation of the old *Conservatoire* concerts.

The orchesta of the *Société* opened with a membership of eighty-four players, distributed as follows:

15 first violins (including Habeneck who conducted
        with violin and bow in hand)
15 second violins
 8 violas
12 cellos
 8 double basses
 4 flutes
 3 oboes
 4 clarinets
 4 bassoons
 4 horns
 2 trumpets
 3 trombones
 1 timpani
 1 harp

There was also a vocal ensemble of 79 voices —

17   sopranos I
19   sopranos II
20   tenors
21   basses

The first concert, on Sunday, March 9, 1828, at two
o'clock, presented the following program:

1.	Symphony No. 3 *(Eroica)*	Beethoven
2.	Duo from *Semiramis*	Rossini
3.	Solo for *cor à piston*	Meifred
4.	Violin Concerto	Rode*
	Soloist: Sauzay	
5.	Air	Rossini
6.	Chorus from *Blanche de Provence*	Cherubini
7.	Overture *Les abencérages*	Cherubini
8.	Kyrie and Gloria from *Messe du Sacre*	Cherubini

The concert was a triumphant success. Those who remembered the old *exercices publics* greeted their return
with enthusiasm, while the young generation of musicians
and connoisseurs experienced a revelation. Fétis, who was
a student of the *Conservatoire* in the early 1800's, wrote a
report in his *Revue musicale* which deserves to be quoted
extensively:[37]

> ... The 9th of March, 1828, will be inscribed as a great day in the annals
> of French music, and as the era of its regeneration. Not only that the
> performance recaptured the stamp of superiority which gave the Conserva-
> toire a European reputation, but a spiritual influence of the highest order
> has developed here ... What verve, what energy, what ensemble, what a
> finish of nuances has the performance of the *Eroica* shown ... A un-
> animity of sentiment, an electric spark animated and directed everyone,
> and the many individuals seemed to be fused into one. The considerable
> difficulties of this great and magnificent composition** were conquered as

---

*This is Rode's last Violin Concerto (No. 13, published posthumously), dedicated
to his old friend Baillot. However, Baillot was indisposed and asked the concert
committee to assign the solo part to the eighteen-year old Éugène Sauzay, a
recent first-prize winner of the Conservatoire. Baillot may have been preoccupied
with the Parisian premiere of the Beethoven Concerto which he was to play two
weeks later.
**The *Eroica.*

if it were nothing but a benevolent symphony by Gyrowetz or Wranitzki. Lightness of runs, majestic effects of *piano* of an immense orchestra, thunders of *forte*, everything was perfect, admirable, in short worthy of the foremost artists of the capital of France. Do you hear, young students? the foremost artists! and you were part of this orchestra! Do not ever forget it, and may this memory be for you one of a great victory . . .

One cannot praise enough the zeal and talent which Mr. Habeneck showed on this occasion as conductor of the orchestra; it is impossible to perceive the composer's general and particular intentions better than this artist has done . . . and at the same time have more self-possession, more assurance in the moments of animation . . . Mr. Habeneck conducts the concerts with the violin. This fact explains the difference which one notices in him when he is at the helm of such an orchestra as compared to his conducting at the Opéra. With his violin he warms up and shares the general thrill; with the baton he remains icy and bored; besides, at the concert, he sees his orchestra while at the Opéra, due to the stupid arrangement there, the orchestra is behind him.

. . . Beethoven's *Eroica* . . . a masterwork of the grandiose, of energy, grace, and originality. One does not know what to admire more: the profusion of motives, the art of presenting them in a prodigious variety of forms, or the novelty of effects. Who could believe, however, that until today this magnificent composition has not been heard in Paris? But how could it be without the reestablishment of the concerts of the Conservatoire? . . . the resolution of the directors of the new concerts to have only new or unknown music played or sung, will add much to the chances of success of these sessions . . . It is impossible to imagine that in any place in Europe one could have a better performance of music.

Fétis erred in saying that this was the first Paris performance of the *Eroica:* it had been played by the *Conservatoire* orchestra in 1811, at one of the student *exercises.* It only proves how completely forgotten those early Beethoven performances were even by men of the older generation.

However, the *Société des Concerts,* and especially its aim to make Beethoven known, met with considerable passive opposition. Many of the French and Italian composers, so we hear from Berlioz, were "ill-pleased to see an altar erected to a German, whose works they deemed monstrosities, and regarded as fraught with danger to themselves and their school." There was "silent opposition, ill-concealed dislike, and ironical reserve" among them, for they considered instrumental music as a "respectable, but distinctly inferior, branch of art, and believed that Haydn and Mozart had achieved all that could be looked for in that direction."[38] Among those cool toward the project Berlioz mentions many well-known musicians — Berton, Kreutzer, Boieldieu, Lesueur, Paer, Catel, and Cherubini. Yet it seems improbable that Cherubini should not have been aware of Habeneck's plan to favor Beethoven's works.

The second concert of the *Société des Concerts,* on March 22, 1828, presented an All-Beethoven program, in commemoration of the first anniversary of his death. The program consisted of a repeat performance of the *Eroica* Symphony, the *Benedictus* from the Mass Op. 86 in C major, the first movement of the Third Piano Concerto in C minor, the vocal quartet from *Fidelio,* the oratorio *Christus am Ölberge* ("Mount of Olives"), and the first Parisian performance of the Violin Concerto, played by Baillot.*

Again Fétis devoted several pages to an enthusiastic review of the concert. He found the Violin Concerto "one of the most beautiful conceptions imaginable . . . a continuous enchantment." Baillot received equal praise: "Never before has this great violinist shown greater mastery . . . It was a veritable triumph."[39]

The next concert, on April 13, brought Beethoven's Fifth Symphony, *"ouvrage colossal",* performed with the usual perfection. "There is only one voice among the foreign artists who abound in Paris at this moment: it is that of admiration for a perfection which almost surpasses the limits of human abilities," reported Fétis.[40] Lesueur, who went to hear it at the insistence of his young student Berlioz, admitted that the symphony had affected him deeply, but said reproachfully, "All the same, such music ought not to be written." Whereupon Berlioz replied, "Don't be afraid, *cher maître,* there will not be much of it produced."[41]

---

*This performance was virtually a rediscovery of Beethoven's Violin Concerto. Since its premiere in Vienna in 1806, it had been played only twice — 1812 in Berlin and 1814 in Vienna, both times by Luigi Tomasini Jr.

During the first four seasons (1828-32), the *Société des Concerts* presented all nine symphonies by Beethoven, most of them in first performances. Here are the dates:

Symphony	No. 3 — March	9,	1828
"	No. 5 — April	13,	"
"	No. 7 — March	1,	1829
"	No. 6 — March	15,	"
"	No. 4 — Feb.	21,	1830
"	No. 2 — Apr.	25,	"
"	No. 1 — May	9,	"
"	No. 9 — March	27,	1831
"	No. 8 — Feb.	19,	1832

Among other composers, Mozart was generally well represented; a special Memorial Concert on April 27, 1828, brought the Symphony in E flat, a piano concerto, the finale from the *Jupiter* symphony, the *Magic Flute* overture, and some vocal excerpts. Haydn, once indispensable on concert programs, was not performed at all during the first year, and sparingly later on; the first concert of the second season (1829) was dedicated to his memory and included one of his symphonies, the *Storm and Calm* from *The Seasons*, as well as the Violin Concerto No. 16 by Kreutzer on themes by Haydn and Cherubini's *Cantata on the Death of Haydn.* * Another concert, in 1830, was dedicated to the memory of Méhul and brought back some of the old favorites, such as the overtures to *Jeune Henri* and *Stratonice*. Weber's overtures were very popular with performers and public. Cherubini received fewer performances than might have been expected, in view of his influential position; after the first concert, which presented three of his works, his name appeared only occasionally.

---

*The two works by Kreutzer and Cherubini were actually composed early in 1805, in spontaneous response to the rumor that Haydn had died. A memorial concert was set in Paris for February 6, 1805, but the program was changed when the news arrived that Haydn was alive and well. Cherubini's *Cantata* was first performed at the Conservatoire in February, 1810, commemorating Haydn's actual death in 1809. Kreutzer played his "Concerto on themes by Haydn" in 1805.

The first years of the *Société des Concerts* were full of exploratory zeal, especially with regard to Beethoven's works. However, once that source was exhausted, the program policy became stale and stagnant. The original resolution of the founders to perform "only new or unknown music,"* was soon buried and forgotten. There was an "ostracism of living composers which imperiled the whole development of music," as the French writer H. Prunières said.[42] New composers were admitted with reluctance; and whenever a novelty was presented, the choice was arbitrary and undistinguished.

The All-Beethoven program of the *Société des Concerts* inspired Berlioz to venture a concert devoted entirely to his own compositions, which no French composer had ever dared. Innumerable difficulties had to be overcome; not the smallest was to obtain the directorial permission of Cherubini for the use of the *Conservatoire* hall.

Cherubini's hesitation** was all the more understandable since Berlioz, still a student of the *Conservatoire,* had failed twice in his attempts to win the *Prix de Rome* (1826 and 1827).*** To make matters worse, the program was to include a cantata rejected as "unplayable" by the Institute,[43] and Cherubini sensed a certain arrogance in Berlioz' request.

Finally all obstacles were overcome; Berlioz copied with his own hand all the parts for chorus and orchestra, which kept him at his desk sixteen hours a day. Although many of his performers participated without remuneration, he spent his last savings on the concert which took place on May 26, 1828. The program included the overtures to *Waverley* and *Francs-Juges,* a vocal excerpt from *Francs-Juges,* the *Choeur et marche des mages,* the "Resurrexit" from his *Mass,* and the *Scène héroique: La révolution grecque.* The "unplayable" cantata had to be taken off the program

---

*See Fétis' review on p. 56.
**In his humorous account of this incident, Berlioz ridiculed Cherubini mercilessly (*Memoirs,* pp. 70-72).
***The first time, Berlioz was eliminated at the preliminary examination.

because of insufficient rehearsal time. Berlioz himself called the concert "futile"; the conductor, Bloc of the *Odéon*, was incompetent, the soloists indisposed or untalented, orchestra and chorus under-rehearsed and unsure, the attendance of the public very poor.

Yet, Berlioz achieved his goal of attracting the attention of influential musical circles in Paris; even Fétis, later one of his most venomous critics, wrote a good review in the *Revue musicale*. After identifying the young composer as a "student at the Royal School of Music," Fétis praised his talent, though with reservations:

> Mr. Berlioz has the happiest of gifts; he has ability, he has genius. His style is energetic and sinewy. His inspirations are often graceful. But still more often the composer — carried away by his young and ardent inspiration — spends himself in search of original and passionate effects ... His originality often borders on the bizarre; his instrumentation is often confused; his melodies are at times arid; grandly he aims at big musical effects, and his exaggeration causes him to overshoot his aim which he could have reached easily by better control of these means.[44]

A few months later, Berlioz entered again the competition for the Rome prize and obtained the second prize (July 1828). His chances to win the first prize the following year were considered excellent. Overly confident, Berlioz decided against making any concessions to suit the "special prejudices" (i.e. the conservatism) of the Academy. This proved to be a mistake, for the jury decided "not to award any prize that year (1829) rather than encourage a young composer who *manifested such tendencies.*" The following day, Berlioz accidentally met Boieldieu, a member of the jury, who told him that he "threw the prize away" by composing a work which was too complicated.[45]

In the meatime, his literary colleagues were more active than ever. In 1829, Hugo published his *Orientales,* Stendhal his *Promenades dans Rome,* Mérimée his *Chronique du règne de Charles IX;* Musset wrote his *Contes d'espagne et d'Italie,* and Dumas succeeded with his play *Henri III et sa cour.* Another important publication of the same year was the *Préface des Etudes françaises et étrangères* by Emile Deschamps, an important manifesto dealing primarily with romantic poetry.

But even more important, from the artistic as well as political point of view, was the year 1830. Victor Hugo obtained a triumphant success with his play *Hernani* (February 25), a success which was literally enforced by the tightly-knit group of *Jeune-France*. The riot in the audience was a veritable fistfight, and that memorable premiere is known, in literary histories, as *La bataille d'Hernani*. However, the press was generally favorable, and the public accepted the victory of the Romantic movement.

In the meantime, Berlioz was intensely at work. "I am preparing an immense instrumental composition of a novel genre," he wrote to his sister; the *Symphonie fantastique* was taking shape. By April, 1830, the work was finished, but the first performance was delayed until December 5.

That summer Berlioz entered the Rome Prize competition for the fifth time. After finishing his assignment, a cantata, in complete seclusion, according to the rules, he left the Academy on July 29, 1830, and found the city in the midst of a Revolution. It was the last of the "Three Glorious Days" — the Bourbon monarchy was overthrown, Charles X was in flight. *Jeune-France* joined the popular movement. Berlioz, stirred by the people's enthusiasm, seized a pair of pistols, but there was no cause to shoot; all was calm. Three weeks later, on August 21, he received the *Grand Prix de Rome*. He was twenty-seven years old.

***

We have reached a turning point in history — political, artistic, literary, musical. Particularly in music, the decade of the 1820's marked the end of an era and the beginning of a new one. Many composers left the scene, either through death or retirement. Weber died in 1826, Beethoven in 1827,

Schubert in 1828. Cherubini and Boieldieu approached the end of their creative career. Lesueur and Catel, Rode and Kreutzer ceased to be active as composers, while Rossini simply decided to retire. Their places were taken quickly by a vigorous young generation: born between 1800 and 1815, they emerged during the 1820's and 1830's — Berlioz, Auber, Halévy, Mendelssohn, Schumann, Chopin, Liszt, de Bériot, Vieuxtemps, Meyerbeer, Wagner. And finally there was the lonely, meteoric figure of Nicolò Paganini who mesmerized Europe with his demoniac virtuosity. In his *Twenty-four Caprices* for violin, published in 1820, technique was raised to the level of art: they were proudly dedicated "To the Artists," and artists everywhere rose to the challenge, not only violinists but also pianists and composers, among them Liszt and Schumann.

To the young generation, Romanticism was no longer a problem but a natural language, the language of their times, which they spoke with ease and fluency. But the preceding generation of composers had to struggle and explore; because they often attempted the new and unknown, because they lived in a time of shifting aesthetic values and changing emphasis, they did not always achieve perfection and balance. Posterity belittled them, rather unfairly, as "precursors" or "pre-Romanticists." Alfred Einstein expressed it so well:

> What good fortune the great have! They endure while lesser figures sink into obscurity; they receive all the credit for things whose origins have been lost to sight. In addition, their lifework stands before us as a totality in which the less important works illuminate the more significant and take on consequence from them. The secondary works of a great composer are more important to us than the principal works of a minor composer ...[46]

The following chapters will deal with works of pioneering composers and "forerunners" who contributed significantly to the eventual flowering of musical Romanticism in the 19th century.

PART II

Instrumental Music
in France

CHAPTER 3

Orchestral Music in France from 1789 to 1830

During the winter season of 1901-02, the *Concerts Colonne* of Paris presented a historical survey of the French symphony. Only three composers prior to Berlioz were given a place on the programs — Gossec, Méhul, and Herold. Far from being impressed with these manifestations of the *génie français,* Julien Tiersot, the distinguished French musicologist, treated them rather condescendingly in one of his reviews.[1]

In planning these programs, the *Concerts Colonne* chose to ignore French symphonic music prior to the year 1774, for the earliest example presented was the *Symphonie de chasse* by Gossec. This had its good reason, for the early symphonies of the 1750's and 1760's are hardly appropriate for performances in modern over-sized concert halls.[2] As for the succeeding decades, the *Concerts Colonne* could make no mistake, for during half a century, from 1780 to 1830, Méhul and Herold were in fact the only symphonic composers in France, if one chooses to exclude — as the Colonne concerts did — the single symphony (1815) of the Franco-Italian Cherubini. It is indeed a strange phenomenon that, while there was an abundance of instrumental music written in France before the Revolution of 1789, we witness an almost complete stagnation and loss of interest during the succeeding period.

The primary reason for this reversal was undoubtedly sociological. During the *ancien régime,* music had three large areas in which it functioned — church, stage, and chamber. The last category included all music that was neither religious nor operatic; thus it comprised symphonies and small ensembles, instrumental as well as vocal. All this wealth of music was performed in the "chambers" of the court, the aristocracy, and wealthy patrons; it was music played in intimate, yet resplendent, surroundings, for a select public of connoisseurs by performers including professionals and skilled amateurs. Even the *Concerts spirituels* preserved a semi-private character, for they were given in one of the halls at the *Palais des Tuileries,* while other concerts were presented at the palatial homes of various sponsors. For these private and public concerts, French composers and publishers provided a steady supply of instrumental music which received eager and frequent performances.

The Revolution of 1789 brought a complete change and the church and chamber musicians found themselves unemployed while the theater musicians were busier than ever. Under the aegis of Napoleon, a new upper and middle class emerged with all the traits of the parvenu and a thin varnish of quickly-acquired "culture." The natural setting for this new society was the opera, with its splendor and make-believe; consequently, French composers turned from the ungrateful task of writing symphonies and chamber music, for which there was so little demand, to the more rewarding field of the lyric stage. However, the interest in virtuoso performances remained strong which encouraged the writing of concertos, *symphonies concertantes,* and brilliant variations on popular operatic airs.

Yet, the lack of demand may not have been the only reason for the dearth of symphonic music in France between 1780 and 1830. To a composer of those days, an opera was not only a more remunerative assignment, but also a more challenging task. The generation of the late 18th and early 19th centuries, among them Méhul, Cherubini, Lesueur, Catel, and Berton, struggled with a new problem — to combine "Gluck's dramaturgical theories with the symphonic ideal,"[3] as represented by Haydn and his motivic-thematic development technique. Always in search of logical dramaturgic development, the French discovered the potentialities of the *leitmotif* as part of dramatic construction. While a theorist like Lacépède[4] discussed its possibilities, a practical musician like Grétry applied it in his opera *Richard Coeur de Lion* (1784). Developing this idea with utmost consequence, Méhul produced *Ariodant* (1799), an opera built on a single fundamental motive called *cri de fureur,* which — and this is significant — was not only used dramatically but also developed symphonically.[5]

> With the adaptation of a symphonic -thematic technique, the leitmotif received a new scope and was to overshadow every other consideration. An instrumental operatic style arose which gradually surrendered the prerogatives of the singing voice to the orchestra.[6]

It seems as if French composers of that generation were so absorbed by the supreme challenge of the symphonic-dramatic opera that they lost interest in the solution of a seemingly subordinate problem, that of the symphony proper. It is noteworthy that both Cherubini and Méhul wrote symphonies toward the end of their careers as successful opera composers, while Herold composed his two symphonies very early in his life, as a preparation for greater things to come. Their efforts failed, on the whole, because their approach was formalistic; it was Beethoven who succeeded in transplanting the magnificent dramatic elements of the French revolutionary lyric drama into the realm of absolute music. Perhaps the French realized instinctively that he succeeded where they failed, and this spiritual kinship may explain the fervent devotion with which Beethoven's music is regarded in France until today.

Whatever skill, talent, and imagination French composers could muster was given to the lyric stage, and theirs was indeed a magnificent contribution. Yet, instrumental music was not excluded, for the French composers found an ideal medium in the operatic overture. Whenever one speaks of French contributions to orchestral music, the overture should be placed first and foremost, for here the French succeeded in fusing operatic and symphonic elements in an astounding way.

The custom of performing overtures on concert programs dates back to the last decades of the 18th century. Once a beginning was made, however, they came so popular that no concert program was complete without at least one overture. It goes without saying that certain overtures did not lend themselves to concert performances; some were too short and designed merely as curtain raisers, others were meant to be played with the curtain actually raised or with action on the stage, while a third type was planned to lead directly without break into the first scene. The great overtures by Gluck, for instance, belonged to the last category and were thus excluded from concert performances until provided with concert endings. Among French composers, however, we find a preference for brilliant endings, and only few close calmly and lyrically.

The transplantation of operatic overtures into the concert hall could not fail to influence the development of the symphony which gradually acquired certain — essentially operatic — elements, such as a richer, more diversified and colorful orchestra, more dramatic and emotional intensity, and a tendency toward tone painting, i.e. program music. In the development of the 19th century symphony, the infiltration of operatic traits played undoubtedly a dominant role.

The opera orchestra was already a highly flexible and sensitive organism at a time when, in the 1750's, the symphony orchestra was in its infancy, trying to find its own laws and potentialities. Many orchestral innovations and new timbres, such as the use of four horns, of clarinets, trombones, massed harps, and diversified percussion, can be traced back to operatic origins. The reason for this spirit of exploration is not difficult to perceive, for the infinite variety of subjects and situations portrayed by the lyric stage stimulated the imagination of the composers into widening and enriching the gamut of orchestral expressiveness.

While the opera thus encouraged the unrestrained use of all orchestral resources, the symphonic orchestra remained, for a long time, restricted in size and tonal volume. The same composers who did not hesitate to use a brass section of nine instruments — four horns, two trumpets, and three trombones — in an operatic climax (possibly with *pavillons levés,* i.e. bells up, to achieve more volume) became subdued when orchestrating a symphony. This holds true of Mozart, Cherubini, and Méhul, even Beethoven and Mendelssohn. A possible explanation for this comparative restraint is the 18th century concept of the symphony as "chamber music" which was carried over well into the 19th century; whereas operas were almost invariably performed in large theaters for a very numerous public. Be it as it may, the juxtaposition, on the same programs, of the richly orchestrated operatic overtures and the comparatively restrained sound of a symphony by Haydn or Mozart must have been startling to even the least initiated listener. No wonder that, for a long time, the loudest among the Haydn symphonies (now known as the "Military," No. 100) was also the most popular; the Parisian public did not tire of hearing this symphony *avec la musique turque.*

The enriched orchestration contributed by the opera served, as we have said, the ultimate purpose of covering a wider range of expression and emotion. The drama, pathos, and poignancy which entered the instrumental style by way of the operatic overture during the 1790's contrasted sharply with the placidity of the average 18th century symphony. Indeed, the difference is so striking that some historians speak of a "revolutionary" instrumental style in discussing the last decade of the 18th century. Whether this stylistic evolution was caused by, or merely coincided with, the political revolution of 1789, is a matter of interpretation; the new trends can be detected in certain pre-revolutionary works such as the overtures to *Démophon* by Johann Christoph Vogel (1787) and by Cherubini (1788), both of which are related to Gluck and particularly to his *Alceste.*

While the overtures to the *tragédie lyrique* generally preserved some of the restrained beauty of its supreme master, Gluck, we see this style vitalized, expanded, and brought to exciting new life in the overtures to the *opéra comique* or — to use a more appropriate term — the *drame lyrique* of the 1790's. The quickened pulse of the revolutionary decade transformed the somewhat static tragedy of Gluck into swiftly moving dramatic action, on the stage as well as in the orchestra. The new mood of the French people, reflected in martial airs, bellicose defiance, stark realism, sweeping passion, and characteristic grandeur and pomp, is so dominant and outspoken in representative operas of the period, that we feel justified in speaking of a French "revolutionary" style.

It is interesting to note that this style appears to be one of the important sources of Beethoven's "dramatic" instrumental style, a fact which has not been emphasized sufficiently by his biographers. Beethoven transplanted the "revolutionary" style, which is essentially sceno-dramatic, into instrumental music. In this he was preceded by men like Cherubini and Méhul who, in their overtures and interludes, made an important contribution to the instrumental style of the 19th century. The influence of the French *opéra comique* on the orchestral techniques of the Romantic era is not yet sufficiently recognized;[7] in fact, 19th century musical Romanticism derived one of its strongest impulses from the French revolutionary opera. It is a historical fallacy — though nurtured by some German historians — that musical Romanticism was a German monopoly; we must at last recognize the important contribution made by French musicians. To the feminine, sweet sadness which is of Austro-German origin, the French added the masculine characteristics of

Romanticism — pomp, passion, sweep, and chivalry, and out
of the fusion of all these ingredients arose the ideal Romantic
style. True, some of the greatest representatives of musical
Romanticism were Germans, not Frenchmen, for the Austro-
German composers absorbed and integrated the French
influence most eagerly, while the French did not accept as
readily the Germanic components of the Romantic style.
Thus, the French role within musical Romanticism is one of
contribution rather than fulfillment; yet, an all-important
contribution it was.

One of the trends favored — if not initiated — by French
composers was that of program music, and here again, the
operatic overture played an important part. The connection
is obvious, for the primary function of the overture is the
setting of a certain mood, the foreshadowing or description
of events and characters expressed through purely musical
means. This was achieved with unfailing musical and dramatic
insight by French composers of the 1790's and 1800's who
created masterpieces of musical characterization and stage-
setting. From a suggestive to a descriptive program was only
a short step which Méhul took in writing *La chasse du jeune
Henri*, an outspoken piece of program music cast in a form
dictated by the course of events rather than musical laws. In
spite of its unparalleled success, there were no immediate
imitations, and program music of such a "realistic" type lagged in France until the advent of Berlioz. By then, the noble
genre of the overture had deteriorated into an artless potpourri of operatic tunes; no wonder that Berlioz sought his
inspiration in the works of Gluck, Méhul, and Spontini.

***

Etienne Méhul

Between 1790 and 1810, the most important and influential composer in Paris, next to Cherubini, was undoubtedly Etienne Méhul. Their achievements have been compared

by many historians, and such comparisons usually tend to favor Cherubini.

Admittedly, the scope of Cherubini's musicianship was more comprehensive, and his technical equipment was superior. Yet, if Méhul's writing was less elaborate, it was also less labored than Cherubini's. There is, in Méhul, a natural flow, an innate musicianship, an almost effortless, intuitive, and yet well-planned, handling of all musical and dramatic problems which is thoroughly convincing and moving. Contrary to Cherubini, whose thematic invention was often contrived and anemic, Méhul's melodies flow with ease and dramatic truthfulness. One must take issue with Carl Maria von Weber's opinion in calling Cherubini "genialer" and Méhul "besonnener"; on the contrary, there is more innate musicianship in Méhul, and more intellectual accomplishment in Cherubini. Let us quote Weber while disagreeing in part with his judgment:

> Méhul unquestionably occupies, next to Cherubini, the first place among the composers who developed and formed their art and career predominantly in France and who, by the truthfulness of their accomplisments, became the property of all nations. If, perhaps, Cherubini has more genius, Méhul has more thoughtfulness, the wisest calculation and use of his means, and a certain solid clarity which testify to his study of older Italian masters and especially the dramatic works by Gluck . . . His characteristic qualities are dramatic truthfulness and lively action without useless repetitions, the accomplishment of great effects, often with the simplest means, and an economy of orchestration which limits itself to what is absolutely essential.[8]

Cherubini and Méhul had one important trait in common — their art was rooted in Gluck; but due to their different background, schooling, and temperament, this influence bore different fruit.

Cherubini's influence on his generation was not so much one of *expression* as of *craftsmanship*. In Méhul's works, technical details seem of secondary importance compared to the dramatic power, flaming passion, and flair for theatrical effects. His youthful sweep, his profound feeling for the innate rhythm and melody of the French language, the vigor and resourcefulness of his orchestration exerted a decisive influence on his contemporaries in France and abroad. Méhul's handling of the orchestra shows constant preoccupation with instrumental colors, knowing exploitation of individual timbres, power and richness without noise; at all times, his instruments are participants, not mere accompanists, in the unfolding of the drama. "Méhul has suddenly tripled the power of the orchestra with a richness always adjusted to the situation,"[9] exclaims Grétry whose scoring of *Richard Coeur de Lion* (1784) looks indeed pathetically thin compared to Méhul's *Euphrosine* (1790). This judicious and imaginative use of the orchestra makes Méhul stand out among his contemporaries. "The interesting orchestration of Méhul is very superior to that of his contemporaries and places him entirely apart from the French composers of his epoch," says Saint-Saëns many years later;[10] "not one instrument too much, not one out of place" (Berlioz).[11] However, these qualities are found primarily in his operas and overtures, while his symphonies are more conventional in the use of the orchestra.

Méhul's significance has, generally speaking, not as yet been fully evaluated by music historians. The few French biographies,[12] more or less accurate in their biographical data, are pitifully inadequate with regard to the analysis of style, form, orchestration, and similar matters. Kretzschmar and Botstiber[13] deal, not always successfully, with his operas and overtures; Lavoix's discussion of Méhul's orchestration contains errors. Strobel's essay on his operas is an important contribution but needs elaboration and ultimate incorporation into a full-length reevaluation of Méhul's creative life.

It is high time that we recognize Méhul in all his importance: he is one of France's truly great composers. But his significance transcends the borders of narrow nationalism: as the most characteristic representative of the French "revolutionary" style he is one of the main sources of 19th century musical Romanticism.

Like Cherubini, Méhul exerted his influence on the Romantic generation of the 1820's and 1803's without being a truly "Romantic" composer in the 19th-century meaning of the term. Méhul's Romanticism is that of the late 18th century, of *Storm and Stress* and the Revolution. After the classicistic recession of the Napoleonic era, many of the attributes of 18th century Romanticism reappeared with different motivation and meaning, in the works of the Romantic composers of the 1820's and 1830's, mainly Weber, Boieldieu, and Berlioz.

Already in his *Euphrosine et Coradin* (1790), still called *comédie,* Méhul widened the limitations of the traditional *opéra comique.* His was a new and virile art, full of vitality, power, and passion, which was recognized immediately by his contemporaries. They were impressed by the dramatic vigor of passionate climaxes which were masterfully underlined and heightened by an imaginative orchestration.

Of particular interest is the Overture which was performed repeatedly on concert programs. Consisting of a slow introduction in the tradition of Gluck, and a brilliant *Allegro* in a lively 18th century style, this overture reveals a flair for musical climaxes and a well-balanced, carefully conceived orchestration, using a comparatively small brass section of two horns and two trumpets. There is no inner link between the noble introduction in D minor and the somewhat conventional *Allegro* in D major; actually, the promise of the opening is not entirely fulfilled in the fast section (ex. III-1, III-2, III-3, III-4).

Example III-1. Méhul, *Euphrosine* (1790).

Example III-2. Gluck, *Iphigenia in Aulis* (1774).

Example III-3. Méhul, *Euphrosine*.

Example III-4. Beethoven, *Sonata for Violin and Piano, Op. 30 No. 2* (1802).

If the novelty and originality of *Euphrosine* attracted general attention, Méhul's next opera, *Stratonice* (1792), placed him firmly at the head of his French confreres. "The style of this young author, perfected every day, is already worthy, in many respects, to serve as model,"[14] said a contemporary critic. Called a "heroic comedy" in one act, the work was actually a "veritable tragedy of a stylistic purity recalling Racine," in the words of a modern historian.[15] This was no longer the conventional *opéra comique:* in Méhul's hands a new type of opera emerged.

The Overture to *Stratonice* was, in its time, one of the most frequently performed concert selections, and with full justification, for it is the most novel, most original and forward-looking composition of the entire revlutionary decade. Not until Cherubini's *Médée* (1797) can we find music comparable in greatness of style; not until Beethoven's overtures to *Coriolanus* (1807) and *Egmont* (1810) was music written that surpassed Méhul in grandeur, agitation, and drama. *Stratonice*, in fact, embodies the quintessence of "revolutionary" Romanticism, carried over into the 19th century, in a sublimized way, by Beethoven (ex. III-5, III-6, III-7).

Example III-5. Méhul, *Stratonice* (1792). Overture.

Example III-6. Beethoven, *Coriolanus* (1807). Overture.

Example III-7. Haydn, *Symphony No. 52 in C minor* (1772). First movement.

The Overture to *Stratonice* consists of two parts — a slow introduction and an *Allegro,* both in F minor, with a brilliant closing section in F major. While there is remarkable uniformity of mood in the two main parts, heightened by the use of the same key, there is structural weakness within the *Allegro* proper where the composer is unable to weld the contrasting themes firmly together. This is a shortcoming to be found often in Méhul as well as Charubini; it took the genius of a Beethoven to invent contrasting themes which do not break the continuity of musical pulse.

The orchestration of *Stratonice* is somewhat fuller than *Euphrosine,* adding a bass trombone to the two horns and two trumpets. Dynamics and nuances are marked with great thoroughness throughout the score; a curious indication is *timballes voilées* (covered kettledrums) prescribed at the beginning, though muffling of the entire orchestra, including the timpani, can be found in older French scores, notably those of Grétry.

Mélidore et Phrosine, a "lyric drama" (1794), has been described by one historian as Méhul's best opera "because of its purest personal content."[16] The work shows certain influences of Cherubini's "motive technique," but exceeds any model by its grandeur, power, and originality of harmony and rhythm.

The overture has almost Beethovenian vigor; strong dynamic contrasts and pulsating rhythms, showing a predeliction for syncopations, keep the interest intensely alive. The brass section of the orchestra uses four horns and one trombone without trumpets. Because of its lyric and calm ending, which foreshadows the actual closing of the opera, the overture was never performed as a concert piece.

The work opens with a slow introduction mixing various moods — grandiose, pathetic, and sorrowful — with clashing dynamic contrasts. A masterful transition leads to an *Allegro,* which has a first theme somewhat related, in character, to *Stratonice,* without being quite as original. The second theme is distinctly weaker in melodic invention. There is no formal development section; an agitated chromatic passage in the basses leads to the recapitulation, which follows the pattern of the exposition with minor variations. After a tonic chord we hear a seven-bar transition which leads to the closing section, a *Grazioso* in 6/8 time, establishing a calm and peaceful atmosphere.

H. Strobel's comments on the *Mélidore* are very enlightening and support our theory that the French revolutionary opera exerted decisive influence on composers like Beethoven, Weber, Mendelssohn, and many of the Romantic musicians. A scene in the second act reminds Strobel of the Dungeon Scene in *Fidelio;* and the end of the Sea Storm in the Third Act, with its thanksgiving after the storm, seems to point toward the *Pastoral* Symphony by Beethoven.[17] Méhul introduces the sea storm by the use of *melodrama,* i.e. spoken words with musical background, an effect often used in the French "terror" opera; such programmatic-pictorial compositions, says Strobel, lead directly to Weber and the *"Wolfsschlucht"* scene in *Freischütz.* The end of the opera, with its mild and peaceful mood, has a melodic line pointing directly to Weber.

Probably the most popular success of Méhul's career was the overture known as *La chasse du jeune Henri* (1797). Redemanded three times at the first performance, a custom was established to play Méhul's work regularly as *entr'acte* music, and for the next decades hardly a week passed without a performance of this overture. Even the sophisticated audiences of the *Conservatoire* concerts enjoyed the piece in the 1830's and 40's.

To judge *Le jeune Henri* objectively, one must forget the exaggerated praise lavished on it by contemporaries and later historians. To term this innocent piece of descriptive music a "symphonic poem," as Pougin[18] and Brancour[19] have done, is a gross exaggeration. Hunting pieces were popular in the 18th century, and Méhul must have known the examples of Haydn and especially Gossec whose symphony *La chasse* was frequently performed from 1774 on. The novelty, in Méhul's case, consisted in the programmatic character of the piece which followed a suggestive pattern of events.

It opens with a peaceful *Andante* in a pastoral mood, picturing the sunrise in the forest; from afar, we hear the beginning of the hunt, played by horns in *pianissimo*. (Incidentally, as many as eight horns were used for the performances of this overture.) The *Andante* returns in a short interlude, after which the hunt gets under way. The music is infectiously fresh, charming, and brilliantly effective although the purely musical content is thin. Yet, the listener has no time for reflection, for he is carried away by the galloping pace of the hunt pictured in gay 6/8 figures or in rushing sixteenth-runs of the violins. Finally the climax is reached when the animal succumbs, with the shot naively marked by kettledrums. A short *doloroso* interlude describes this sad event, after which the victorious shouts of the returning hunters bring the overture to a rousing close.

This colorful picturization charmed the French audiences who were always receptive to tone painting. But even nowadays a hearing of the recording by the Paris Lamoureux Orchestra is enjoyable. The ingenuity of Méhul in adjusting his music to a program rather than a standardized musical pattern is an important step toward program music as developed in the 1830's and 40's. However, the overture is too long for its thin musical content (on the record, the piece is slightly shortened); especially the piano reduction exposes mercilessly the poverty of material, while the orchestral version is carried by the brilliant use of instrumental colors.*

An important milestone is *Ariodant* (1799) which bears a dedication to Cherubini. The large score of 319 pages, worked out in every detail, has a preface by Méhul urging his colleagues to comment more freely on their artistic intentions and thus guide the public in musical matters. However, the significance of *Ariodant* lies not in words but in deeds: the consistent use of a *leitmotiv* (called *cri de fureur*), introduced dramatically throughout the opera, makes it a work of epochal importance in the history of the opera (ex. III-8, III-9).

Example III-8. Méhul, *Ariodant*. Introduction to Act III.

Example III-9. Méhul, *L'Irato* (1801).

The work has no formal overture; each of the three acts opens with a short instrumental prelude setting the mood and leading into the first scene without break. The prelude to the first act, scored for full orchestra including four horns,

---

*A more positive evaluation is given by Alexander Ringer who writes that the *Allegro* section in Méhul's *La chasse du jeune Henri* "offers the first satisfactory compromise between the sonata outline and the expressive demands of the underlying topic." (See "The *Chasse* as a musical topic of the 18th century," *Journal of the American Musicological Society* VI (1953), pp. 158-159).

two trumpets, and one trombone, consists of a short *Adagio* in G major, opening with three solo cellos accompanied by a fourth cello and double bass. Lavoix' mention of a trombone participating in the beginning is based on misreading of the score.[20] From this calm beginning, tenseness arises and a beautiful climax is built up; after the *fortissimo* is reached, a sudden *piano* changes the mood, and the curtain rises.

The prelude to the second act is described by Cherubini as "very original, a prelude to a nocturnal festival";[21] it leads directly into the chorus *Oh nuit*. A long instrumental prelude precedes the third act preparing in a sublime way the mood of the ensuing aria by Edgard. In this powerful, agitated piece, with its fiery expression and dramatic emotion, Méhul foreshadows Beethoven in a startling way, showing once more the strong ties between Beethoven and the masters of the revolutionary French opera (ex. III-10, III-11).

Example III-10. Méhul, *Ariodant.* Introduction to Act III.

Example III-11. Méhul, *Ariodant.* Introduction to Act III.

At the peak of his success as dramatic composer, Méhul suddenly decided to try a different style. Beginning with *L'Irato* in 1801, he wrote several operas in the *buffo* and *comique* genre — unpretentious works on a smaller scale, using a reduced orchestra. Realizing that such a shift would be questioned and perhaps criticized, he supplied the engraved edition of *L'Irato* with two prefaces: the first, a dedication to "Général Bonaparte, premier consul de la République française," the second, a note addressed to his public. In the dedication, he credits Bonaparte with having inspired him to write in a lighter vein; in his *Note* he denies any "conversion" and says that any genre is justified as long as it is "agreeable and truthful." In fact, one wonders why Méhul should be so apologetic about writing a comic opera since this was not his first attempt in this genre: one of his early successes had been the humorous *Le jeune sage et le vieux fou* (1793) (ex. III-12, III-13).

Example III-12. Méhul, *L'Irato* (1801).

Example III-13. Mozart, *Le nozze di Figaro* (1786). Overture.

Méhul's shift from the dramatic to the comic genre had several reasons of which Bonaparte's avowed preference for Italian music was only one. The public taste was moving away from the revolutionary "terror" style toward lighter, gayer entertainment — today one would call it "escapism." Méhul was very much aware of public trends; he longed for a truly popular success which, despite all acclaim by the connoisseurs, he had not achieved with his serious works. His comic operas had a measure of success though some contemporary critics, including Cherubini, considered his talent more suited to the dramatic genre. Yet, his lighter efforts were acclaimed not only in Paris but also in Germany;

Weber[22] lauds particularly *Les aveugles de Tolède* (1806) which has a piquant and delightful overture, built on a bolero rhythm and filled with Spanish color.

It would lead too far to discuss or even enumerate all of Méhul's operas, for he was enormously productive: between 1790 *(Euphrosine)* and 1807 *(Joseph)* he composed some twenty-five operatic scores, aside from other music. We shall limit ourselves to a few which, for various reasons, deserve special attention, namely *Héléna, Uthal, Gabrielle d'Estrée,* and his masterpiece, *Joseph.*

Héléna, a typical "rescue" opera based on a libretto by Bouilly (the author of the original *Leonore* text), was first presented in Paris early in 1803 and reached Vienna less than six months later. This is an important fact, for we find in the overture to *Héléna* a startling parallelism with Beethoven's *Leonore* which had its premiere three years later, in 1806. Méhul preceded Beethoven in using trumpet calls as musical anticipation of the rescue; separating these trumpet signals appears a musical episode in which the generally sunny atmosphere of the overture changes to a darkened mood.[23] The similarity of procedure between Méhul's Overture to *Héléna* and Beethoven's Overtures Nos. 2 and 3 to *Leonore* is too obvious to be accidental; however, it must be said that the whole episode acquired, in Beethoven's hands, a dramatic significance which by far exceeded Méhul's playful idea.

Méhul's orchestral imagination is shown in *Uthal* (1806), based on a libretto taken from Ossian, the literary fashion of the period. In order to suggest the dark-hued atmosphere of the setting, Méhul excluded the violins entirely and assigned the top parts in the string section to divided violas. The idea, however, was not appreciated by his contemporaries; after the premiere Grétry made the sarcastic remark, "a *louis d'or* for an E-string!"[24] *Uthal* could not compete in public favor with Lesueur's *Ossian,* based on a similar topic and produced with enormous success two years earlier.

Equally unsuccessful was *Gabrielle d'Estrée,* given in 1806, whose failure was attributed to a poor libretto. The overture, pompous and brilliant, shows Méhul to be well versed in the splendid and hollow style of the Empire; he clearly foreshadows Spontini, usually considered the typical representative of that period, whose *La vestale* did not reach the stage until the following year (1807). Although the thematic material of Méhul's overture appears stilted and not overly inspired (especially in the slow introduction), it shows such care in the treatment and development of various motives as to make it almost a symphonic movement. The scoring is thinner than that of Spontini who likes the brilliant brass; Méhul uses in this overture only four horns without trumpets or trombones.

The work which should make Méhul's name truly immortal was *Joseph* (1807). Although not entirely characteristic of Méhul's dramatic power (which is more evident in a work like *Ariodant*), *Joseph* nonetheless represents the sum total of his art, for here he succeeds in fusing the purity and pathos of Gluck's music drama with the serious elements of the *opéra comique* which had undergone such an ennobling transformation during the 1790's and early 1800's.

The overture to *Joseph* is not one of the most inspired works of Méhul. The music lacks a certain natural flow and seems at times somewhat uninspired and contrived. Divided into three large sections of almost equal length and importance, the overture thus deviates from the standard "slow-fast" pattern. An *Adagio,* scored for strings alone, leads into an *Allegro moderato,* built on a theme of Gregorian mood, showing the noble restraint so characteristic of the entire opera. The final section, *Allegro,* has more life and brilliance; especially effective are the fanfares of trumpets and horns toward the end. Although the overture has a "concert" ending, it was never performed as a separate piece on any contemporary program, for its specific character, so admirably adapted to the subject of the opera, was not well suited for the concert hall.

***

Despite the success of *Joseph,* Méhul abandoned the stage temporarily and turned his attention to instrumental music. Between 1808 and 1810, four symphonies by Méhul were presented in Paris. These, however, were not his first essays in the symphonic genre. As early as 1797, on January 28, the *Concerts Feydeau* played a symphony by Méhul, an event which was described in one sentence by a contemporary reporter: "The second part of the concert began with a charming symphony by Méhul."[25] This is indeed a statement of exasperating vagueness. We know that the performance was so well received that the work was repeated at the next concert on February 7, but further details are lacking.

Some historians (including Pougin) conjecture that this early symphony might be identical with the Symphony in G minor, published as No. 1 some ten years later, but this theory is untenable on stylistic grounds. More plausible is the tentative identification recently made by David Charlton: he links the symphony of 1797 with two symphonic movements by Méhul (an *Andante* in F and a *Presto* in C) written "clearly in the style of Haydn." The autograph is preserved in the *Bibliothèque nationale* in Paris.[26]

For many years it was assumed that a symphony by Méhul was played at the *Conservatoire* on January 30, 1802 — a date given by Constant Pierre. However, recent research in contemporary journals has revealed that it was a symphony by Haydn, not by Méhul, that was played at that concert. Hence, we must discard this date from the calendar of early Méhul performances.

On November 3, 1808, more than a year after the great success of *Joseph,* Méhul presented a manuscript symphony (later published as No. 1 in G minor) at the inaugural concert of a new concert society, the *Cercle musical de la Cour de Mandar.* It was "covered with applause and was judged very beautiful," according to the *Journal de L'Empire.* Another symphony by Méhul, probably No. 2 in D major, was played at the *Cour de Mandar* on December 1 of the same year.

Encouraged by the success, Méhul now turned to the *Conservatoire* for further performances. The First Symphony in G minor was heard again on March 12, 1809, the Second Symphony on March 26 (with repeat performances on April 2 and April 23) while the premiere of the Third Symphony in C major took place shortly thereafter, on May 21. The following year, on March 18, 1810, the *Conservatoire* presented Méhul's new Symphony No. 4 in E major. The numbering of the symphonies corresponds to that used by the composer who chose not to count his early symphony of 1797.

Only the symphonies numbered 1 and 2 (in G minor and D major) were published in Paris in 1810 (the First also appeared the same year in Leipzig). The Third Symphony was withdrawn from publication by the composer though a plate number had already been assigned to it. The Fourth Symphony also remained unpublished. After a single performance, both were shelved and were considered lost until rediscovered by David Charlton in 1979. In his words,

These 'missing' symphonies never in fact went very far astray...They have been found to survive, but only in the form of non-autograph manuscript orchestral parts, in the collection of the former Conservatoire orchestra, now the Orchestre de Paris.

It is all the more puzzling that this material has remained undetected for over one hundred years. Pougin, while preparing his Méhul biography in the 1880's, may have seen scattered orchestral parts (he reports a "trace" of four symphonies), but he did not pursue the matter, nor did later historians investigate any further. The rediscovery of two additional symphonies is an important musicological find; until now, the evaluation (or, better, undervaluation) of Méhul as symphonic composer was based on incomplete evidence.

Charlton, in summarizing his impression, says:

> It is...gratifying to see that the rediscovered symphonies of Méhul are in overall character more free than nos. 1 and 2 from Viennese influences of an obvious kind ... [They] admit a greater degree of formal and expressive variety than their predecessors..."

We shall return to a more detailed discussion of the music.

***

Méhul's symphonies were applauded warmly by the public to whom he was known as a successful opera composer. The critics recognized the high quality of his writing but reacted with some restraint: they seemed surprised and somewhat disconcerted by the sudden appearance of a French symphony composer. Since the early 1790's, the tradition of French symphonic writing had been interrupted, to be replaced by the works of the inexhaustible Haydn, interspersed occasionally by Mozart. Méhul — who deserved to be acclaimed as the worthy successor to the 18th century tradition of French symphonists — was treated instead with benevolent condescension. The official *Moniteur universel* printed a lengthy discourse by its critic François Sauvo. He asserted that Haydn took over the orchestras of Europe as his uncontested domain while Mozart (in the opinion of "well-informed men") followed in considerable distance; as for Beethoven, he had a number of followers among the professionals claiming that he was the most able of all. Among these masters, according to Sauvo, Méhul must be placed in the first rank; without imitating Haydn, he belonged to his school. Méhul's work, so we read, excited much interest; one listened with attention and judged with severity which honors the high regard for Méhul's talent. If the work had been written by someone else, it would have produced more enthusiasm; yet one found Méhul worthy of himself which is already much, and one admired particularly an *Andante* which was very beautiful and contained charming details.

This is the essence of Sauvo's review after the performance in 1809 of Méhul's First Symphony in G minor. Typical for the actual lack of understanding is the statement concerning the *Andante* which is the least personal, the most "Haydnesque" of the four movements, and, therefore, was most readily understood. Méhul felt compelled to reply. His letter to Sauvo is modest, almost deferential. He professed to be a "passionate admirer" of Haydn and continued:

> I felt the dangers of my enterprise; I foresaw the reserved reception given to my symphonies by the music lovers ... For next winter, I plan to compose new symphonies, and I shall try ... to persuade the public to believe that a Frenchman can follow, from afar, Haydn and Mozart.[27]

The carefully phrased letter reads like a statement designed to appease any further criticism. Méhul avoids mentioning the name of Beethoven who was still a highly controversial figure. But we know that he had experienced the impact of Beethoven when he heard his early symphonies at the *Conservatoire* in rehearsals and performances conducted by Habeneck. Much later, in 1840/41, Habeneck told Anton Schindler:

> ... Of all the artists who heard us play these symphonies [Beethoven's Nos. 1 and 2], Méhul alone showed himself impressed; in fact they inspired him to write similar works of his own — he composed three symphonies of which one was particularly meritorious and successful.[28]

Actually, Méhul's real problem was not so much how to "follow" Haydn and Mozart as how to come to terms with the genius of Beethoven.

Other critics were more generous than Sauvo, so for example the *Journal de Paris,* assigning to Méhul the place he deserved:

> ... Mr. Méhul has actually attempted to recapture for France a field of music that had been completely abandoned. Formerly, Mr. Gossec used to make the symphonic form a vehicle for his fine talent. But ever since Haydn's numerous productions began to charm and amaze all of Europe, Mozart alone succeeded in arousing comparable interest. Mr. Méhul, without actually trying to imitate these two famous composers, has based his work upon his brilliant imagination while bringing to bear an extraordinary musical craftmanship ... We feel compelled to state in all sincerity that a *French symphonist* has risen after all, and that the concert reported here can truly be said to have turned into a personal triumph for him.[29]

Sauvo, after hearing Méhul's Second Symphony in March 1809, became more positive in his appraisal. It may well be that this work, being musically more conventional than the First Symphony, appealed to his conservative taste. We read in the *Moniteur universel* :

> This new symphony was even more applauded than the first: it seemed to have more of the characteristic imprint of the master. The first movement may be a little mannered in the use, or better contrast, of instruments; the *Andante* has an agreeable but not very original theme which is varied in many ways with rare skill. This is Haydn's secret, but when the master uses it, the chosen theme is usually of exquisite freshness and enchanting melody: this is a prime condition. Méhul's *Presto* is ingenious and brilliant; but the movement which won most favor is doubtless the *Minuet* ... Conceived with enthusiasm, it has a single idea, well invented and well treated; the *Trio* is particularly delightful ...[30]

Méhul's Third Symphony followed on the heels of the Second — less than two months separate the two premieres. The new work "had everyone's approval," according to the *Journal de l'Empire,* while the *Journal de Paris* extols its "melodious, pure themes, brilliant passages, and learned transitions." Both critics praise the "noble and touching" slow movement "of an absolutely new type: one of those epoch-making pieces of which one does not tire." Yet, despite so much approval, the Third Symphony was not repeated, nor was the Fourth Symphony, presented a year later. This is particularly regrettable in the case of the Fourth since the last two movements were completely rewritten by the composer after the premiere. The critics continued to be benevolent, but there is no indication that they perceived any particular growth in Méhul's stature as a symphonist. The following quotations concern the Fourth Symphony.[31] First the *Journal de l'Empire*:

> Méhul is one of our most capable composers and best harmonists; he is neither a Haydn nor a Mozart, but has qualities unique to himself, his own physiognomy and character . . .

The *Journal de Paris* is more perceptive:

> His talent is distinguished by the noble purity of his motifs, by the learned, the finished and the beautiful nature of his orchestral writing; no one has known how to make use of the cellos with greater success than Méhul; these instruments give to the majority of his compositions a color and an expression which are quite particular, and it is in this above all that he shows his originality."

Méhul's expressive writing for cello is also praised by the critic of the *Tablettes de Polymnie* though some negative observations are added:

> The first movement . . . is worthy of the greatest masters; the theme of the *Andante*, for cello solo, at first too deprived of accompaniment and too long, is varied in the style of Haydn, with much taste and skill in the treatment of the orchestra. The *Minuet*, in canon form, has original effects, although there are a few conventional spots in the woodwind solos of the *Trio*; as for the *Finale*, it is a masterwork of science, overloaded with fugal imitations, counterpoints, and transitions which may be very beautiful but so involved that the imagination and receptiveness (of the listener) get tired without experiencing enjoyment . . .

This criticism of the *Minuet* and the *Finale* may have prompted Méhul to compose second versions of these two movements though they did not reach the public.

Praising the balance and harmony of the works by Haydn and Mozart, the critic of the *Tablettes* continues with this warning:

The surprising success of Beethoven is a danger sign for music. The contagion of Teutonic harmony seems to sweep the modern school of composition formed at the Conservatoire. They believe in producing effects by writing the most barbaric dissonances and by noisily employing all the instruments of the orchestra . . .[32]

Why the *Conservatoire* was singled out for criticism is not at all clear; teachers like Cherubini, Méhul, Catel, and the old Gossec certainly did not lead their students astray. In the absence of a symphonic school in France, the enlargement of orchestration was carried forward by operatic composers, primarily Spontini who had no connection with the *Conservatoire*. Such unjustified criticism undoubtedly hurt and discouraged Méhul.

Sensitive to criticism, Méhul was also racked with self-doubts. Because of artistic dissatisfaction, he withdrew his Third Symphony from publication. We have seen that he discarded the last two movements of his Fourth Symphony after the premiere in order to rewrite them. A projected Fifth Symphony remained incomplete, and he ultimately abandoned symphonic writing altogether.

***

Méhul's posthumous fame all but ignored his symphonies. Cherubini, his oldest friend who professed to have loved him "like a brother", dismisses Méhul's symphonies (together with his ballets and cantatas) as being of minor interest; in fact, he ascribed only three symphonies to him, a rather thoughtless error.[33]

Nor did Habeneck show any interest in reviving Méhul's symphonies though he was at the helm of the *Conservatoire* orchestra when they were first played in 1809. He ignored the opportunity of reviving one of the symphonies in 1830 when a Méhul Memorial Concert was given at the *Société des Concerts du Conservatoire*.

The negative attitude of Habeneck found support with Fétis who wrote in the *Revue musicale*:

> We can only applaud the decision not to perform one of Méhul's symphonies. Nature has not endowed this great master to deal successfully with this genre of music. Enchanted by the beauties of Haydn's symphonies, he wanted to create them according to the same system, and while he wanted to show an abundance of developments, he succeeded in being merely dry and pretentious. His genius was made for the dramatic style.[34]

In repeating this negative evaluation in his *Biographie universelle*, Fétis perpetuated it for generations:

> They [i.e. the symphonies] were the result of the idea, predominant in Méhul's mind, that there are set procedures to write all kinds of music. He saw in Haydn's symphonies nothing but a theme which was presented and worked out in all possible forms. Thus he took themes, developed them carefully, and provided the listener with not a single emotion. It was a chain of formulas, well arranged but without charm, melody, abandon. The small effect produced by the symphonies...caused Méhul very much distress.[35]

Incidentally, Fétis mentions six symphonies by Méhul without identifying them in any way.

Pougin, who published the first full-length monograph on Méhul in 1889, rejects Fétis' judgment as unfair. He gives a sympathetic description of the Symphony No. 1 in G minor without actually appreciating all its remarkable qualities; his analysis offers very little tangible information and gives instead an abundance of picturesque words like *allure, éclat, feu, élégance*. On the whole, Pougin considers Méhul's symphonies very "honorable" works born out of a "noble ambition"; they are interesting attempts which deserve sincere respect although they do not add to Méhul's glory.

Tiersot,[36] who heard both the first and second symphonies by Méhul performed at the *Concerts Colonne* during the season of 1901-02, considers them well-schooled efforts though far from giving an adequate measure of the author's genius. Tiersot castigates the singular error of French composers who consider the symphonic form as a purely academic genre, a sort of a school assignment for prospective Rome Prize winners. He also blames the *Académie:* while a fugue and a symphony were expected from the young contestants, the committee of judges attached very little importance to either assignment. Pointing to the simultaneous writing of Méhul's and Beethoven's symphonies, Tiersot charges Méhul with being inhibited by formulas which he considered necessary; thus he suppressed whatever genius there was in him. Tiersot admits that both symphonies by Méhul contain interesting parts, especially the No. 1, but it is evident to him that Méhul's primary concern is workmanship *(écriture);* none of the admirable *cantilenas* of *Joseph,* nor the triumphant *éclat* of the *Chant du départ,* nor the Romantic poetry of *Ariodant* were carried over into the symphonies.

Another biographer, Brancour,[37] deplores the fact that Méhul, in writing his symphonies, did not use his gifts for the "descriptive" and the "picturesque," which he displayed in his *Jeune Henri.* In discussing the orchestration, Brancour asserts that Méhul uses a richer orchestra than that of Haydn, which is incorrect, for Méhul's orchestration is actually smaller than Haydn's. However, Brancour alone notices the kinship between Méhul and the much younger Mendelssohn.

All these eminent music critics of the past and present display the aggravating tendency of deploring that Méhul's symphonies are not what *they* think they should have been; thus they all miss the essential points while harping on minor deficiencies.

Not that Méhul lacked eminent admirers. Beethoven, for one, showed continued interest in his operas which were given in Vienna. (We have pointed out the parallelism between Méhul's *Héléna* and Beethoven's *Fidelio,* and there are other affinities). Carl Maria von Weber directed the production of Méhul's *Joseph* in Dresden in 1817 and wrote a warmly appreciative introduction. Richard Wagner admitted that, as a young man, he was deeply moved by the nobility of *Joseph.*

As late as 1852, Berlioz wrote a perceptive essay on Méhul, praising him with certain reservations. But it was Robert Schumann who alone sensed Méhul's potential as a symphonic composer.

During the winter season of 1837-38, the celebrated Gewandhaus Orchestra of Leipzig, conducted by Mendelssohn, gave four historic concerts of music from Bach to Weber. A Méhul symphony was played on March 1, 1838.* We have a review by Schumann:

> ... the most interesting (number) was a symphony by Méhul ... so different from the German symphonic style, as it appears to us, and yet so thorough and so clever, although not without mannerism. We recommend this piece most warmly to other orchestras. Noteworthy was the similarity of the last movement with the first movement of Beethoven's C minor symphony (No. 5), and also the similarity of the scherzos of both works — in fact so much that there must have been a conscious reminiscence from one side or the other; on which side I am unable to say since I do not know the birthyear of Méhul's work.[38]

Although Schumann does not mention key or number of the Méhul symphony played in Leipzig, it can only have been the First in G minor which, in the last two movements, bears a remote similarity to Beethoven's Fifth Symphony. Strange as it may seem, there was no "conscious reminiscence" on either side, only a surprising coincidence. Both symphonies were first performed in the year 1808 — Méhul's on November 3 in Paris, Beethoven's on December 22 in Vienna; neither was printed until the following year. (Constant Pierre made a grievous error when he listed a Parisian performance of Beethoven's Symphony in C "minor" on April 10, 1808; the symphony performed on that date was "en ut," namely the First).

While any direct reminiscence must be ruled out in this case, there were certainly mutual affinities between Beethoven and Méhul. Beethoven knew and used the musical vocabulary

*However, this was not a premiere: Méhul's Symphony in G minor was played at the Leipzig Gewandhaus as early as May 13, 1810, and repeated the same year on November 22.

of the French revolutionary opera typefied by Méhul – in *Coriolanus, Fidelio* and elsewhere – and he maintained his interest in Méhul's works even after the composer's death. As for Méhul, he became gradually aware of the expansion of the symphonic idiom sparked by Beethoven's early symphonies. Certainly, Méhul's Second Symphony in D major has a kinship with Beethoven's Second (also in D) in terms of pace, spirit, and temperament.

Méhul approached the composition of symphonies (we mean those written between 1808 and 1810) at the height of his career, as a mature and experienced composer who, for some twenty years, had explored every aspect of stage composition and every angle of orchestral expressiveness. Compared to the impact of some of his overtures, Méhul's symphonies sound somewhat tame and restrained. Attuned, in his operas, to a world of emotion, Méhul was obviously hampered in expressing himself within the standardized, circumscribed architecture of the symphony which he adopted without questioning. There can be no doubt that Méhul was very conscious of the fundamental difference between operatic and symphonic style; perhaps it was this effort to avoid the rhetoric of the stage which drove him at times into adopting an excessive reticence.

Yet, Méhul did not exclude all operatic trends from his Symphony in G minor; in fact, he transmuted some of the passionate sweep of the revolutionary opera into the language of instrumental music. This transfer, already effectuated in his overtures, is now partly achieved in a symphony: the "drama" steps from the operatic stage into the concert hall – something Beethoven achieved in a grander, bolder manner.

To say that Méhul sounds "Beethovenian" or "Mendelssohnian" is just as meaningless as describing certain Haydn movements as "Beethovenian" or Johann Schobert as "Mozartian"; it is putting the cart before the horse. On the other hand, such "foreshadowings" do not mean necessarily that the younger artist imitated the older; often this kinship is subconscious or coincidental, and even more often it merely indicates a common point of departure. In the case of Beethoven and Méhul, this common point was the French revolutionary opera; in the case of Méhul and Mendelssohn, it may have been Cherubini. But there is that remote possibility that Mendelssohn actually knew Méhul's First Symphony (published in 1810) when he wrote his own First Symphony in C minor in 1824 or his First Piano Concerto in 1831. Be this as it may, there are affinities between Méhul and Mendelssohn that are often startling. Méhul, in 1808, succeeded in projecting a mood which was to become typical of Mendelssohn's classicistic Romanticism — agitation without much fire, passion without much intensity, but also elfin grace and knightly nobility. Mendelssohn had an additional advantage: he had fully absorbed Beethoven. The first French composer to do so was Berlioz.

The symphonies of Méhul bridge the gap between Gossec and Berlioz and are a distinguished contribution to the French symphonic repertoire. Méhul is the earliest French representative of classicistic Romanticism — an early manifestation of Romanticism based on preservation of the traditional forms while widening the emotional gamut. Far from being a mere epigone, his contribution is distinctly personal.

Unfortunately, Méhul did not create any "school." His most talented student, Ferdinand Herold (a Rome Prize winner) composed two youthful symphonies in 1813-14 which reveal little, if any, influence exerted by his teacher. The next French symphonist, George Onslow, enlarged the orchestra by adding trombones but remained essentially within the Viennese tradition. A new plateau of symphonic writing is reached by Berlioz and his *Symphonie fantastique,* but he owed nothing to Méhul.

***

Méhul's Symphony No. 1 in G minor is scored for strings, a full woodwind section (pairs of flutes, oboes, clarinets, and bassoons), two horns, and timpani. This is a comparatively small orchestra, smaller than Haydn used in some of his "London" symphonies. The use of timpani without trumpets is unusual, for it had become customary, since the 1750's, to treat the combination trumpets-timpani as a unit in symphonic scores. We also note the continued absence of trombones in Méhul's symphonies; he was unaware that Beethoven had broken with tradition by employing them in his Fifth and Sixth symphonies of 1808.*

Méhul's restraint in the scoring was self-imposed, for he had handled far larger orchestrations in his operas. He must have felt that the thematic material of his Symphony in G minor did not require a heavier orchestration; perhaps he thought of Mozart's Symphony in G minor (K. 550), orchestrated on an even more intimate scale.

The economy of orchestration, apparent in all of Méhul's works, aroused the admiration of many musicians, including Carl Maria von Weber and Berlioz. However, this discretion, so successful in his operas, proved less so in his symphonies, for Méhul apparently did not realize sufficiently that in a symphony the orchestra is not mere support, but the actual protagonist.

The Symphony No. 1 in G minor opens with an *Allegro* in *alla breve* time. The first theme is fiery and proud, the mood agitated, sweeping, and powerful. This beginning is somewhat reminiscent of Cherubini's *Médée* and clearly foreshadows Mendelssohn's Symphony No. 1 in C minor as well as his First Piano Concerto in G minor. Thus Méhul forms a link between the early revolutionary Romanticism of the 1790's and the classicistic Romanticism of the 1820's (ex. III-14, III-15, III-16, III-17, III-18).

*Charlton found some evidence that an earlier version of this symphony may have used a larger brass section: four horns, two trumpets, and one trombone. See his preface to the score of Méhul's Symphony No. 1 in G minor (A-R Editions, in preparation).

Example III-14. Méhul, *Symphony No. 1* (1808). Opening theme.

Example III-15. Cherubini, *Médée* (1797). Overture.

Example III-16. Mendelssohn, *Symphony No. 1* (1824). Opening.

Example III-17. Méhul, *Symphony No. 1* (1808). First movement.

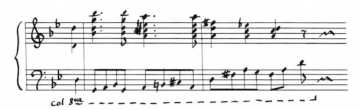

Example III-18. Mendelssohn, *Piano Concerto No. 1 in G minor* (1832).
First movement.

A bridge passage leads to a second theme in B-flat major which is quite "Mozartian" in its flowing and yet singing motion. No repeat bars separate the exposition from the development, which opens in B-flat minor and modulates through various keys. The recapitulation begins with the second theme in G major, after which the first theme reappears in the home key of G minor. A brilliant coda, bristling with diminished seventh chords, brings the movement to an effective close.

The reversal of first and second theme in the recapitulation is a device often used in the French operative overture, especially by Cherubini and by Méhul, and offers a very effective modification of the traditional *sonata-allegro* arrangement. By having the contrasting second theme follow the modulating development section, the composer achieves a welcome change of mood, while the usually more virile first theme leads effectively into the coda without breaking the continuity. Other composers have not accepted the transplantation of this overture device into the symphony; it shows Méhul's independence of judgment and forms a definite link between his operatic and symphonic works.

The second movement, an *Andante* in B-flat major, is truly an homage to Haydn, for the form, melodic invention, orchestral treatment, and many details are handled in the Haydn tradition. The movement is a set of variations on a simple, songful theme;* the variations — one of them in *mineur* — do not wander far from the theme and consist mainly of contrapuntal embellishments assigned to various instruments. The woodwinds are treated with discretion and imagination. Technical details, such as the balance of major and minor, certain transitions, the leading of the bass line, are handled in a masterful way. The extended coda is another sign of the Haydn influence. The movement is somewhat overly long, which causes the interest to lag toward the end.

The third movement is easily the most original part of the entire symphony. Though entitled *Minuet,* it has definite *scherzo* character and is mentioned as such in Schumann's review. Its originality is not materially diminished by a certain resemblance to the third movement of Beethoven's Fifth Symphony, such as the use of pizzicato strings with a few added woodwinds, or the heavy bass figure in the Trio; on the other hand, the character of Méhul's movement is less demoniac than that of Beethoven; it is more elfin, more airy, once again pointing toward Mendelssohn's future style (ex. III-19, III-20).

Example III-19. Méhul, *Symphony No. 1* (1808). Third movement.

Example III-20. Beethoven, *Symphony No. 5* (1808). Third movement.

*Charlton traces this theme to a variant of the traditional French noël "Venez, divin Messie." Méhul followed the example of Haydn who used a French tune in his Symphony No. 85 (*La Reine*). See preface, *op. cit.*

The finale, an *Allegro agitato* in *alla breve* time, could be called a "perpetual motion," for a figure in eighth notes runs throughout the entire movement, heightening the mood of agitation and occasional dramatic vehemence. The form is that of a *sonata-allegro,* however without contrasting second theme; the development technique is somewhat reminiscent of Mozart's mature period (e.g. the Symphony No. 40 in G minor) and shows a master's touch, enhanced by a superior handling of the orchestra.

The similarity between this finale of Méhul and the first *Allegro* of Beethoven's Fifth Symphony, mentioned by Schumann, is a superficial one consisting merely in the repeated use of the "short-short-short-long" motive; as for the mood, Méhul's music is agitated without having any of Beethoven's explosive intensity. More significant is the pronounced affinity between Méhul's finale and that of Mendelssohn's First Symphony, written some fifteen years later (ex. III-21, III-22, III-23).

Example III-21. Méhul, *Symphony No. 1.* Last movement.

Example III-22. Beethoven, *Symphony No. 5.* First movement.

Example III-23. Mendelssohn, *Symphony No. 1* (1824). Last movement.

The four movements of Méhul's First Symphony are far from being stylistically homogeneous. The first movement, kindred in spirit to Cherubini's *Médée,* could well have been written as early as 1797, and the same can be said about the Haydnesque second movement. The stylistic break comes with the last two movements which doubtlessly belong to the first decade of the nineteenth century. It is fairly evident that Méhul's First Symphony was composed in 1807-1808, after the completion of *Joseph,* though some thematic material might be of older vintage.

***

Méhul's Symphony No. 2 in D major was the most successful of the four; it received three consecutive performances, and the contemporary critics were more laudatory.* Its appeal consisted probably in a certain conventionality as compared to the originality of the First Symphony. The orchestration is the same in both symphonies; again Méhul dispenses with trumpets and trombones.

The work opens with a slow introduction, *Adagio,* in ¾ time, of stately and dignified character, built on an ascending scale motive. After this promising opening, the ensuing *Allegro* is somewhat disappointing; the themes are undistinguished and not sufficiently contrasted; throughout the movement there is a lack of rhythmic variety. As in the First Symphony, there is no double bar to separate the exposition from the development which is built primarily on the first theme of the *Allegro.* The recapitulation follows the regular pattern of the exposition, without the reversal of the two themes which characterized the First Symphony. Despite the length of the movement, the end comes rather abruptly; there is no coda but simply a repetition of the codetta

---

*Modern editions of Méhul's Second Symphony published in Paris in 1922 (piano score) and 1957 (full score).

already heard at the end of the exposition. As we have said before, this movement has a certain kinship to Beethoven's Second Symphony.

Superior to the somewhat undistinguished first movement is the ensuing *Andante* (B minor), undoubtedly the best part of the entire symphony. It has the melancholic grace of an old air, stately and yet supple; the simple theme foreshadows the sad sweetness of a *Moment musical* by Schubert. Méhul's *Andante* brings another symphonic movement to one's mind — the *Allegretto* from Beethoven's Seventh Symphony: there is the same persistence in the use of a rhythmic figure, the same simplicity of melodic line, and a certain similarity in the counterpoint embellishing the return of the theme. Méhul's Second Symphony was written in 1808-09, Beethoven's Seventh in 1812; it is improbable (though not impossible) that Beethoven saw a score of Méhul's work, which did not create any stir outside of Paris. So we must accept these affinities as pure coincidence; yet they are significant, for they prove a similarity of mood which was pervading Europe from Paris to Vienna, and which Méhul suceeded in capturing (ex. III-24, III-25, III-26, III-27).

Example III-24. Méhul, *Symphony No. 2* (1808-9). Second movement.

Example III-25. Méhul, *Symphony No. 2*. Second movement.

Example III-26. Beethoven, *Symphony No. 7* (1812). Second movement.

Example III-27. Beethoven, *Symphony No. 7*. Second movement.

The third movement bears — similarly to the First Symphony — the misleading title *Minuet* while being actually a *scherzo*. The thematic invention is weak, yet the instrumentation is so clever, the orchestral colors are contrasted so knowingly, the mood is so gay and good-humored, that the movement produces an excellent effect. Particularly noteworthy is the deft handling of the woodwinds in the Trio, and the characteristic, truly "Beethovenian" treatment of the timpani.

The finale, an *Allegro vivace* in 2/4 time, has an infectious gaiety reminiscent of finales like Haydn's Symphony in D (No. 104) or Beethoven's String Quartet Op. 18 No. 5; an even better analogy, perhaps, is the *Anacréon* Overture by Cherubini. It is merry without being boisterous, brilliant without being shrill. The movement opens with a timpani figure which runs for eight bars, on a low D, and this note is continued, bourdon-like, while the other instruments intone the theme. The rhythmic figure of the timpani is exploited in the development section and returns at the very end of the movement. While undistinguished in thematic invention and somewhat overly long, this finale has enough momentum to carry it through its weaker parts.

***

The Symphony No. 3 in C major uses a larger orchestra, reinforcing the wind section with a pair of trumpets. The rediscovered orchestra parts reveal that the bassoons and the horns were doubled. Thus, four bassoonists and four horn players participated in the performance. In keeping with this rich instrumentation, the opening *Allegro* (marked *ferme et modéré*) is dominated by a martial, fanfare-like first theme that recurs throughout the movement. One can perceive it as a reflection of the glitter and pomp of life during the Empire, but it leaves the listener with a feeling of emptiness. While the quiet, intimate second subject offers welcome relief from the brass flourishes, its invention is weak and undistinguished.

Méhul redeemed himself with the second movement, a lovely *Andante* of melancholy tinge, in A minor, with a central section in A major. For once, Méhul abandoned his preferred variation form in favor of a ternary structure. As the movement unfolds in a leisurely fashion, it gains in density and grows more complex. The climactic point is a surprising chromatic progression much favored by Méhul in the course of these symphonies. The entire mood of the *Andante* is what Schumann once called "provençal" in describing a Beethoven quartet movement. The contemporary critics were enraptured with Méhul's *Andante,* and Charlton calls it "perhaps Méhul's best ever symphonic movement, astoundingly Beethovenish in spirit, ingenious and subtle in its growth."

Omitting a *minuet* or *scherzo,* Méhul chose a three-movement structure for this symphony. The final *Allegro* is a piece of great brilliance, a kind of *moto perpetuo* using a sixteenth-note motion in ¾ time. The second theme offers a graceful contrast but does not materially enrich the thin musical content of this movement. The over-all structure is a *sonata-allegro* without offering much development or diversity. Everything is predictable. The outer movements of this symphony adhere to a formula with little creative originality. Méhul may have felt the musical emptiness of much of his symphony and withdrew it from publication as being inferior to the first pair of symphonies. Charlton offers this thought:

> In the case of this finale, it throws excessively into relief those motifs which are, once again, related to Mozart's *Jupiter* Symphony. It may be this feature as much as any other which caused the composer to withdraw it from publication. The symphony is not in any way undeserving of performance, but neither is it as satisfying as that mercurial masterpiece, No. 1 in G minor.

***

Méhul's Fourth Symphony in E major (ca. 1809-10) is "an achievement of profound and entertaining utterance," according to Charlton.[39] In this work, he returned to the traditional four-movement form. Once again he reduced his orchestra to exclude the trumpets, and he used the timpani only briefly in the last movement. This restrained use of orchestral resources (already noticeable in his operas of the early 1800's) is in strong contrast to the orchestral opulence and dramatic power evident in his pre-1800 operas and overtures. Historians have pointed out the stylistic evolution in Méhul's artistic outlook which Charlton describes as "a new musical aesthetic of economy." Having briefly deviated from this new posture in his Third Symphony, Méhul returned to it in his Fourth.

The first movement is organized along the lines of a traditional *sonata-allegro,* with a double bar and a repeated exposition — the only example of its kind in Méhul's orchestral allegros. It opens with a brooding *Adagio* introduction; one hears a "truly germinal phrase . . . a thematic series of chords in triple meter." The principal theme of the movement is, in Charlton's words, "primarily contrapuntal . . . typical of many of our composer's themes: by virtue of consisting of at least two contrasting strands, they may either be developed in part or treated in invertable counterpoint." The entire movement contains an abundance of thematic material (comparable to his First Symphony in G minor). He often uses a type of theme that is not singable but of an idiomatic orchestral texture. (Compare the finale of his Second Symphony which is similarly orchestral). The second movement begins with a cello melody accompanied by the double basses playing pizzicato. The "thudding bass footsteps" remind Charlton of Berlioz' *Harold in Italy*. At the first performance, only two solo cellos were used. The cello melody, fifty-six measures long, forms the first section of a ternary form, but the cellos are also used prominently in the middle section of this movement. One critic recalled a similar effect in Méhul's opera *Stratonice,* dating back to 1792.

The last two movements are preserved in two entirely different versions. Both versions can be reconstructed from existing parts, and in each case, the new version is a decisive improvement. Judging by the published newspaper reports, it was the first version that was heard at the premiere.

Originally, the third movement was a *Minuet* and *Trio* in E major, the former written in canon, the latter containing "some commonplaces in the wind soli" (to quote a contemporary criticism). The rewritten *Minuet* stands in E minor and has a different theme. Halfway through the *Trio* there is a false reprise of the *Minuet*, after which the *Trio* resumes — a formal subtlety one is likely to find in Beethoven. A substantial coda rounds out the repeated *Minuet*. The rewritten *Minuet* is on the same high level as Méhul's minuets in his First and Second Symphonies — perhaps not as "superficially startling" but "at least equally imaginative," in Charlton's judgment.

The two versions of the finale are even more revealing of Méhul's self-critical mind. Originally he had written a "Haydnesque" *sonata-rondo* compared in style to "village songs" by the *Journal de Paris.* But another contemporary critic explains Méhul's stylized movement as a deliberate homage to Haydn who had recently died. Méhul may have been inspired by Cherubini's *Chant sur la mort de Haydn,* acclaimed at the *Conservatoire* in February 1810. (Actually, Cherubini's memorial cantata was written in 1805, in response to a false rumor of Haydn's death, as was Kreutzer's Violin Concerto No. 16 on themes of Haydn). We do not know what motivated Méhul to compose the finale anew, whether criticism or self-dissatisfaction. Be this as it may, a new final movement was written and copied in parts; judging by players' markings it must have been played through if not performed. Charlton, who examined both versions, describes the second one with enthusiasm:

> This movement proved to be a triumph of gaiety and profound wit . . . The more he pleases us with abundant ideas, the more he seems to have drawn inspiration from his original basic shape [see below]. The Finale, a $^2/_4$ *Allegro* of such colorfully conceived music that it is quite impossible to give any idea of it at the keyboard, is also cast in a highly unorthodox form: almost a cross between sonata-rondo and sonata proper, with bits of its six main ideas returning at wrong moments.

The "basic shape" mentioned above is derived from the introduction of the Symphony, transformed into the main subject of the new finale and subsequently used in the development section. The device of reminiscence-motif was used by Méhul in his early operas and by French composers before him. However, the idea of using it in a symphony was a novelty — if we disregard Beethoven's precedent of which Méhul knew nothing at the time. It testifies to Méhul's innovatory mind and makes one regret that he did not pursue his symphonic explorations.

Indeed, Méhul's Fourth Symphony has never been properly evaluated, for the version played at the premiere had been partly discarded by the composer. One wonders why Méhul, one of the founding members of the *Conserva-*

toire, was not offered an opportunity for hearing his revised symphony performed. Or did he not press the matter?

Undaunted, Méhul embarked on yet another symphony which he gave the number 5, in A major. Only the first movement is preserved: an introductory *Andante* (48 measures) and an *Allegro* (242 measures). Charlton, who examined the fragment, comments, "This lone movement shows Méhul still at the height of his symphonic powers, and moreover returning to the monothematicism that had characterized his pre-Revolutionary piano sonata in A minor." The undated autograph score is in the Vienna Nationalbibliothek. The date of composition appears to be 1810-1811, judging by the watermarks of the paper used.

One wonders what caused Méhul to abandon the projected symphony and to turn his back on symphonic writing. Was it self-criticism? Was it disillusionment with the skepticism he encountered? Even an old friend and associate like Cherubini minimized his efforts as a symphonist. Méhul's dissatisfaction with the social and artistic conditions in Paris of the 1810's may have contributed to his withdrawal: a French composer had to be a pure idealist to spend time and talent on symphonies — played for small circles of connoisseurs — while the public at large filled the opera houses.

London established a Philharmonic Society in 1813 as a center for the performance of instrumental music, but Paris had to wait until 1828 when the *Société des Concerts du Conservatoire* was founded to fill a long-standing void. It was the lack of such a musical center that delayed the acceptance of Beethoven's music in Paris. As for French composers, there was no incentive to write symphonic music since there was no forum to perform it. Méhul was only too well aware of these conditions: even the famed *exercises* of the *Conservatoire* in the years 1800 to 1815 were, in fact, only semi-professional performances.

Be this as it may, Méhul turned away from the genre of the symphony and resumed his career as an opera composer where he had gained his early fame. His last few stage works were well received. He died in 1817 at the age of fifty-four. The memory of his symphonies was kept alive, not by the French, but by foreign musicians like Mendelssohn, Reinecke, and Hallé, among others.

***

Luigi Cherubini

Cherubini's position among his contemporaries was unique. Perhaps no other composer was more universally respected during his lifetime by his colleagues; among his admirers were Haydn and Beethoven, Méhul and Viotti, Mendelssohn and Schumann, Spohr and Weber — not to mention the host of students and devoted friends in Paris; they have all testified to their indebtedness and respect for the great master. A belated indirect tribute was paid him by Hans von Bülow who called Brahms "the heir of Luigi and of Ludwig," i.e., of Cherubini and Beethoven.

But this high regard was not entirely shared by the public of Paris where his works were often criticized as being too learned and lacking in emotional appeal. After enjoying a measure of success during the 1790's and early 1800's, Cherubini encountered growing indifference of the public and Napoleon's court. During the Bourbon Restoration, he devoted most of his efforts to church music, thus addressing himself to a limited audience. At the time of his appointment as director of the *Ecole royale* (the old *Conservatoire*) in 1822, Cherubini was respected and feared but rarely performed. During the seething 1820's and 1830's, he began to lose touch with his times; in the midst of the Romantic movement, at a time when composers like Boieldieu, Auber, Meyerbeer, and Berlioz were in the forefront, Cherubini seemed strangely old-fashioned — a great man who witnessed his own oblivion.

It is not easy to ascertain the roots of Cherubini's art. Kretzschmar poses the question without offering a satisfactory answer; but at least he succeeds in abolishing the prevailing legend of a predominant German influence.[40] True, Cherubini knew Haydn's thematic development technique but he used it unconvincingly and sparingly, for his development sections are usually brief. Nor did Cherubini accept the instrumental *cantabile* style of Mozart to whose influence he succumbed only occasionally in the treatment of vocal parts. As for Beethoven, "he dreaded him, like the antichrist of art," according to Berlioz; even if this statement were an exaggeration, it is clear that Cherubini did not consider Beethoven of sufficient importance to be used as model.

It is generally assumed that Cherubini's chief inspiration was Gluck, yet it is well to remember that he did not come in contact with Gluck's music until 1786, when he first visited Paris. By that time, the twenty-six year old Cherubini was already well known as a composer of operas and church music. True, his music was undistinguished until he settled in Paris in 1788. Here he found the musical scene in full fermentation and the Gluck-Piccinni controversy still alive. Cherubini's decisive stimulant was not merely Gluck but, more specifically, the Parisian Gluck, the master of the *tragédie lyrique* with its century-old tradition. Yet Cherubini wrote only one work in this genre, *Démophon* (1788), which was unsuccessful; all his other operas which established his fame, from *Lodoiska* (1791) to *Water Carrier* (1800) were French dialogue operas, *opéras-comique,* and he deeply absorbed the spirit and tradition of this typically French product. To this may be added the vigorous new concepts of life and society promulgated by the French Revolution. All this stirred the young Cherubini profoundly and molded his musical personality. Italian, German, French — Cherubini is a true representative of the supranational musical style envisioned by Gluck himself, without "the ridiculous distinctions between music of different nations."[41]

Yet if we persist in classifying composers by nationalities, Cherubini unquestionably belongs to the French orbit. He lived in Paris from 1788 until his death in 1842; there he spent the greatest part of his life — a long life span which began in 1760 when Mozart was but four years old, and ended after Richard Wagner had completed *The Flying Dutchman*. Cherubini lived in France through two revolutions, through wars, glory, defeat, and reconstruction. He became part of France, and France became part of him, though he never quite learned to master the language completely. For over forty years, he was connected with the *Conservatoire*, guiding generations of young French musicians. Like Lully, Cherubini truly belongs to France and its musical history.

***

The question — Cherubini, classic or romantic? — has been posed often and persistently. His biographers Hohenemser[42] and Schemann[43] found both classic and romantic elements in his music: on one side classic preservation of form, moderation of affect, symmetry of architecture; on the other side romantic passion and sweep, tone painting, vivid orchestral colors, bold harmonies and modulations.

Yet it is dangerous to judge Cherubini with the standards of 19th century Romanticism, for all his important works were written between 1788 (*Démophon*) and 1806 (*Faniska*); after that, his contribution to musical "progress" was negligible and the leadership passed into other hands. Cherubini's fundamental attitude was that of a classicist; whatever Romantic tendencies are found in his works belong to the Romanticism of the revolutionary 1790's rather than the Romantic school of the 1820's and 1830's. In the former, he was an active leader, in the latter, a passive onlooker.

He planted many of the seeds of Romanticism, yet he did not participate in its full harvest.

Actually, Cherubini can be considered one of the main inspirers of 19th century musical Romanticism. Beethoven and Schubert, Weber and Mendelssohn are deeply in his debt. Mendelssohn, a sincere admirer of both Beethoven and Cherubini, said:

> In looking through the score of *Fidelio,* as well as listening to the performance, I perceive everywhere Cherubini's dramatic style of composition. It is true that Beethoven did not ape that style, but it was before his mind as his most cherished pattern.[44]

Hugo Riemann agrees, "Beethoven's *Fidelio* . . . is closer to Cherubini than to any other composer."[45]

Among the "rauschende Ouvertüren"[46] Franz Schubert played every evening during his school days at the Seminary were certainly some by Cherubini, and *Médée* was one of the first operas he heard.[47] Weber testified to his love for Cherubini in many essays, aside from the living testimony of his music. Mendelssohn's overtures to *Midsummer Night's Dream* and *Fingal's Cave* show unmistakably Cherubini's influence. In France, his principal disciples were Boieldieu, Auber, Herold, and Halévy.

Though Cherubini was predominantly an operatic composer, it was his treatment of the orchestra which seems to have impressed his contemporaries most of all. He handled every instrument in a highly individualized and idiomatic manner; especially his treatment of the French horns became characteristic for the entire Romantic generation. His orchestra is a marvel of color and flexibility, of balance and expressiveness. He operates with such economy of means that he seems to strive at all times for maximum effect with minimum effort. There is no needless blaring nor undue thickening of the texture. In this respect, his use of the brass section is highly revealing, both as to number and choice of instruments. We find the following combinations in his best known overtures:

4 horns	in *Médée, Eliza*
4 horns, 1 trombone	in *Deux journées*
2 horns, 2 trumpets	in *Faniska*
2 horns, 2 trumpets, 1 trombone	in *Lodoiska, Hôtellerie portuguaise*
4 horns, 2 trumpets, 3 trombones	in *Anacréon, Abencérages*
4 horns, 4 trumpets, 3 trombones, 1 ophicleide	in *Ali Baba*

In his *Concert Overture* he uses the heavy nine-instrument combination of four horns, two trumpets, and three trombones, while his Symphony employs only four brasses — two horns and two trumpets.

In many instances, four or five brass instruments filled Cherubini's need for this particular timbre. Occasionally, by eliminating trumpets altogether and substituting two additional horns, Cherubini achieved greater homogeneity of sound at the expense of brilliance, which is also true of the combination of four horns and one trombone (without trumpets) used in his masterpiece *Les deux journées*. Whenever Cherubini employs only one trombone, he notates it in bass clef and uses it primarily for supporting the bass line. In later years, Cherubini increased the size of his brass section in keeping with the trend of the times, but he always retained a predilection for the poetic sound of the French horn.

One weak point in Cherubini's technique of orchestration is a certain monochromic tendency heightened by calculated restraint. He juxtaposes rather than mixes orchestral colors which results in occasional monotony. Especially the string instruments are often entrusted with long episodes, unrelieved by any change in sonority. The fact that Cherubini was able to transcribe his Symphony for string quartet illustrates this point sufficiently. This certain lack of boldness and colorfulness is counterbalanced by superior skill and intelligent planning.

Cherubini's style is personal and well-defined from *Lodoiska* (1791) on. He tends toward the contemplative and the lyrical, the intimate and the filigree, but is able to achieve occasionally impressive dramatic effects. His harmonies are often original, unusual, and even audacious in certain dissonant combinations; his counterpoint is skillful and expert. Unfortunately, only too often the total effect is weakened by a paucity of melodic invention which tends to be uninspired and artificial; too often he expends his skill on a third-rate theme which no amount of art can bring to life. Despite this lack of natural melodiousness — ofttimes criticized by his contemporaries — some of Cherubini's melodies are ingratiating, warm, even romantically tinted.

Aside from one Symphony (1815), Cherubini's contribution to orchestral literature consists of a number of overtures, some of which — like *Médée* and *Anacréon* — are still played today.

Cherubini handled the overture form in a free and imaginative way; in fact, his treatment is so individualized that he seems to have searched for a different solution of formal problems in each of his works. Thus he contributed immensely toward keeping the overture form free from the shackles of standardization — a fate which the genre of the sonata and the symphony did not entirely escape.

The only standardized pattern which Cherubini observed in all his overtures, except *Médée,* is the subdivision in a slow introduction and a spirited fast section. Within this *Allegro,* which constitutes the main section, we find a variety of procedures. Some consist of two quasi-symmetrical parts (A^1 and A^2), both complete with two or three themes connected by extended bridge passages, without any development section; others have a short development section which is handled without particular skill. Occasionally, as in *Lodoiska,* Cherubini treats the form quite freely; we find, too, that some of the overtures are tightly-knit, while others are almost potpourri-like. Sometimes an extended coda is attached to the *Allegro* section; at other times the order of first and second theme, in the recapitulation, is reversed and the first, usually brilliant, theme serves as ending. At all times, the closing section is handled with supreme skill and dramatic flair.

***

Cherubini's overture to *Démophon* (1788) is a significant and important composition, by far the finest and noblest piece of music heard in Paris since Gluck left in 1778. Written in C minor, it sustains a tragic rather than dramatic mood and has the nobility and seriousness so characteristic of Cherubini. Its form is traditional: a slow introduction followed by a fast movement in the *sonata-allegro* pattern. Cherubini makes an attempt at unification by using the same theme in both the introduction and the *Allegro,* but he cannot prevent the composition from appearing disjointed. This inability to weld a piece together is a characteristic weakness of Cherubini. Stylistically, this overture — preceding the first major opera of Méhul by two years — clearly presages the "revolutionary" style of the 1790's though Cherubini could not as yet free himself entirely from the somewhat static tradition of the Gluck style. The orchestration, too, is still sober: no clarinets are used in the overture, although they appear later in the course of the opera, and there are no trombones.

Abandoning the field of the *tragédie lyrique,* Cherubini turned to the genre of the *opéra comique* and achieved a great and legitimate success with his next work, *Lodoiska,* presented in 1791 at the small *Théâtre Feydeau* which became the home of all his future productions. The score of *Lodoiska* was considered a revelation by his colleagues, but the public seemed to prefer Rodolphe Kreutzer's opera on the same subject, presented a few weeks later at the *Comédie Italienne.*

The overture to Cherubini's *Lodoiska,* once one of his most popular works, nowadays appears strangely faded. A conspicuous weakness is the melodic invention which is often undistinguished and stilted; his themes, furthermore, are not clearly defined but consist often of drawn-out theme sections. Occasionally, however, Cherubini expands with a melody full of charm such as the second theme of the *Allegro vivace* which, in its quiet melancholy, has an almost Schubertian quality. Presenting a theme in the minor mode and repeating it immediately in major is a device used effectively by Cherubini and adopted later by Schubert, who makes extensive use of it. Cherubini is definitely more "harmonist" than "melodist"; his harmonic treatment has originality and often achieves surprising effects with unexpected modulations which again brings Schubert to our mind.

The orchestration of *Lodoiska,* with its individualized treatment of the woodwinds and horns, has already a Romantic tint. Cherubini uses a full woodwind section including clarinets, and a brass section of five instruments — two trumpets, two horns, and one trombone in bass clef. This trombone is not merely doubling other bass instruments but is handled with a certain independence.

As far as form is concerned, Cherubini frees himself from the pattern established by Gluck. Although he keeps the fundamental arrangement slow-fast, he enlarges the fast section by subdividing it into several independent parts, as can be seen from the following chart:

Adagio (D major)	— a slow introduction of little distinction
Allegro vivace (D major)	— consisting of two approximately symmetrical parts, without interpolated development section. Two contrasting themes are introduced, the second in the minor mode.
Moderato	— a short section introducing new thematic material.
Allegro vivace	— a short, coda-like section (eleven bars) reaffirming the D-major tonality and bringing the work to a brilliant close.

Of greater significance is Cherubini's next opera, *Eliza* (1794). Schemann calls it a "child of the terror era" and considers it a key to the understanding of the composer's personality.[48] His attempt to paint nature through music is a characteristic Romantic trait. Even more so is his treatment of the orchestra, especially the four horns which he uses in haunting calls, sustained notes, and characteristic intervals. The French horn, in the words of Alfred Einstein, is "the Romantic instrument par excellence; and solely through its use in instrumentation one could trace the development of the Romantic in music."[49]

The overture, though somewhat long for its content, has remarkable dramatic flair, and its basically undistinguished melodic invention is made attractive by interesting harmonic treatment.

Again the form is handled freely: a long *Maestoso* introduction containing some unusual harmonic progressions brings an ingratiating theme which reappears later. A tense transition — a masterpiece of almost Beethovenian suspense — leads into an *Allegro spiritoso*. Although the first theme is weak, the section is made more interesting by original harmonies and imaginative orchestral colors, with the string and woodwind instruments grouped against each other in interplay. A bridge passage tries to "work out" a motive from the first theme but succeeds only in showing Cherubini's limited development technique. The second theme section reintroduces the theme of the *Maestoso* played by the entire orchestra, with a counterpoint in the violas, cellos, and bassoons, both beautiful and effective.

A development section as such is lacking, for the *Allegro* consists of two symmetrically arranged parts, A^1 and A^2. However, when the first theme reappears in A^2, it is transformed and dramatized in a sort of amplified recapitulation. An appended *Piu mosso* section, motivically related to the *Allegro spiritoso,* is actually an extended, brilliant coda. Clipped chords, separated by long rests, foreshadow Beethoven's coda technique.

"Peculiar — almost strange, grand — almost immense, rich — almost limitless"[50] — such was the impression created by *Médée,* Cherubini's masterpiece. Fifteen years later, the judgment is more sober; Weber speaks of the overture as "magnificent, mildly passionate."[51] Indeed, much had happened between 1800 and 1815, and compared to the true savagery of Beethoven's *Coriolanus* or *Egmont,* Cherubini's *Médée* appeared certainly "mild."

Yet these comparisons are unavoidable and necessary, for Beethoven's dramatic style grew directly from such works as *Médée* or Méhul's *Stratonice.* The spiritual affinity between Beethoven on one side and Cherubini and Méhul on the other side cannot be over emphasized. The similarity of style is startling; the difference is merely one between talent and genius. While Cherubini and Méhul are often unable to sustain the impact of their first inspiration, Beethoven develops, molds and unifies his ideas with relentless concentration.

The opening of *Médée* has the hallmark of true greatness. With the first F minor chord, the overture steps immediately into the drama with powerful impact. There is no slow introduction, nor is there a coda; the whole piece is concise and unified. The first theme, passionate and sweeping, definitely has Beethovenian grandeur. As the tension subsides, the interest begins to lag during the drawn-out middle section using undistinguished thematic material. Although artfully interwoven and imaginatively orchestrated, the bridge passage and second theme section are anti-climatic. A short development section utilizes the first theme in various keys without displaying particular imagination; yet the dramatic impact is temporarily recaptured. The recapitulation reverses the order of main and subsidiary theme by starting with the bridge passage followed by the second theme; then at last the principal theme reappears in the home key of F minor and brings the overture to a rousing climax.

The orchestration calls for the usual strings, woodwinds, and timpani; but in the brass section, Cherubini limits himself to four horns. This adds homogeneity to the orchestral sound but robs it of projection and impact, and one cannot help but feel that the piece would have gained by the inclusion of trumpets and trombones. Yet one must admire the transparency of orchestration which is powerful without being noisy.

Cherubini, who had never excelled in wild and fiery music, startled his contemporaries with *Médée* to such an extent that one critic found "reminiscences and imitations" of Méhul's style.[52] Indeed, Méhul was known for his powerful, highly dramatic manner while Cherubini was generally more lyric and contemplative. Cherubini was obviously stimulated by the prevailing dramatic style in French music of which Méhul was then the foremost exponent, although "imitation" is certainly too harsh a word. Méhul himself rose to the defense of his friend in an open letter to the critic, saying that the inimitable author of *Lodoiska, Eliza,* and *Médée* had no need of imitating anyone.[53] Incidentally, Cherubini had dedicated his *Médée* to Méhul who reciprocated with the dedication of his *Ariodant* to Cherubini.

The following year (1798) Cherubini completed an opera in one act, *L'hôtellerie portuguaise,* which met with little success because of a poor libretto. The overture, a gay piece with a "quaint, mysterious" introduction,[54] was played frequently on concert programs, although it is less artful than other of his overtures. All the more surprising is the inability of Hugo Botstiber to identify this overture: he quotes the beginning in his *History of the Overture,*[55] but does not recognize the characteristic *folies d'Espagne* theme. In general, Botstiber's discussion of Cherubini's overtures in twenty-eight lines is wholly inadequate; he relies entirely on Kretzschmar's essay[56] to which he refers the reader.

The most interesting part of this overture is the introductory *Larghetto* which is largely taken up by the contrapuntal treatment of the *folies d'Espagne* theme, played by the string section alone. The ensuing *Allegro spiritoso* starts with a running figure in the violas which later reappears as a transition passage. When the full orchestra enters at last in the eleventh bar of the *Allegro,* the effect is overpowering. Unfortunately, the *Allegro* suffers from melodic anemia and a potpourri-like looseness of form. However, there is much effective writing for orchestra, and the typically operatic coda, rolling in a "snowball" crescendo, brings the work to a rousing close.

With *Les deux journées* (also known as *The Water Carrier* or *Der Wasserträger*), Cherubini succeeded at last in obtaining a truly popular success. Aided by a good libretto (which earned the literary approval even of Goethe), the work received more than two hundred performances in Paris alone within the first four years after its premiere in 1800. In Germany it was given on every operatic stage. For once, the public agreed with the experts:[57] the work was held in high esteem by Beethoven who kept the score on his piano, by Spohr who was "intoxicated with delight," by Weber who published an admiring analysis.

The overture is considered, by some biographers, the best among Cherubini's many works in this genre. Schemann,[58] for instance, finds it equal to the finest examples — *Iphigenia, Don Giovanni, Freischütz;* he calls it typical of the new overture style because it portrays the essence of the entire drama. Another authority, John Ella,[59] comes to an entirely different conclusion: the overture, with its "grand, heroic inspiration," does *not* adequately represent the mood of the libretto with its "sentimental, pastoral character." Incidentally, the overture has no thematic connection with the opera itself.

The overture opens with the traditional slow introduction, an *Andante molto sostenuto,* of great beauty and sustained interest. A masterful, tense preparation leads to the fast section, *Allegro,* which consists of two symmetrical parts without any development section. Three themes are presented: the first, brilliant, in E major; the second, an extended theme group, partly in E minor, punctuated by brutal *fortissimo* chords; the third again brilliant with interesting harmonic progressions which, at times, are quite dissonant. The second half of the *Allegro* recapitulates the first rather faithfully. An appended *Presto* of eighteen bars uses the first theme, taken at a faster speed, and brings the piece to an effective close.

The deviation from the conventional sonata form did not escape the attention of some historians. "The classical form is of secondary importance, — everything is filled with soul," remarks Schemann. Less impressed is G. A. Macfarren who accuses Cherubini of being generally deficient in principles of musical construction and therefore unqualified for success in the field of instrumental music. Diametrically opposed is the opinion of Richard Wagner who calls Cherubini "probably the greatest musical architect, . . . a bit stiffly symmetrical, but so beautiful and assured."[60]

The orchestra employed in this overture consists of the customary strings and woodwinds, while the brass instruments are limited to four horns and one trombone, omitting trumpets. Weber reports that trumpets were added in the overture when he heard the opera performed in Munich in 1811; in his opinion, their use might be justified in the *Allegro* section, but not in the introductory *Andante*.[61]

Among Cherubini's overtures, none had a more enduring success than *Anacréon;* it occupied a favored place in the orchestral repertoire throughout the 19th century and is still performed today. The overture survived the work for which it was written: the opera-ballet *Anacréon,* first performed in Paris in 1803, was a failure which Cherubini attributed to "the infernal clique directed against all who are connected with the *Conservatoire*."[62]   However, this was obviously not the only reason, for the work was also unsuccessful in Vienna where it was given in concert form in 1805.

Unaffected by these failures, the overture was received enthusiastically wherever it was played. At the first performance in London in 1815, the public demanded to hear it three times in succession. Melodious and uninhibited, it is indeed an irresistible piece of music, bursting with life and vigor, orchestrated in vivid colors. The brilliance is enhanced by the key of D major and the use of an extremely powerful orchestra. For the first time, Cherubini employed the heaviest brass section of his days: four horns, two trumpets, and three trombones. An equally large brass section is used by Beethoven in the *Leonore* Overture No. 3, written three years after *Anacréon*.

The powerful, majestic opening chords of the introductory *Largo assai* set the stage; sustained horns, a few solo woodwinds provide a contrast. The opening of the ensuing *Allegro* is a masterpiece of calculated suspense. For forty-seven bars, the orchestra remains *pianissimo,* at first the strings alone, then joined by a few woodwinds, obstinately repeating the same motive on a pedal point. Finally, a gradual *crescendo* sets in, with a mysterious timpani roll as background; and when, after twelve additional bars, the *fortissimo* climax is reached at last, the effect is overpowering. The second theme flows out of the first, and no contrasting material is introduced. The development section is modulating and uses a bridge passage from the exposition as principal material. Finally, the D major tonality is re-established and the second theme reappears. For added interest, a new one-bar motive is introduced consisting of a simple scale passage used later as countersubject and also in the final *stretta*. This closing section is a typical operatic "steamroller," musically empty, aiming merely at display of orchestral power and brilliance.

On the whole, the *Anacréon* overture is less labored, more naturally flowing than any of the other overtures by Cherubini, but it is also less refined, more flashy. Kretzschmar hears in this overture "demonic lightnings," "eruptions" which remind him of Beethoven, of the Symphonies Nos. 4 and 9, of the *Leonore* overtures; the entire Romanticism as to tendencies and means, so he claims, was ready in Cherubini's mind.[63] This cannot be accepted without qualification: true, the means were ready (we can find, in Cherubini, the germs of most of the Romantic techniques), but the tendencies were classicistic.

With some twenty operas to his credit, with an important post at the *Conservatoire,* Cherubini was not truly popular in Paris. Treated with indifference by Napoleon who bestowed favors on other artists, involved in a discriminatory battle directed against the *Conservatoire* of which he was a member, mistrusted by some of his French colleagues who considered him a "foreigner," his situation was not enviable. This was the man to whom, as a contemporary said, "one owes so much thanks in Paris and whom one thanks so rarely! whom the public understands so little! who, like Mozart, is praised by musicians and amateurs but not truly enjoyed."[64]

Under these circumstances, Cherubini was undoubtedly pleased to receive a commission to write an opera for Vienna where his works were highly popular. The libretto, *Faniska,* was in German, a language foreign to Cherubini, and we may assume that he composed the Italian translation which later appeared in the published score.

Cherubini arrived in Vienna in July 1805, and was received with great honors. He met most of the prominent musicians, including Haydn and Beethoven, who both professed admiration for their eminent confrere. Whether Cherubini had equally high regard for Beethoven, we do not know; personally they did not become friends because they were both of a somewhat gruff and unapproachable character.

It is interesting to note that both *Fidelio* and *Faniska* were composed, rehearsed, and performed almost simultaneously. Cherubini witnessed the unsuccessful premiere of *Fidelio* on November 20, 1805. In the meantime, Napoleon and his troops had entered Vienna on November 13, 1805. When the French Emperor heard that Cherubini was in

Vienna, he ordered him to direct his private musicales, but their relationship did not improve.

Three months later, on February 26, 1806, Cherubini's *Faniska* received its premiere and was warmly applauded by the Viennese, though with less enthusiasm than some of his earlier works. A month later, Beethoven presented his revised *Fidelio* (March 29, 1806) which fared little better than the first version.

The opinions about *Faniska's* value are divided. Kretschmar, for instance, considers it "among Cherubini's terror operas, the most remarkable, most original, most powerful achievement,"[65] thus placing it above *Eliza* and *Les deux journées*. Schemann, on the other hand, calls *Faniska* the weakest of all of Cherubini's mature works although he admits that the overture is not "disgracing" the composer.[66]

It is this overture which concerns us here. Bellasis considers it one of Cherubini's most finished works.[67] It is certainly worked out with particular care, as if Cherubini had made a special effort to be worthy of the city of Haydn and Mozart. After the somewhat shrill brilliance of *Anacréon,* we find *Faniska* more intimate, careful of details, conceived and written in the spirit of Mozart. The brass section is reduced to five instruments — two horns, two trumpets, and one trombone.

The dignified introduction, *Largo assai,* makes effective use of contrasts between powerful *tutti* chords and lovely fragments of melody played by woodwind soloists, and also juxtaposes the string section with the woodwinds. The ensuing *Allegro* is gay and graceful, and uses the orchestra with great economy. The theme is announced by the first violins, supported sparingly by the second violins, violas, and horns.   A beautifully built-up *crescendo* culminates in an impressive climax of the full orchestra, after which a Mozartian bridge passage leads to the second theme, "strange, weird, yet lovely . . . repeated with delightful persistency and with an airy accent."[68] Despite its indisputable originality and some expert three-part writing, this second subject is ineffective and too extended.

A short development section, built on a motive taken from the bridge passage, moves in beautiful, well-chosen modulations with occasional dramatic accents. A charming transition leads back to the first theme. In this recapitulation, the order of bridge and second subject is reversed, and the powerful bridge episode is used as a brilliant ending.

After his return to Paris in 1806, Cherubini ceased to compose for almost two years, allegedly because of the continued neglect by the Imperial Court. "He found Paisiello installed as new director of the Imperial chapel and Paer in charge of Napoleon's private music," asserts the *Encyclopédie du Conservatoire*.[69] At least the first half of the statement is erroneous, for Paisiello had left Paris and Napoleon's employ in 1804. It is possible that Paer's appointment discouraged Cherubini; on the other hand, Napoleon was not entirely inattentive to Cherubini for he commissioned him to write *Pimmalione* for the Italian opera at the *Tuileries* which was given, without success, in 1808.

Cherubini's last major effort in the operatic field was *Les abencérages,* given at the *Opéra* in 1813; this work, too, did not succeed and was removed from the repertoire after some twenty performances. Again, professional experts disagree with the public's verdict; as late as 1839, Mendelssohn writes admiringly of "the sparkling fire, the clever and unexpected transitions, and the neatness and grace with which he writes . . . It is all so free, so bold and bright."[70] More than in words, Mendelssohn shows his indebtedness to Cherubini in some of his music.

For a long time, the overture to *Les abencérages* remained a favorite repertoire piece of many conductors. Less unanimous are the historians: while Otto Jahn, the Mozart biographer, praises the "mixture of dashing fire and refined esprit, of grace and strictness," the *Quarterly Music*

Magazine calls it "the least attractive of any he has written, though it still contains many indubitable proofs of the ability . . ."[71]

An examination of the score makes this divergence of opinions understandable: there are admirable sections side by side with stilted and outmoded parts. This unevenness may have been caused by Cherubini's subconscious realization of the shifting musical style. Much had happened between 1806 and 1813, between *Faniska* and *Les abencérages;* no more were Cherubini, Méhul, Lesueur, Catel in the forefront of the young generation; the new leader was Spontini, and his glittering, pompous style the fashion of the day.

The overture to *Les abencérages* starts with the traditional slow introduction, *Largo,* which seems cold and stilted. The full orchestra punctuates episodes of woodwinds and strings. However, the picture changes for the better with the *Allegro spiritoso.* A chivalrous theme, presaging Weber's *Invitation to the Waltz,* is full of sparkle and life, and makes one forget the intrinsic weakness of its melodic invention. A slightly mannered bridge passage leads to a melancholy second theme of faded beauty, played by the strings alone. A third theme follows, built like the first on a simple triad, but made extremely attractive by an interplay of strings and woodwinds, foreshadowing Mendelssohn and his *Fingal's Cave.* A freely treated development section utilizes the triad idea of the first theme and the expanded bridge passage, modulating through various keys. The recapitulation begins with the second theme in D minor, followed by the third theme in the main key of D major. An extended closing section, motivically related to the first theme, with powerful chordal progressions, brings the overture to a brilliant ending.

The orchestration is as large as the of *Anacréon,* with a full brass section of four horns, two trumpets, and three trombones.

The following year (1814), Cherubini received a commission from The Philharmonic Society in London to write
several works for its concerts. A similar commission was
extended to Beethoven; thus the Society, then in its second
year, honored the two most famous living composers.
It is well known how Beethoven disappointed his friends
and admirers in London by sending three of his overtures
which were neither new nor particularly worthy of his
talent; after one rehearsal, the works were laid aside.
Cherubini took far greater pains with his commission
though the ultimate result was not much more satisfying.
He spent several months in London, from February 25 to
June 8, 1815, which kept him away from Paris during the
turbulent "Hundred Days" reign of Napoleon. Once in London, he completed the Concert Overture in G, the Symphony
in D, and a Pastoral Cantata; much of this music was probably sketched prior to his arrival in London.
In judging the Concert Overture, one should not measure
it with Beethovenian standards. "One expects more than one
is justified to expect," remarks Schemann philosophically.[72]
Scored for large orchestra, with nine brass parts (four
horns, two trumpets, three trombones) but using only one
flute, the work does not show any signs of having been
written in haste. Its workmanship is polished and well-
balanced, yet all the artfulness cannot hide the intrinsic
weakness of melodic invention which is often bloodless,
unoriginal, and outmoded.
The slow introduction, *Larghetto* (G major), is music
in the style of Haydn, i.e. some twenty-five years behind its
time. After a *pianissimo* fade-out and a long pause, an *Allegro
spiritoso* erupts with suddenness, coupled with a surprising
shift to G minor. The style is reminiscent of "Storm and
Stress," it has energy and drive but sounds neither convincing
nor like genuine Cherubini; the composer seems to force
himself into an *agitato* mood not unlike the "revolutionary"
style of the 1790's which, in 1815, sounded somewhat
belated and dusty.

The second theme is in the same key of G minor and is slightly reminiscent of early Beethoven (e.g., Piano Sonata Op. 2 No. 3). Leading to the third theme is a bridge passage introducing new material which is utilized in the short development section. The recapitulation follows the pattern of the exposition; however, the bridge passage is expanded and now contains an effective climax.

A general pause prepares for the closing section, a *Presto*, using the typically operatic device of "snowballing" an insignificant motive in constant repetition and adding instrumental entrances. The final *stretta* is built on commonplace triad and scale material, with tonic and dominant chords following each other in rapid succession.

The whole piece is by no means unworthy of Cherubini and could be played effectively even today; but it is a work of retrospective, belated tendencies.

The Symphony in D was begun in London in March, 1815, and finished on April 24 of the same year.[73] Although Cherubini had made some preliminary sketches in Paris, he had to work very fast, and the manuscript shows signs of great haste. Joseph St. Winter, who edited the score in 1935 after the original manuscript,[74] reports that Cherubini's copy resembles in many places more a sketch than a finished work, especially in the last movement, while the second movement is full of changes and corrections.

Despite this haste, the composition as such must have satisfied the composer, for when he decided to transcribe the Symphony for string quartet some fifteen years later, he made only negligible changes, usually necessitated by the change of instrumentation, rather than a desire to improve the quality of the work.

Historians generally interpret this transcription as a tacit admission of the composer that the work, in its original form as symphony, was a failure. In fact, the premiere in London was not successful, and a performance in Vienna was received coolly. The programs of the Paris *Conservatoire* offer no evidence that the Symphony was performed in the

French capital, which may be another proof that Cherubini did not care to have it performed, at least not in its original symphonic form.

While most biographers tend to agree with the verdict of the composer as far as the preference for the quartet version is concerned, there is one protesting voice: Robert Schumann calls any such transcription "a sin against the original divine inspiration."[75] Being a creative artist, Schumann considered it unthinkable that a piece of music, conceived in a particular medium, could be transplanted without harming its original concept.

Leaving aside the justification of any transcription, a comparison of the Symphony score with the quartet arrangement leads to interesting conclusions.

The first movement, especially the *Allegro* following the slow introduction, shows, in the symphonic version, a very sparing use of wind instruments which are employed in a somewhat old-fashioned *tutti* manner, i.e. mainly in *forte* passages. There are extended sections where the string instruments are used exclusively, and only in the development section are winds and timpani permitted to participate more actively. Although the slow introduction makes more imaginative use of wind instruments, one must admit that the material of the first movement is by no means unsuited for string quartet.

As for the second movement, Cherubini made his own decision, and a wise one it was: he did not attempt to transcribe the *Larghetto cantabile* of the Symphony, but composed a new (and very lovely) slow movement for the quartet version.

The third movement underwent a few revealing changes: in the symphonic version, it was called *Minuet* with a tempo marking *Allegro non tanto;* in the quartet version, the movement became a *Scherzo* with the tempo accelerated to *Allegro assai.* The music, curiously enough, remained exactly the same. The original title was decidedly a misnomer, for the movement has definitely a *scherzo* character. The faster tempo is appropriate for the quartet version: a group of four players can afford a faster tempo without loss of clarity and precision.

Actually, the last two movements suffer in the quartet arrangement, for they depend to a large degree on the colors of wind and percussion instruments; their essentially weak thematic invention is laid bare in the monochromic timbre of the string quartet. The *Trio* of the *Minuet,* based almost entirely on woodwinds, loses most of its charm when played by strings; and the *Finale,* with its typically orchestral *brio* strengthened by brass and timpani, becomes anemic and tiresome in the quartet version.

* * *

The neglect of Cherubini's Symphony has been criticized repeatedly; as early as 1863, Anton Schindler, the friend and biographer of Beethoven, registered his protest.[76] A revival of the work in Vienna in 1865/66 elicited from Eduard Hanslick, the critical oracle of the Austrian capital, a cool comment: "artful...accurate...noble...but still a wig."[77] Biographers of Cherubini, among them Bellasis and Schemann, urged re-evaluation of the Symphony, although admitting certain shortcomings in the score.[78] A well-balanced evaluation was made by Karl Nef who finds the attraction of Cherubini's Symphony in the tension between old and new; the slow introduction is pervaded with Romantic longing, while the old-fashioned comfort of the *Larghetto* is suddenly interrupted by stormy agitation, as if the 18th and the 19th centuries were clashing.[79]

In our opinion, there is actually very little "Romantic longing" and very much "old-fashioned comfort" in this Symphony. It is remarkable, almost puzzling, how Cherubini succeeded in remaining coolly detached and undisturbed in the face of the strong new currents pervading

European thought and art. In his hands, classicistic purity became sterility, and transparency became rarefied to such an extent that all life seems to have escaped. But the world, already in the midst of the birth pangs of a new era, refused to accept a sugarcoated pill as a cure for all ills. Cherubini, who in the 1790's and 1800's had been a beacon and a guide, appears in this Symphony of 1815 as the custodian of a bygone era.

It is obvious that, in composing his Symphony, Cherubini let himself be guided almost exclusively by the symphonic conception of Haydn as to form, technique, and expression. Other composers, too, were subjected to the same influence — Mozart, Beethoven, Méhul, for instance; but what, to others, was merely a point of departure, became in the case of Cherubini a dominant factor. Cherubini's Symphony came twenty years too late: what might have been admired in 1795 was found epigonal in 1815.

Very revealing, in this respect, is a comparison between Cherubini's Symphony and his Concert Overture, composed at the same time. Being a master of the overture form, he needed no models, whereas in the field of the symphony, being a novice, he leaned heavily on well-tried examples; thus, the Overture shows much more independence of mood, construction, and orchestration. The latter is much heavier in the Overture than in the Symphony: nine brass instruments as compared to four (two horns and two trumpets), while the remainder of the orchestra is the same in both works. Curious is Cherubini's use of only one flute while the other woodwinds are in pairs, similar to Mozart's Symphony No. 40 in G minor. Although the prejudice against the use of trombones in symphonies had been broken by Beethoven, Cherubini still avoids their use — a characteristic difference between "operatic" and "symphonic" concept.

***

Cherubini's Symphony opens with a short introduction, *Largo,* which is pervaded by a peaceful, pastoral atmosphere of sustained lyricism. The "Romantic longing" of the opening phrase foreshadows Mendelssohn's "Nocturne" from the *Midsummer Night's Dream* music, written almost thirty years later (1843) (ex. III-28, III-29). Weber, too, learned from Cherubini how to blend woodwinds and horns into a timbre of shimmering, silvery beauty.

Example III-28. Cherubini, *Symphony in D* (1815). Introduction to First movement.

Example III-29. Mendelssohn, *A Midsummer Night's Dream* (1843). Nocturne.

The ensuing *Allegro* has some of the joyful spirit which many compositions in the key of D major have in common. The first theme is contrasted in itself: four-and-a-half bars of fiery *forte* are followed by some sixteen bars of lyric melody played by the strings alone. A bridge passage leads to the second theme in A major, again dominated by the strings, and a third theme in the same key, presented first by the strings, then repeated by the woodwinds. An extended closing section rounds out the exposition which has no repeat signs.

The development is based mainly on the first theme which lends itself so well to a working-out because of its dual, contrasting character. A transition leads gradually and unobtrusively into the recapitulation which follows the pattern of the exposition closely; however, when the first theme reappears, it lacks the first four energetic bars and begins immediately with the lyric section of the subject.

As already mentioned, the treatment of the wind instruments in the *Allegro* is rather traditional: they appear primarily as reinforcement, except in some sections of the development where their use is more distinctive and individualized. The workmanship is expert but somewhat dry and uninspired; nothing unforeseen happens, everything unfolds in a thoroughly conventional manner. The thematic invention, as so often in Cherubini's works, is somewhat pale and anemic; particularly impersonal, in this movement, is the third theme. Some parallel fifths which escaped the composer's eye in the haste of preparing the work for performance were covered up in the quartet version (ex. III-30a, III-30b).

Example III-30a. Cherubini, *Symphony in D* (1815). Parallel fifths in First movement.
Example III-30b. Cherubini. Same fifths, here avoided in quartet version (1828).

The second movement, *Larghetto cantabile* in G major, is a piece of haunting loveliness, in the Haydn tradition, with powerful orchestral climaxes and many exquisite details. The form is ternary: A′ — B — A″. The first section

(A') has two themes, in G major and D major; the second section (B) consists of an elaboration of the first theme and culminates in a beautifully conceived climax. An artful transition leads back to the last section (A'') which is merely an elaboration of the first part. Throughout this movement, the woodwinds are handled with individuality and independence; the melodic line is distributed among various instruments which are often given solo parts. In view of this idiomatic treatment, it is not surprising that Cherubini omitted this particular movement in the quartet version of the Symphony.

The *Minuet* (actually a *scherzo,* as we have said before) derives much of its color and effect from the brilliance of the wind instruments, particularly the middle section (*Trio*) which depends entirely on the woodwinds while the strings are totally subordinate.

The finale, *Allegro assai,* has been called "inadequate" by Schemann.[80] It is indeed, but only as a quartet movement, while the original symphonic version is effective, though somewhat superficial. Brass instruments and timpani are assigned essential parts and add to the sweep and fire of the movement. Again, the thematic invention is not overly original (especially the second theme is weak), but the Anacreontic spirit carries the movement to a brilliant finish.

***

Throughout the entire Symphony, one cannot but admire the superior craftsmanship, the prudent (perhaps overly cautious) distribution of climaxes, the fine balance within each movement and between the movements. The fatal weakness of the work is the often conventional thematic invention and the generally restrained orchestration. The transcription for quartet eliminated the latter, but left the musical content untouched (except for the new slow movement). Thus the composition did not achieve any more popularity as a quartet than as a symphony. That Cherubini was able to write a truly fine string quartet is proved by his Quartet No. 1 in E flat, composed in 1814, one year prior to the Symphony.

"There are few things more strange in musical history than that Cherubini, so great a master in the orchestra, should have failed in his one symphony," says Bellasis.[81] This relative failure, however, is small indeed if compared to Cherubini's invaluable contribution to the orchestral idiom which is revealed most fully not in his symphony, but in his operatic overtures.

***

The Symphonies of Ferdinand Herold

About the same time that Cherubini wrote his Symphony in London, a young Frenchman, Ferdinand Herold (born in 1791), composed a number of instrumental works, including two symphonies. Herold, whose chosen instrument was the piano, had written some piano music in 1811 while still a student of Méhul at the *Conservatoire*. The following year he obtained the Rome Prize which meant a prolonged stay in Italy. There he composed symphonies and string quartets; the first symphony was written in Rome in 1813, the second in Naples in 1814. In a letter to his mother Herold writes:

> The Symphony (No. 2) which I am sending to the Institute, has been played here in Naples three times with success, by a mediocre orchestra...[82]

The *Institut de France* was highly pleased with the achievement of they young prizewinner, as we can see from the following report.

> We have received from Mr. Ferdinand Herold . . . a symphony and three quartets. This young composer deserves nothing but praise and encouragement. The Music Division is very pleased with these pieces . . . The Symphony has energy and originality, and everywhere his writing is broad, correct, and easy-flowing . . .[83]

However, Herold himself, according to his biographer Pougin, did not attach much importance to these early instrumental works; his entire ambition was to achieve success on the operatic stage. This success came to him slowly and late: after some fifteen operas which met with mediocre approval, he finally obtained a brilliant success with *Zampa* (1831) and *Le pré aux clercs* (1832); the following year he died of consumption, at the age of forty-two.

Tiersot, who heard the revival of one of these symphonies (probably No. 2) at the *Concerts Colonne* in 1902, does not show himself particularly impressed:

> It is a pleasant composition which aims no higher than to renew some of the amenities of Haydn's symphonies; the themes are graceful, but that is not sufficient to fulfill the expectations which we have nowadays for the noble genre of the symphony.[84]

In the course of his article, Tiersot reproaches the older generation of French composers for considering the symphony a "school assignment," cultivated only for the purpose of fulfilling the Rome prize obligations: "it was a singular error of the French musicians of those times to see in the symphony merely a scholastic genre."

Herold's symphonies illustrate this point. Both were conceived in the spirit of Haydn and Mozart, reflecting a bygone era. Though Herold must have heard (and even participated in) performances of Beethoven's first two symphonies by the *Conservatoire* student orchestra, there is no trace of it to be found in his scores. Even more surprising is the absence of any influence by his teacher Méhul whose four symphonies were played in Paris shortly before Herold left for Italy; and Méhul as symphonist had some original ideas.

Writing his symphonies under the Mediterranean sun, young Herold had no ambitions of opening new vistas nor did he have sufficient experience in expressing himself through the absolute language of the symphony. Thus he chose a comfortably traditional idiom and well-tried classical forms and techniques. His writing is fluent and graceful, the themes are pleasant though not truly inspired, the workmanship is skillful, the orchestration is transparent and idiomatic (the violin was his secondary instrument). Next to the customary string and woodwind sections, Herold uses only two French horns and timpani, excluding trumpets — the same intrumentation to be found in Méhul's First Symphony. Herold once described his orchestral writing as "difficult" which is an exaggeration: the technical demands are actually below those of a Haydn symphony. Nevertheless, the Roman musicians faltered at the first rehearsal of his First Symphony while a "mediocre" orchestra in Naples played his Second Symphony in 1814.

In terms of form, Herold allows himself a few minor liberties, though all sanctioned by the Viennese tradition. The First Symphony (C major) is cast in four movements opening with a concise *Allegro,* without repeat of the exposition, and with a shortened recapitulation beginning with the second theme in the tonic key. An *Andante* in F major is very much in the Haydn style. There follows a *Minuetto* in C minor, with a *Trio* in E major, without tempo indication; the movement was praised by the Institute as having "une originalité piquante." The final *Rondo Vivace* is described by some as the best, by others as the weakest of the movements; its charm lies in its brisk animation while the themes are rather uninspired. One original touch is the initial phrase consisting of three measures which is asymmetrical and perturbed the jury of the Institute; the young composer was admonished to invent in the future "irreproachable" themes suitable for elaboration.

Although only one year separates the two symphonies, the Second Symphony (D major) shows marked progress in the composer's mastery of the symphonic language. It is conceived in three movements, each of ampler proportions. The first opens with an impressive *Introduction* (*Largo*) of twenty-six measures in the best Haydn style, ending on the dominant in *fortissimo*. The theme of the ensuing *Allegro molto* enters *pianissimo*, in 3/4 meter, creating a strong contrast. The movement is a fully worked out *sonata-allegro*, with repeated exposition (the sinuous second theme has a Schubertian quality!), a forceful development, and an imaginative recapitulation where the above mentioned second theme reappears in B-flat major. (Schubert took similar liberties with key relationships; in fact, it is worth remembering that Herold and Schubert composed their first symphonies during the years 1813/15, unbeknown to each other). The second movement, *Andante* (F major) is very much à la Haydn, with clarinets omitted and a mood reminiscent of the *Surprise Symphony,* even to the point of a sudden *fortissimo* chord creating a rude interruption. The final *Rondo* is one of those "running" movements, with contrasting episodes in longer note values, full of wit and playfulness, with a brief section in imitative style. This Symphony was the crowning achievement of his academic studies at the *Conservatoire* and earned him the praise of the Institute.

After his return to Paris in 1815, Herold plunged into the operatic life as pianist-coach and composer. The symphonies were forgotten and there is no record that they were played during his lifetime. He died young, in 1833. His youthful works, written at the *Conservatoire* and in Italy, were published posthumously in 1870-90 by his family, including the scores of his symphonies,* and it may well be that the performance of 1902 in Paris was a premiere.

French historians continue to evaluate Herold's position as an instrumental composer in a condescending manner. A

---

*A new edition of Herold's symphony scores, with an introduction by Boris Schwarz, was recently published by Garland Publishing, Inc., New York, 1981.

generalized statement can be found in the *Encyclopédie du Conservatoire:*

> These works (symphonies, quartets, etc.) have neither long breath nor profound inspiration, but they contain occasionally interesting ideas. A closer examination proves that Herold could have cultivated the symphonic genre with real distinction if he had directed his efforts toward this aim.[85]

Unperformed and unpublished in their time, Herold's symphonies exerted no influence. But they deserve to be noted by historians as lonely outposts, standing between Méhul's traditionalism and Berlioz' innovative spirit, though closer to his teacher Méhul by training and disposition.

***

Catel and Boieldieu

The overtures of Cherubini and Méhul almost monopolized the concert programs in Paris between 1800 and 1815, and comparatively little attention was paid to overtures by other composers. A work which was able to hold its own was the overture to *Semiramis* by Charles-Simon Catel.[86]

Catel's fame rests primarily on his *Traité de l'harmonie* (1802) which, on Cherubini's recommendation, was adopted by the *Conservatoire* and remained a standard text for almost fifty years. This reputation as theorist was detrimental to his career as composer, for his detractors branded his works as "too learned." *Semiramis,* Catel's first opera, had its successful premiere in 1802. The overture outlived the opera and remained a concert favorite until the 1850's.

Scored for a large orchestra including seven brass parts (two horns, two trumpets, three trombones), the overture shows effective handling of the instruments. It opens with a *Lento* full of tension, suspense, and powerful contrasts which is actually the most originally conceived section of the entire overture. The ensuing *Allegro maestoso* is animated, brilliant, and dramatic in parts, although the bloodless second theme weakens the initial favorable impression. In the middle of the *Allegro,* the introduction reappears, after which the *Allegro* returns. An extended closing section, part of which is built on a pedal point growing from *pianissimo* to *fortissimo,* brings the overture to a brilliant and effective close.

The whole piece is well conceived and solidly constructed, full of life and fire. Without having the spark of genius, this overture is nevertheless historically important, for it shows how firmly established and well handled, even by secondary composers, the new instrumental style was — that style based on the Gluck tradition and enlivened by the dramatic vividness of the revolutionary opera.

Another primarily operatic composer who found a place on concert programs through his overture is Adrien Boieldieu. His early *Calife de Bagdad* (1800), written at the age of twenty-four, has a youthful charm and naiveté which is entirely lacking in his *Jean de Paris,* produced in 1812 after his prolonged sojourn in Russia. Why this work impressed the usually so discerning Schumann[87] is incomprehensible. The overture shows the pauperization of craftsmanship in the *opéra comique:* the orchestration is primitive, the harmonization elementary, and the melodic invention, which could save a work of this kind, is conspicuously weak. One can understand Berlioz who, in speaking of Boieldieu, says ironically that he "expressed the most childish surprise at any combination of harmonies outside the three chords with which he had trifled all his life."[88] This, however, did not prevent Boieldieu from writing *La dame blanche* (1825), one of the most successful operas of all times, which received three hundred performances in less than two years — a work which has been called "the French Freischütz" by a German historian.[89] The overture, however, is an artless potpourri, fashioned hurriedly by the composer with the aid of two students, one of whom was Adolphe Adam.[90]

***

Lesueur and Spontini

Two important musicians of that period remain to be discussed — Lesueur and Spontini. "Spontini was the last classic of the old school, Lesueur the first romantic of the new," says Lavoix, a statement fallacious in its sweeping generalization.[91]

La caverne, Lesueur's first opera, was presented in 1793 and received more than one hundred performances within fifteen months. It is a characteristic product of the political environment — "the fearfully oppressed atmosphere, feverish excitement, wild energy."[92] *La caverne* was one of the first and purest examples of the "terror" and "rescue" operas which dominated the French scene for a decade. "Everything is original, grand, much too unusual and new in forms and means," says Kretzschmar.[93]

Lesueur is a dramatic composer par excellence. His music, when divorced from action, has little intrinsic interest. This is most noticeable in his overtures and instrumental entr'actes: they fulfill their purpose of establishing a certain mood without offering much of purely musical value. Thus, his overtures are not effective in the concert hall and, in fact, were never performed separately. Nevertheless they are eminently interesting from the historic point of view, for they represent the "revolutionary" instrumental style in all its strength and weakness.

Most important in all of Lesueur's works, however, is the spirit in which they are conceived. There is a constant earnest search for the new and the unusual, a conscious avoidance of the down-trodden path of routine. It is this relentless spirit of adventure, more than details of crafts-manship, which Lesueur succeeded in transmitting to his student Berlioz. Master and student have certain traits in common — ardent and poetic imagination, love for grandiose sonorities, and eagerness for innovations.[94] However, by 1822, when Berlioz first came in contact with Lesueur, the old master was only a feeble reflection of his former artistic self — the fiery reformer and pamphleteer of the 1790's and 1800's had become a placid, resigned man who liked to be left alone with his thoughts, patiently attending to his duties as teacher and church composer, but actually forgotten as a creative musician. He shared this fate with his entire genera-tion — Catel, Berton, Kreutzer, Méhul, even Cherubini — all "revolutionary romanticists" who, in their last years, were left behind — bewildered and disillusioned — by the swiftly moving current of new music. Here we discover the fallacy of the above-quoted statement by Lavoix: Lesueur was not "the first romantic of the new school," but the last romantic of the old school, of that 18th century romantic generation which we have called "revolutionary romanticists." Lesueur's connection with the "new" Romantic school was tenuous and his only loose link was his student Berlioz. Persuaded by Berlioz to attend a performance of Beethoven's Fifth Sym-phony, Lesueur — though visibly impressed — disguised his emotion: "All the same, such music ought not to be written." "Don't worry, master," Berlioz replied, "there is not much danger that it will."[95]

***

Equally questionable is Lavoix's statement with regard to Spontini: he was not the "last classic of the old school," but a representative of that classicistic trend prevalent in French art during the Napoleonic Empire and even a few years beyond it.

Spontini presents, in some ways, the same phenomenon as Cherubini and Viotti: an Italian, trained in the musical atmosphere and tradition of Italy, transforms himself, upon contact with the Parisian musical scene, into a "French" musician, and soon becomes the symbol and leader of French music. To trace and analyze the fusion, the interpenetration of Italian heritage and French tradition in the works of these three composers is a fascinating task. All three preserved their Italian heritage to a certain degree, although with varying intensity.

Spontini came to Paris in 1803, at a time when the French capital was once again divided into two musical camps —pro-Italian and pro-French. This time, the Italian party had the support of Bonaparte and his influential circle, but the French musicians fought back fearlessly. No wonder that Spontini was not received with open arms by his French colleagues; even the established Cherubini was considered by some with misgivings.

During the next few years, Spontini underwent a considerable musical transformation. Under the impression of the French *tragédie lyrique,* Spontini molded his style to French taste and tradition, emerged as a rejuvenated, modernized Gluck, with an Italian's gift for melody and the French flair for pomp and splendor (ex. III-31, III-32, III-33).

Example III-31. Vogel, *Démophon* (1787). Overture.

Example III-32. Lesueur, *La caverne* (1793). Overture.

Example III-33. Spontini, *La vestale* (1807). Overture.

Spontini's first success in Paris, and in many respects his finest work, was *La vestale* (1807) where the various components of his art — Italian, French, and German — appear in beautiful balance. The overture, an imposing piece of orchestral writing, adheres to the traditional formal pattern — a slow introduction followed by an extensive fast movement. The opening *Andante sostenuto,* in D minor, is beautifully sustained, carefully wrought, and minutely worked out in dynamics and orchestration. It leads directly into a *Presto assai agitato,* an extended piece with two contrasting themes (in D minor and D major), a development section, recapitulation, and coda. Towering climaxes are reached toward the end of the exposition and the recapitulation where a prolonged pedal point prepares a pompous, march-like outburst; and the ending of the overture is tremendously brilliant and effective.

It is strange that this impressive overture did not receive frequent concert performances; in fact it was played only once at the *Conservatoire,* in 1818, more than ten years after the premiere of the opera, at the height of Spontini's career. Perhaps Weber was right in saying that "music meant for scenic effect loses this effect to a great extent in the concert hall."[96]

These words referred to a concert performance of the overture to *Fernando Cortez,* Spontini's second major opera written for Paris and presented in 1809. The *Académie impériale* spared no effort to give the new work a brilliant presentation. With unmistakable irony, a contemporary correspondent wrote shortly before the premiere:

Now a new work is being studied, *Fernando Cortez,* and one assures us that it will surpass everything in beauty — of scenery.[97]

Despite some adverse criticism, however, the new work established Spontini as the dominating personality of the Paris *Opéra* for more than a decade.

Fernando Cortez shows Spontini in a somewhat new light. The Gluck tradition, still preserved in *La vestale,* appears weakened and is replaced by a brittle, steel-like brilliance which often seems cold and calculated for utmost effect. The overture to *Fernando Cortez* abounds in martial rhythms and crashing climaxes. Without any slow introduction, the piece starts immediately with a fanfare-like theme. On the whole, the melodic invention is undistinguished, the transitions are weak, and the entire overture too long for its thin musical content. In all its glittering and yet empty pomp, *Fernando Cortez* is a typical product of the Napoleonic era.

Much in the same style is *Olympie,* Spontini's last opera for Paris, given in 1819. Napoleon was gone, but much of the Napoleonic spirit remained. The defeat of 1815 was forgotten, France's courage was unbroken. Spontini's grandiloquence appealed to Bourbon France just as much as it had to the Empire. In *Olympie* we have the same cold pomp and calculated construction, brought to life by a superb flair for the theater, the drama, the scenic effect — nowadays called showmanship. Weber, this sensitive and yet practical musician, had the highest regard for *Olympie* and staged its performance in Dresden; in fact, Weber's *Euryanthe* overture seems to have some of Spontini's dashing action.

The overture to *Olympie* is a textbook example of an operatic overture: linked with the opera by thematic material, it captures the essence of the entire work. The form deviates from the traditional pattern of the French overture and adopts instead the arrangement of the Italian overture — fast — slow — fast. Following Spontini's example, Berlioz cast some of his most effective overtures (e.g. *Carnaval Romain*) in the same mold.

The piece opens with an *Allegro marcato con fierezza* which immediately activates the entire orchestra in a tremendous *tutti*. Contrasts between *fortissimo* and *pianissimo,* interrupted by long silences, heighten the tension. After a sudden break, a new mood appears; a slow section, *Andante religioso,* with a peaceful, pastoral atmosphere. The English horn joins the woodwinds, with muted strings as background. A modulation leads directly into the third section, *Allegro molto agitato,* in the original key of D major. Starting with a transition very much in the Italian style, building up a tremendous *crescendo* on a pedal point, the first theme is brought back, fiery, brilliant, march-like. After a calmer second theme of insignificant melodic invention, Spontini attempts a development section with somewhat awkward modulations. The recapitulation is built into a tremendous climax, whipping up more and more excitement on a long pedal point (in fact, there are six-and-a-half pages of continuous *fortissimo* and triple *forte* in the score). All the resources of the orchestra are thrown into the ending. Here are the foreshadowings of Berlioz' *Fantastique,* of Wagner's *Rienzi,* of Liszt's *Les Préludes;* in Spontini, we find the true source of the colorful orchestral brilliance which would become so typical of the 19th century. Berlioz, an ardent admirer, analyzed it in a perceptive essay:

> Spontini's orchestration ... is in no way derivative from anyone. Its special coloring is due to the use of the wind instruments ... The important as well as novel role assigned by the composer to the violas, now massed together, now divided like the violins ... is likewise characteristic of his orchestration ... The moderate but exceedingly ingenious use of trombones, trumpets, horns, and kettledrums, the almost total omission of the shrill high notes of the piccolos, oboes, and clarinets — all impart to the orchestration ... a tone of grandeur, an incomparable energy and power, and often a mood of poetic melancholy. [98]

In *La vestale, Fernando Cortez,* and *Olympie,* Spontini uses practically the same large orchestra: strings (with divided violas); woodwinds, including piccolo, English horn, and third bassoon; a powerful brass section with four horns, two trumpets, and three trombones; and a large assortment of percussion instruments. The handling of this large body of instruments is masterful though of varying quality, as Berlioz remarks:[99] "The orchestration, which is of sober richness in *La vestale,* grows complicated in *Cortez* and is overdrawn with a number of useless lines in *Olympie,* to the point of occasionally making the instrumentation heavy and confused." The orchestral writing was considered very difficult in its time, and Spontini was faced with bitter complaints and open enmity from the musicians, which he overcame with ruthless determination.*

Spontini is called the musical personification of the Napoleonic Age. This is a convenient, and yet ambiguous label. True, his music captured the spirit of Napoleonic France which was martial, aggressive, proud, energetic, pompous, and passionate. Yet, the pompousness, usually attributed indiscriminately to the Empire and Spontini alike, was a prerogative neither of France nor of Spontini. Actually, it was the new Italian opera, headed by Simon Mayr and the Venice school,[100] which first introduced and emphasized the overloaded orchestra and the effect at all costs. Nor did this brittle glitter affect Spontini alone, for similar traits can be found in later works of Méhul (*Gabrielle d'Estrée*) and Cherubini (*Les abencérages*), though applied with more discrimination and refinement.

Considered from a more comprehensive point of view, it might be more accurate to ascribe Spontini's massive settings and imposing splendor to the typical Romantic tendency toward luxuriance of expression. The fact remains that Spontini is neither epigone nor precursor, neither "last classicist" nor "first romanticist," but the perfect personification of his times — that contradictory era when reaction and progress existed side by side, in politics as well as in the arts.

---

*Spontini left Paris in 1820 to accept a royal appointment in Berlin.

Spontini's nature was opposed to consciously Romantic art, to the abandonment of certain limitations, to the uninhibited self-proclamation, for his was an art of calculated order, measured balance, and rigorous method. Off the stage, however, in his unpretentious songs, he shows an almost Schubertian grace and warmth, and some of his melodic lines point toward the sweetness of Bellini. Moreover, Spontini furnished the principal tool of Romantic music which was eagerly accepted by Berlioz, Liszt, and Wagner: the rich luxuriance of the orchestral palette, with a wealth of colors and shadings, with flexibility and crashing power transcending anything his predecessors or contemporaries had to offer. "It was Spontini who invented the colossal *crescendo,*" exclaimed Berlioz in admiration.[101] Standing as a "classicist" between two "romantic" generations, Spontini reaches out in both directions, connecting the 1780's with the 1830's, an important and indispensable link between the old and the new.

***

Young Berlioz as Instrumental Composer

"An artist . . . without ancestry and without posterity" — this is how Ernest Newman characterized Berlioz.[102] What Newman meant to say with this brilliant (if arguable) aphorism is the uniqueness of Berlioz within the context of French music. Certainly Newman was well aware of Berlioz' musical "ancestry" — his studies with Lesueur and Reicha, his admiration for Gluck, his methodical exploration of the scores by the "three modern masters, Beethoven, Weber, and Spontini."[103] Yet, the sum-total of his apprenticeship explains merely the technical aspects of his art; it fails to explain the startling newness, the exciting originality of his early works. French music of the 1820s was mired in mediocrity, dominated by cheap pursuit of sensationalism, tyrannized by finger acrobats posing as virtuosos.

Suddenly, Berlioz emerges in 1828 — a firebrand in his twenties, articulate and agressive, determined to create a musical revolution. "I took up music where Beethoven left it," he is reported to have said to Fétis.[104] He arranges a concert entirely of his own works, on 26 May 1828, which is well reviewed but does not open any official doors.* He wins the Rome Prize in 1830 after several failed attempts which enhances his stature but does not advance his career. To hear his works performed, he must arrange concerts at his own expense. Only once did Habeneck present one of Berlioz' compositions — the *Rob Roy* Overture — at the concert of the *Conservatoire* on 14 April 1833, but it was poorly received and later discarded by the composer. He had to wait until 1849 to hear another of his works performed at the staid *Conservatoire* — fragments from the *Damnation of Faust.* There is evidence of a deliberate exclusion of Berlioz.

***

Within the framework of our topic, we shall limit our discussion to Berlioz' instrumental works completed by 1830 — the overtures to *Francs-Juges* and *Waverley,* and the *Symphonie fantastique.*

Berlioz composed the two overtures in 1827-28 and included them on his concert program of 26 May 1828. (The concert was played by an orchestra of volunteers under the direction of Bloc of the *Odéon.*) Mediocre though the performance was, it gave Berlioz the opportunity of hearing the actual sound of his scores.

*See p. 60

At that time, Berlioz was (in his own words)

> ignorant of the mechanism of some of the instruments . . . Neither of my
> masters taught me anything about instrumentation. Lesueur's ideas on the
> subject were most limited. Reicha understood the qualities of most of the
> wind instruments; but I don't think that he had any real conception of
> grouping them in larger or smaller bodies."[105]

Berlioz acquired his prodigious knowledge of orchestration by purely empirical means: he turned to friends in the
orchestra who demonstrated their instruments for him, he sat
in the orchestra pit reading the score during performances.
Not being a pianist, Berlioz skipped the intermediate stage of
a "piano score"in writing for the orchestra: his imagination
unfolded in purely orchestral timbres. Played in a piano
reduction, a score by Berlioz loses its essential quality. This
was recognized by Schumann:

> Berlioz' music must be *heard;* even an examination of the score is not suf-
> ficient for its understanding, and it is labor lost to make it out on the
> piano. He appears to get results in spots by mere tone effects . . .[106]

Nevertheless, Schumann's remarkable analysis of the *Symphonie fantastique* was done after Liszt's piano score.

Both of Berlioz' earliest overtures require a very large
orchestra. In the woodwind section he uses two bassoons
plus contrabassoon in *Francs-Juges,* four bassoons in *Waverley.*
The brass section calls for four French horns, three trumpets
(including one modern valve trumpet), three trombones, and
one or two ophicleides. The percussion instruments are the
customary timpani and, in *Francs-Juges,* also cymbals and
bass drum. To balance this big wind section, Berlioz prescribes
a minimum number of required string instruments — "at least
15 first and 15 second violins, 10 violas, 12 cellos, and 9
double basses."

Yet, this large orchestra is used with restraint and discrimination, saving the power of the full orchestra for certain
climaxes and providing effective contrasts. A fine example of
juxtaposed sonorities is the slow introduction (*Adagio*

sostenuto) of the *Francs-Juges* Overture. Berlioz keeps the first nineteen measures thin and transparent, limited to strings and a few selected winds. The sudden entrance of a dozen brass instruments in triple *forte,* unison or in octave doublings, reinforced by clarinets and bassoons, produces an almost terrifying effect. One is hard pressed to find a precedent for such a kind of orchestral scoring.

The ensuing *Allegro assai,* in the same key of F minor, follows a classical *sonata-allegro* pattern: three themes, a brief development section, and a traditional recapitulation plus coda. Within this framework, however, Berlioz takes extensive liberties, especially in the recapitulation. The themes are effectively contrasted: the first in a rushing *agitato* mood, the second a haunting melody borrowed from one of his youthful compositions. When this melody is repeated in the woodwinds, the first theme is used as counterpoint in the strings — a skillful combination. The third theme is a series of prayer-like sustained chords in the flutes and clarinets while the strings furnish a background of excited tremolos and snatches of the first theme. In the score, Berlioz provides the following explanation, "The orchestra takes a double character there. The stringed instruments must, without covering the flutes, play with a rude and wild accent, the flutes and clarinets however with a soft and melancholic expression." In the ensuing elaboration of this theme, Berlioz achieves an ominous effect by having the timpani beat a ¾ rhythm against the ⁴/₄ motion of the orchestra.

Despite a few signs of inexperience in some awkward transitions, the *Francs-Juges* Overture is an astonishing work for a young composer trying his wings in a new idiom.

It is interesting to juxtapose two opinions about the work, one by Mendelssohn, the other by Schumann. Mendelssohn had a low opinion of Berlioz' talent (they met in Rome in 1831) though he mellowed in later years and treated Berlioz "like a brother" in Leipzig in 1843. But there is nothing brotherly in the following letter addressed to Moscheles in 1834:

> Whta you say about Berlioz' Overture [*Francs-Juges*] I thoroughly agree with. It is a chaotic, prosaic piece, and yet more humanly conceived than some of his others . . . His orchestration is such a frightful muddle, such an incongruous mess, that one ought to wash one's hands after handling one of his scores . . .[107]

Schumann, on the other hand, is symphathetic though not uncritical. He heard Berlioz' overture in 1837 in Leipzig played by the Euterpe Society:

> . . . the overture to the *Vehmic Judges* which is being proclaimed as a monstrosity, whereas I cannot find in it anything but the work of a French musical genius, well cut in clear style although still immature in some details; there are however occasional strokes of lightning, like precursors of the glorious storm that is thundered forth in his symphonies.[108]

The word "glorious" was eliminated in the collected edition of Schumann's articles as if he had changed his mind. The readers of the journal *Neue Zeitschrift für Musik* were familiar with Berlioz' name through Schumann's perceptive analysis of the *Symphonie fantastique* in 1835.

While the overture *Francs-Juges* was part of an unfinished opera, *Waverley* is an early example of a "topical" overture for the concert hall. It was inspired by the novel of Sir Walter Scott which Berlioz read in translation. The manuscript contained several quotations from the novel, but the first published edition of the score is prefaced only by the motto

> Dreams of love and lady's charms
> Give place to honour and to arms.

Love and war, the two contrasting moods, are beautifully captured by the composer. The tender and peaceful opening *Larghetto* is contrasted to the chivalrous theme of the *Allegro vivace,* with dashing violin passages in the spirit of Weber's *Oberon* Overture. The orchestration grows in richness until a fiery bridge section is reached. Breaking off suddenly, a second theme is introduced, of rather weak invention. On a deceptive cadence, the full orchestra enters in *fortissimo,* all the more startling because much of the brass section had been silent until then. The character is martial and fanfare-like. There is no development to speak of, and the first two themes reappear in the home key of D major. After some interplay between both themes there comes the brilliant reaffirmation of the chivalrous first theme. In preparation of the coda, the second theme is heard in scurrying diminution, building toward the rousing close that unleashes the full power of the orchestra.

On the whole, the *Waverley* Overture is a more conventional piece, but it impressed the critics at the first hearing. Both overtures contradict the notion that Berlioz was technically inexperienced or insufficiently schooled. True, there are some weaknesses in harmonic progressions and in awkward transitions, but obviously Berlioz knew exactly the effects he wanted to achieve, and he quickly learned how to achieve them.

The perceptive Schumann reviewed Berlioz' youthful composition in reverse order: first the *Symphonie fantastique* in 1835, then the *Francs-Juges* overture in 1837, finally the *Waverley* overture in 1839. By then he was fairly familiar with Berlioz' style, yet the review of *Waverley* reveals a slightly puzzled state of mind:

> ... Under careful scrutiny certain thoughts, taken by themselves, often appear commonplace, even trivial. But the whole exercises an irresistible charm on me despite much that is repellent and unusual to a German ear. In every one of his works, Berlioz shows himself different: in each one he ventures on new ground; it is hard to know whether we should term him a genius or a musical adventurer. He dazzles like a flash of lightning, but he leaves behind him the smell of brimstone; he sets great sentences and truths before us, and directly after, he begins stammering like an apprentice ... Nevertheless, let everyone now hasten to make his acquaintance; for in spite of all its youthful shortcomings it is, in grandeur and originality of invention, the most remarkable creation in the domain of instrumental music that France has lately produced.[109]

* * *

The *Symphonie fantastique,* completed and first performed in 1830, is a work of overwhelming originality. It
was written by a young man — about twenty six — younger
than either Haydn or Beethoven when they approached the
symphony. Moreover, he was not fettered by older models.
He had few roots in the past: "he believed in neither God
nor Bach," complained Ferdinand Hiller.[110] He disliked
Handel, he was cool toward Haydn and Mozart. But in
1828 he discovered "the giant form of Beethoven . . . [who]
opened before me a new world music."[111] This encounter
with Beethoven's music in 1828-1830, during the genesis
of the *Symphonie fantastique,* provided the decisive stimulation for Berlioz' striking growth as a composer. While
he was inspired by Beethoven, he did not consciously imitate
him. Cairns observes:

> The influence was not directly stylistic . . . Rather, it was the example that
> was decisive — the revelation of the immense new possibilities open to the
> symphony, through thematic generation, contrast, rhythm, and expressive
> use of the orchestra: these things and the triumphant demonstration of an
> art in which each work is a unique dramatic statement.[112]

It may well be that Beethoven's Fifth Symphony and its
cyclic structure provided the stimulus for the *idée fixe.* It is
conceivable that the mildly programmatic nature of the
Pastorale and its expanded five-movement form encouraged
Berlioz to proceed in a similar manner in his *Symphonie
fantastique.* Beethoven's "Scene by the brook" and Berlioz'
"Scene in the country" share an affinity in their communion
with nature. Nevertheless, the *Symphonie fantastique* is a
work of musical independence and artistic self-reliance. And
it came at a time when, aside from Onslow, no French composer gave any serious thought* to the symphonic genre.
The idea of an "immense instrumental work"[113] came to
Berlioz in June 1829. But the *Symphonie fantastique* did not
grow organically: it is a composite work, and various sections
were written at different times and for unrelated purposes.

*/Farrenc a little later
(L)

After surveying the disparate musical material, he conceived the device of a literary comment to unify the various elements. On 6 February 1830 he wrote, "I was just going to begin my great symphony (*Episode in the Life of an Artist*) to depict the course of this infernal love of mine. I have it all in my head, but I can write nothing. . ."[114] By that time, the movements had become stages in the life of "an artist" with whom he identified himself. While some of the music may have been written first, there came a point where music and story began to interact and to influence each other. On 16 April 1830, barely ten weeks later, he announced, "I have just written the last note."[115] Not only the music was completed but also the literary comment that was to explain the meaning of the symphony.

Clearly, the *Symphonie fantastique* is not a piece of ordinary program music. The music is not meant to illustrate the words, but the words serve to clarify and unify the structure of the symphony. In an explanatory note distributed at the first performance, Berlioz stated clearly that he intended to express "passions and feelings," not images or abstract ideas.[116] But his caveat failed, the public "discussed what they read and not what they heard."[117] He was never able to shake off the image of a "program" composer.

The *Symphonie fantastique* is too well known to require formal analysis. Each of the five movements has its own form, shaped equally by musical logic and extramusical connotations. Certainly, Berlioz was aware of "sonata form" (he had used it in his early overtures, though somewhat freely). In fact, the first movement of the *Fantastique* suggests a modified sonata form. But there is no need to apply a traditional mold to Berlioz' music which was alien to his freely roaming imagination. Ernest Newman presents the case convincingly:

> Berlioz did not put together his music in the conventional German way, not because he had not the craftmanship for it, but because it simply did not appeal to him. He saw no sense in plodding away at a "form" that had no

real relation to what he had to say . . . He could construct logically enough
in his own new way . . . avoiding the bogus sort of manipulation that passes
for "working-out" in the schools . . .[118]

Berlioz' musical logic and formal coherence is often un-
derestimated. A recent analysis by Edward T. Cone reveals
a wealth of thematic cross relations beyond the *idée fixe*.[119]

A few words about his orchestration are in order. The
Symphonie fantastique requires a large orchestra which is
handled with restraint. The heavy brass instruments (three
trombones and two ophicleides) are held in reserve until
the last two movements. The opening movement uses a
classical orchestra except for the added two cornets. The
second movement has two harp parts, each of which should
be played by "at least" two harps — an indication usually
disregarded. The third movement requires four kettledrums
and two players, creating those magical timpani chords. The
full orchestral resources are unchained in the two final movements. The orchestral bells in the finale could be replaced by
two grand pianos, as the composer stipulated. Once again, as
in the overtures, Berlioz specified the minimum of string
players — no fewer than 15-15-10-11-9. For his early performances of the *Symphonie fantastique* in Paris, Berlioz
assembled as many as 125 players. When he conducted the
work abroad, he had to make concessions as to the size and
quality of the orchestra. Even in such a musically advanced
city as Leipzig, Berlioz encountered difficulties in 1843 when
he conducted his own works: no two harps were available
and Mendelssohn had to play the parts on the piano; the
English horn was so badly out of tune that a clarinet was
substituted; no ophicleides were available and had to be
replaced by additional trombones. In smaller cities the situation was undoubtedly worse.

Berlioz has received much unwarranted blame for orchestral "orgies." The heavy use of brass instruments was
not his invention: it was a Parisian fashion that preceded him.
Spontini and Cherubini indulged in it as did other operatic

composers. When Mendelssohn read Cherubini's score of his last opera *Ali-Baba,* he criticized the brass-heavy orchestration as a concession to the "rotten new Parisian taste ... throwing three or four trombones around as if the people had not ear drums, but real drum skins ... until it hurts."[120] Nowhere can the orchestration of the *Symphonie fantastique* be called noisy: it is a model of well calculated dynamic variety, much admired by later masters of orchestration such as Rimsky-Korsakov and Richard Strauss. An apt summary is offered by Cone:

> Not only was [Berlioz] assigning quasi-dramatic roles to one instrument or section after another, but he was assembling, from the orchestral ensemble as a whole, one huge virtuoso instrument ... Berlioz' sound has been in the ears of composers ever since, even when they have reacted most strongly against it.[121]

The *Symphony fantastique* was indeed the first "concerto for orchestra" where individual and collective virtuosity was required from the performers.

Considering the unaccustomed difficulties of the score, Berlioz had reason to be pleased with the first performance on Sunday afternoon, 3 December 1830. The orchestra was led by Habeneck, at the time the foremost conductor in Paris.* Berlioz wrote to a friend, "I had a wild success. The *Symphonie fantastique* was received with shouts and acclamations; they had to repeat the *March to the Scaffold...*"[122] More sober is his recollection in the *Memoirs;* he admits that "the performance was by no means perfect, as two rehearsals are wholly insufficient for such complicated works."[123] Nor was he pleased with the impression created by the third movement, the "Scene in the country," and he later rewrote it. Still, it was a "sensation;" indeed, it opened a new era in the history of music.

***

*It is regrettable that Habeneck, a fine musician, is rather unfairly portrayed in Berlioz' *Memoirs* due to their estrangement during the 1830's.

Onslow as Symphonist

George Onslow (1784-1853) is best know as a chamber music composer. By 1830 he had published forty opus numbers of ensemble music — works in the classical mold though not without individual touches — and he was highly regarded in his native France and in Germany. Stimulated by the upsurge of interest in orchestral music generated by the newly-founded *Société des Concerts du Conservatoire*, Onslow turned his attention to the symphonic genre. Although Habeneck, the founder-director of these concerts, was primarily interested in the music of Beethoven, a few select living composers were admitted to the programs, and the first Frenchman thus honored was Onslow. He completed his First Symphony in July 1830 and dedicated it to the *Société des Concerts* and to Habeneck: the first performance was given on April 10, 1831 and received favorable reviews. [124] Onslow turned immediately to the composition of a Second Symphony which he dedicated to the Philharmonic Society of London, in gratitude for the honorary membership bestowed on him; the premiere was given in Paris and London in 1832. The critical reception was more favorable in Paris than in London. Published in Leipzig, Onslow's two symphonies found their way almost immediately into the German repertoire, and before long the Germans adopted Onslow as their own. Mendelssohn as conductor and Schumann as critic took a liking to Onslow's music. Of course the critics realized that his style was classicistic and essentially retrospective, but they approved of his well-mannered traditionalism and his expert instrumental writing. His acceptance of Haydn and Mozart as models was considered an asset; of course he was also aware of the works of Beethoven whose

*Onslow's first two symphonies are republished, with an introduction by Boris Schwarz, by Garland Publishing, Inc., New York, 1981.

earlier style left his mark on Onslow. In terms of orchestration, Onslow surpassed his models, for he consistently used
three trombones in addition to four horns and two trumpets — a rather heavy instrumentation that was fashionable
in Paris (much to Mendelssohn's complaint!). In terms of
form, Onslow followed the customary pattern of four movements without any programmatic connotations. Onslow's
Third Symphony, which followed in 1834, was his own
orchestration of his String Quintet Op. 32 in F minor "with
considerable changes," as he remarked. Toward the end of his
career, in 1847, he wrote his last symphony, the Fourth. By
that time, his style was considered rather old-fashioned.

What is remarkable about Onslow's symphonic works of
the early 1830s is the fact that they achieved acceptance at a
time when Berlioz struggled for recognition. Habeneck, who
"sponsored" the Onslow symphonies, was unwilling to do
the same for Berlioz. Compared to a single performance of a
Berlioz overture (*Rob Roy*) in 1833, Onslow's symphonies were
premiered and repeated at the *Conservatoire*. It was precisely
during the 1830's that Onslow was the most often performed
living French symphonist in Paris. Onslow's career was
crowned in 1842 by this election to the *Académie* as successor to
Cherubini.

***

The Symphonie Concertante

The *Symphonie concertante* is a genre that flourished —
primarily in Paris — between 1770 and 1830. As the name
implies, it absorbed elements of the symphony and the
concerto — one could call it a symphony with several prominent solo parts — though it is closer to the concerto
principle. The *Symphonie concertante* is not a hybrid form

but developed its own character — extroverted, optimistic, displaying unabashed virtuosity and competitiveness among its soloists. Many of these works have only two rapid movements, omitting the customary slow movement. The solo instruments most commonly used were two violins, but the number and variety of soloists expanded, particularly as wind instruments joined the ranks of solo performers.

The *Symphonie concertante* reached the peak of its popularity during the 1780's. At the *Concert spirituel* there was hardly a program without a "concertante." Mozart, while visiting Paris in 1778, was eager to write such a piece for four wind players and orchestra (now known as *Sinfonia concertante* K. 297b) but through some intrigue it was not performed at the time. On April 8, 1787, a "nouvelle symphonie concertante" by Haydn was on the program, for violin, cello, oboe, flutes and horn obbligato.* That same season, Viotti presented two of his *Symphonies concertantes* at the *Concert spirituel;* the two solo violin parts were played by Guerillot and Imbault.

At the competing *Concerts des amateurs* (later renamed *de la Loge Olympique*) the Chevalier de Saint-Georges, a brilliant violinist, was in charge and produced a dozen of his charming *symphonies concertantes,* mostly for two solo violins and orchestra, between 1775 and 1784.

After the Revolution, the production of *symphonies concertantes* declined sharply though the public continued to enjoy them. Barry Brook, the chief historian of the *symphonie concertante,* has compiled a statistical survey listing no fewer than 46 Parisian composers with over 200 *symphonies concertantes,* mostly before the Revolution.[125]

---

*This work is not identical with Haydn's *Concertante* for violin, cello, oboe, and bassoon as solo instruments (Hob. I: 105), composed and first performed at the Salomon concert in London on March 9, 1972.

As compositions they had an ephemeral life but for a time they outnumbered the symphonies produced in France. Brook offers the following interesting explanation:

> After the Revolution, the production of symphonies came to a virtual standstill as princely patrons headed for England or the guillotine. The *symphonie concertante* persisted, however, for the obvious reason that it was essentially a bourgeois rather than an aristocratic art form.[126]

We need not concern ourselves here with the *symphonie concertante* outside of France — they were produced in Mannheim, London, Vienna, and Berlin, but in much smaller numbers. Essentially, the *symphonie concertante* is a Parisian phenomenon, as Brook points out convincingly. Of post-revolutionary composers, we may mention Rodolphe Kreutzer who wrote two *symphonies concertantes* for two violins in the 1790's, followed by two more in the early 1800's. They were played, to the delight of the Parisian public, by the composer and his colleague, the eminent Pierre Rode. Kreutzer's "concertantes" remained popular; as late as 1816, Paganini and Lafont chose to perform one of Kreutzer's "concertantes" at their joint concert in Milan (often described as "contest.") Other composers who took interest in the *symphonie concertante* after the turn of the century were Catel, Baillot, Reicha, and the pianist Louis-Emmanuel Jadin who drew the pianoforte into the solo ensemble. Last but not least, Beethoven's so-called Triple Concerto Op. 56, composed in 1803-04, is basically a *symphonie concertante*.

***

CHAPTER 4

The French Violin Concerto (1780-1830)

During the period under discussion, France made a notable contribution in the field of the violin concerto. French violinist-composers treated the genre in such a characteristic way that the so-called French Violin Concerto became a model for two generations of European violinists and composers.

The label "French," however, needs to be qualified. True, the genre saw its fullest bloom on French soil, and French musicians made a decisive contribution, yet its roots reach across the borders into Italy and Germany. From Italy came the concerto's basic form and structure, firmly established by Tartini. Germany's contribution, emanating mainly from Mannheim and Vienna, consisted of a more symphonic treatment, a subtler organization of the first movement, and a richer orchestral palette. In the hands of French violinists, the genre acquired Gallic traits — verve, brilliance, drama, and piquancy. Thus, the "French" Violin Concerto represents a fusion of various heterogeneous elements — a fusion which was attempted by violinists and composers of many lands. In France, the pioneers of the concerto were Jean-Marie Leclair and Pierre Gaviniès, followed in the 1770's by Simon Le Duc and Chevalier de Saint-Georges.

They were all overshadowed by the Italian-born Giovanni Battista Viotti who established himself in Paris in 1782. His role has been compared, by some historians,[1] to that of

Lully; yet it is well to remember that Lully, who came to Paris at the age of fourteen, became French to a degree which Viotti, merely a visitor in Paris for ten years, never achieved. Although Viotti reached his full maturity under French influence, his strong Italian background is always discernible: he remains the last representative of the great tradition of Corelli, Tartini, and Pugnani. For this reason, the purest representative of the French Violin Concerto is actually not Viotti, although he is often called its "father," but his most illustrious disciple, Pierre Rode, whose native French temperament surpassed his master's acquired Gallicism. For it was the spirit rather than any formal aspects which gave the genre its typical character, described by Schering in the following words:

> Conceived primarily as virtuoso piece, the French concerto abandons the rivalry between solo and tutti: the soloist of the *Concert spirituel* was interested exclusively in the display of his technical skill. The first movements are subdivided into the usual four tutti and three solos. New, however, is their outlook. Brilliance and splendor, grandeur and dignity — these are the characteristics expressed so well by the opening march tuttis in their pompousness. These are the sediments of that partly heroic, partly lowly *soldatesque* mentality which led the French minds to daringly disregard religion and morals during the time of the Revolution. The French Violin Concerto is a product of the revolutionary atmosphere, closely related to the youthful operas of a Cherubini and Méhul and represents similarly the best characteristics of the French nation . . .[2]

While this description is adequate, one can take issue with several points. Admittedly, the French concerto was a virtuoso vehicle, but nonetheless its best representatives — Viotti, Rode, Kreutzer, and Baillot — elaborated their orchestral parts with great care. True, the old "rivalry" between solo and tutti was abandoned, only to be replaced by a new, and not necessarily inferior, principle: the projection of a brilliant solo part against the background of a symphony orchestra. This corresponds to the displacement of the old *concerto grosso* by the new *symphonie concertante*. The virtuoso principle, stressed by the French Violin Concerto, remained the model throughout the 19th century, although there are a few exceptions in the violin literature where the "symphonic" element is emphasized. Let us not criticize too harshly the virtuoso tendencies of the French concerto, for despite occasional exhibitionism, the French were generally guided by their innate good taste in the treatment of the genre.

Schering's self-righteous indignation with the "lowly *soldatesque*" mentality of the Revolution is slightly amusing, particularly since he contradicts himself in the next sentence by saying that the revolutionary operas, like the French Violin Concertos, represent the French nation at its best. We have pointed out repeatedly that the defiant and martial mood of the young French Republic is reflected in the music of the period, both in the fields of opera and instrumental works; whether this was done with or without regard for "religion and morals" is wholly unimportant. The fact remains that the French Violin Concerto of the 1790's is as much a reflection of the revolutionary period as are the "terror" and "rescue" operas of Méhul, Lesueur, and Cherubini.

While drama, fire, pathos, and brilliance dominated the first movements of the concertos, we find sweet lyricism in the slow movements; the occasional overembellishment of a simple melodic line merely followed the generally accepted practice of the day. The last movements, usually *rondos,* show the imagination of French composers at its best: sparkle, humor, piquancy, and rhythmic verve alternate with occasional melancholy. The *rondos* were often cast in the rhythms or colors of foreign lands; fashionable were the polonaises, boleros, *rondeaux russes,* tambourins, Hungarian and Spanish tunes.

***

The history of French violin playing in the 18th century is one of fabulously rapid ascent from backward beginnings to unrivaled mastery. At the start of the century, there was no French violinist able to cope with the sonatas by Corelli, for ever since Lully, French violinists were trained for ensemble playing rather than solo performance. By the middle of the century the French had closed the gap which separated them from their Italian confreres, and a master like Leclair (1697-1764) can be mentioned in the same breath as the great Tartini (1692-1770), though the French still had no one to match the virtuosity of Locatelli (1693-1764) until Pierre Gaviniès (1726-1800) appeared. The apex of a century of violinistic progress was reached when Viotti arrived in Paris in 1781, to remain for ten years. His presence stimulated a whole generation of young French violinists, led by the incomparable triumvirate Rode, Kreutzer, and Baillot. Their appointment to the faculty of the *Conservatoire* in the 1790's resulted in a unified teaching method and the establishment of extraordinarily high violinistic standards. From then dates the hegemony of the French violin school which remained unchallenged, despite the meteor-like appearance of Paganini or the notable achievements of Spohr and Joachim. In fact, the Austro-German school could never quite compete with the Franco-Belgian school, for it lacked the singleness of method centered in the Paris *Conservatoire.*

Viotti was born in 1755 and received his musical education in Turin, where he studied with the celebrated Gaetano Pugnani. After serving five years in a subordinate position in the royal orchestra, Viotti joined his teacher Pugnani on a concert tour in 1780-81. They played successfully in Switzerland, Germany, and Poland, and finally reached St. Petersburg. On their return trip, they separated in Berlin: Pugnani returned to Italy while Viotti proceeded to Paris. On March 17, 1782, he made his memorable debut at the *Concert spirituel* and "struck like lightning."[3] The sophisticated public of the French capital, professionals, amateurs, and critics alike, were unanimous in their praise. For eighteen months, Viotti's success in Paris continued unabated; during that period he was heard twenty-seven times, always in his own concertos. Suddenly, after an appearance on September 8, 1783, he decided to withdraw from public concerts. For the next nine years, he performed only in private circles, at the court of Queen Marie Antoinette in Versailles and as leader of the private orchestra of the Prince de Soubise. Much of his time was spent in composing and teaching.

In 1788, Viotti was appointed director of a new opera theater, the *Théâtre de Monsieur*. His administration was successful, but the revolutionary events became so threatening that he left hurriedly for London in July 1792.

Here he resumed his career as soloist and composer. Viotti's debut at one of Salomon's concerts on February 7, 1793, was highly acclaimed and he became the favorite solo performer for the entire series. The following season (1794) he shared the limelight with Haydn. In 1795 he was appointed director of the new Opera Concerts where Haydn's last symphonies were performed, and continued to be active in London during the next few years. His playing was described in the following words:

> Viotti is now probably the greatest violinist in Europe. A strong full tone, indescribable skill, purity, precision, shade and light coupled with the most charming simplicity characterize his playing . . .[4]

At the height of his success, in 1798, Viotti became the victim of a political intrigue and was ordered to leave England. He spent several years in seclusion near Hamburg, occupied mostly with composing. In 1801 he returned to London but he never resumed his musical career. Short visits to Paris, in 1802 and 1814, proved that he was unforgotten; his friends and disciples received him as if a "father rejoined his children".[5]

In 1819, Viotti was appointed director of the Paris *Opéra* but resigned under pressure in 1821. Two years later he returned to London where he died in 1824.

***

The period during which Viotti exerted a direct influence on the French violin school was comparatively short, from 1782 to 1792. During this decade, by his performances, compositions, and teaching, he completely rejuvenated the French approach to the violin, both in playing and composition. Yet this was not accomplished by any concentrated, ambitious drive on his part, for he was gentle and modest; he merely appeared at a moment when circumstances were rife for a re-orientation for which his musical personality served as guide and model.

His initial success in Paris was due primarily to his superb playing which was an inimitable blend of virtuosity, musicianship, and personal charm. The acclaim of the highly sophisticated Parisian public proves that he must have been far superior to local and visiting virtuosos like Saint-Georges and Gaviniès, Jarnowick and Mestrino. As a composer, however — and it goes without saying that Viotti, following the custom of his period, was heard primarily in his own works — his success was neither immediate nor unanimous:

> The music by Viotti baffled somewhat the Parisian public which was little accustomed to a cantilena so noble and pure, to a style so firm, broad, and so free of impishness.[6]

Far from being an explanation, this statement by Pougin is merely a well-sounding platitude, for there is no reason why the Parisian public, so well versed in musical matter, should have been unable to comprehend the concertos by Viotti. We are inclined to believe that his rapidly growing success as composer was due to a quick adjustment, on his part, to French musical taste. Before coming to Paris, he had published one concerto in Berlin (later revised as No. 3), and he may have made his debut with this older work. Once in Paris, he composed and published concertos in rapid succession.

The relationship between Viotti and French music was not only one of "giving," but also of "receiving."

The modern school of violin opened with Viotti, but he could not have completed his work without the laborious preparation of many pioneers. . .[7]

If this statement by La Laurencie tends to overemphasize the contribution of French violinists between 1750 and 1780 (for they are his "pioneers"), we must remember that the French of the 1780's expected to find, in their instrumental music, a mixture of drama and sentimentalism, fire and piquancy — traits that were alien to Viotti's rather placid early style. Once he acclimatized himself to Parisian taste, the public was quick to acclaim his works as well as his performances. The cosmopolitan brilliance of the French capital, the superb performances of the operatic stages, the virtuosity of orchestral playing, the array of international celebrities — all this must have impressed Viotti as it did artists before and after him. It is remarkable how rapidly Viotti shed the last vestiges of provincialism, to grow within a few years into an artist of cosmopolitan stature.

Of course, there are also dissenting voices among historians. Andreas Moser takes issue with the figurative title "father of modern violin playing" often applied to Viotti. Moser contends that Viotti did not enrich the violin technique with a single innovation, and that many older violinists (especially the Mannheim School) are actually far more modern in their handling of technical matters than Viotti.[8] These objections can be refuted easily. For one, greatness in music is not contingent on innovations; if this were true, a man like, say, Mondonville, the inventor of harmonics, should be counted among the great. Some of Viotti's predecessors may have treated the violin in a more difficult way; but the point is not how difficult a passage is but to what use the composer puts it. Viotti discarded virtuosity for its own sake and integrated the technique into the fabric of his compositions. The public, tired of the empty exhibitionism of virtuosos, followed him, for Viotti appeared at a moment when the esthetic conception of the role of music was changing: music, according to the new reasoning, should not merely astonish, but primarily move the soul. This explains the acceptance of Viotti's art as revelation of a new kind, despite the absence of any violinistic pyrotechnics.

An important factor in establishing Viotti's lasting influence was his teaching. Strangely enough, Viotti did not give any lessons in the conventional sense of the word; his teaching was done along the lines of stimulation and inspiration, rather than actual lessons, of the student. He had disciples, not pupils; surrounded by a group of eager young violinists, he gave his generous advice whenever he discovered real talent, and these lessons were given without fee. "On sait que Viotti ne donnait jamais de soins intéressés," says Miel.[9] Although the number of those privileged to receive his personal advice was very limited, the achievements of those chosen few carried the fame of Viotti's school rapidly through Europe. In Paris, his method was perpetuated by the *Conservatoire*. Although founded three years after Viotti left Paris, the violin classes were in the hands of his foremost disciplines — Rode, Kreutzer, and Baillot — resulting in a remarkable unification of method among the young generation of French violinists. How entrenched his influence was is illustrated by the fact that until the year 1853 (with one interruption in 1845) concertos by Viotti were selected exclusively for the public contests at the *Conservatoire*.

***

In evaluating Viotti as a composer, it must be remembered that most of his works were written before 1800, though he lived until 1824. Yet, coming late in the century, he absorbed the influences of *Sturm und Drang* and, partly, of the revolutionary decade, which brings him close to the Romantic period; in fact, he is one of the most important pre-Romantic composers.

Viotti's catalogue of works, compiled by Remo Giazotto,[10] contains 157 numbers, including much chamber music, several *symphonies concertantes,* and a few vocal selections. Most important, however, are his twenty-nine violin concertos which served as models for an entire generation of violinist-composers. Even Beethoven let himself be influenced by Viotti when he wrote his own Violin Concerto. Ten of Viotti's violin concertos were arranged for piano by prominent pianists; others were transcribed for flute.

Viotti's concertos fall into two large categories, the "Paris" concertos (Nos. 1 to 19) and the "London" concertos (Nos. 20 to 29). The dividing line is the year 1792; in fact, the Concerto No. 20 was begun in Paris and completed in London. Further sub-divisions are needed for a fuller understanding of Viotti's evolution as a concerto composer.

The first six concertos were all published in Paris in 1782; they represent his "early" period. Some may have been composed earlier; we know that at least one (later numbered 3) was published in Berlin in 1781 though it was revised for the Paris publication. Baillot suggests that it was written when Viotti was only fourteen. The rapid publication in 1782 suggests that Viotti had several concertos ready when he arrived in Paris. These "early" concertos are well-made but rather conventional in style and technique.

The next six concertos (Nos. 7 to 12) belong to the years 1783 to 1787. Some of them may have been played by Viotti at the court of Versailles after he withdrew from the *Concert spirituel.* This group of concertos shows a certain growth but no decisive step forward as yet. The writing is extremely polished, both for the orchestra and the solo instrument; the style is predominantly *galant.* A characteristic example is Concerto No. 7 in B flat major, recently republished in a modern score edition.[11]

With the concertos Nos. 13 to 19, which belong to the years 1788 to 1791, Viotti entered a new phase as concerto composer. He enlarges the symphonic scope, especially in the opening *tutti* section; he enriches the solo parts and expands the slow movements; and above all he intensifies the expressive range by the use of minor modes. Of the seven concertos belonging to this period, no fewer than five are in a minor key. His thematic invention acquires drama and tension, grandeur and sweep, nostalgia and sadness — a whole new palette related to the French opera of the day. His close friendship with Cherubini may have influenced his development as a composer. This group of concertos shows the full extent of French influence on Viotti; at the same time he absorbed the impact of Haydn whose "Paris" symphonies had recently arrived in the French capital. Without surrendering his Italian heritage, Viotti created the prototypes of the "French" violin concerto. We must single out the Concertos No. 14 in A minor, No. 16 in E minor (which attracted Mozart's attention), No. 17 in D minor, No. 18 in E minor, and No. 19 in G minor. These late Parisian concertos are the legacy that Viotti's French disciples continued to use as models and inspiration. While the choice of minor keys is not, *per se,* a sign of "Romanticism," it does signify a premonition, a changed mood, especially when it appears as consistently as in the case of Viotti (ex. IV-1).

The change was not limited to the character of the thematic material, for its handling, too, underwent modifications. In the first movement of the Concerto No. 14, we

Example IV-1. Viotti, *Violin Concerto No. 14* (ca. 1783).

find a regular development section in place of the hitherto customary introduction of new material. While a development section is not necessarily a criterion of quality or progress, its use in a concerto was comparatively rare and novel. Viotti was one of the first to apply the motivic development technique to the genre of the violin concerto, a procedure which was generally adopted by succeeding generations; yet, he is not consistent, for many of his later concertos dispense with a development.

The first movement of the 14th Concerto is a model of concentration. Built in four *tutti* and three *soli*, it opens with an extended *tutti*, in ternary form, containing the two main themes which return, partly varied, in the first solo. The focal point of the movement is the development, centered in the second solo. The recapitulation, strongly abbreviated to the exclusion of the second theme, begins with the third solo when the soloist restates the first theme, however not in his own modified version, but as originally stated by the orchestra. There is no provision for the usual cadenza at the end of the movement, which emphasizes its conciseness.

The second movement, a nostalgic *Siciliano* in E minor in pure Italian tradition, contrasts the cantilena of the solo violin, played on the silvery E string, with the dark-hued accompaniment of the orchestra. Even the final *Rondo,* in A minor, has wistful and melancholic overtones.

From the viewpoint of violin technique, this Concerto No. 14 is easier than some of its predecessors, for it has less variety in bowings, fewer double stops, and generally less brilliance. The passages are subordinate to the mood of the work — the virtuoso bows to the musician. Viotti — never a friend of break-neck virtuosity — obviously strives toward a spiritualized technique which becomes ennobled, better integrated, more supple and sonorous, while at the same time being simpler and less intricate.

A particularly ingratiating work is the Concerto No. 16 in E minor. In the mid-1780's, it found its way to Vienna where it came to the attention of Mozart. He found it so attractive that he planned to have it performed at one of his academies. Mozart proceeded to enrich the original orchestration (which had two oboes and two French horns) by adding trumpets and timpani. These Mozartian parts are preserved and listed in the Köchel catalogue as No. 470a. Who was the violinist for whom Mozart undertook the work? Perhaps it was Johann Friedrich Eck, a friend of Mozart and an admirer of Viotti, who visited Vienna in 1786. At any rate, we do not know whether the performance in Vienna took place. But the fact that Mozart bothered to work on the concerto by Viotti is a sign of his esteem for the composer. In 1971, Viotti's Concerto No. 16, with Mozart's retouched orchestration, was recorded by Andreas Röhn and the English Chamber Orchestra under Charles Mackerras;[12] it sounds splendid, for Mozart's added parts are most appropriate to the character of Viotti's work.

Equally satisfying are the next three concertos, Nos. 17, 18, and 19. Viotti's favorite pupil, Pierre Rode, introduced them to the Parisian public in 1791 and they aroused boundless enthusiasm. "Then only did one perceive the violin in all its beauty and eloquence," said Baillot.

Never was more exaltation, more grandeur, more fire combined with more
gracefulness. These concertos, of so noble and so pathetic a character, exalt
the soul . . .[13]

In fact, these concertos, particularly Nos. 18 and 19, have
many hallmarks of pre-Romanticism: agitation and sweep,
nostalgia and sentimentalism, drama and power. Viotti, essentially a lyricist by nature, shows occasional weakness in
the dramatic aspect; actually he never equalled the monu-
mentality of his 14th Concerto. But there is warmth and
intimacy in his music, even an occasional streak of larmoyance
in his use of the augmented second. Characteristic and revealing, too, is Viotti's more frequent use of the diminished
seventh chord; "as late as 1840, the diminished seventh chord
had something specifically New-Romantic...," says Schering;[14] how much more was this the case in 1790. In fact,
some sections of Viotti's 18th and 19th Concertos could have
been written by a youthful Beethoven.

In the first movement of the 17th Concerto, Viotti uses a
second theme which is but a variant of the first, and there is
hardly any contrast between the themes. While such a procedure tends to unify a movement, it also entails the danger
of monotony unless used with the skill of a Haydn — a
danger which Viotti did not quite escape. All the more contrasts are contained in the first movement of the following
Concerto (No. 18) where a first theme (in E minor) of partly
heroic, partly lyric character is juxtaposed with a sunny
second theme in the major mode.

Original and imaginative is the second movement of this
18th Concerto — a kind of nature or mountain theme,
reminiscent in mood of the *Ranch des vaches,*[15] like a Swiss
shepherd's call, echoing from one mountain peak to the other.
The mood is comparable to the third movement ("Scene in
the country") of Berlioz' *Symphonie fantastique,* written
some forty years later.

Noteworthy, too, are the finales of the 17th, 18th, and 19th Concertos. To write an effective finale in the minor mode is not easy; some composers simply avoid the problem by writing the first movement in minor and the last movement in major, as, for instance, Mendelssohn (Violin Concerto) or Schumann (Piano Concerto). Viotti chose minor keys for all three above-mentioned finales; he invented graceful and piquant *rondo* themes of wistful charm and pulsating agitation, at times foreshadowing the finale of Beethoven's *Pathétique,* Opus 13.

***

Viotti's "London" concertos fall into two unequal groups. The Concerto No. 20 was, as we have seen, begun in Paris and completed in London. The Concertos No. 21 to 27 were composed in the years 1792 to 1797 for Viotti's personal use while he was active as successful soloist in London. However, the last two concertos, No. 28 and No. 29, were written in the early 1800's, after his return from exile. Perhaps he intended to use them for his reappearance in London, but such a plan (if it ever existed) was not realized. A concert allegedly given by Viotti on November 23, 1803, at the King's Theatre in London (listed in Giazotto's biography)[16] cannot be traced in the newspapers of that period. When the Philharmonic Society of London was founded in 1813, Viotti's name appears among the sponsors but he was not invited to perform as soloist; his name appears far too rarely, only as a chamber music player and leader of the orchestra. But we know through Baillot's account that Viotti performed his last concerto, No. 29 in E minor, for his Parisian friends in 1818; for that occasion he seems to have written a new slow movement.[17] The two last concertos were not published until 1823 and 1824, shortly before the composer's death.

Let us turn to the earlier group of the "London" concertos. They show Viotti as a consummate master of the genre. He addressed himself to a different public, less excitable and volatile, more classically oriented through their continuing admiration for Handel and their recent enthusiasm for Haydn.

Viotti's stay in London coincided with Haydn's second visit in 1794-95. Both Haydn and Viotti appeared at the Salomon concerts, and it speaks for Viotti's stature as performer and composer that he was not dwarfed by the great master. The professional relationship between Haydn and Viotti was quite cordial. When Salomon decided, early in 1795, to discontinue his concerts, Viotti saved the situation by organizing the Opera Concerts for the spring season 1795. He assembled the best orchestra ever heard in London and gave Haydn the opportunity to introduce his last symphonies. Viotti appeared as soloist at many of these concerts (as did other fine artists) but he was not actively involved in leading the orchestra.

Viotti's "London" concertos are, perhaps, less exciting than the best of his Parisian works, but they are more refined, more finished in workmanship (particularly with regard to his treatment of the enlarged orchestra), and more classically oriented. There can be no doubt that the close contact with Haydn and his acquaintance with Haydn's "London" symphonies had considerable influence on Viotti as composer. He felt challenged, and he rose to the challenge.

The last nine "London" concertos by Viotti have one trend in common: a freer handling of the concerto form, specifically a closer connection and integration of the three movements. Modest as Viotti's experiments in this direction were, he nevertheless deserves the credit of having been one of the first to loosen the rigid construction of the concerto. The 19th century accelerated such "reform" attempts which aimed at closer connection between movements (e.g. Beethoven's and Mendelssohn's violin concertos), contraction of three into one movement (as in Spohr's *Gesangscene* and de

Bériot's First Concerto), or expansion into four movements (Vieuxtemps' No. 4).

Five of Viotti's last nine concertos -- Nos. 20, 21, 25, 26, and 29 — have certain, though modest, deviations from the conventional concerto form.

In the pastoral-like Concerto No. 20, Viotti terminates the second movement on a dominant chord, followed without interruption by the *finale;* the soloist begins with an *Allegretto,* to be played *ad libitum sin al tutti,* when the orchestra starts the actual final movement in *Allegro vivo;* yet, the *Allegretto* theme returns several times within the *rondo finale.*

The same drawing-together of movements is achieved in the 29th Concerto where Viotti precedes the *finale* (*Allegretto*) with an orchestral slow *Introduzione* of 19 bars, modulating from C major — the key of the second movement — to E minor, the key of the *finale,* not unlike Mendelssohn's transition in his Violin Concerto some fifty years later.

The same is achieved in a much simpler way in Viotti's 26th Concerto in B-flat major: the *Andante,* in G minor, modulates toward the end to B-flat major and closes on the dominant chord, whereupon the *finale* enters in the main key of B-flat.

The 21st Concerto brings a motivic connection between the first and the last movements: the composer quotes in the *finale* a charming *minore* passage from the first movement.

Very interesting is the form of the first movement of the Concerto No. 25 in A minor. The first *tutti* opens with a 13-bar *Andante* in *Siciliano* rhythm (6/8), followed by a ternary *Allegro vivace assai* in A minor. After a return to the Tempo I (6/8), the soloist enters with a heart-warming *cantilena.* This is followed by a renewed tempo shift, back to *Allegro vivace assai,* this time however in A major and introducing entirely new thematic material — almost like a new movement. Yet, the composer obviously considered A minor the main key of the concerto, for he chose it for the *finale.* The middle movement, *Andante sostenuto,* is in D major.

However, as far as the inner structure of the first movement form is concerned, Viotti did not go beyond his Paris period; so we find developments only in Nos. 22 and 24.

Modest as they are, these formal innovations are not the only premonitions of the approaching new era in Viotti's London concertos. Already in his Paris concertos we observed a broadening of the expressive gamut by dramatic, heroic, or tragic accents, by lyric, nostalgic, or melancholic tints. In his last period, the expressiveness of his palette gained further in wealth of colorings and moods. Although there are conventional "relapses" — as in the thematic material of his 21st or 23rd Concertos — Viotti comes increasingly closer to the Romantic ideal through his expansively expressive (though never sentimental) melodies and his tender, almost effeminate, harmonies. Most pronounced are these tendencies in his last two Concertos, Nos. 28 and 29, which have a certain resigned lyricism in common. Romantic, too, is the pseudo-dramatic first *tutti* of the 28th Concerto, with its agitated diminished seventh chords; in fact, the first theme of the 29th Concerto is, in rhythm, melodic line, and harmonization, a surprising premonition of Mendelssohn and Schumann. Other romanticizing traits are the occasional use of imaginative *fermatas* on certain pivotal notes of the melody, and short interpolated cadenzas for the soloist — sometimes even with accompaniment — as in the *finale* of No. 29 or the *Cadenza con sentimento* in the 28th Concerto (ex. IV-2, IV-3, IV-4).

Example IV-2. Viotti, *Violin Concerto No. 28* (ca. 1805). Opening of First movement.

Example IV-3. Viotti, *Violin Concerto No. 28.* First movement.

Example IV-4. Viotti, *Violin Concerto No. 29* (ca. 1805).
Mendelssohn, *Violin Concerto* (1844).
Schumann, *Piano Concerto* (1841-45).

At the same time, however, we find, even in Viotti's last period, entire movements written wholly in the 18th century tradition; in fact, the 23rd Concerto (nicknamed "John Bull") is conceived in an intentionally retrospective, almost Handelian, style which does not make it any less dusty and dull. Sometimes, stylistic contrasts are juxtaposed in the same movement; one need only compare the monumental first theme with the gracefully Mozartian second theme in the opening movement of the 24th Concerto.

Viotti's compositorial workmanship shows particular care in the works of his last period, though it never reached particular distinction: voice leading, counterpoint, and harmony (with a predilection for chromaticisms) are handled with a sure hand. Whether or not his close friend Cherubini assisted him in matters of orchestration, as was often rumored, is impossible to ascertain; even if it were true, it could have applied only to his Paris concertos, not to those written in London.

Violinistically speaking, Viotti's London concertos are less difficult and partly less brilliant than those of his Paris days. The passage work often receives musical justification by serving as counterpoint or embellishment for thematic material played by the orchestra, as in his famous 22nd Concerto. Even in his early works, Viotti never required excessive technique if compared to Tartini and Gaviniès, the great technicians of their period. Yet, this simplification can be considered a progress; for while other violinists pushed their technical exploits beyond the limits of satisfying sounds, Viotti kept always the resulting sonorities in mind which, at all times, were to remain pleasant and agreeable. Thus, he invented passages which were richly sonorous and effective while being only moderately difficult. His "secret" was to utilize more fully the idiomatic potential of the violin; he avoided double stops in very high positions, but did not hesitate to play a *cantilena* high on the G string for the sake of sonority; as a rule, he wrote double stops in the lower positions using open strings for added resonance; passages in high positions were invented in such a way as to avoid dangerous shifts — they could be played by remaining in one position; interesting and characteristic bowing added variety to ordinary runs. (However, the so-called "Viotti stroke" may not have been invented by Viotti.) Not a maximum of difficulty, but a maximum of sonority was obviously Viotti's criterion in designing his technical passages. That he never stooped to virtuosic trickeries, like his contemporaries Lolli or Duranowski, was already mentioned; he remained at all times the noble artist.

Among Viotti's London concertos, the No. 22 in A minor must be singled out as his masterpiece; it was held in the highest esteem by Brahms and Joachim. We hear that

Brahms "did not rave as passionately even about the Beethoven Concerto" as he did about Viotti's No. 22. Then Joachim continues:

> During my bachelor years in Hannover, when we played together up in my room, I had to play it for him two and even three times in a row. With red face, raised shoulders, and groans of comfort he delved into the keyboard while accompanying and was happy that "such a thing existed in this world." That is why I always called this piece *his* concerto by Viotti.[18]

While working on his own violin concerto, in May 1878, Brahms had obviously the Viotti Concerto on his mind, for he wrote to Clara Schumann:

> The A minor Concerto by Viotti is my particular enthusiasm ... It is a glorious piece of a remarkable freedom of invention, sounding as if improvised, and yet everything so well planned ... That people in general do not understand nor respect the very best things, such as Mozart's concertos and that concerto by Viotti — that's how men like us live and become famous. If people only suspected that they receive from us *in drops* what they could drink there to their heart's delight![19]

We know through Joachim that Brahms' particular admiration of the 22nd Concerto by Viotti was based "next to the charming invention, primarily on the perfectly balanced relationship between minor and major in the construction of the first movement." Joachim then continues to summarize his own opinion:

> The fact that this concerto does not require too much finger velocity in the highest positions has led to its wide use as study material for pupils; nevertheless, a spiritual (*durchgeistigt*) performance of its passages requires a considerable amount of technical proficiency in left and right hand. One has become used to banish this work into the study room and has forgotten its high poetic value. With its abundance of beautiful melodies and its uncommonly original form, it belongs, in my opinion, in the very first rank of violin concertos . . .[20]

As usual, Andreas Moser, loyal disciple of Joachim, echoes his master and even surpasses him by attempting to rank various violin concertos as to musical quality. In this — rather useless and naive — procedure, Viotti's 22nd Concerto is assigned third place, immediately following the concertos by Beethoven and Mendelssohn, and in preference to the concertos by Brahms and Mozart.[21] How rapidly such esteem can change is proven by the fact that, only twenty-five years later, the eminent Leopold Auer does not even mention Viotti's name in his book *Violin Master Works and Their Interpretation.*[22] On the other hand, Carl Flesch, no less an authority, chooses the first movement of Viotti's 19th Concerto for discussion in his *Kunst des Violinspiels* and deplores the complete neglect of Viotti's works in the modern concert repertoire.[23]

During the first half of the 19th century, any composer attempting to write a violin concerto had to be acquainted with Viotti's works. This holds true even of Beethoven whose Violin Concerto (1806) shows specific resemblances with certain of Viotti's concertos; one need only compare the slow movement of Viotti's 22nd Concerto with that of Beethoven or Viotti's *Rondo* of the 20th Concerto with Beethoven's final movement.

With all due admiration for Beethoven's Violin Concerto — undoubtedly the greatest work of its type written — one must admit that its technical passages lack specific violinistic invention; the fact that Beethoven later transcribed the entire work for piano solo and orchestra emphasizes this point. Although he played the violin, he was not a violinist in the professional sense of the word, and thus his technical treatment of the violin was influenced at times by Viotti, Rode, and Kreutzer. Theirs was the dominant violin style of the 1800's, and Beethoven — not an expert in this field — preferred to adapt himself rather than experiment on unsafe grounds.[24]

While any reminiscences in Beethoven's Concerto are probably subconscious, we can find a resemblance between a transition in Brahms' Violin Concerto and Viotti's 22nd Concerto which Joachim considers intentional (ex. IV-5a,

IV-5b). In a footnote to his analysis of the Brahams Concerto, Joachim says:

I cannot suppress the remark that this transition seems to me an intentional echo of the one connecting the first and second movements of Viotti's 22nd Concerto, a work for which Brahms had always a particular predilection.[25]

Example IV-5a. Viotti, *Violin Concerto No. 22* (ca. 1792-97).

Example IV-5b. Brahms, *Violin Concerto* (1878).

***

Pierre Rode

Among Viotti's students, Pierre Rode (1774-1830) was closest to his master's style. Born in Bordeaux, young Rode came to Paris in 1787 and attracted Viotti's attention. Obviously, Viotti thought highly of Rode's talent, for he entrusted him with the first performances of several of his latest concertos. The sixteen-year-old Rode made his debut at the *Concert spirituel* on April 5, 1790, quickly followed by a performance at the *Théâtre de Monsieur* on May 2; both times he played a concerto by Viotti (probably No. 13). During Holy Week of 1791 and 1792, Viotti arranged concerts at the *Théâtre de Monsieur* to replace the defunct *Concert spirituel;* among the soloists were Rode, Kreutzer, and Alday. Rode outshone all: he played the new Concertos by Viotti (Nos. 17 and 18) "avec tout le charme et toute la pureté qui distingue son talent," as his colleague Baillot wrote.[26] It was the beginning of a great career.

By 1800, Rode occupied such coveted positions as professor at the *Conservatoire,* solo violinist of Bonaparte, and (briefly) soloist at the Paris *Opéra.* He won the Parisian public with his masterful Concerto in A minor (No. 7) and was considered the foremost French violinist. Since Rode traveled extensively, his style became known throughout Europe and was eagerly imitated by the younger generation of violinists. Even Spohr, always a rugged individualist, admits having succumbed for a time to the fascination of Rode, whom he heard for the first time in 1803:

> The more I heard Rode, the more I was carried away by his playing, so that I did not hesitate to prefer his style — at that time a perfect reflection of his great master Viotti — to that of my teacher Eck. Thus I endeavored to absorb Rode's style by the most careful study of his compositions. In this I succeeded quite well, and until the time when I gradually acquired my own style, I was probably the most faithful copy of Rode mong the young violinists of the day.[27]

Among others who have pointed out the similarity of styles between Viotti and Rode are J. F. Reichardt[28] and an anonymous critic in the *Allgemeine musikalische Zeitung,* who writes, after having heard Rode in Berlin in 1802-03:

> ....All who have heard his famous teacher Viotti confirm without dissent that he possesses to perfection his teacher's own interesting style, but with more mildness and more refined feeling.[29]

A few years later, the same journal praises Rode's

> ... incomparable tone, always even and beautiful in all imaginable modifications; the noble, dignified taste which discards all that is merely amusing or startling; and the utmost perfection in every aspect of his playing.[30]

From 1804 to 1808, Rode resided in St. Petersburg as solo violinist of the Tsar and enjoyed enormous popularity. He was active as soloist, quartet leader, and teacher. It was primarily due to his influence (later continued by his successor Charles Lafont) that Russian violin playing acquired a distinctly French style.

Rode returned to Paris in 1808 and tried to reestablish his former pre-eminence with a concert on December 22, but it was a disappointment. The critics found that "his playing left much to be desired from the point of view of fire and inner life."[31] Vienna, too, received him coolly when he returned there in 1812-13, and his old admirer Spohr was particularly disappointed, for he found him "cold and mannered."

> I missed the old audacity in the handling of great difficulties and felt particularly dissatisfied with his performance in cantabile . . .[32]

In 1814 Rode settled in Berlin; in 1819 he returned to France without resuming his career. "Rode refuses to touch the violin," wrote Mendelssohn in 1825. An ill-fated attempt, in 1828, to play in Paris embittered his last years; he died in 1830.

***

It was during the period of violinistic decline that Rode came into closer contact with Beethoven. They probably knew each other from Rode's earlier visit to Vienna in 1801-02 when Beethoven — according to unconfirmed reports — wrote one of his violin romances for the visiting Frenchman. In 1812, Beethoven completed a major work for Rode, the Violin Sonata Op. 96, which received its first performance on December 29, 1812, with Archduke Rudolph as pianist. During the preceding week, Beethoven was obviously perturbed; he decided to send the violin part to Rode for practice purposes and yet was afraid that the violinist might take offense. Even the writing had to be adjusted to Rode's style:

> In our finales we like to have fairly noisy passages, but Rode does not care for them — and so I have been rather hampered.[33]

This is indeed strange testimony, for it shows Beethoven advocating a virtuoso *finale* to which Rode obviously objected. The performance was not an unqualified success; "Mr. Rode's strong point is apparently not this type of music, but the interpretation of concertos," writes a contemporary reporter.[34]

Yet, we must not imagine Rode as one-sided virtuoso; he played quartets assiduously, both privately and in public, and his favorite repertoire consisted of string quartets by Haydn and Mozart. No less a connoisseur than Count Lobkowitz said in 1801 that he never experienced greater musical pleasure than while listening to Rode's quartet playing.

As composer, Rode devoted himself almost exclusively to the violin although some of his themes became so popular that they were sung publicly by celebrated singers. Most important among Rode's compositions are thirteen violin concertos and two books of études, including the *24 Caprices,* a vademecum of violin instruction. There are also a number of *thèmes variés,* some with orchestral accompaniment, others written as *quatuor brillant,* i.e. a solo violin part with string trio accompaniment. Three collections of duos for two violins and a Fantasy op. 24 for violin and orchestra round out the list of Rode's compositions.

There is no noticeable development or ascending curve in Rode's creative work. His first Concerto in D minor, published when he was twenty, in 1794, is a remarkably mature work, molded firmly in Viotti's pattern from which he deviated but little in later years. Though his handling of form became more concentrated, his expression more supple, his technique more finished, he remained unchanged in the fundamental as-

pects of his musical personality, and any later progress seems
small compared to his astonishing Opus 1.

Of course, the quality of his thirteen concertos is not
evenly high. After the grandiose No. 1 follow two weaker
concertos, in E major and G minor, though the third has a
certain grandeur. The ingratiating Concerto No. 4, in A major,
shows him to greater advantage: the invention is more original,
the form more concentrated. Similar in its pastoral character
is the Fifth Concerto, in D major; yet it does not come to life,
despite a certain symphonic attitude. With the following
three concertos, however, Rode reaches his peak: the festive
No. 6 in B-flat, the expressive No. 7 in A minor (his most
celebrated work), and the equally beautiful No. 8 in E minor.
Compared to these achievements, the Concerto No. 9 in C
major appears much weaker, and the same can be said about
the No. 10 in B minor which he presented to the Parisian
public in 1808, after an absence of five years. The work did
not please, as can be seen from the following review:

> In the choice of concerto Rode was not particularly wise. He wrote it in
> St. Petersburg; and it seemed as if the cold of Russia was not without
> influence on this work.[35]

Rode's next concerto, No. 11 in D major, belongs to his
best works; in fact, it is the favorite of his biographer Friedrich
Moser. The Concerto No. 12 in E major shows a creative
decline, as does his last Concerto in F-sharp minor/A major.
Rode dedicated his last concerto to his old friend and colleague Baillot who had promised to give the first performance at the opening concert of the new *Société des Concerts
du Conservatoire* on March 9, 1828, under the direction of
Habeneck. Baillot, feeling indisposed, asked his son-in-law,
Eugène Sauzay (a recent prize winner of the *Conservatoire*)
to play the solo part. The work was received with respect, a
succès d'estime without consequences. It was published
posthumously.

The influences which molded Rode's musical development are not difficult to identify: there are his teacher

Viotti, his friend, the cellist-composer Luigi Boccherini, and the theorist Antonin Reicha. The latter settled in Paris in 1808, and many well-established musicians sought his advice in matters of composition. Rode's contact with Reicha, which must have taken place after the virtuoso's return from Russia in 1808, was probably informal; yet it is entirely possible that the increased solidity of craftsmanship, noticeable in Rode's 11th Concerto, was due to Reicha's influence. Rode's inclination toward the Viennese classicists, which became increasingly strong from his 9th Concerto on, was certainly encouraged by Reicha. While Viotti seems to have leaned more toward Haydn, Rode shows a closer affinity to Mozart. Needless to say, both were unaffected by Beethoven who, at that time, was still a controversial figure.

Rode's creative life can be divided into two periods. During his first decade as composer, between 1794 and 1804, he is the typical "revolutionary romanticist," subjected to the same influences and environment as young Méhul, Cherubini, and Lesueur; this period produced his concertos Nos. 1 to 8. After 1804, Rode — like many other musicians — goes through a period of classicistic reorientation during which the Viennese influence settles and clarifies his style; to this second period belong his concertos Nos. 9 to 13.

Viotti's influence on young Rode was understandably strong and can be traced easily. Thus, there is a close affinity of mood between Viotti's dramatic Concerto No. 14 and Rode's Nos. 1 and 3, between Viotti's pastoral-like 20th Concerto and Rode's Nos. 4 and 5. Viotti's famous 22nd Concerto and Rode's masterpiece, the 7th, are closely related in their combination of lyricism and drama, while Rode's 8th Concerto has an elegiac mood similar to Viotti's last concerto, No. 29.

On the whole, however, we find that the thematic invention of Rode is less romanticizing, less lyrically expansive than that of Viotti; there is often a certain classicistic coolness and detachment in Rode's themes, even in his early period, pointing toward Vienna's classical school. On the other hand, Rode has sometimes more pathos, festiveness, and *brio* which, in his Concerto No. 11, is akin to Weber. Occasionally, Rode surprises us by daredevil sweep juxtaposed with a sweet Italian *cantilena* whose nostalgic sighs sound almost as sentimental as de Bériot's cloying sweetness of some twenty-five years later. In general, Rode's melodic line is likely to be more embroidered and artificial than that of Viotti; we may assume that Rode preferred to work out his embellishments in advance while Viotti relied more on improvised elaboration of the melody.

Most personal is Rode in his final movements which sparkle with gracefulness, piquancy, and impishness. The invention is charming, the elaboration artful, and the whole treatment unconventional, in contrast to the occasional formality of the first two movements. To heighten the final effect, the soloist is sometimes permitted to end the concerto together with the orchestra, rather than have the usual short *tutti* as closing. The virtuoso element predominates in these *finales,* but the passages are always interesting and in good taste.

Following the fashion of the day, Rode introduced foreign tunes and rhythms into his *rondos;* thus we find three *polonaises,* of which the one in the First Concerto is the most attractive (probably influenced by a similar movement in Viotti's Concerto No. 14). Less successful is Rode in two *rondos russes.* In his Fifth Concerto, he introduces a Russian folk tune which appears also in Beethoven's "Variations on a Russian dance from the ballet *Das Waldmädchen*" (Wo071); both Rode and Beethoven make changes in the original tune. Thoroughly distorted, however, is the well-known Russian folk tune, "In the Field Stood a Little Birch Tree" (used by Tchaikovsky in the *finale* of his 4th Symphony) which appears in the *finale* of Rode's Concerto No. 12; here, the Frenchman misunderstood completely the character of the Russian theme. The other Russian tunes used in the same movement are rather weak and unidentifiable, aside from a quotation of the *Waldmädchen* theme.

Infinitely more successful is Rode in his freely invented *finales,* such as the characteristic *rondo* theme of No. 2 with accents on the weak parts of the measure; the transparent, good-humored *rondo* of No. 4 with a pastoral theme based on *musette* fifths (truly worthy of a Haydn); the charming final *Allegretto* of No. 6 with an undertone of Viennese *Gemütlichkeit* (slightly reminiscent of Mozart's Piano Quartet in G minor); or the piquancy in the *rondos* of Nos. 7, 8, 11, and 13 — there is always an abundance of imagination, sparkle, and good humor.

While charming in the invention of themes, Rode is not particularly strong in their harmonization or development. His harmonies are generally simple and uncomplicated, and very rarely does he strive toward originality. Contrapuntal workmanship is totally absent, and he is almost equally disinterested in development technique. Only one among the thirteen concertos, the sixth, shows an attempt at development where, in the course of the second solo in the first movement, the orchestra plays fractions of the second theme, accompanied by the soloist with characteristic triplet passages. In the 7th Concerto, the development consists merely of a reappearance of the principal theme, played by the soloist in a slightly altered version in B minor, instead of the original A minor; a similar procedure — which can hardly be called a "development" — is adopted in the 11th Concerto. In all his other concertos, Rode prefers to introduce new material into the second solo of the first movement in place of a thematic development. Obviously, Rode was not particularly intent on unifying the first movement form, for he used different — or only faintly related — thematic material for the first tutti and the first solo. In other words, he disregarded certain attempts of Viotti and others to construct the first movement of the concerto according to the *sonata-allegro* pattern, and preferred to proceed more freely.

In matters of violin technique, Rode did not materially expand the limitations set by Viotti, but his passages are more supple, more sonorous and idiomatic than his master's. There is more variety in the use of different bowings, including a very rapid and brilliant solid *staccato* which Rode uses often and with great effect. Judging by his compositions, Rode must have had a masterful command of his right arm; in fact, his *24 Caprices* established a code of bowing technique which will remain valid as long as the violin is played. Based on Rode's example and tradition, the French school of violin playing has preserved, until today, a particular variety and suppleness of bowing.

In matters of left hand technique, Rode is comparatively conservative. Double stops are used rarely except for occasional passages in thirds, broken octaves, and tenths. Generally, he prefers rapid runs and arpeggios, some of which utilize the highest positions. Rode likes the rich sound of the G string and uses it for long *cantilenas* as well as brilliant passages, foreshadowing Paganini's sensational use of one-string technique; he dares to have the soloist occasionally finish a movement on the G string, in preference to the traditional high register for a brilliant ending. Whenever Rode succeeds in freeing himself from the somewhat stereotyped technique of the Viotti school, his passages assume a glitter pointing toward the later de Bériot, but as a rule, his violinistic demands are limited. An exception is Rode's 11th Concerto which requires a more highly developed technique of left and right hand. Yet, even during his lifetime, Rode saw himself outdistanced by younger men like Lafont, Spohr, and de Bériot, not to mention Paganini.

***

Rodolphe Kreutzer

Rode has been often compared to Rodolphe Kreutzer, his contemporary, who won fame as violinist, conductor, and composer. Rode's style is typically French — sparkling, polished, elegant, brilliant, yet somewhat cool and detached, showing himself at his best in the piquant *finales* while being least convincing in slow movements. Kreutzer, of German origin though born in France, is more rugged and powerful, warmer and more daring, yet not without occasional academic dryness; his strength lies in the first movements, especially in development sections. Undoubtedly, Rode was the more naturally gifted performer, while Kreutzer had a certain pedestrian perfection. Incidentally, both were on friendly terms; during the season of 1799-1800 they were heard in a *Symphonie concertante* for two violins and orchestra, composed by Kreutzer especially for the occasion. A contemporary report describes this memorable event as follows:

> Mr. Kreutzer courageously entered the arena with Rode, and both artists offered the connoisseurs a most interesting contest . . . One could clearly observe that Kreutzer's talent was more the fruit of long study and untiring effort, while Rode's art seems to have been born with him, for he overcomes the greatest difficulties with all ease and effortlessly . . . Kreutzer is probably the only one who could be compared to Rode.[36]

Gerber reports that it was fashionable to take sides and to favor one or the other of the two virtuosos. Although a contemporary of Kreutzer, Gerber never heard him play but reprints the following judgment of a "colleague":

> The manner of Viotti is also that of Kreutzer; he has the same large tone and the same broad bowings in the *Allegro,* and his execution of the most difficult passages is precise and extremely clean. In the *Adagio* Kreutzer shows himself even more to be a master of his instrument . . .[37]

We see that Kreutzer, like Rode, was compared to Viotti; however, since they were very different in their approach and temperament, the question arises *who* of the two actually possessed the true "manner of Viotti."

In comparing Kreutzer to his famous confreres, Fétis found that he lacked the elegance, charm, and purity of Rode or the versatile technique and deep feeling of Baillot; yet, Kreutzer had an "originality of sentiment and style"[38] unsurpassed by anyone — qualities which invariably moved the listener. A modern French historian, Henri Expert, summarizes his opinion in the following words:

> A man of verve, enthusiasm, and vehemence, Kreutzer revealed himself entirely in his magnificent and passionate playing.[39]

German historians tend to emphasize Kreutzer's German descent; Gerber even asserts that he was born in Germany[40] which is incorrect, for Rodolphe Kreutzer was born in Versailles in 1766, the son of a German musician in French military service. His early violinistic training was in the hands of Anton Stamitz (the younger son of the famous Johann Stamitz of Mannheim) which introduced a German factor into Kreutzer's development. Stamitz taught Kreutzer so well that he was able to appear at the *Concert spirituel* in Paris at the age of thirteen: on May 25, 1780, he played a concerto of his teacher, and the enthusiasm of the public was such that he had to repeat a movement. In 1784, he made his debut as a composer, performing his own concerto at the *Concert spirituel.* The following year he was appointed member of the Royal Orchestra in Versailles and enjoyed the patronage of Queen Marie Antoinette.

Thus, Kreutzer's career was well advanced by the time Viotti arrived in Paris which may explain the fact that he never actually studied with the great master. However, there can be no doubt that Kreutzer belonged to the circle around Viotti and that his development as violinist and violin composer profited greatly by this contact.

While Rode preferred the life of a traveling virtuoso, Kreutzer's career was centered on Paris. Recognized as one of the best violinists of his generation, he occupied such prestigious positions as solo violin at the *Opéra* and at Napoleon's court, professor at the *Conservatoire,* conductor and artistic director of the *Opéra.* He undertook only two concert tours abroad: one in 1796 to Italy where he met and encouraged a Genovese prodigy, Nicolò Paganini; the second to

Vienna in 1798 where he made the acquaintance of a young composer, Beethoven. This casual encounter (which impressed Beethoven, if not Kreutzer) led to Beethoven's dedication of his Violin Sonata Op. 47 to Kreutzer in 1804. By that time Kreutzer was back in Paris and showed no interest whatsoever in the dedication. In fact, Kreutzer seems to have had a certain antagonism toward Beethoven's compositions and resisted the performance of Beethoven's symphonies at the *Opéra* concerts during the 1820's, while his colleague Habeneck advocated their acceptance. Kreutzer wielded great power at the *Opéra,* as young Berlioz found out to his sorrow when he received a blunt rejection.

As a composer, Kreutzer was more versatile than either Viotti or Rode: aside from his vast output for the violin, he wrote a multitude of stage works, and his operas and ballets remained in the active repertoire from 1790 to 1825. If we are to believe Fétis, Kreutzer wrote his early and most successful operas (including *Lodoiska* in 1791) without having studied harmony. Only after his appointment to the *Conservatoire,* so Fétis asserts, did Kreutzer "feel the obligation to be learned" which merely impaired his imagination and originality.[41] All this is malicious nonsense, for Kreutzer reached his peak as composer in his last two violin concertos, Nos. 18 and 19, written about 1806-09. It almost seems as if this eminent scholar resented any natural creative talent — something he himself so sorely lacked, despite his many learned books on musical theory and his numerous dry-as-dust compositions.

As for Kreutzer, it is well possible that he began to compose as autodidact, for some of his earliest compositions — six duos for violin and viola (1783) and his Concerto No. 1 (1784) — show a certain lack of experience which is not surprising in a young man of seventeen. Yet, his subsequent studies not only failed to "impair his imagination," but enabled him to write some of the most solidly constructed violin compositions of his time. His instrumental catalogue includes 19 violin concertos, four *symphonies concertantes,* 15 string quartets, sonatas, trios, and a number of variations. He was also co-author (with Rode and Baillot) of the Violin Method of the *Conservatoire.* In our days, his name is immortalized by the famous *Etudes ou Caprices,* a study work of incomparable pedagogical insight.

Kreutzer's versatility as composer is recognized by Gerber who describes him not only as "one of the foremost virtuosos of his instrument, but also one of the most popular composers of vocal and instrumental music."[42] "His works . . . are distinguished by expressivity, warmth, and picturesqueness," says Expert.[43] More than that, they show the same qualities which characterized his playing — fire, impetuosity, sweep, and grandeur, but there are also pages that are dry, stilted, and antiquated.

In Kreutzer's creative life, we can distinguish three periods: the youthful first where he worked under the guidance of his teacher Stamitz; the developing second when his style changed under the influence of Viotti; and the mature third when he showed an increasing classical orientation colored by his individuality. His admiration for the Viennese masters, Haydn and Mozart, is apparent in his instrumental works, while as operatic composer, he belonged to the "revolutionary romanticists" of the 1790's — Cherubini, Méhul, and Lesueur. Obviously, Kreutzer was naively impressionable, for we are told that after hearing a composition by Mozart, he would immediately write a work in the same style. His fondness for Haydn found tangible expression in his 16th Concerto, based on themes by Haydn. Despite occasional deviations into a sort of pre-Romanticism, Kreutzer was — like Rode — fundamentally a classicistic artist and contributed little to the evolution of a new style.

The chronology of Kreutzer's concertos begins with No. 1 in 1784, the work he played that year at the *Concert spirituel.* He was reengaged twice during 1785, and three times in 1786; these dates might account for his concertos

Nos. 2, 3, and 4. He played again at the *Concert spirituel* in 1787 and 1789, corresponding roughly to his concertos Nos. 5 and 6. Two concertos, Nos. 7 and 8, are attributed to the 1790's.

A whole string of Kreutzer's concertos appeared in Leipzig in the early 1800's; by 1805 the total number had reached No. 15. A curious work is the Concerto No. 16 on themes by Haydn. In 1805, the rumor of Haydn's death swept through Europe. A memorial concert was planned by the grieving French musicians, and special compositions were prepared by Cherubini and Kreutzer. Before the concert took place, Haydn declared that he was alive, and Cherubini cancelled the performance of his *Chant sur la mort de Haydn,* but Kreutzer saw no reason of abandoning his "Haydn" Concerto and played it as an homage to the master on February 6, 1805. The work is a kind of medley but put together with skill. By 1806, Kreutzer had completed his 17th Concerto, which he performed for the first time on July 21, 1806, at a concert of the famous singer Mme. Catalani to whom the work is dedicated. His last two concertos, Nos. 18 and 19, were composed within the next few years, probably before 1810, the year Kreutzer broke his arm and retired from active concertizing.

***

Kreutzer's first five concertos offer nothing unusual from the point of view of form: each consists of three separate movements, except for No. 5 where the second and last movements lead into each other without break.

The first movements contain the usual four *tutti* which frame three *soli,* and have ternary structure — exposition, development, and recapitulation. In contrast to most of his confreres, Kreutzer makes serious attempts at developing his thematic material, undoubtedly under the influence of his Mannheim-trained teacher. In fact, even Kreutzer's thematic invention shows a streak of German "burgher" rather than French "salon" atmosphere. Kreutzer's youthful immaturity is noticeable in his overdependence on models and a certain conventionalism of expression; yet there is no apparent awkwardness in compositorial matters which seems to belie Fétis' assertion that he owed everything to his "instinct" and nothing to "schooling." For an "autodidact," his craftsmanship is indeed remarkable; already his harmonies show occasional originality, as for instance in the first movement of the 3rd Concerto, and his motivic workmanship has ingenious details, like in the *rondo* of the 4th Concerto where the rhythmic pattern of the soloist's theme reappears frequently as an accompaniment figure.

Kreutzer's slow movements have varying titles: *Pastorale, Sicilienne,* or *Romance,* the latter a particularly fashionable type. His gamut of expressiveness is still conventionally limited; only the *Romance* of the 5th Concerto shows more warmth and sentiment. In his final *rondos,* Kreutzer still lacks the sparkling verve of his French contemporaries, and his invention tends more toward the German good-humored homespun.

As far as violin technique is concerned, Kreutzer shows considerable imagination in designing technical difficulties which, however, are frequently dry and musically unrewarding. All too often, passages in his concertos sound like quotations from his *études.* Kreutzer lacked, to a certain degree, Viotti's and Rode's supreme gift of integrating the inevitable virtuoso element into a musical whole; "music" and "technique" stand side by side, instead of interpenetrating.

Yet, Kreutzer's technical equipment is impressive and solid. His left hand, judging by the technique he favored, must have been large and strong; there are frequent tenths, as well as thirds and broken octaves. His position work is well developed; surprising jumps from low to high registers (an effect used often in French violin concertos) show his assurance on the fingerboard; he exploits the higher positions even on the G and D strings, and does not avoid the 2nd and 4th positions, considered awkward by many other violin composers. His bow arm, too, is strong and favors rich sonorities; his choice of bowings, somewhat too uniform at first, gains in variety from the 5th Concerto on. Kreutzer likes to spice his passages with syncopations, occasionally emphasizing them with double stops. His treatment of the violin is thoroughly idiomatic; themes and passages sound as if composed with violin in hand. How rich, how full and sonorous is already the opening theme of his First Concerto, utilizing the lower open strings in powerful chordal support of the brilliant E string.

From the 3rd Concerto on, Kreutzer begins to lose a somewhat homely touch in thematic invention and technical treatment; with the 6th Concerto in E minor — the first in the minor mode — he opens a new phase in his creative life. Viotti's influence comes finally to fruition, and we can see Kreutzer abandon Stamitz and the Mannheim tradition to follow Viotti and the Vienna classical school. At the same time, Kreutzer — like Viotti and Rode — could not escape the current mood of the French musical scene, exemplified in the operas around 1790, and some of the heroic, militant, pathetic, and passionate mood penetrated into his instrumental music.

Similar to Viotti, Kreutzer shows a sudden and decisive predilection for minor keys: among his last fourteen concertos (Nos. 6 to 19), seven are in minor. Hand in hand goes a shift in general mood which changes from the energetic or pleasant to dramatic sweep and pathetic grandeur, while preserving the virile strength of his early style. This prevailing atmosphere, most noticeable in his subsequent minor key concertos, the Nos. 8, 9, and 10, is contrasted occasionally with supple and expressive themes, nostalgic suspensions, and whole sections of decidedly pre-Romantic sentiment.

In his concertos in major keys, however, Kreutzer shows himself in an entirely different light: here he is close to the

Viennese classical school, especially to Haydn, in keeping with the Parisian taste of the 1790's and 1800's when Haydn's popularity was at its peak. Practically in every one of Kreutzer's works we can find sections and whole movements filled with Haydn's spirited limpidity and good humor. Mozart's lyricism was more alien to Kreutzer's nature, despite all admiration; a curious, almost literal quotation from *Figaro* in Kreutzer's Concerto No. 14 may have been accidental. There was more affinity between Kreutzer and the young Beethoven: as youths, both were subjected to French and Mannheimist influences, and both approached the heritage of Haydn and Mozart with freshness and virility. There is a kinship of mood and spirit between the first movements of Kreutzer's Violin Concerto No. 11 and Beethoven's Piano Concerto No. 1; there is even a passing similarity of themes. When Kreutzer visited Vienna in 1798, Beethoven was just working on his concerto, and it may well be that the French violinist heard him play it privately. This does not imply, however, that Kreutzer was necessarily on the receiving end; on the contrary, we feel that Beethoven is actually much indebted to Kreutzer. Many a passage from Beethoven's Violin Concerto can be found in similar patterns in earlier works by Kreutzer whose technical storehouse provides more inspiration for Beethoven than either Viotti or Rode (ex. IV-6a, IV-6b, IV-7a, IV-7b, IV-8a, IV-8b).[44] The fact that Beethoven chose Kreutzer, not Rode or Baillot (both of whom he knew at the time) as recipient of the dedication of his Sonata Op. 47, seems proof that he felt the kinship between the mighty spirit of that work and Kreutzer's virile style. As for Kreutzer, he left the discovery of Beethoven to his colleagues Habeneck and Baillot and did not take any active part in the promotion and performance of Beethoven's works in Paris.

In compositorial craftsmanship, Kreutzer surpasses his more celebrated confrere Rode; this is especially obvious in his development sections of the first movements where he excels in motivic working-out technique, as well as more

Example IV-6a. Rode, *Violin Concerto No. 1* (1790).
Example IV-6b. Beethoven, *Violin Concerto* (1806).

Example IV-7a. Kreutzer, *Violin Concertos Nos. 4 and 14* (1786, 1804).
Example IV-7b. Beethoven, *Violin Concerto.*

Example IV-8a. Kreutzer, *Violin Concerto No. 16* (ca. 1805).
Example IV-8b. Beethoven, *Violin Concerto.*

careful and knowing treatment of the orchestral parts. Yet,
in natural endowment, in charm, *esprit,* and originality of
thematic invention, Kreutzer is far weaker; though there are
exceptions, like the enchanting *Bolero* of the 17th Concerto
which has irresistible melodic and rhythmic attraction.

Kreutzer's most notable achievements, however, are his
last two concertos, the 18th in E minor and the 19th in D

minor, for they are the culmination not only of his creative life, but of an entire generation of French violin composers. Next to Viotti's 22nd and Rode's 7th Concertos, the 19th Concerto by Kreutzer is the most perfect example of the French Violin Concerto. What Rode achieved, almost without effort, in his very first concerto, Kreutzer reached only in his last: the perfect integration of all the components which make a great violin concerto — balance between musical content and virtuoso display, between soloist and orchestra. Typical, too, are the moods of the three movements: drama and grandeur in the first, soulful *cantilena* in the second, brilliance and sparkle in the *finale*. The result was a model concerto which, in its type, remained unsurpassed. Joseph Joachim included the 19th Concerto in his Violin Method (volume III) and has the following comment:

> Kreutzer manifests in his first movement that bold decision for which his playing was so much admired by his contemporaries . . . It is a beautiful example of that kind of pathos which among French masters so often manifests itself in sudden shifts from high to low registers or *vice versa*, without exceeding the natural limits of expression of the instrument . . .[45]

The slow *Andante* is praised for the "warmth of its *cantinella*" and the *Rondo* for its "playful grace."

Technically, the last two concertos show Kreutzer at his best: the form is clear, concentrated, and well organized; the development sections reveal excellent workmanship; his harmonies are original and often bold. There is one formal innovation in the first movement of No. 18: between the development and the recapitulation, the composer inserts a — thematically independent — *Grave,* a sort of recitative of the solo violin, sixteen bars long, projected against orchestral *tremolos.* The effect is original and decidedly romanticizing, if not Romantic. Noteworthy, too, are several short cadenzas of the solo violin in the last two movements of both the 18th and 19th Concertos — a procedure which we have already found in some of Viotti's concertos.

The violinistic equipment required by these concertos is not excessive; yet, Kreutzer's type of technique is so different and often so intricate that a special conditioning is needed. This is even more true in the case of some of his earlier concertos which abound in fast trills, exposed arpeggios, difficult double stops, and a variety of bowings. He himself realized that his concertos needed special technical preparation, for many of the technical problems in his famous *40 Etudes ou Caprices*[46]* seem like quotes from his concertos; their original purpose was probably that of "preparatory exercises." Needless to say that the *Caprices* have proved their worth far beyond this limited scope, for they constitute the vademecum of every violinist. While musically less imaginative than Rode's 24 *Caprices*, Kreutzer's collection of *études* is more systematic; he deals with certain technical problems in a more thorough manner.

***

Pierre François Baillot

Among the contemporaries of Rode and Kreutzer, only one violinist-composer can bear comparison — Pierre François Baillot (1771-1842). Although his creative talent was less original and easy-flowing, he nevertheless attained a unique position in the musical life of Paris.

Baillot was not so much a virtuoso as a versatile musical personality: soloist, quartet player, composer, writer, pedagogue, he seems at home in every field of musical endeavor.

As performing violinist, Baillot represented a comparatively new type: the re-creative artist. The virtuosos of the

---

*The original edition of Kreutzer's *Etudes* (reportedly 1796) has not been found. The earliest extant edition is dated c. 1803, Leipzig, Breitkopf & Härtel, plate No. 373, owned by the *Hochschule für Musik* in Berlin. Later editions increased the number of etudes to 42.

18th and early 19th centuries, when performing in public, usually limited themselves to their own compositions which fitted closely their peculiar style and personality. To adapt oneself to another style, to attempt the interpretation of a strange work by probing for the composer's intentions was an art almost unknown. In contrast to the often arbitrary attitude of the virtuoso, Baillot was a true "interpreter" of great music of various periods: he made a careful study of the violin classics of the 18th century, he played the quartets of Haydn and Mozart, and he performed the music of his contemporaries — Beethoven, Cherubini, Reicha, Spohr, and Mendelssohn. It was Baillot's adaptability which aroused the admiration of his listeners; so says Fétis who heard him play often:

> ....a rare, I should say unique, talent which permitted him to adopt as many manners of playing as there were styles in the music he performed ... Baillot as quartet player was more than a violinist: he was a poet.[47]

Other contemporaries speak of Baillot's artistry with similar enthusiasm. Here is an excerpt from a letter written in 1815 by pastor Karl Amenda to his friend Beethoven:

> There, in Mitau, I also heard Baillot from Paris. Oh! what a mighty instrument is the violin when it speaks through the soul of Baillot. Not since I heard you play at Zmeskall's the last time was I ever so shaken by a mortal as I was by Baillot. He told me that he was in Vienna some time ago, and spoke of you with enthusiasm; nothing gives him greater pleasure than to play your works, and he confessed that he played for you only once, but in great embarrassment ...[48]

Baillot's devotion to Beethoven's genius was genuine, not merely a conversational phrase; next to Habeneck, he did more than anyone else to make Beethoven's works known in Paris: the Violin Concerto* and many of the sonatas and

---

*First performed in Paris at the *Société des Concerts du Conservatoire* on March 22, 1828.

quartets were heard for the first time in France through his interpretations.

Baillot's natural talent for the violin was not as strong and inborn as that of Rode or Kreutzer; yet, through intelligence and perseverance, he developed into one of the "most perfect" players, as a Viennese critic called him;[49] even Spohr, a man very hard to please, has only praise for Baillot's playing.

Contemporary reports describe his style as virile and bold, his tone as large but at times somewhat harsh and not always agreeable because of too much bow pressure.[50] His interpretations were serious, broad, austere, and lacked the grace or piquancy of a Rode, while his attitude toward the public was uncompromising and commanded attention. His technical equipment was formidable though there was a lack of lightness.

Baillot's relationship to Viotti was one of disciple and master rather than student and teacher. As a boy of twelve, Baillot heard Viotti play and was deeply impressed; soon afterwards, however, Baillot left Paris, not to return until 1791, the year before Viotti left for London. By that time, Baillot was already so accomplished a violinist that Viotti placed him in the orchestra of the *Théâtre Feydeau.* After five months Baillot decided to abandon temporarily the active career of a musician without, however, losing interest in the violin. Whether or not Baillot had actual lessons with Viotti cannot be established, but there is no doubt that he belonged to Viotti's inner circle during 1791-92. Their friendship lasted through the years; they exchanged affectionate letters,[51] and Baillot's *Notice sur Viotti,* published in 1825, after the master's death, is a warm and admiring tribute.

Most characteristic of Baillot's musical inclinations was his lifelong interest in chamber music. As early as 1795, he was heard in some trios of his own composition at the *Maison Wenzel*[52] and, we may assume, also in other ensemble music. In 1814, Baillot established regular quartet concerts in Paris, patterned after Schuppanzigh's concerts in Vienna, which became a most valuable — though at the time unappreciated — contribution to the musical life of France. How apathetic the public was toward this type of music can be gathered from the following Paris report of the *Wiener Musikzeitung* of 1817:

> Quartets are not popular at all here. Baillot, at present the idol and one of the most finished players, gives a subscription series during the winter for an audience of fifty people; that is all one can gather in this colossal city for this branch of music.[53]

Obviously, Baillot was not the man to be discouraged by this lack of response, for we read in the *Revue musicale* of 1829 the program of one of his soirées consisting of a quintet by Boccherini, a quartet by Haydn, a Quintet "original" in G minor by Mozart (probably the String Quintet K. 516), the Quartet in A major by Beethoven, and a Fantasy on a Theme by Plantade — certainly quite a fare for one evening.[54]

Baillot continued this pioneer work in his home where many friends and musicians gathered regularly to hear chamber music performances; there Berlioz was initiated into the late quartets by Beethoven. Other soirées took place at the home of the publisher Schlesinger, the violist Urhan, and the pianist Hiller. Mendelssohn, who played his music with Baillot in 1825 and again in 1831-32, speaks with great warmth about him; Chopin calls him a "rival of Paganini." On November 24, 1834, Baillot played the following program with Hiller at the latter's home: two sonatas by Bach (including the third in E major), and the "Kreutzer" Sonata by Beethoven; among those present were Cherubini, Meyerbeer, and Chopin. In a letter to the editor of the *Gazette musicale,* a certain Fr. Stoepel describes the "indescribable joy of admiration and enthusiasm" of those present and adds, "There is only one Baillot in this world . . . the prince of French violinists."[55]

As composer, Baillot found much less recognition. Fétis ascribes it to the fact that Baillot refused to make concessions to the taste of the public which found his music bizarre and lacking in charm. This alleged bizarreness, so Fétis continues, was merely originality which, perhaps, did not always appear in the right place[56] — a somewhat naive statement. That the exorbitant difficulties of Baillot's compositions prevented their wider popularity (as Fétis assumes) is unlikely, for Baillot's technique, though more elaborate, does not exceed in general the limits of Kreutzer.

Spohr comes closer to the truth when he says:

> Baillot's compositions have correctness which set them apart from those of most other Parisian violinists; they also have a certain undeniable originality; but there is something artificial, mannered, and antiquated in his style which leaves the listener mostly cold.[57]

By "correctness" Spohr undoubtedly means a certain accuracy of compositorial craftsmanship which Baillot acquired in his studies with Catel, Cherubini, and Reicha.

A good summary of the composer Baillot is given by Wasielewski:

> His works show a musically educated mind, careful planning, and highly efficient treatment of the violin. But they lack the ingratiation of creative musical soulfulness, that natural spontaneousness which moves the hearts ... His temperament is spirited, yet controlled by reflective speculation ... He tends toward a certain sophisticated refinement of effect ...[58]

These words contain the essence of Baillot's creative work: it is the product of intellect rather than inspiration; his originality is intentional and therefore artificial and calculated. Yet, because of his high intelligence and alert mind, he often succeeded in creating new and unusual effects and colorings; and though he himself did not create anything of lasting beauty, he certainly stimulated his students to avoid the commonplace and obvious.

***

Among Baillot's many instrumental compositions, his nine violin concertos are the most important. The first could have been published shortly after 1795 since the composer is designated, on the title page, as member of the faculty of the Conservatoire. However, it may have been composed somewhat earlier, since Fétis reports[59] that Baillot found success with his concertos even before he joined the Conservatoire. The 5th Concerto bears a dedication to a Russian nobleman and was probably written during Baillot's sojourn in Russia, i.e., between 1805 and 1808. The 8th Concerto is dedicated to Kreutzer and must have been written after his return to Paris. The 9th Concerto was published after 1815, for the title page describes Baillot as member of the Royal orchestra and professor of the *Ecole royale de musique.* A detail pointing toward an even later date (possibly 1817 or 1818) is the fact that the 9th Concerto bears precise metronome markings; the metronome of Maelzel was patented in 1816, and the inventor settled in Paris in 1817.

Thus, Baillot's last concertos were written years after both Viotti and Kreutzer ceased to write in this form; Rode, too, did not publish any concertos after ca. 1811, for his last ones are posthumous.

One can divide the nine concertos by Baillot into two groups — the "brilliant" and the "intimate." To the first group belong the Nos. 1, 3, 5, 7 — here he follows well-tested models, especially Kreutzer, whose broad, virile style was closest to him. Here are the old, well-known ingredients of the French violin concerto: pompousness, pathos, grandeur, and virtuosity, though in Baillot's hands they appear somewhat diluted and less spontaneous.

In the second group, however (e.g. Nos. 6 and 8), Baillot abandons all superfluous brilliance, reduces the virtuoso passages to an absolute minimum, and uses themes of chamber music-like intimacy; even the finales stress musical rather than virtuoso aspects. In these works Baillot may have been influenced by Viotti's late works, possibly also by the chamber music style of the Viennese masters.

Undoubtedly Baillot reveals himself in a more personal, original, and characteristic manner in these "intimate" concertos which have many pre-romantic tinges. However, French violin music did not follow his lead and developed in the other, the brilliant, direction; only in matters of technique did Baillot exert any influence on the younger generation of violin composers.

As far as the concerto form is concerned, Baillot followed the traditional pattern. All of his concertos are in three strictly separate movements, and he does not attempt to connect the movements more closely. The first movements are usually subdivided into four *tutti* and three *soli;* occasionally, as in Nos. 7 and 8, there are only three *tutti* and two *soli.* Most of the opening movements (except Nos. 3 and 5) have development sections in which the principal themes are worked out, especially fine is the powerful development of the 9th Concerto.

Baillot's slow movements show particularly careful workmanship; they are usually rather extended and demand not only tonal beauty and expressiveness but pose also technical problems, like the 4th Concerto where the solo part of the *Adagio* is polyphonic throughout. He also likes to incorporate into his slow movements sections with fast passages as well as solo cadenzas. At other times, he writes slow movements of great simplicity and noblesse, like the two *Romances* of the Concertos Nos. 6 and 9; especially the first-named is quiet, peaceful, and of an introspective, almost religious, mood. The form of the second movements is generally ternary (A-B-A), very rarely binary (e.g. No. 7).

The finales consist of the usual *rondos,* often with national coloring such as *Polonaise, Rondo russe, Rondo on a Moldavian air.* The workmanship is careful and imaginative, though many of the finales are excessively long. One of the best finales is the *Presto agitato* of the Concerto No. 4 in E minor, where the composer emphasizes musical values rather than brilliant display. On the other hand, we find that all the episodes in the *Rondo russe* consist of virtuoso passages, separated only by the single Russian theme.

Baillot's thematic invention is less inspired and significant than either Rode's or Kreutzer's; yet, because of his concern to avoid the commonplace, he often succeeds in achieving a remarkable degree of originality, especially with regard to new colorings and timbres. His gamut of expression ranges from energetic, sweeping grandeur to elegiac submission; strangely enough, he is less subject to the influence of the Viennese classical school than, e.g., Kreutzer, though the style of Haydn and early Beethoven left its traces on some of his movements, especially in the 8th and 9th Concertos. On the other hand there are movements pervaded with Schubertian lyricism and nostalgic sentimentalism; there is a softening and suppling of the melodic line which prophesy the coming Romantic period. Pointing in this same direction are Baillot's frequent use of the diminished seventh chord as expression of drama, increased chromaticism, and his unusual sense for timbres.

Yet, despite all his compositorial ambitions, it is in the field of violin technique that Baillot made his most important contribution. Liberating himself from the stagnant tradition of the Viotti school, he succeeded in inventing truly original passages and in enriching the violinistic idiom, especially in the field of multiple stops. He does not shun awkward, hard-to-play intricacies which make his technique sound less smooth, less idiomatic than that of Rode or Kreutzer. Though Baillot did not introduce anything fundamentally new, he nevertheless made an important contribution toward the evolution of violin playing, for his was a free, bolder, more sovereign concept of technical matters. Not only violinists learned from him, but also composers like Mendelssohn and Saint-Saëns, for instance.

There is no need to go into further analyses of Baillot's works, for they do not reveal any new facets of his artistic personality. Reared in the tradition of Viotti, firmly anchored in the musical heritage of Haydn and Mozart, Baillot was by no means a mere "traditionalist": he championed music of his contemporaries; he showed the way toward a more effective and brilliant exploitation of violinistic possibilities; and he transmitted the sum-total of his experience to a host of young violinists. True, his accomplishments as composer are more labored than inspired, yet they stimulated others who were creatively more gifted. Baillot was the intermediary between the older and the younger generation, equally beloved and admired by both.

***

Charles Lafont

Charles Lafont stands, like Baillot, between two generations of violin composers — the classical, devoted to the ideals of Viotti, and the rising Romantic, represented by de Bériot. While Baillot, by age, background, and temperament, tended more toward the old school, Lafont, young, daring, phenomenally gifted for the violin, came close to the Romantic ideal.

At the height of his career, during the decade between 1807 and 1817, Lafont was considered the most accomplished of all French violinists, notwithstanding the fact that among his active competitors were virtuosos like Kreutzer, Rode, and Baillot. According to Fétis,[60] Lafont's playing had impeccable purity, great technical assurance, and a silken, though at times unenergetic, tone, used irresistibly in enchanting *cantilena*.

Even more weight is carried by the opinion of Spohr[1] who judges his colleague with professional severity. Obviously impressed by Lafont's "perfect execution,"[1] Spohr says:

> Lafont combines in his playing a beautiful tone, utmost purity, vigor and grace, and he would be a perfect violinist if, coupled with these excellent qualities, he could muster a deeper feeling...

More convincing than any verbal testimonials, however, is the fact that Lafont was able to compete with Paganini in a thoroughly creditable manner. Our sources for this musical *rencontre,* which took place in Milan on March 11, 1816, are varied. Both protagonists left retrospective accounts (dated almost fifteen years later) which are remarkably objective. However, Paganini's friends and admirers embellished the story, making it appear as a defeat for Lafont, and as such it went down in history. Here are the facts:

Paganini had travelled from Genoa to Milan early in 1816, eager to hear Lafont who had the reputation of being the best violinist of France. His first impression was decidedly cool, as he reported to his friend Germi in a letter of February 3, 1816: "He plays well, but he does not surprise." Recalling the entire event to his biographer Schottky many years later, Paganini is more generous toward his French colleague. Here is Paganini's account:

> I enjoyed Lafont's playing very much. A week after his concert, I gave mine in the *La Scala* theater so that he would have an opportunity to hear me. The next morning Lafont suggested that we give a joint concert. At first I refused, saying that such affairs were dangerous, for the public would consider it a "duel" in which there would have to be one victor and one vanquished; in our case this would be even more inevitable since Lafont was considered the best violinist of France while I was considered, without merit, the best Italian violinist. Lafont, however, did not accept this reasoning, and I had no choice but to accept. I left the arrangement of the program to him, but refrained voluntarily from playing on *one* string to keep the competition fair. I started with a concerto of my own composition, which was followed by Lafont's playing of one of his concertos. Next we appeared both in a double concerto by Kreutzer; here I kept strictly to the printed page wherever the two violins played together, but improvised in my solo sections which my rival did not like at all. As next

number on the program, Lafont played his variations on a Russian theme, and I concluded the program with my variations *Le Streghe*. Lafont, perhaps, had a more beautiful tone, but the applause of the public showed me that I was by no means the vanquished in this competition.[62]

Rossini, a close friend of Paganini, embellished the story and retold it to Ferdinand Hiller:

Lafont came to Milan with the strange prejudice that Paganini was a sort of charlatan whom he could dispose of in no time. Thus he invited him to play something together in his concert in *La Scala*. Paganini came to Rossini and asked him whether he should accept. "By all means," was the reply, "so that Lafont would not think that you lack the courage to compete with him." Lafont sent Paganini the solo part; but Paganini did not want to see it and said that the orchestra rehearsal would be sufficient. At this rehearsal Paganini played his part at sight quite correctly. However, at the concert, he repeated the variations, which Lafont played before him, in octaves, thirds, and sixths, so that the poor Frenchman became thoroughly confused and did not play as well as he could. Rossini reproached Paganini with this lack of musical conscience, but he only laughed. Lafont returned to Paris completely infuriated and spread the opinion of Paganini's charlatanery until the Parisian public had an opportunity to judge otherwise.[63]

Fourteen years after the event, Lafont felt compelled to take a stand against the persistent rumor of his "defeat." In 1830, he published an open letter in the *Harmonicon* of London telling his side of the story:

In March 1816, I gave in conjunction with Paganini a concert in the great theater *La Scala* in Milan, and far from making a cruel trial of the powers of my adversary or of being beaten by him ... I obtained a success the more flattering as I was a stranger in the country ... I played with Paganini the concerted symphony of Kreutzer in F major. For several days previously to the concert we rehearsed this symphony together and with the greatest care. On the day of the concert it was performed by us as it had been rehearsed and with no change whatever; and we both obtained an equal success in the passages executed together or separately. On coming to the *phrase de chant* in F minor ... there was a decided advantage for one of us. The passage is of a deep and melancholy expression. Paganini performed it first. Whether the strong and brilliant character of the piece was ill suited to the ornaments and brilliant notes which be gave to it, or whatever else was the cause, his solo produced but little effect. Immediately after him, I repeated the same passage and treated it differently. It seems that the emotion by which I was then agitated caused me to give an expression more effective though more simple, and it was so felt by the audience that I was overwhelmed with plaudits from all parts of the house. During the fourteen years I have been silent on this trifling advantage obtained over Paganini in this instance, only in the symphony and probably rather by the superiority of the school than by that of talent. It is painful for me to speak of myself . . . I was not beaten by Paganini; nor he by me. On all occasions I have taken pleasure in rendering homage to his great talent; but I have never said that he was the first violinist in the world. I have not done such injustice to the celebrated men, Kreutzer, Rode, Baillot, and Habeneck. And I declare now as I have always done that the French school is the first in the world for the violin.[64]

For a balanced report we must rely on a contemporary critic, the Milan correspondent of the *Allgemeine Musikalische Zeitung:*

A few days ago Paganini and Lafont gave a concert together. There was a great rush for seats. Everyone wanted to witness the duel between the two artists and, as might have been foreseen, the result showed that when it comes to artificiality, to technical mastery, Paganini is without a peer, Lafont being far behind him in this respect. Both, however, are about equal when it comes to beauty of tone and fine sensitive playing, with the odds perhaps on the side of Lafont. Both artists received extraordinary applause.[65]

Combining the stories, it appears as if Paganini used a somewhat questionable method in embellishing his part in the Kreutzer work with technical trickeries. Be it as it may, Lafont's eagerness and courage were admirable but ill-advised, for he could never expect the excitable Italian public to favor him above their own artist. The truth of the matter is, however, that Lafont's conventionally accomplished playing was no match for the erratic genius of Paganini who, fifteen years later, in 1831, took Paris by storm.

Being a performer of decidedly virtuosic tendencies, Lafont was interested primarily in a maximum of effect and brilliance when composing for his own instrument. His compositions abound in technical intricacies and violinistic fireworks, but are musically far below the standards of Kreutzer, Rode, and Baillot. Lafont's principal accomplishment lies in his expansion of violinistic possibilities, paving the way for the violin style of de Bériot. His career coincided with the general trivialization of music which gripped Europe in the 1820's and 30's, and his production of potpourris, *rondos,* and fantasies on operatic melodies certainly contributed their share. According to the fashion of the day, Lafont was not even the sole author of these pieces, but usually joined hands with some reputable pianist, like Herz, Moscheles, or Onslow, who would provide the necessary dose of brilliance for the piano part, while Lafont belabored the violin — a procedure foreshadowing our age of specialization. Lafont's name became almost a byword of virtuoso brilliance, as can be gathered from the following quotation of Robert Schumann:

...I count Bohrer among the virtuosos who habitually compose in a brilliant style, so to speak a German Lafont...[66]

Nevertheless, Lafont — like Henri Herz — had certain compositorial ambitions which he satisfied by writing a number of larger works, notably seven concertos for violin and orchestra which, in the opinion of Schering,[67] were modeled after those by Rode. This is not surprising, for Lafont's style, emphasizing sweetness and elegance rather than vigor, was akin to that of Rode.

Yet, despite all serious intentions, Lafont's concertos are far below the standards set by his teachers, Kreutzer and Rode. His treatment of the concerto form is thoroughly conventional, his compositorial craftsmanship rather primitive, his thematic invention undistinguished, and even his violin passages are not as brilliant as one would expect from a virtuoso of his standing; in fact, his technical treatment of the violin in the concertos is so tame that one would never suspect the author of having competed seriously with Paganini. True, Lafont's technique is fluent, but it is not really difficult. In a way, Lafont is the initiator of a special brand of violin virtuosity: making passages sound more dazzling and difficult than they actually are.

In his slow movements, Lafont stresses the sentimental, sweetish, nostalgic mood, a certain abandon to feeling and affect which borders on affectation and triviality. This differs from the noble restraint of Kreutzer and Rode and heralds the approach of the sentimental age. Being a professional singer as well as a violinist, it was only natural for Lafont to transmit the mood of the French *romance* from the voice to the violin, making his slow movements sound at times like "songs without words." While his inventive powers were not sufficiently original to insure the survival of his melodies, he is obviously much more at ease in writing a sentimental *romance* or a sparkling *rondo* than in laboring over an academic first movement. Recognizing this fact, one publisher, F. Hoffmeister of Leipzig, included fragments of Lafont's concertos, namely the second and third movements of Nos. 2, 5, and 6, in a collection entitled *Douze compositions brillantes par Ch. Lafont.* Of his other concertos, only the third in E minor acquired a certain reputation, although it was obviously modeled after two famous examples — Viotti's No. 22 and Rode's No. 7. It is amusing to note that, while Viotti begins his masterpiece on the E string in third position and Rode with a similar theme in fourth position, Lafont outdoes both by climbing into eight position, without being able, however, to cover up the paucity of his invention.

Summarizing Lafont's accomplishments, we see him occupy an intermediary position between the — fundamentally classicistic — school represented by Viotti with his disciples Rode and Kreutzer, and the Romantic violin school initiated by de Bériot and brought to its apex by Vieuxtemps. By allowing himself to be influenced by Paganini, Lafont broke away from the violinistic inbreeding among the French disciples of Viotti, and removed the staleness which enveloped the group of violinists around the *Conservatoire.* De Bériot continued on this path until the personal appearance of Paganini in Paris, in 1831, tore the French violinists out of their smug complacency.

***

Charles de Bériot

Charles de Bériot (1802-1870) can be called the first Romantic of the violin, for beginning with his first published composition, the *Air varié* Op. 1, he belonged entirely to the Romantic age. Standing on the shoulders of men like Baillot and Lafont, who did important spadework, he made a definitive break with the Viotti tradition which had dominated the violin for almost four decades, from 1780 to about 1820.

De Bériot's appearance, in the 1820's, came at a time when Romantic ideas and concepts were far advanced and ripe for public acceptance. Yet we must not imagine him as a musical and intellectual giant, comparable to Liszt or Berlioz; in fact, he does not seem to have taken any active interest in the Romantic movement as such. De Bériot's Romanticism was of modest proportions; unhampered by intellectual complications, he had an innate gift for inventing sweet melodies and tinkling passages. All the more remarkable are his achievements: he made important changes in the form of the violin concerto, he revitalized the short character piece and the *air varié,* and — most important of all — he regenerated and modernized the technique of the violin.

De Bériot's singular originality in the treatment of the violin can, perhaps, be traced to the fact that he was almost self-taught. Aside from some early lessons with a local teacher in his home town of Louvain (Belgium), he did not have any instruction until he came to Paris in 1821, at the age of nineteen. Even then, he attended Baillot's classes at the *Conservatoire* merely as an auditor for only a few months. Viotti, who heard him play, gave him the following advice: "You have a beautiful style, try to perfect it; listen to all violinists of talent, but do not imitate anyone."[68] De Bériot certainly took this advice literally and persisted to preserve his violinistic independence; a short study period with André Robberechts, a compatriot and former student of Viotti and Baillot, did not alter his fundamental approach.

De Bériot's most ambitious compositorial efforts were his ten violin concertos in which he used three different types of concerto form: the traditional three-movement concerto (Nos. 2 and 3), the one-movement concerto (Nos. 1, 4, and 5), and the three-movement form welded into one without breaks between movements (Nos. 6, 7, 8, 9, and 10). Such attempts at liberalizing traditional forms were typical of the Romantic school, and de Bériot was one of the first to apply new principles to the violin concerto.

The first type does not need any lengthy explanation, for it is the conventional concerto form with an *Allegro* as first movement, subdivided into only three *tutti* and two long *soli,* a slow movement in the center, and a *rondo* as *finale.*

The second type, the concerto in one single movement, can be described as a *Konzertstück,* to use the German term, or — as it is called sometimes — a *Concertino.* In piano literature, this type became popular since Weber introduced his *Konzertstück* (F minor) in 1821, though he conceived the initial idea of this piece as early as 1815.

De Bériot, apparently the first to use the *concertino* form for the violin, does not handle it too well at first: his Concerto No. 1 (Op. 16) lacks somewhat inner coherence although a certain ternary pattern (major key — minor key — major key) is discernible. Better welded is his 4th Concerto Op. 46 which shows a definitely symmetrical arrangement (A-B-A). Organized into three *tutti* and two *soli,* it has an exposition with two themes, a middle section marked *Poco piu lento* introducing a new theme of heroic character, and an abbreviated recapitulation beginning with the second theme of the exposition. Basically, this form is not too different from a first movement, except that it lacks a development section.

Completely mature from the formal point of view is the 5th Concerto Op. 55 (D major) which shows a fully developed *concertino* type. Again we find a A-B-A pattern: A^1, marked

Allegro moderato, contains an introductory *tutti,* an extended *solo* with three themes, and a short orchestral transition to an *Adagio* (B) given entirely to the soloist. After a *fermata* the orchestra returns to the initial *Allegro moderato* (A^2), joined by the soloist playing an abbreviated version of his first *solo* which concludes the entire work.

No less interesting is the third concerto type used by de Bériot, namely a three-movement form played without interruption. This type, actually a combination of the one-movement and the three-movement forms, was de Bériot's favorite, for he used it in five of his ten concertos. The idea of connecting separate movements was not new; as we have seen, Viotti, Kreutzer, and Rode use it occasionally, as well as Beethoven and Spohr. Yet, de Bériot not only eliminated breaks between movements but also connected them motivically by using thematic fragments from the first movement in the *finale* (e.g., in Nos. 7 and 9); incidentally, a similar attempt was made by Viotti in his 21st Concerto. As to the structure of the first movements, de Bériot contracted them at times into only two *tutti* and one *solo* (the latter containing two themes and extensive passages, as in Nos. 7 and 9), while the last two movements have normal length.

Not only in matters of musical form was de Bériot a child of the Romantic era, but also in melodic invention and harmonic treatment. Forgotten are the stilted classicistic stereotypes of a bygone era: now everything sings, speaks, sighs, stomps, and shouts with complete abandon. The gamut of expression is wide and obviously influenced by the *opéra comique*: there are themes of march-like military pomp, theatrical sweep, melting melancholy, or graceful piquancy. True, de Bériot's emotions are at times shallow, his inspiration trivial, his pathos theatrical, his melancholy affected; yet, everything seems ennobled by Gallic charm, good taste, and gentlemanly nonchalance. While compositorial workmanship is generally not de Bériot's strong point, he makes an obvious effort in some of his concertos (notably Nos. 2, 3, 7, 8, and 9) to give them careful finish and to preserve a certain dignity worthy of the traditional concerto form.

Truly creative, however, is de Bériot in his technical treatment of the violin; here, his imagination appears inexhaustible. It is as if the violin bow, usually solid and pedestrian, suddenly acquired wings: it hops, bounces, and flies with disrespectful impishness, or it hits daringly three strings simultaneously in flashing up-and-down strokes. De Bériot discards the heavy *détaché*, the broadly detached bowing on the string, as well as the hammered *martelé*, and stresses instead the *spiccato* and *sautillé* (both bouncing), and the flying as well as the thrown (*ricochet*) *staccato*.

In left hand technique we find, in place of conventional scales and arpeggios, a multitude of double stops and chords, made more sonorous by frequent use of open strings. Broken octaves and tenths in highest positions, chromatic double stops played with only two fingers sliding across the finger board, artificial harmonics, and *pizzicatos* plucked with both right and left hand now become standard equipment. While all these effects were known and used before, de Bériot raises them from the level of parlor tricks to a more dignified, though still trivial, art. Previously, composers generally refrained from using technical trickeries in concertos; even Lafont reserved his virtuoso fireworks for his operatic fantasies and *airs variés*. De Bériot abandons all such restraint and fashions the concerto into a glittering virtuoso vehicle, a development which became symptomatic for the 19th century.

Yet, despite all brilliance, de Bériot's technical requirements are actually often modest; their effectiveness lies in their idiomatic invention. Of all violinist-composers, his writing is probably the most violinistic. Undoubtedly, his imagination was stimulated by Paganini's exploits; yet, de Bériot's style was actually firmly set from his Opus 1 on, before he had any contact with the Italian wizard. Later, de

Bériot and, to a greater extent, his student Vieuxtemps, succeeded in absorbing and Gallicizing the technical advances made by Paganini. De Bériot's compositions have completely disappeared from today's concert programs, and rightly so, for his virtuoso style was continued and perfected by violinist-composers of greater talent, like Vieuxtemps, Sarasate, and Wieniawski. However, de Bériot's concertos and *airs variés* are still very useful as study material, for they introduce the budding violinist to the virtuoso treatment of his instrument, counterbalancing the heavier fare of Viotti, Kreutzer, and Rode. While realizing de Bériot's musical limitations, we must guard ourselves from underestimating his influence: as head of the important Belgian school he molded a generation of violinists; beyond that, he adapted the violin to the requirements and the mood of the Romantic age, giving it an elf-like, iridescent quality.* Mendelssohn's conception of the violin, not only in his Violin Concerto but also in the violin parts of his orchestral and chamber music, shows a definite technical affinity to de Bériot, of course infinitely ennobled and made subservient to musical ideas (see examples IV-9a, IV-9b, IV-10a, IV-10b).

Example IV-9a. De Beriot, *Violin Concerto No. 3* (ca. 1835).
Example IV-9b. Schumann, *Phantasiestücke*, Op. 12 (1837). "Aufschwung."

*De Bériot was professor of violin at the Conservatoire in Brussels from 1843 to 1852. He was the teacher of Vieuxtemps. The Belgian School produced some of the greatest violinists of the century, e.g. Vieuxtemps, Artôt, Prume, Léonard, Marteau, Massart, Marsick, Ysaÿe, and César Thompson. Through Marsick and Massart, who were appointed to the faculty of the Paris Conservatoire, the influence was extended to the French School, although the two schools were generally so closely linked that one usually speaks of a "Franco-Belgian" School.

Example IV-10a. De Beriot, *Violin Concerto No. 3.*
Example IV-10b. Mendelssohn, *Violin Concerto* (1844). First, second, and third movements.

***

CHAPTER 5

Pianoforte Music (1780-1830)

In the field of keyboard music, France was strangely unproductive for about one hundred years. There is a mysterious gap between the last clavier compositions of Rameau (1741) and the first piano works of César Franck (1842) during which France produced very few piano composers and not a single piano virtuoso of international stature. This is all the more strange since the interest in the pianoforte was ever increasing in Paris; while there were only 68 teachers of harpsichord or pianoforte in the French capital in 1788,[1] there were 1800 piano teachers in 1832 and "still not enough."[2] Chopin was dismayed when he arrived in Paris in 1831:

> I don't know where there can be so many pianists as in Paris, so many asses, and so many virtuosi . . .[3]

Despite this intense interest, the leadership in piano composition and virtuosity remained in the hands of foreign pianists, mostly of German origin, who flocked to Paris in search of fame and fortune.

Yet, French influence was by no means eliminated; on the contrary, these foreign artists absorbed much of the Gallic spirit, shed their provincialism, and acquired the polish and brilliance indispensable to success in the sophisticated atmosphere of Paris. Their music acquired a character decidedly different from that of their confreres across the border: it was music more rounded, more ingratiating, and more cosmopolitan. Here again, as so often, France withstood an artistic invasion by absorption and assimilation; and the French style, far from disappearing "within ten or fifteen years" as Leopold Mozart had predicted in 1764,[4] emerged in new luster and richness.

> In every century France has attracted crowds of foreigners and has as-similated them . . . France shapes her inhabitants in her own image, and these, in turn, carry forward the existence and the unique character of France down the ages.[5]

The influx of German keyboard artists began in the 1750's, about the same time that German wind players were engaged to fill important positions in French orchestras. Just as German clarinet and horn players brought new techniques and new skills to Paris, so the German clavierists introduced a new expressive style which favored the supple pianoforte rather than the rigid harpsichord. Within a few decades, the French keyboard style, based on the proud tradition of Couperin and Rameau, was obliterated and transformed, and the few native French composers who clung to the ornate *style rocaille* sounded hopelessly outdated.

Among the German pianists who settled in Paris prior to the Revolution, the most important were undoubtedly Johann Schobert and Nicholas Hüllmandel. The influence of Schobert, who arrived in the French capital about 1760 and died suddenly in 1767, extended far beyond the short span of his life: until the Revolution, his compositions could be found on every piano in Paris. That the boyhood style of Mozart was strongly influenced by Schobert was established by the research of Wyzewa and Saint-Foix.[6] While in Paris, Schobert was the favorite of the salons, and the "sentimental character" of his success was compared to that of Chopin some seventy years later.[7]

Another compatriot for whom young Mozart had high regard was Nicholas Hüllmandel, an Alsatian pianist-composer who settled in Paris in 1776. Mozart saw some of his piano sonatas during his Parisian visit in 1778 and wrote to this father in Salzburg:

> Write and tell me whether you have ... Hüllmandel's sonatas. If not, I should like to buy them and send them to you. Both works are very fine.[8]

Having studied with C. P. E. Bach before coming to Paris, Hüllmandel was a well-schooled musician of solid craftsmanship which he fused with Parisian taste. His historic position is that of an intermediary between Schobert, whose clavier style was still a compromise between harpsichord and pianoforte, and Clementi, whose approach to the keyboard was purely pianistic.

Hüllmandel's compositions, consisting mainly of eight collections of keyboard sonatas (many with optional violin accompaniments) were published in Paris between 1776 and 1788. During the Revolution, he left for London where he died in 1823.

Hüllmandel was not a composer of marked originality, but his inborn taste, his craftsmanship, and an intuitive understanding of French musical style make him stand out among his Parisian colleagues. Beginning with his Opus 1, he shows a polished perfection of technique, noble expression, and a feeling for balance. Despite the brilliance of his piano writing, it never degenerates into mere glitter; thus he is a bulwark against the inroads of trivial virtuosity. In many of Hüllmandel's works, C. P. E. Bach's well-ordered spirit is noticeable, and while the disciple lacks the genius of the teacher, he is less severe, more ingratiating, more "French."

Hüllmandel handles the sonata form in a flexible and varied way: some are built in three movements, others are limited to two. His opening movements are either binary or ternary, and the same holds true of his *finales,* unless he prefers to close with a *rondo.*

There is quiet dignity and often touching expression in his slow movements which not only left their imprint on Mozart but at times even foreshadow Beethoven (ex. V-1,

V-2, V-3, V-4). The kinship between Hüllmandel's keyboard style and Mozart's "Parisian" piano compositions of
1778 is curious and revealing. Yet, one dare not speak of a
direct influence of Hüllmandel on Mozart; rather one may
assume that Mozart, once in Paris, adjusted himself to the
prevailing Parisian taste of which Hüllmandel was at the
time an important exponent. For Hüllmandel was not an
isolated case but mirrored, in his works, the general trend in
French music during the pre-Revolutionary decade: a certain
sorrow, nostalgia, and noble grandeur, flowing from the
works of the prophetic Schobert toward the Revolution in an
ever-increasing stream.

Example V-1. Hüllmandel, *Piano Sonata* (before 1788).

Example V-2. Mozart, *Piano Sonata K. 545* (1788).

Example V-3. Hüllmandel, *Piano Sonata.*

Example V-4. Beethoven, *Piano Sonata Op. 2 No. 3* (1795).

Fairly typical of these tendencies are the early piano sonatas by Etienne Méhul[9] who, after 1790, was to become France's leading operatic composer. Méhul came to Paris at the age of sixteen, in 1779, where he attracted the attention of Gluck. On the verge of leaving Paris, Gluck recommended young Méhul as a student to Johann Friedrich Edelmann, an Alsatian pianist-composer who had settled in Paris in the 1770's.

Méhul's career began in 1782 when his *Ode to Rousseau* was performed at the *Concert spirituel*. The same year, the *Journal de clavecin* published some of his keyboard arrangements of popular operatic excerpts. Such transcriptions were common practice among young pianist-composers of the day — a practice which was reflected in their original works. Indeed, the keyboard compositions of that period succumb frequently to the influence of the operatic stage, and Méhul is no exception. Noticeable, too, is a certain orchestral conception of the keyboard, undoubtedly encouraged by such transcriptions of operatic scores.

The following year (1783), Méhul published his first series of three sonatas "for the harpsichord or pianoforte," followed by a second series of three sonatas (with optional violin accompaniment) in 1788. These works show a decisive flair for pianistic writing and are clearly designed for the pianoforte rather than the harpsichord; the optional choice of instrument indicated on the title page appears to be a mere formality. In view of the remarkably high standard of these youthful works, it is particularly regrettable that Méhul's operatic success made him abandon the field of piano composition.

The first series of sonatas, published when the composer was twenty years old, consists of three works, in D major, C minor, and A major, of which the third — actually the least characteristic of the set — has been reprinted in modern editions.

Two of the sonatas, the first and third, are built in three movements: *Allegro, Andante, Rondo* in No. 1, *Allegro, Minuet, Rondo* in No. 3. The second sonata consists of only two movements: *Allegro, Minuet.*

The First Sonata should not detain us too long; it is music of little consequence, though pleasant, well-proportioned, and of fresh inspiration. The Second Sonata, however, is particularly interesting because of its dramatic, essentially "scenic" style which Pougin describes in the following words:

> In these tormented and vivacious rhythms, in the expressive and plaintive harmonies, in the passionate *allure* and general character, one can already discern the dramatic sentiment full of emotion, ardor, and intensity which will constitute the strength and originality of Méhul.[10]

The opening movement of this sonata, *Allegro,* is built on three themes of which the first and third are used in the dramatic development section forming the core of the movement. The recapitulation is shortened to a minimum and serves simply as coda. The whole movement has noble pathos and symphonic sweep. As a contrast, the *Minuet* is in the major mode (with a *Trio* in minor) and shows traces of Schobert's influence or, at least, a similarity of mood.

The Third Sonata was chosen by several modern editors (e.g., Köhler, Pauer) for republication. Their attention was probably attracted by its Mozartian character which, in fact, makes the work appear less dated than the scenic style of the Second Sonata. The first *Allegro* has a frank, engaging freshness, and the melodic invention is full of charm. Again, the *sonata-allegro* form is preserved; the development section uses the first theme as well as some new material, and the recapitulation is shortened by the omission of the second theme. A *Minuet,* standing in second place, has the *cantabile* style of Schobert and Mozart, while the *minore Trio* shows some of the "pre-Beethovenism" so cherished by French musicologists (ex. V-5, V-6). The final movement, a *Rondo Allegretto,* is more conventional and unexciting, though well written. Throughout the work, the handling of keyboard problems is skillful but technically not very advanced.

Example V-5. Méhul, *Piano Sonata Op. 1 No. 3* (1783).

Example V-6. Beethoven, *Piano Sonata Op. 27 No. 2* (1801).

The second series of Méhul's sonatas, published five years later, shows remarkable progress in every respect. The first sonata, a grand and brilliant piece in D major, expands the first-movement form by introducing four themes; to preserve a balance, the development is kept short while the recapitulation is extensive. The second movement, an *Andante,* is a set of double variations alternating between major and minor mode, built on two themes. The final *Rondo* is slightly reminiscent of the "Turkish" music so popular at the time; otherwise it is a rather mediocre piece.

The Second and Third Sonatas of this set show again the operatic influence already noticeable in the first series. The first movement of No. 2, *Allegro moderato,* sounds like a piano transcription of an actual operatic overture — with a theme that seems to speak, haltingly, in a *recitativo* style, with breaks, silences, and suspense. Nothing quite so personal had as yet appeared in French piano music. The middle movement, a *Siciliano,* is very short, while the final *Allegretto* is vivacious and pianistic, though not particularly impressive.

The Third Sonata,* too, reveals obvious dramatic intentions of the composer, and again Méhul's fundamentally orchestral conception of the keyboard becomes apparent. The core of the first movement is a development section built skillfully on two pedal points, with interesting enharmonic modulations. The *Adagio* has noblesse and feeling, while the final *Rondo* succeeds in covering its weak thematic material by pianistic brilliance, using hand crossings effectively.

Without wishing to overestimate these early, and necessarily immature, works, we must nevertheless recognize the significance of Méhul's six sonatas within the framework of French pianoforte music; for here, a young artist of essentially French temperament succeeded in absorbing various foreign influences and fusing them with his French heritage. A new element was the infiltration of certain operatic devices and moods into piano music which was to become increasingly pronounced in the ensuing decades, with Weber its most notable representative. In the case of Méhul, this tendency appears natural, almost unavoidable, considering his intense preoccupation with the stage and his profound admiration

---

*This sonata (Op. 2, No. 3, C major) has been reedited by Mme. Maurice Gallat (Paris, ca. 1925).

for Gluck. Otherwise, Méhul was rather conservative, especially with regard to piano technique which he kept within the confines of solid, traditional musicianship, achieving brilliance without shrillness and controlling virtuosity by excellent taste.

**

With the establishment of the *Conservatoire* in 1795, French piano playing and instruction — like that of all other instruments — found at last a center of methodization. Lacking a towering personality comparable to that of Viotti in the field of the violin, French piano playing did not immediately produce spectacular results; nevertheless, the group of pianist-composers affiliated with the *Conservatoire* exerted considerable influence, establishing excellent standards of technical proficiency and somewhat lesser ones of musical taste.

Among the earliest piano instructors at the *Conservatoire* was Jean-Louis Adam who was appointed in 1797 and remained on the faculty until 1842. His *Méthode de Piano,* published in 1802-04, served at the *Conservatoire* for many decades and was translated into German by Czerny in 1826. Among Adam's students were such celebrities as Kalkbrenner and Herold, both prize winners of the *Conservatoire.*

Adam,[11] an Alsatian like Hüllmandel and Edelmann, was born in 1758, began his music studies in Strasbourg, and continued them in Paris from 1777 on under the guidance of Edelmann. Adam's early compositions, published after 1778, were still under the influence of harpsichord concepts, with titles such as *Les regrets, Les tendres plaintes,* reminiscent of early French harpsichordists. Beginning in 1781, however, obviously under the impression of Clementi's brilliant appearance in Paris, Adam adopted a new pianistic style, evidenced in his Sonatas Op. 4 (1785) which are vigorous, dramatic, expressive, and effective. Typical of the — already mentioned — infiltration of operatic elements into piano music is the title of a lost work by Adam, *Sonate dans le genre d'ouverture.* In later years, Adam succumbed to the temptations of shallow virtuosity at the expense of musical values. His was by no means an isolated case, for the sensational success of the German pianist Daniel Steibelt, who settled in Paris in 1790, almost irresistibly forced his confreres into imitating his exhibitionist virtuosity. These were the days of potpourris and operatic fantasies, of bacchanales for piano with triangle and battle pieces where the noise of cannons, the cries of the wounded, and the chant of victory were described through puerile musical means. The new pianoforte, with its improved pedals, seemed ideally suited for these exploits. Even solid musicians like Clementi and Cramer had to bow occasionally to such demands, while publishers and composers hastened to cater to the fashion of the day.

It is appalling to see one serious pianist after another succumb to the popular trend. Aside from Adam, there were the brothers Jadin[12] — Hyacinthe (1769-1802) who, during his short life, was a favorite of the Parisian salons, and Louis (1768-1853) who succeeded his brother on the faculty of the *Conservatoire.* Louis Jadin, whose early compositions — published between 1787 and 1795 — were serious and highly promising, exhibited his "descriptive" talents also in the field of orchestral music, for in 1806, the *Conservatoire* orchestra performed his symphony *La bataille d'Austerlitz,* barely three months after the actual battle had taken place. Another fashionable pianist-composer was Louis Pradher, also a member of the *Conservatoire* faculty where he succeeded Boieldieu in 1803. Pradher is sometimes called "the true father of salon music,"[13] for among his students were such coryphaei as Henri Herz, Rosellen, and Hünten.

This generous trend toward fashionable popularity among the piano instructors of the *Conservatoire* makes one wonder whether this flightiness of musical standards was not, perhaps, responsible for the unimpressive showing of the French piano school during the early 19th century. This becomes particularly evident by comparing it to the spectacular achievements during the same period of the French violin school where such aberrations of taste were the exception rather than the rule. True, pianistic standards were high and technical proficiency was perfected constantly, but they did not serve musical ends. No wonder Chopin was appalled in viewing "so many virtuosi and so many asses."

***

In such an atmosphere of trivial shallowness, a figure like François-Adrien Boieldieu is indeed a relief. A friend and protégé of Louis Jadin, he nevertheless preserved his independence in matters musical. Born in Rouen in 1775, Boieldieu — like Méhul and so many other prominent French composers — received his first musical instruction from an organist; his teacher was the reputable Charles Broche, also well known as composer and harpsichordist.

Before coming to Paris in the fall of 1796, Boieldieu established an excellent reputation as pianist and composer in his home town of Rouen. Here he became acquainted with visiting celebrities, like the violinist Rode and the singer Garat, who facilitated his first steps in the capital. Garat introduced him to Louis Jadin who proved a most generous friend.

With the help of Jadin, Boieldieu was able to find a publisher for his first piano sonatas; and within the next few years he established his reputation as a pianist so firmly that he was appointed to the piano faculty of the *Conserva-*

toire in 1798. Although his position was that of a professor of "second class," this was indeed a high distinction for a young man of twenty-three, recently arrived from the provinces.

As a young piano teacher, Boieldieu was not a model pedagogue. One of his pupils, Fétis, writes about his students:

> Too occupied with his career as dramatic composer to take interest in lessons of instrumental technique, Boieldieu was a rather bad piano teacher; but his conversation was studded with very fine remarks on his art, full of interest for his students, and not without profit for their studies.[14]

To which Saint-Foix adds understandingly:

> I imagine that, while he was neglecting a bit his piano class, it is mainly about Mozart that he spoke to his students.[15]

At the time Fétis studied with Boieldieu, around 1800, the master was occupied with the composition of his opera *Le Caliphe de Bagdad:*

> Often he consulted us [so Fétis says] with charming modesty, and the piano lesson was spent while we grouped around him to sing the ensemble numbers of his latest opera.[16]

Most of Boieldieu's piano compositions[17] were written either shortly before or during his early tenure at the *Conservatoire.* The list of his instrumental works, published between 1795 and 1803, is impressive: some fifteen sonatas for pianoforte solo (Opp. 1, 2, 4, 6) and pianoforte with violin accompaniment (Opp. 3, 7, 8); a trio for piano, violin, and cello (Op. 5); numerous duos for harp and pianoforte; and a piano concerto, one of his earliest works, written in Rouen in 1792 and later published in Paris with a dedication to his friend Louis Jadin.

In contrast to the general trend toward virtuosity, Boieldieu maintains a noble dignity, seriousness of purpose, and sincerity of emotion. While his early piano works require an expert player, they do not overstress technical brilliance which is controlled by refined musical taste. There is no particular concession to the public taste, no lowering of musical standards, no yielding to the temptation of showmanship.

The date of Boieldieu's Sonatas Op. 1 is not definitely established. If we are to believe Jadin's claim[18] that he helped Boieldieu sell these sonatas to a publisher, their publication must have taken place after Boieldieu's arrival in Paris, i.e. in the fall of 1796; of course they may have been written earlier, in Rouen. For unexplained reasons, Favre[19] gives the publication year as 1795, but we tend to believe Jadin's statement although it was made almost forty years after the actual events took place.

Judging by the silence of contemporary French journals, the publication did not attract any particular attention. A few years later, the *Allgemeine musikalische Zeitung* printed a review of these early sonatas by Boieldieu who, in the meantime, had won considerable success in the field of opera:

> To practice these sonatas will be especially useful since they contain many very brilliant concert passages; yet they lie so well in one's hand that an expert player can get them at sight without spoiling his hands, as is the case with so many new sonatas of our modern German composers. The author is known as an agreeable composer for the voice in and outside of Prias, but not as instrumental composer; we may add that he seems to come from Clementi's school and his style is similar to that of this master, but he does not have Clementi's depth, wealth, and originality. Incidentally the sonatas are very long and could have been improved if the author had not repeated certain favorite sections, also if he had written at least one *Adagio*. However, he must have felt that his strength lies in the effective and the brilliant; and this may be true, for the *Andante* of the second sonata (the only one in the collection) is very insignificant.[20]

On the whole, praise and criticism are distributed fairly in this article. Perhaps the writer was not aware that he was reviewing the works of a twenty-year-old composer which, necessarily, were immature. Rather than compare them to the finished products of Clementi, we should like to draw a parallel between Boieldieu's Opus 1 and the early sonatas by Méhul of 1783-88. The works of these two young Frenchmen, both only twenty when they first grappled with the problems of the piano sonata, have certain traits in common: a definite refinement of piano writing, restraint in the use of virtuoso effects, and a tendency to carry sceno-operatic moods into instrumental music. Boieldieu, while somewhat inferior in the handling of sonata form and thematic development technique, takes greater interest in pianistic brilliance, and his thematic invention shows at times a martial and defiant mood so characteristic of the 1790's. For between the sonatas by Méhul and those by Boieldieu lies the Revolution; and while we do not wish to overstress the direct influence of certain historic events on artistic expression, it cannot be denied that the revolutionary events were almost immediately reflected in French music, adding vehemence and passion to the somber pathos and dignified nobility of the pre-revolutionary decade.

Boieldieu's sonatas show him from a most characteristic side: being a "natural" composer, he is obviously at ease when inventing a charming melody or expressing a nostalgic mood, but he becomes awkward when the sonata form requires intellectual accomplishment. Consequently, his expositions are usually full of ingratiating freshness, while he has little of interest to convey in his development sections. Strangely enough, Boieldieu avoids slow movements where his melodic gift could have expressed itself so happily, and cultivates the two-movement sonata. Such is the case in two of the three sonatas constituting Boieldieu's Opus 1.

The first, in G minor, consists of a *Moderato* and a *Rondo.* An "ardent and passionate"[21] mood pervades the opening movement which shows imagination and fluency in the handling of the keyboard. The *finale,* with an enchanting refrain, is vivacious, sparkling, and full of capricious rhythms. The French composers of that generation lavished particular care on their final *rondos* which show their Gallic spirit to best advantage, and Boieldieu was no exception.

The Second Sonata (in F major) has three movements— *Allegro moderato, Pastorale,* and *Prestissimo.* The opening movement is unusually long and starts with a beautifully lyric, singing, and expansive theme. A brilliant bridge leads to a less significant second theme, after which another set of transitory passages prepares an extensive *codetta,* or rather third theme, of an exquisite, pensive quality. The development section deals primarily with the first theme, interpreted dramatically and at times orchestrally, while the recapitulation follows the pattern of the exposition. The technical passages, brilliant and effective, are based mostly on broken chords, interspersed with some octaves and thirds; and being musically unimaginative, these passage sections appear overly long.

The second movement, a *Pastorale* in C major, is also too extended for its rather naive and slightly faded content. The form is that of a *rondo,* A-B-A-C-A-D-A-B-A, with the D section in contrasting minor.

The finale, *Prestissimo,* is not *"en rondo,"* as Favre erroneously states,[22] but in A-B-A form. Conceived as a sort of perpetual motion, it is keyed to sparkling velocity. The exuberant mood is akin to the *finale* of the so-called "Lark" Quartet by Haydn, with similarly continuous motion in rapid sixteenths. Most of the technical display is entrusted to the right hand while the left participates only occasionally. Harp-like use of broken chords, distributed among both hands, and some broken octaves constitute the most spectacular technical feats which, if measured by Clementi's standards, are modest indeed.

The third and last sonata of Opus 1, in B-flat major, returns to the two-movement pattern. The first movement, *Allegro brillante,* opens with a march-like, chivalrous theme which is followed by a contrasting lyric subject. In the development section, new material is introduced, adding variety and interest. The final movement, a *Rondo,* has the usual polish and fluency.

Boieldieu's Opus 1 was followed almost immediately by a second series of three sonatas, published as Opus 2, which show the composer in a partly different light.

Undoubtedly the most interesting work in the new set is the First Sonata, in F minor. The two movements, *Andante doloroso* and *Allegretto (Rondo),* represent late 18th century Romanticism in characteristic form: melancholic sadness and sentimental — almost tearful — expression, wistful charm and restrained emotion pervade the entire work (ex. V-7, V-8). Yet there are structural deficiencies impairing the over-all impression. By keeping both movements in the same key and mood, even to the point of abandoning virtuoso display, the composer is unable to stave off a certain monotony; here a contrasting middle movement would have brought welcome variety. Within the first movement, Boieldieu handles the sonata form somewhat mechanically: in the exposition, the themes appear strung together; the development lacks imagination, for it consists mainly of transposing the first theme into the major mode; and the recapitulation repeats the exposition almost literally. Thus, the first movement appears overly long, for the thematic material — somewhat bloodless though ingratiating — is unduly stretched and diluted. Yet there are charming details, such as the almost Chopinesque coda of the first movement, or the imaginative preparation of the last re-entry of the *rondo* theme.

Example V-7. Boieldieu, *Piano Sonata Op. 2 No. 1* (1796-97). First movement.

Example V-8. Boieldieu, *Piano Sonata Op. 2 No. 1.* Coda of First movement.

The Second Sonata of Opus 2, in E-flat major, employs a three-movement pattern: *Allegro moderato, Adagio non troppo,* and *Rondo.*

The first movement opens with a heroic theme in a dotted, march-like rhythm. Preserving this rhythm while changing the mood to gracefulness and piquancy is the second subject, which resembles a motive from an *opéra comique* rather than a sonata theme. Compared to the First Sonata, the melodic invention has less originality, but there is more technical brilliance.

The slow movement, in B-flat major, is pervaded by Mozartian serenity which expands with beautiful intensity in a middle section in F minor. There is no drama, only warmth and emotion; particularly noteworthy is the sensitive and meticulous distribution of nuances. The whole movement is a small, perfectly finished gem.

The final *Rondeau* (the word is spelled variously with either the Italian "o" or the French "eau" at the end) is a gay and brilliant movement, with a *minore* section stressing broken octaves, especially in the left hand.

As No. 3 in this set, we find a Sonata in C major which is less conventional in its sequence of movements. A short, introductory *Andante avec grâce* leads into an *Allegro brillante più Presto,* followed by a *Minuet* and a *Polonaise.*

The first *Allegro,* in keeping with the adjective *brillante,* surpasses all previous pieces by Boieldieu as to pianistic difficulty. Octaves, thirds, and other double stops are used frequently, while hand-crossings and velocitous passages add to the technical problems. The development section is more interesting than usual and modulates into distant keys, wandering as far as D-flat major. The abbreviated recapitulation begins with the second theme and uses the first theme as coda — a reversal often found in French operatic overtures of that period. The mood of this first movement is fiery, brilliant, and often orchestral.

The *Minuet,* in C minor, marked *Presto,* is actually a *scherzo.* While the term *minuet* continued to be used for *scherzo*-like movements during the early 19th century, this misnomer by Boieldieu is in fact a rather early example. To be sure, *minuets* — in the hands of Schobert, Haydn, and Mozart — had long ceased to be a courtly dance, but while these masters changed the dance character toward the lyric, dramatic, or folky, Boieldieu adds a "somewhat brutal rudeness."[23] A pleasant *Trio,* in C major, offers a well-planned contrast. The whole movement has almost orchestral vigor.

Little can be said about the *finale,* a *Polonaise,* which is overly long, thematically weak, and lacking in variety of harmony and rhythm — indeed much inferior to Schobert's imaginative treatment of this dance. Nevertheless, the whole sonata leaves an excellent impression.

Even more impressive are the *Deux grandes sonates* in D major and A minor, published as Opus 4, which testify to Boieldieu's continued growth as composer. His new position as professor at the *Conservatoire,* his closeness to Cherubini, and the rapidly increasing standards of piano virtuosity must have spurred him into making a special effort. His treatment of the sonata form becomes more supple while preserving charming details such as the extended *codetta;* his themes acquire amplitude without losing their occasional comic opera tinge; and his piano technique gains in brilliance and modernity. In discussing the Sonatas Op. 4, Favre says:

> More finished than the previous works, more personal in melody, richer and more varied in harmony, these sonatas certainly count among the best of Boieldieu. They reflect clearly his Romantic tendencies, and often foreshadow the art of a Weber.[24]

Saint-Foix comes to the same conclusion and calls Boieldieu "the French anticipation of Weber," enumerating such common traits as warmth, enthusiasm, chivalry, drama, caprice, and pianistic polish.[25]

A significant tendency, pointed out by Saint-Foix, is the ever-increasing length of Boieldieu's works: the first movement of Opus 1 No. 2 has 259 bars, the first movement of Opus 4 No. 1 has 282 bars, while the *Allegretto* of his *Grande sonate* Op. 6 (ca. 1802) has 394 bars. Saint-Foix considers such expansion a characteristic trait of the new century and calls it "Romantic" length. One need only compare the length of Beethoven's and Schubert's sonatas and symphonies with those by Haydn and Mozart to realize the truth of this observation. Unfortunately, the "new length," in the case of Boieldieu, did not always coincide with an expansion of content, and so we often find long stretches of insignificant, though effective, passage work.

In closing our discussion of Boieldieu's piano works, we may quote the excellent summary of Favre:

> Although written almost entirely in the closing years of the 18th century, Boieldieu's piano works actually belong to the 19th century, for they inaugurate brilliantly its tendencies and new spirit. The Romanticism which one could already discern in the works of Charpentier, Adam, and L. Jadin, affirms itself here more strongly, in the conception of form as well as in the character of ideas. If, by the spontaneity of inspiration, these compositions seem often akin to those of Mozart, they also announce, at times, the fantastic spirit of Weber. It is, therefore, regrettable

that Boieldieu ceased so early to write for piano in order to devote himself entirely to the theater. The rich promise of his youth awakened hopes for perfect works in his maturity which doubtless would have placed him on the same level as the great Romantic foreign pianists of the early 19th century. Nevertheless, his work, abundant and varied, holds an enviable place in the instrumental production of the period. Furthermore, by its chivalry and frankness, by its juvenile charm, it possesses an originality which is essentially French. [26]

**

With the beginning of the 19th century, the trend toward exhibitionist virtuosity increased enormously. London, Vienna, and Paris became training centers for pianists, while publishers flooded the market with trivialities. This trend increased, rather than diminished, as the century progressed, and seemed at a peak during the 1830's, when Robert Schumann tried in vain to stem the tide, using scorn and ridicule in the pages of his *Neue Zeitschrift für Musik.*

German historians, self-righteously, often blame the Parisian "salons" for the deterioration of musical taste, but they choose to overlook the fact that German virtuosi were among the leaders of the day — Steibelt, Hünten, and the brothers Herz. True, Paris accepted them with open arms, but so did Germany; the artists are to blame, not the public, exclaims Schumann.

One discusses so often the corruption of the public, but who has corrupted it? you the composer-virtuosos. I do not know of a single instance where the public has fallen asleep during a Beethoven concerto. [27]

While French participation in these pianistic "orgies" was comparatively modest, Paris continued serving as schooling center for pianists as well as providing an insatiable market for their virtuosic exploits. That the most prominent among the salon composers received their musical education at the *Conservatoire* is noteworthy and somewhat puzzling: Kalkbrenner, Jacques and Henri Herz, Franz Hünten, and Henri Rosellen were all alumni and prize winners of the *Conserva-*

toire. Their technical schooling was superb, yet they were obviously not taught how to utilize their pianistic proficiency for musical ends.

In castigating the "three arch-enemies" of music, Robert Schumann classified them as follows: (1) those without talent, (2) the "dime-a-dozen" talents, (3) the talented multi-scribes.[28] Obviously, Schumann judged every musician indiscriminately according to his accomplishments as composer, disregarding the fact that the distinction between composers and performers became increasingly pronounced. To judge virtuoso performers like Steibelt, Herz, and Thalberg mainly on the basis of their compositions — as Schumann often did — means to misrepresent their role. Their significant contribution was in the field of piano technique, and their compositions were merely a pretext to exhibit their virtuosity. To use the heavy artillery of formal musical analysis in discussing their innumerable musical products is futile, for their objective was not to create musical values but to explore and expand the technical potentialities of the pianoforte, and within these limitations they accomplished an important task. During the entire 19th century, there were, perhaps, only two artists equally great as composers and performers — Chopin and Liszt — and both abandoned the concert stage in favor of creative work.

***

Before the ascent of Liszt and Thalberg in the 1830's, the two most prominent pianists in Paris were undoubtedly Kalkbrenner and Henri Herz. Though of German origin, they became, by schooling and career, completely Gallicized and belong to the Parisian scene.

Friedrich Wilhelm Kalkbrenner, born near Berlin in 1785, entered the Paris *Conservatoire* at the age of fourteen and graduated two years later with the first prize. His teachers were Jean-Louis Adam in piano and Catel in harmony. In 1803, his father sent him to Vienna where he was befriended by Haydn and Albrechtsberger, Hummel and Clementi. Returning to Paris in 1806, Kalkbrenner established himself as successful performer and teacher. From 1814 to 1823 he lived in London, but the climax of his career came after he moved back to Paris in 1824, where he remained until his death in 1849.

When Chopin arrived in Paris in 1831, he was deeply impressed by Kalkbrenner's playing and ranked him higher than any pianist he had heard. So he wrote in a letter:

> ... I am very intimate with Kalkbrenner, the leading European pianist, whom I am sure you would like. (He is the only one whose shoelaces I am not fit to untie: all these people like Herz, etc. — I tell you they are mere boasters; they will never play better than he.)[29]

In another letter Chopin compared Kalkbrenner to Paganini. It is interesting to note that Herz's elegant brilliance impressed Chopin less than Kalkbrenner's steel-like perfection; perhaps he admired in Kalkbrenner what he lacked himself: impeccable control of mechanism, independent of mood or disposition.

Chopin's admiration found tangible expression in the dedication of his Piano Concerto in E minor to Kalkbrenner, who reciprocated by writing variations on a mazurka by Chopin. In Schering's opinion, Chopin's dedication had an "inner reason,"[30] for he believes that Chopin's E minor Concerto was influenced by Kalkbrenner's Concerto Op. 61 in D minor; indeed there are certain affinities of thematic invention and pianistic treatment.

The total list of Kalkbrenner's compositions is long and varied; among the more important works are four piano concertos, chamber music for piano and various instruments, and valuable *études* and studies. As a composer he was not without talent; unfortunately, the youthful freshness and spontaneity of his early works disappeared in later years, to be replaced by pompousness and technical display. In reviewing Kalkbrenner's Piano Concerto No. 4 (Op. 127), Schumann gives the following interesting opinion:

> If I were to say that I was ever a great admirer of Kalkbrenner's composi-tions, I should tell the untruth; nor can I deny that, in my younger years, I often enjoyed hearing and playing them, especially his first, spirited, really musical early sonatas which promised excellent things for the future and where there was not as yet any of the artificial pathos and that certain affected profundity which make us dislike his later greater compositions. Now that we have a clear picture of his accomplishments, we can see that the D minor Concerto was his highest peak, the work which showed all the bright sides of his pleasant talent, but also his limitations . . . Yet it is laudable that he did not lose the courage (though perhaps the strength) to struggle forward a few more steps. Here we find the rare case that an older composer attempts to follow a younger. In this Concerto (Op. 127) we can see unmistakably the influence of the young Romantic world... It does not work, it does not suit him; he has no talent for Romantic im-pudence . . . He should keep to his old, well-deserved reputation as one of the cleverest piano composers, a master in his work for fingers and hand — we prefer it to his four-voice fugatos, insincerely nostalgic suspen-sions, etc.[31]

This article was written in 1836. By that time, Kalkbren-ner's elegant and graceful style began to appear faded, for a new thundering generation, led by Thalberg and Liszt, began to occupy the foreground of the pianistic stage. Kalkbrenner's method of playing, based on exclusive finger technique, his flying octaves and sixths produced solely by the wrist, were not geared to the orchestral sonorities of the younger genera-tion; these young titans refused to be tamed, pianistically speaking, by such mechanical devices as the *chiroplast,* a machine recommended by Kalkbrenner to enforce an im-mobilized position of the hand at the keyboard.

Kalkbrenner was not alone in being displaced from the Olympus by Thalberg and Liszt; there was also Henri Herz, fifteen years his junior, whose reign as pianistic idol of Paris between 1825 and 1835 was shaken. Born in Vienna in 1803, Henri Herz entered the Paris *Conservatoire* in 1816 where he studied with Pradher and Reicha, and graduated two years later. During the height of his career, Henri Herz surpassed in popularity every rival, not only as one of Europe's most celebrated virtuoso, but also as an immensely successful composer of "salon music" for the piano. In his innumerable fantasies, *rondos,* potpourris, and variations, Henri Herz deliberately catered to the musical fashion of the day; yet he had certain compositorial ambitions as can be seen from his eight piano concertos, sonatas, chamber music, and various study works. That his reputation in Paris was durable and firmly established is proved by his appointment to the faculty of the *Conservatoire* in 1842, a post which he held until 1874. In 1845 he undertook an extensive concerto tour through North and South America and described his — often amusing — adventures in a book entitled *Mes voyages en Amérique* (1866). He died in Paris in 1888, eighty-five years old.

The compositions of Henri Herz must be taken as a typical reflection of the public's taste during the 1820's and 1830's which, as we have said before, was deteriorating steadily, especially in matters concerning the piano. That such decline should take place while Beethoven, Schubert, Weber, Mendelssohn, and Schumann were writing master-works for the piano is a curious historical paradox. Viewing the crazed success of Herz and his consorts, one can only admire the steadfastness of contemporaries like Mendelssohn and Schumann who refused to compromise. No writer spoke more vigorously against the perversions of "salon music" and its idol Herz than Schumann; no other artist was riled more mercilessly in his *Zeitschrift für Musik* than Herz. One can discuss him (1) sadly, (2) humorously, or (3) ironically, says Schumann in one of his reviews, meaning that one can discuss him in any way but seriously.

> The Second Concerto by Herz is in C minor and may be recommended to those who like the first. Should on the same program a certain C minor symphony be presented, one would do well to play it *after* the concerto.[32]

Yet, even Schumann realized that it was pointless to harp on the compositorial weakness of Herz, and admitted that the study of his bravura pieces raised the general technical level, an advance which, some day, would be used for better purposes. "All this has its good points even for us Beethovenians."

Herz' true significance lies in his furtherance of piano technique which he treated in a glittering and velocitous, rather than ponderous, way.

Already Chopin used broken chords and passages with the greatest sensibility — frequently with the melody in the middle voices; with Herz, this art celebrated its greatest orgies. Aside from Liszt, hardly anyone, up to then, had utilized jumping technique and lightning-fast tone repetitions more systematically than Herz.[33]

This paragraph by Schering makes it appear as if Herz merely followed in the footsteps of Chopin and Liszt; actually he preceded both of them, and his keyboard style possesses already many characteristic traits which we admire so much in Liszt, Chopin, and — to a lesser degree — in Thalberg. Indeed, Herz' piano style is quite "modern," much more so than Kalkbrenner's, who never freed himself completely from the drawing room technique of Hummel and his Viennese school. There is a certain piquancy and coquettishness in Herz' piano style which is reminiscent of de Bériot's violin style; both belong to the 1820's. Just as de Bériot stands between the older French School of Rode-Baillot and the Romanticist Vieuxtemps, so Herz forms the connecting link between the older school of Clementi-Hummel-Kalkbrenner and the modern triumvirate Liszt-Chopin-Thalberg.

***

CHAPTER 6

Chamber Music

In discussing chamber music of the late 18th and early 19th centuries, one should be aware of a certain cleavage which appeared in the 1750's and persisted for almost one hundred years: on one side, chamber music favoring one "solo" instrument at the expense of its partner or partners; on the other side, chamber music based on equal partnership among the participating instruments.

Belonging to the first, the "solo" type, are the keyboard sonatas with violin accompaniment, so popular between 1740 and 1790; the trios and quartets for clavier with accompanying (at times optional) string instruments, represented mainly by Johann Schobert and his school; and the *quatuor brillant,* i.e. string quartets with a brilliant first violin and three subordinate string parts, cultivated primarily by violinist-composers.

As for the keyboard in ensemble music, it must be said that neither Haydn nor even Mozart succeeded quite in curbing its domination, and a truly equal partnership between pianoforte and string instruments was not established until Beethoven's Trios Opus 1 appeared in 1795. Long afterwards, however, fleet-fingered pianists like Hummel, Kalkbrenner, and Herz continued to compose "chamber" music in which a few timid string or wind players would be cowed by a thundering pianist. Even Chopin's Piano Trio Op. 8 (1828-29) and Cello Sonata Op. 68 (1847) or César

Franck's early Piano Trios Opp. 1 and 2 (1841-42), though musically far superior, still favor the piano; and remnants of this tendency can be detected in some of Mendelssohn's and Schumann's chamber music works for piano and strings.

The Parisian composers between 1780 and 1830 cultivated both types of chamber music. While the virtuoso composers, pianists and violinists alike naturally favored their instruments at the expense of their partners, there was a group of serious-minded composers — Cherubini, Reicha, and Onslow — who wrote their chamber music works in the tradition of equal partnership established by the Viennese classical school.

∗∗∗

Many of the sonatas by Hüllmandel, Méhul, and Boildieu, published in Paris between 1775 and 1800, were composed for harpsichord or pianoforte with violin accompaniment; however, the violin parts were so subordinate, if not optional, that it would be futile to discuss these works as "chamber music."

An important step toward equalization of partnership was made by Boieldieu in his Trio Op. 5 "for forte-piano with accompaniment of violin and cello obbligato," written around 1800 and originally published under the title Sonata.[1] Although the piano is still favored, the string instruments are holding their own, and the cello is occasionally used for the presentation of themes.

The work consists of three movements, somewhat unusual in the case of Boieldieu who preferred a two-movement arrangement, omitting a slow part. The well-constructed opening *Allegro* is followed by a short, slow *Lamentabile con espressione* which leads without interruption into the finale, *Allegretto con spiritoso*. The second movement, a pretty but superficial "lamentation," evokes exaggerated praise from Saint-Foix[2] who finds it

so poignant in its expression that one begins to regret the almost complete absence of *adagios* in the instrumental works of Boieldieu: it is a
kind of plaint, of supplication so intense that one wonders by which
means the author arrives at such a pathetic, yet so simple and effective,
result.[2]

The corner movements are vivacious and lively, and the
themes have occasionally a comic opera gaiety. The sonata
form is handled adequately though somewhat mechanically;
in order to fill a larger form, Boieldieu resorts to diluting,
rather than developing, its content. There are extended
stretches where the music just idles along, as for instance
the middle section of the *finale,* filled with chordal progressions in the piano part (about four measures given to each
chord) while the cello provides an occasional *pizzicato* and
the violin supplements some harmonies. Yet, this "development" which, to us, appears so dull and unimaginative, found
an admirer in Favre who describes it as "extremely ingenious,
well conducted, and where the dramatic vigor is combined
with very curiously chosen sonorities."

If the Trio by Boieldieu lacks the occasional sparks of
genius which characterized the chamber music of Schobert,
it shows greater maturity in the handling of the ensemble
idiom. Schobert was a pioneer in the field of keyboard chamber
music; during the thirty years separating him from Boieldieu,
the idiom lost its experimental character and acquired tradition and assurance. While Haydn's contribution in the field of
keyboard chamber music is relatively small, Mozart — standing firmly on Schobert's shoulders — evolved an idiom which
was to remain the code until superseded by Beethoven's
larger concepts.

The significant fact about Boieldieu's Trio is its comparative independence from Vienna and, more specifically,
Mozart. Disregarding the detour via Vienna, Boieldieu chose
to take his inspiration directly from Schobert and the Parisian
tradition. Yet, his work is by no means entirely retrospective;
written at the juncture of two centuries, it has the serenity
of the 18th century intermingled with a languorous, somewhat affected sentimentality pointing toward the 19th

century and the approaching Romantic period. Boieldieu's position, transitional and pivotal, can be compared — within the French orbit — to that of Weber.

An important facet of Boieldieu's talent is his feeling for balance and measure, controlled by his innate good taste. In general, French composers resisted the deterioration of musical taste so widespread during the early 19th century. The Parisian "dégringolade musicale," described so contemptuously by young Mendelssohn in 1825,[5] did not affect the fundamental musical culture of France. Composers like Boieldieu, Auber, Méhul, and Herold, while writing popularly in the best sense of the word, never compromised their traditional French taste and resisted any encroachment of triviality, whether it came from beyond the Rhine or the Alps.

Examples of both can be found in the chamber music works of Ferdinand Paer, Friedrich Kalkbrenner, and Henri Herz.

Paer's *Trois grandes sonates pour le piano-forte avec accompagnement de violon et violoncelle* were published around 1811. Riemann called them erroneously "Violinsonaten mit Cello at libitum:"[6] actually both string parts are designated as optional and completely subordinated to the piano which is treated with great brilliance. The style of the music is decidedly hybrid: it retains a somewhat faded 18th century gentility, covered by a heavy make-up of aggressive 19th century piano virtuosity. This was the piano style of the new century, developed by men like Steibelt, Clementi, and Dussek — the first generation of pianists, not harpsichordists, who were building the new technique of the keyboard; and Paer took full advantage of these achievements. With regard to structure, Paer employed the classical sonata form for all three trios.

In Kalkbrenner's chamber music works, we find a combination of French brilliance tempered by Viennese tradition. The latter influence became weaker the more his career centered on London and Paris; therefore his earlier chamber music works, written under the fresh impression of his study years in Vienna, show better comprehension of chamber music style than those composed later.

Among his chamber music works with piano, we may single out a few characteristic examples: the Quartet Op. 2 for piano and strings; the Septet Op. 15 for piano, string quartet, and two horns; the Piano Quintet Op. 81 with clarinet, horn, cello and double bass; and the Trio No. 4, Op. 84, for piano, violin, and cello.

The Piano Quartet Op. 2 has a certain unpretentious freshness, especially in the first movement, although style and content are definitely faded. There is an attempt at unifying the movements by introducing a motive from the first movement into the *finale*. The piano part dominates, as is to be expected; yet, the violin is treated adequately and participates in the presentation of themes, as well as in some virtuoso display. Definitely subordinate are the viola and the cello. Although brilliant, the piano part offers nothing spectacular; the passages consist largely of scales, arpeggios, and broken octaves.

In the Septet Op. 15 in E-flat major, the ensemble balance is shifted in favor of the piano to such an extent that it could be called a piano concerto. This is already indicated on the title page; while the Quartet Op. 2 mentions all participating instruments on an equal footing, the Septet is entitled "for pianoforte with accompaniment of . . ." Despite all prominence, the piano part does not require any excessive technique and seems less difficult than contemporary works by Clementi.

In the *Grand Quintetto* Op. 81, the piano is "accompanied" by clarinet, horn, cello, and double bass. The clarinet part is written in C and can be played by a violin, while an alternate part is provided for viola to replace the horn, if necessary. The music — loud and furious, bombastic and inflated — is repellent in its pretentiousness. To make matters worse, the work is overly long, especially in the last movement which seems interminable and even includes a *fugato;* time and again, the pianist resumes his brilliant tirades. Aside from a short section in the slow movement entrusted to the accompanying instruments, the piano dominates from beginning to end. The keyboard technique employed in this Quintet is decidedly more advanced than in previous works.

Equally brilliant and overcharged with technical display is the Trio Op. 84; as an innovation, not only the piano but also the violin and cello are assigned a more virtuosic role. For this reason, we may assume, the term "accompaniment" was not used in the title. Takes as a whole, Kalkbrenner's ensemble compositions are typical manifestations of the virtuoso style in chamber music which was widespread during the first three decades of the 19th century.

Into this same category belongs the *Grand Trio* Op. 54 for piano, violin, and cello by Henri Herz, dedicated to "Monsieur L. Cherubini, Directeur du Conservatoire de musique," an homage from a successful alumnus to the director of his alma mater. Actually, this trio by Herz is less pretentious, more pleasant music than Kalkbrenner's inflated opus. The thematic invention and the technical passages are reminiscent of de Bériot's violin style: there is the same lilting, coquettish gracefulness, the same bounce and verve. The piano technique is elegant, fluent, and effective without being noisy. Although the violin and cello parts are designated as optional, they have a good deal to say, and a performance for piano alone, even with the cued-in notes provided for such an exigency by the composer, would prove very unsatisfactory.

***

Let us now turn our attention to chamber music without participation of the piano. Gossec, the most prolific French composer between 1750 and 1780, wrote a number of string trios and string quartets which, without being singularly original, preserved the intimacy and balance so essential for true chamber music. Yet the following generation could not resist the general trend toward virtuosity. In the hands of violinist-composers like Rode and Kreutzer, the string quartet became a display piece for the first violinist while the remaining three string parts were relegated to an accompanying role. This fad was by no means limited to France; even a solid musician like Spohr contributed to the hybrid genre of the *quatuor brillant* which, in fact, can trace its ancestry to the early string quartets of Haydn. Even in later years, Haydn occasionally favored the first violin, so that certain of his quartet movements resemble solo pieces for violin with string trio accompaniment. Violin virtuosos of those days took advantage of such opportunities with eagerness, and we have contemporary reports describing performances of some Haydn or Mozart quartet by a famous virtuoso (occasionally standing on the stage) "accompanied" by three unnamed players.

Yet, on the whole, the *quatuor brillant* had only an ephemeral existence, limited to the early decades of the 19th century; and none of the works written in this genre achieved any widespread popularity.

Among those who contributed to the repertoire of the virtuoso quartet was Pierre Rode, the leading violinist of his days. Cobbett[7] lists four string quartets (Opp. 11, 14, 15, and 16) without taking into consideration that some of these opus numbers may have contained more than one work, according to the custom of the period. At least, such is the case in Opus 11, consisting of two complete quartets which are typical examples of virtuoso quartet writing: the first violin plays a veritable concerto to the accompaniment of a string trio. The musical style is derived from the Viennese tradition of Haydn and Mozart, though diluted and deprived of all emotional intensity, flowing along smoothly and fluently without offering anything of particular interest or originality. Rode's inborn talent for composition was considerable, as some of his concertos show, but his limited schooling prevented him from dealing effectively with the difficult medium of the string quartet.

More productive was Rodolphe Kreutzer: fifteen published string quartets, six string trios (for two violins and cello), six sonatas for violin and cello, and a quintet for string quartet and clarinet or oboe are among his chamber music works. It becomes immediately obvious that Kreutzer's compositorial expertise was far greater and more diversified than Rode's; one need only examine his Quartets Op. 1 and 2, each consisting of six works. Opus 1 still clings to the brilliant style, for the title reads *quatuors concertans*. This qualifying adjective is dropped in the title of Opus 2 where we find better balanced workmanship, more artful elaboration, and an obvious desire to avoid the commonplace.

Five of the six quartets contained in Opus 2 are built in four movements, with a *minuet* in second place, which might be due to Mozart's influence. Opus 2 No. 5 follows a more independent pattern: it opens with an *Adagio* in G major, has an *Allegro agitato* in G minor as center movement, and closes with a *Grazioso* in ¾ time, not unlike a *tempo di minuetto*.   Fundamentally, Kreutzer does not deviate from the Haydn-Mozart tradition which seems to paralyze French instrumental composers into a kind of frozen conventionalism as late as the 1830's (e.g. Onslow). Yet, this idiom is handled with such assurance by Kreutzer that one is surprised by the early opus numbers. The Quartets Op. 1 are dated ca. 1790, when the composer was twenty-four years old; by that time he had already written several violin concertos and started to compose for the stage. The Quartets Op. 2 were published ca. 1795-1798 when Kreutzer competed successfully with Cherubini and Méhul as a favorite opera composer, not to mention at least eight violin con-

certos completed and performed. Thus, the early opus numbers must not deceive us: these are clearly the works of an
experienced composer. The Quintet for strings and clarinet
or oboe also belongs to the 1790's, as well as the sonatas for
violin and cello. Among his earliest works are some duos
for violin and viola, written in Versailles in 1783 at the age
of seventeen; we are reminded that young Kreutzer played
the viola professionally and in fact entered the Royal orchestra as a viola player in 1783 because there was no vacancy
in the violin section. In later years, Kreutzer followed the
trend of the time and collaborated with the harpist Charles
Bochsa in writing six *Nocturnes concertans* for harp and
violin (1822). Kreutzer was a composer of serious accomplishments and deserves to be remembered.

The chamber music works by Baillot, insignificant in
number and quality, need not detain us. While his creative
gifts were limited, he was supreme in other fields of musical
endeavor, especially in the performance of chamber music.
Thus, it is not surprising that Cherubini chose him as recipient of the dedication of his first three string quartets,
for they were conceived and written with Baillot's playing
in mind.

Cherubini's string quartets are among his best works. As
quartet composer, he stands between Haydn and Mozart on
one side and Beethoven on the other side. While accepting
the formal structure of the 18th century masters, he fills
these forms with more rhapsodic, more colorful content —
music that is often Romantic in mood and spirit without
losing its classicistic outline; in fact, he rarely deviates from
traditional patterns. In sheer craftsmanship, Cherubini is
the equal of any of the great masters: his quartet writing
is lucid, intelligent, and well-balanced, his thematic workmanship varied and interesting, and his gamut of expression
personal and often unconventional. His shortcomings are a
somewhat pallid melodic invention and his occasional in-

ability to weld a work together, to create unity out of various components; thus, his works in larger forms appear at times fragmentary and lacking in cohesion.

The First Quartet, in E-flat major, was composed in 1814 but not published until 1835. Bellasis[8] asserts that the work was "revived" by Baillot around 1829 without having received any previous performance; but it is unlikely that Cherubini withheld his first quartet for fifteen years without letting Baillot play it. This particular work, considered by many to be his best quartet, was a favorite of Schumann, Mendelssohn, and especially Joseph Joachim who performed it frequently.

At the time Cherubini composed his first quartet, the first ten of Beethoven's string quartets were already published, including the Opus 74 in E-flat major. Though we do not know which of these ten quartets were at the time known to Cherubini, we may assume that he was familiar with most of the important foreign publications.

In view of the identical key signatures of Cherubini's first and Beethoven's tenth quartet, it is tempting to search for similarities, but there is hardly any kinship between the works. One can point to the fact that both quartets start with a slow introduction, and that both first *Allegros* are built on a triad theme, but these are superficial — and probably accidental — similarities. Actually Cherubini maintains remarkable independence. His first movement, though not of startling originality, has freshness and spontaneity. The second movement, a *Larghetto sans lenteur* in B-flat major, consists of a set of variations which are much closer to Haydn than to Beethoven and impress the listener by their wide gamut of expression which ranges from lyric tenderness to powerful drama. The third movement, a *Scherzo* in G Minor, is perhaps the most Romantic of the four movements, for it heralds the elfin mood that was to become such a characteristic part of *Oberon* and the *Midsum-*

mer Night's Dream. Compared to the *scherzo,* the last movement appears somewhat dry and academic.

Biographers of Mendelssohn have occasionally pointed toward an alleged affinity between his first string quartet (Op. 12 in E-flat major) and Beethoven's Quartet Op. 74. Actually there are more obvious ties between Mendelssohn and Cherubini which can be easily seen when comparing their first string quartets. Mendelssohn's *Canzonetta* from Op. 12 resembles Cherubini's above-mentioned *Scherzo* in a startling way, especially in the fast-moving middle section where pairs of string instruments bounce along in a light *spiccato* bowing. We know of Mendelssohn's immense pleasure while playing viola in Cherubini's first quartet.[9] He may have become acquainted with it in 1825, during his visit to Paris; at that time, Cherubini's quartet was as yet unpublished, but the manuscript must have been available to Baillot with whom Mendelssohn was on friendly terms. Mendelssohn's string Quartet Op. 12 was completed in 1829, six years before Cherubini's first quartet was published; yet we are convinced that Mendelssohn knew Cherubini's work when writing his own quartet.

Cherubini's Second Quartet in C major, written in 1829, was merely a transcription of his Symphony in D major of 1815. Although fourteen years separated the Symphony from the quartet adaptation, Cherubini made hardly any changes in the music itself and limited his retouchings to minor adjustments (see pp. 130-134). The most important change consisted in replacing the original slow movement of the Symphony, unsuited for transcription because of its orchestral character, with an entirely new movement in A minor.

As a symphony, Cherubini's work was unsuccessful, and it did not fare much better as a quartet. Its thematic material, conceived along straightforward orchestral lines, did not lend itself easily to polyphonic treatment; thus, lacking both the

orchestral color of the symphony and the contrapuntal
finesse of a true quartet, the music often sounds monotonous
and uninspired. Robert Schumann expresses it in the following words:

> ... as symphony, this music sounded too much like a quartet; as quartet,
> it sounds too symphonic, and indeed I am averse to all such transmuta-
> tions, which I consider an offense against the divine first inspiration.[10]

Yet it would be wrong to underestimate this work which
shows a master's touch even in its weaker spots.

> A few dry passages, the work of intellect alone, can be found here as in
> most of Cherubini's works; but even then, there is still something interest-
> ing — be it in the setting, a contrapuntal finesse, an imitation; something
> that gives you food for thought. There is most spirit and masterful life
> in the *Scherzo* and the last movement. The *Adagio* has a strikingly in-
> dividual A minor character, something of a *Romanza,* something Provençal.
> After repeated hearings its charm opens up more and more; and the closing
> is such that you begin listening again though you know that the end is
> near.[11]

This *Adagio* which pleased Schumann so much is the
movement composed especially for the quartet version,
substituting for the *Larghetto* of the Symphony. It is doubtless the most inspired and imaginative movement of the entire
quartet, somehow evocative of the haunting mood of the
slow movement (also in A minor) of Beethoven's Quartet
Op. 59 No. 3. However, Cherubini does not sustain this mood
of pensive nostalgia but breaks the continuity by introducing
a somewhat vociferous section in A major. After modulating
to C major, new thematic material is introduced, the character
of which is at first lyric, then dramatic, with a slight overdose
of brilliance. The first theme returns in all its loveliness,
followed by the lyric part of the C major episode transposed
into A major. A coda of bewitching beauty closes the movement.

As for the other movements, they are singularly ineffective
in the quartet version, for most of their atraction consisted

originally in a typically orchestral *brio* and contrasting instrumental timbres.

Infinitely superior is the Third Quartet (in D minor) which Cherubini completed in 1831, at the age of seventy-one. All the more surprising is the youthful vigor, fire, and animation pulsating in this work. Form and idiom are handled with supreme mastery, the flow of melodic inspiration seems more abundant than usual, and the quality of the four movements is of such consistent excellence as to make this easily the best among Cherubini's quartets.

The first movement, *Allegro comodo,* opens with a theme of dual character: first a questioning, hesitating phrase, repeated twice (in its pattern slightly reminiscent of the opening of Mozart's String Quintet in G minor), followed by an agitated motive which, after six bars, is cut short by a sustained phrase. These three components of the first theme (or, better, theme group) are used skillfully in the development section, while the second theme — a rather capricious motive set against a clear-cut rhythmic background — is dropped until it reappears in the recapitulation. Of particular beauty and imagination is the extended coda which contains a condensation of the principal themes. The movement closes brilliantly in D major.

The slow movement, *Larghetto sostenuto,* in A-B-A form, is akin to Haydn, but achieves an almost orchestral climax toward the middle. Again we must admire the extended coda, wrought with exquisite finesse.

The ensuing *Scherzo* is an elaborate movement of considerable length, actually the longest of the four movements. The opening is treated as a *fugato,* with the theme played first by the cello, then by the viola, finally by the violins in octaves; and although the fugal technique is abandoned after the third entry of the subject, the *Scherzo* abounds with contrapuntal playfulness, such as imitations, canons, and so forth. As a complete contrast appears the middle section, *Moderato sans lenteur,* which is quite homophonic, graceful, bouncing, dominated by a coquettish theme in the first violin. The recapitulation of the *Scherzo* is even more elaborate and interpolates, toward the end, the motive of the middle section (*Moderato*). The vitality, humor, and drive of this movement are wholly admirable.

The finale, *Allegro risoluto* in D major, is fresh and engaging without offering any problems; the writing is less refined, the score resembling in parts a reduced version of an orchestral movement. However, after the significance of the first three movements, this *finale* serves its purpose to relax and release tension, and brings the work to an effective close.

Published as a set in 1835, these three quartets by Cherubini were generally well received and frequently performed, especially the first and third. However, the opinions of German musicians as to the value of these works were at least divided, and the reservations were made abundantly clear in an article by Schumann, written after a hearing of the first quartet in 1838. The question was one of style: used to the quartet idiom of Haydn, Mozart, and Beethoven which was established as a model, any deviation was resented, even if the originator was a master as universally admired and respected as Cherubini. In Schumann's every word we can feel the reticence of uttering a critical word about someone he esteemed so highly; yet he says:

> I confess that, after hearing this quartet (No. 1) for the first time, especially after the first two movements, I felt very uneasy; this was not what I had expected, many things seemed operatic and overloaded, others appeared small, empty, and peculiar (*eigensinnig*); perhaps it was the impatience of youth which kept me from understanding immediately the often strange language of the old man; for on the other hand I felt of course the dominating master . . . Certainly many will feel the same way; one must come to know the specific character of this, *his* quartet style; it is not the friendly mother tongue in which we are being addressed, but it is the noble foreigner who speaks to us; the more we learn to understand him, the higher we shall respect him . . .[12]

***

Between 1834 and 1837, Cherubini composed three additional string quartets which were not published until after his death. We can treat these posthumous works more summarily, for they show definite signs of declining creative power. He composed them more for himself than the public; "it keeps me busy and amuses me, for I do not have the slightest pretension"[13] wrote the seventy-seven year old master to his young friend Hiller in 1837. Of course, there is the usual craftsmanship which, however, cannot compensate for the withering of creative inspiration. The most satisfying of the set is the Sixth Quartet in A minor; in the *finale,* Cherubini introduced what, to him, was an innovation, namely a brief recapitulation of the principal themes from the three previous movements — a procedure which, after Beethoven's Ninth Symphony, became increasingly frequent as the century progressed. The other two quartets, No. 4 in E major, and No. 5 in F major, offer nothing remarkable; they seem less ambitious and elaborate than their predecessors and cannot claim more than historic interest.

Following the last quartet, Cherubini completed a string quintet (with a second cello) which remained unpublished. The work, in E minor, was begun on July 30, 1837 and finished on October 28, 1838; the same season it was played for a select circle of friends, with Baillot as first violinist, and created a deep impression. Cherubini's biographer Schemann[14] speaks highly of this work which he finds full of freshness and imagination, and far superior in concept and inspiration to the last quartets. Incidentally, Cherubini planned to write several string quintets, as he confided to Hiller in a letter, but never came to realize this project. Thus, this string quintet remained the "swan song" of the great master, full of autumnal beauty, crowning a rich creative life.

***

The towering personality of Cherubini dwarfs contemporaries like Reicha and Onslow. Yet, though their works are now largely forgotten, they contributed considerably to the literature of chamber music and enjoyed the respect of their fellow musicians and connoisseurs.

Antonin Reicha (1770-1836) spent altogether thirty years of his life in Paris. His first visit was comparatively short: he arrived in 1799, as a young composer in search of recognition, and left rather disappointed two years later. The second time, more mature and settled, he made Paris his permanent home and remained there from 1808 to his death in 1836. His main source of livelihood was teaching, at first privately, then — from 1817 on — as member of the *Conservatoire.* His prestige as teacher of theory and composition was such that many leading Parisian musicians, long past their study years, sought his guidance and advice. Yet, Reicha's influence transcended that of teaching; reared in the same tradition and environment as Beethoven — both studied with Neefe in Bonn and with Haydn in Vienna — Reicha was the foremost exponent, in Paris, of the Viennese school and tradition; he was also considered an authority on Bach and Handel, then almost unknown in France. Reicha and his circle provided a bulwark against the inroads of shallow salon music sweeping Paris during the early 19th century; it is certainly no mere coincidence that, among his disciples, were Baillot and Habeneck who contributed so immeasurably to the propagation of good music in Paris. One of Reicha's biographers, Emmanuel, ascribes the "spiritual formation of Habeneck"[15] to Reicha, which certainly goes too far, for Habeneck — as well as Baillot — knew and performed Haydn, Mozart, and Beethoven long before they came into closer contact with Reicha.

Incidentally, Reicha's attitude toward Beethoven was by no means uncritical; he rarely mentioned the name of Beethoven in his theoretical treatises and never quoted examples from his works. Berlioz, who studied counterpoint with Reicha at the *Conservatoire,* left us the following testimony:

> ...I have often heard Reicha speak rather coldly about the works of Beethoven and comment with ill-disguised irony on the enthusiasm which they caused.[16]

Nevertheless, Reicha's compositions written during his stay in Vienna (1802-08) show Beethovenian influences and even "direct reminiscences."[17]

Through his teaching and his theoretical works, Reicha transmitted the sum-total of his experience and schooling to a generation of young French musicians who generously testified to his singular gifts as pedagogue. Adolphe Adam, composer of the popular *Postillon de Longjumeau,* says in his *Souvenirs* (1857):

> Reicha was as quick as Eler [co-professor of counterpoint at the Conservatoire] was slow. In his class one covered the counterpoint in one year; in Eler's one needed five.[18]

Berlioz expresses himself similarly:

> Reicha's lessons in counterpoint were singularly lucid; in a short time he taught me a great deal, without waste of words; and unlike most masters, he generally explained to his pupils the meaning of the rules he wished them to obey.[19]

To have formed such divergent students as Onslow, Rode, Liszt, Gounod, Berlioz, Adam, and César Franck, testifies to Reicha's flexibility of pedagogical approach. Aside from giving his students a solid craftsmanship, he imbued them with his own indefatigable quest for unusual harmonic and rhythmic combinations. He prided himself on his intellectual, quasimathematical, approach to musical composition, and appears almost like a predecessor of Joseph Schillinger. Berlioz quotes Reicha as saying:

> It is by the study of mathematics that I have succeeded in achieving a complete mastery over my ideas; by this means I have subdued and tem-

pered my imagination which used to run away with me; and now that it
is controlled by reason and reflection, it has doubled its power.[20]

Unfortunately, little of this reasoning penetrated into
Reicha's own compositions, which are partly academic and
conventional, partly stilted and contrived. He either "followed
the routine which he despised"[21] or became artificial and, at
times, impalatable in his quest for originality at all costs.

Among the works Reicha wrote in Paris between 1808
and 1826 were a symphony, performed at the *Conservatoire*
in 1809; several overtures and operas; and many chamber
music works for various combinations, including his famous
twenty-four wind quintets (Op. 88, 91, 99, and 100), written
between 1810 and 1820.

The first of these quintets (for flute, oboe, clarinet,
bassoon, and French horn) was begun in 1810 but did not
satisfy the composer. After further studies, he completed,
within the next four years, a set of six wind quintets (later
published as Op. 88), one of which was performed at the
Conservatoire in 1814.

The following year, five prominent Parisian wind players
joined forces to present regular subscription concerts in the
foyer of the *Théâtre Italien* in order to make Reicha's quintets
known. Since four of the players had received Reicha's
instruction in composition, they brought special devotion to
their task. At first, these concerts aroused widespread interest,
but gradually the novelty wore off so that only thirty subscribers remained in February 1819, after which the series
was ended.

Nevertheless, Reicha's quintets continued to be performed at irregular intervals in small circles of connoisseurs,
for Spohr reports that he was present in 1821 at a rehearsal
of the Quintets Op. 100 during which lists were circulated
"to fish for subscribers."[22] The quintets were also heard occasionally at the *Concerts spirituels* and the student concerts
of the *Conservatoire*.[23]

There was nothing particularly new about the idea of composing for wind ensembles, considering the rich literature of serenades, cassations, and divertimenti by Haydn, Mozart, Beethoven, and a host of minor composers. A model particularly close to Antonin Reicha was the *Parthien* of his uncle Josef Reicha,[24] published in the 1780's, which employed similar combinations of instruments. Antonin Reicha differed from his predecessors inasmuch as he abandoned the rather loose sequence of serenade-like movements, which he replaced by the stricter four-movement pattern of the sonata form. In other words, he shifted his quintets from the lighter divertimento genre into the more serious one of chamber music. In workmanship and effectiveness, his wind quintets were compared to the string quartets by Haydn, as the following contemporary review proves:

The effect produced by these quartets (sic!) of our gifted compatriot, is in its way the most perfect I ever witnessed, as far as musical execution is concerned. It is impossible to imagine a more coordinated, discreet, and yet sparkling precision, a more effective performance . . . If it were possible to surpass Haydn in the composition of quartets and quintets, it would have been achieved by Reicha with these quintets. It seems to me impossible to combine more correctness and clarity with more invention and originality.[25]

Much more reserved is Berlioz' comment:

His quintets for wind instruments were the fashion for a time in Paris. They are interesting, but rather cold.[26]

More thorough in his observations is Spohr, who finds Reicha's quintets

rich in interesting harmonic sequences, truly correct in matters of voice leading, and effective in the individualized use of the wind instruments, however often faulty in matters of form. Mr. Reicha is not sufficiently economical with his ideas and presents, often at the very beginning of his piece, four to five themes, each of which closes on the tonic chord. Less abundance, in this case, would mean more wealth. His periods, too, are often poorly connected and sound as if he wrote one yesterday, the other today. However, his minuets and scherzos, being short pieces, are less susceptible to these objections, and some of them are, in form and content, real masterpieces.[27]

It is strange indeed that, despite all erudition and self-criticism, Reicha was unable to eliminate these shortcomings; for it is true that most of his first movements suffer from an over-abundance of thematic material obscuring the musical structure while, at the same time, precluding any true development of themes.

His slow movements are usually kept simple, in *lied* form or theme and variations, while his *minuets* lean toward the character of a *scherzo* or waltz. The *finales* often transgress the limits of chamber music by being frankly operatic in the choice of thematic material.

Reicha's treatment of the five wind instruments is highly idiomatic which seems natural considering the fact that he was a professional flutist. In his scoring for quintet, however, he does not always succeed in spreading the material evenly among the five instruments, and there is a tendency of favoring flute and oboe at the expense of the lower instruments which are frequently confined to accompaniments. Despite Reicha's obvious endeavor to be unconventional, particularly by means of harmonic piquancies, his musical language is fundamentally that of an epigone of the Viennese classical school, of Haydn and Mozart, with an occasional pre-Romantic, "Schubertian," coloring.

Reicha's numerous chamber music works — piano trios, string quartets, and compositions for mixed groups of string and wind players — do not show him in any new light. His reputation rested firmly on his wind quintets which were admired even by those who, like Cherubini, were otherwise cool toward his creative efforts. In fact, Reicha's appointment to the *Conservatoire* was primarily due to the success of these quintets.

***

"There was no better master; he knew the full important secret of teaching,"[28] George Onslow said of his master Reicha. Onslow studied privately with Reicha for only a few months during which he supposedly covered the field of harmony and composition — indeed a record for speed, if not for thoroughness.

However, Onslow did not come to Reicha entirely unprepared: he had already composed three string quintets, a string quartet, some piano trios, and a piano sonata; yet he had written these works as autodidact, guided mainly by assiduous studies of Haydn and Mozart. At the age of twenty-two, Onslow wrote his first string quintet and — being independently wealthy — had it published almost immediately, in 1807. Only later did he realize his technical shortcomings and sought Reicha's advice. Such was his gratitude to his master that he refused to be considered for the *Académie* ahead of him; this highest honor was bestowed upon Onslow in 1842 when he was elected to succeed Cherubini.

Three nations lay claim to Onslow: England, because he was a grandson of the first Lord Onslow and because his father was British; France, for he was born in Clermont-Ferrand and his mother was French; and Germany, because of his affinity to German music. The German historian Riehl says in an essay on Onslow:

His works belong...to the realm of German music...as an artist he is naturalized with us...Only two masters of foreign nationality have chosen the string quartet as their main field — Boccherini and Onslow.[29]

There is a certain justification in this claim; despite the fact that Onslow spent years in London where he studied piano with Dussek and Cramer, and that he lived in France during most of his mature life, his music is steeped in the German, or — more precisely — in the Viennese tradition. Although he spent only a few years in Germany, he was aware of the progressive trends in German music and knew the works of Beethoven, Spohr, and Mendelssohn. Yet, in his music there are very few, if any, traces of "modernism": occasionally a chromatic progression, a rhythmic intricacy, a mannered melodic twist indicate a desire for more originality, but this seems affectation rather than conviction. At heart, Onslow was a classicist, almost entirely content in following Haydn, Mozart, and the younger Beethoven, using their forms and language without questioning their validity. Occasionally, his French temperament breaks through, so in the day, *chanson*-like *finales* in duple time or in the *Minuet* of the String Quartet Op. 10 No. 2 where he uses an "Air de danse des montagnes d'Auvergne" (he was born in the Auvergne). In his String Quintet No. 15, Op. 39 of 1829 he attempted a bit of program music: having suffered a hunting accident while the work was in progress, he included movements describing Pain, Suffering, and Recovery. The Quintet became known and popular as the "Quintet of the bullet." Onslow arranged his String Quintet No. 10, Op. 32 for full orchestra; it became his Third Symphony (1834).

Onslow's works, though epigonal, are well-proportioned and agreeable, and written with considerable fluidity and elegance. Too well-bred to be either passionate or dramatic, Onslow prefers to remain on the surface rather than probe any depths of feeling — a charming *causeur* who knew how to talk fluently without saying much. The remarkable fact about Onslow is that his limited talent was taken so seriously for so long by so many: not only did his quartets and quintets remain popular with amateurs during most of the 19th century, but even a critic of Schumann's stature admits Onslow into the inner circle of chamber music composers. In discussing the "strangeness" of Cherubini's quartet style, Schumann says:

> Now one has become accustomed to the manner of the three well-known German masters (Haydn, Mozart, Beethoven), and has — in fair recognition — admitted to this circle also Onslow and Mendelssohn as followers of the former.[30]

The list of Onslow's chamber music works, as given by Cobbett,[31] comprises no less than 34 string quintets, 36 (*recte:* 35) string quartets, six violin sonatas, three cello sonatas, to which — not mentioned by Cobbett — should be added ten trios for piano, violin and cello. Onslow also wrote a few works for combinations of string and wind instruments: a nonet for flute, oboe, clarinet, horn, bassoon, string quartet, and double bass (*ad libitum*); a septet for piano, flute, oboe, clarinet, horn, bassoon, and double bass; and a sextet for the same combination of instruments without the oboe.

The string quintets, which have remained his most popular works, calls for two cellos (following the model of Boccherini rather than Mozart, who doubled the viola); however, a double bass can be substituted for the second cello. The idea to include a double bass in a string quintet seems to have been accidental, as Chouquet recounts:

At a certain performance in England the second violoncello failed to arrive, and it was proposed that Dragonetti should play the part on his double-bass. Onslow positively refused, saying the effect would be dreadful. However, after waiting some time, he was obliged to consent, and after a few bars was delighted with the effect. After this he wrote them [the quintets] for cello and double-bass, and the preceding ones were then rearranged in that way under his own inspection by Gouffé, the accomplished double-bass of the Paris Opéra.[32]

Onslow's chief merit lies in his persistence in upholding the serious standards of chamber music composition during a period when French music was swept by glittering salon pieces. In resisting this trivialization of taste, Onslow thus joined a small but important group of musicians — among them Cherubini, Méhul, Baillot, Kreutzer, Habeneck, and Reicha in the 1810's and 1820's, reinforced in the 1830's by Berlioz, Chopin, Liszt, Urhan, and Franchomme. That even Chopin and Liszt compromised occasionally with the "salon," only proves the strength and temptation of the modish genre and adds significance to Onslow's uncompromising attitude.

***

Music for violin and piano
The Duo brillant

Among French composers of the time, the sonata for violin and piano never gained much favor. The genre did not lend itself to virtuoso display, and there was little demand for such works. It was the custom for violin soloists to appear with orchestra or with string quartet, very rarely with piano. True, Baillot played the sonatas by Beethoven at his chamber music soirées, but there was no comparable French repertoire to speak of.

As the pianoforte grew in popularity, so did the combination of piano and violin. More and more often, two famous virtuosos — one a pianist, the other a violinist — would appear in joint concerts and create their own repertoire. The genre became known as *Duo brillant,* usually under joint authorship. How the actual compositional work was done remains a mystery, but the technical aspects were clearly divided, each virtuoso taking charge of his own instrument. The objective was to impart a maximum of idiomatic brilliance to each of the parts. The over-all framework was usually an operatic fantasy, a set of variations on themes from one of the popular operas of the day.

The genre became particularly popular in the 1820's, in keeping with the general trend toward increased virtuosity. If one of the two authors was also a good composer (like for example Moscheles), the resulting work might be quite respectable. Suffice it to name some of the collaborators: Charles Lafont with Ignaz Moscheles and Henri Herz; Charles de Bériot with George Osborne and Sigismond Thalberg; H. W. Ernst with Stephen Heller; Vieuxtemps with Anton

Rubinstein. The genre disappeared, to be absorbed by the sonata for violin and piano which in turn gained in brilliance.

The Violin Duo

A peculiar type of chamber music, which flourished during the late 18th and early 19th centuries, was the violin duet, i.e. works for two violins without accompaniment. They were usually written by violinist-composers, either for public performances (the *Duo brillant*) or, more modestly, as chamber music and for teaching purposes. The most valuable contribution in this specialized field was made by Viotti who wrote more than fifty such duets. Although less personal than his violin concertos, they contain nonetheless a great deal of ingratiating music written in the Haydn-Mozart tradition. Many of his disciples, among them Kreutzer and Baillot, recognized the pedagogical value of such an instrumental combination and continued in his footsteps, though in a less prolific way. Most productive in this field, however, were Ignace Pleyel and Féréol Mazas, whose duos, some very easy, others of medium difficulty, are still widely used today; and indeed many of these unpretentious works are tuneful, piquant, and ingenious in their deliberately limited exploitation of the instruments. Pleyel (1757-1831), Austrian by birth, French by adoption, was one of the most popular composers in the 1780's and 90's, and his works earned the approval even of Mozart and Haydn. In 1795 Pleyel settled in Paris where he entered the music publishing business, to which he added the manufacturing of pianofortes, and so he gradually ceased to compose. Mazas (1783-1849), on the other hand, devoted his life to the violin, concertizing and teaching, and his many *études* and compositions, full of melodic charm, are still highly valued and universally used.

***

Summary and Conclusion

The roots of musical Romanticism in France reach back to the 1760's when the brooding, dark-hued, expressive style of Johann Schobert, the German-born keyboard master, became fashionable, obliterating the traditional *style rocaille* of the French. Despite Schobert's premature death in 1767, his influence remained strong until the Revolution, as evidenced in the keyboard compositions of Edelmann, Hüllmandel, Méhul, and Mozart. Similar trends toward sentimentalism can be found in French violin music of the 1760's and 1770's while, on the other hand, the symphonic school, headed by the prolific Gossec, remained blissfully unaffected by any emotionalism. This co-existence of *style galant* and pre-Romantic *Empfindsamkeit* in 18th century music is the norm, rather than the exception, throughout Europe, and can be traced in the works of C. P. E. Bach, Johann Stamitz, Giuseppe Tartini, Joseph Haydn, and W. A. Mozart.

While Europe regained its composure after the emotional upheaval of Storm and Stress, while Haydn and Mozart succeeded in fusing and sublimizing *style galant* and *Empfindsamkeit* into a style of classical perfection, we see French music follow its own independent course and continue its search for emotional expressiveness. During the 1780's the French predilection for tragic, pathetic, or nostalgic accents increased rather than diminished. Under the impact of the Revolution of 1789, the dark-hued undercurrent in French music erupted into a musical style of dramatic drive, impassioned action, fiery defiance, and militant assertiveness. Characteristic of the turbulent revolutionary decade were the "terror" and "rescue" operas; the masters of the new style were Méhul, Cherubini, Lesueur, Kreutzer, Berton, and Gaveau — the group of "revolutionary Romanticists," as we have called them. This style found its immediate reflection in French instrumental music, notably the violin concertos of Viotti, Rode, and Kreutzer, and — naturally — in the operatic overtures which were also used as independent concert pieces and influenced the evolution of symphonic style.

Thus, French music during the 1790's presents a picture markedly different from that of the general European scene. Mozart died in 1791, without experiencing (though prophetically foreshadowing) the new trends; Haydn was too settled in his own ways to remold his style. It was Beethoven who absorbed the full impact of the French revolutionary Romanticists — a fact not always recognized in all its significance by his biographers. After Beethoven, we see Weber and — to a lesser degree — Schubert and Mendelssohn accept certain French influences.

While the musical style of French revolutionary Romanticism spread throughout Europe, spicing the Austro-German sentimental nostalgia with chivalrous, dramatic, and realistic accents, the French themselves experienced a classicistic recession during the 1800's and 1810's. We see Cherubini strive toward Mozartean balance and perfection (*Faniska,* 1806), Méhul turn toward Italianized *opera buffa* (*L'irato,* 1801) or biblical repose (*Joseph,* 1807), while Spontini personifies the cold, massive pompousness of the Napoleonic Empire (*La vestale,* 1807; *Fernand Cortez,* 1809). Only Lesueur's *Ossian* retains some of the pre-Romantic flavor, but the work was written before the turn of century, though not performed until 1804.

Weber's *Freischütz* (1821), the first truly Romantic opera, found the French unprepared, for they still admired the cold glitter of Spontini's *Olympie* (1819). When Weber's master-piece reached Paris in 1824, it was received coolly at first, and its growing success was due partly to a quick adaptation of the work itself to French taste, and partly to a gradual conditioning of French taste to Weber's musical language.

Within a short time, Romanticism conquered the French lyric stage. *La dame blanche* (1825) by Boieldieu is called the "French counterpart" of the *Freischütz* by a German historian.[1] Boieldieu's contribution is a vivid illustration of the inner link between the 1790's and the 1820's: born in 1775, he spent his formative years in revolutionary Paris where he produced his first opera in 1796. *La dame blanche* was not the work of an exploring newcomer, but the mature product of a composer steeped in the tradition of Cherubini and Méhul. The same can be said about Auber and Herold who followed in his path.

In the field of instrumental music, French Romanticism lagged until Berlioz entered the scene with the overtures to *Waverley* and *Francs-Juges* (1827-28). And he remained alone, unless we choose to include Liszt and Chopin in the French orbit — alone among his French confreres in his devotion to instrumental music, though he attempted to widen its ex-pressive gamut by the addition of vocal parts or an explana-tory program. Next to his towering personality, such mani-festations as de Bériot's and Vieuxtemps' violin compositions, César Franck's immature Piano Trios Opp. 1 and 2 (1841-42), or Félicien David's infantile quintets and the naive sym-phonic ode *Le désert* (1844) appear decidedly second-rate.*

It is strange indeed that the French, whose musical style of the 1790's stimulated and propelled European Roman-ticism, failed to participate more fully in the consumma-tion of musical Romanticism. For Berlioz is a seemingly isolated phenomenon, neither accepted by his contem-poraries as truly representative of France, nor even con-sistently Romantic in his own life work — "an artist without ancestry and without posterity," to repeat Ernest Newman's

* for better music,
try
Louise Farrenc
Leon Krautzer

quote.[2] Yet the isolation is not as complete as it appears at first glance; upon closer study, we discover the threads connecting the grandiosely flamboyant Berlioz of the 1830's and the revolutionary Romanticists of the 1790's — the kinship between the *style énorme* of the revolutionary festival and the *Symphonie funèbre et triomphale,* between the multiple vocal and instrumental choirs of Lesueur and Méhul and the *Requiem,* between the picturesque, evocative "nature" music of Cherubini and scenes in the *Fantastic Symphony* and *Harold in Italy.*

This continuity is important for a full comprehension of French musical Romanticism. One can compare it to a majestic mountain range with two peaks separated by a valley; despite certain differences of outline and consistency, both peaks belong to the same mountain range. The first peak, gently prepared between 1760 and 1789, was reached during the revolutionary decade of the 1790's, while the second arose rather suddenly between 1825 and 1830. Separating the two is the classicistic recession of the 1800's and 1810's. Contemplated in such a manner, French musical Romanticism of the 1830's ceases to be a belated step in the wake of similar European trends and appears as a second flowering, obviously related to its first manifestation during the 1790's when the French revolutionary Romanticists boldly expanded the gamut of musical expressiveness.

***

Notes on Sources

Introduction

1. Julien Tiersot, *La musique aux temps romantiques* (Paris, 1930), p. 18.
2. Ernst Bücken, *Handbuch der Musikwissenschaft* (Leipzig, 1928-1934), vol. VI, pp. 135-36.
3. Michel Brenet, *Les concerts en France sous l'ancien regime* (Paris, 1900; reprint ed. New York, 1970).
4. A. A. Elwart, *Histoire de la Société des Concerts du Conservatoire impériale de musique* (Paris, 1860).
   Arthur Dandelot, *La Société des Concerts du Conservatoire de 1828 à 1897* (Paris, 1898).

Chapter 1

1. *The Letters of Mozart and His Family*, trans. Emily Anderson (London/New York, 1938), vol. II, pp. 706-7.
2. Cf. Brenet, *Les concerts en France sous l'ancien regime*.
   Constant Pierre, *Histoire du Concert Spirituel* (Paris, 1975).
3. M. de Chabanon, *Observations sur la musique* (Paris, 1779), quoted in L. Striffling, *Esquisse d'une histoire du goût musical en France au 18e siècle* (Paris, 1912), pp. 259-60.
4. Michel Brenet, "La librairie musicale en France de 1653 à 1709," *Sammelbände der Internationalen Musikgesellschaft* VII (1907), pp. 401-66.
   G. Cucuel, "Quelques documents sur la librairie musicale au 18e siècle," *Sammelbande der Internationalen Musikgesellschaft* XIII (1912), pp. 385-92.
5. Cf. C. Pierre, *Les facteurs d'instruments de musique* (Paris, 1893).
6. J. de La Borde, *Essai sur la musique ancienne et moderne* (Paris, 1780), quoted in Striffling, p. 270.
7. A. E. M. Grétry, *Memoires ou Essais sur la musique* (Paris, 1789), vol. I, p. 78, quoted in Striffling, p. 271.
8. E. F. Curtius, *The Civilization of France*, trans. O. Wyon (New York,

1932), p. 87.

9. J. Combarieu, *Histoire de la musique* (Paris, 1935), vol. II, p. 402.

10. A. V. Arnault, *Souvenirs d'un sexagénaire,* quoted in A. Pougin, *Méhul* (Paris, 1893), pp. 86-88.

11. J. Gaudefroy-Demombynes, *Histoire de la musique française* (Paris, 1946), p. 188.

12. Dandelot, p. 2. However, the *Concerts Feydeau* were still in existence in 1797 when a symphony by Méhul was played there.

13. "Maîtrises," *Grove Dictionary*, 5th ed.
Octave Fouque, *Les révolutionnaires de la Musique* (Paris, 1882), pp. 14-16, sets the figure at 800.

14. The letters patent, dated 29 March 1672, permitted Lully to organize special music schools wherever necessary for the good of the Opéra. Cf. Combarieu, vol. II, p. 423.

15. F. Hellouin, *Gossec et la musique française à la fin du 18e siècle* (Paris, 1903), p. 50.

16. Cf. C. Pierre, *L'école de chant à l'Opéra de 1672 à 1807* (Paris, 1896).

17. *Chronique de Paris*, 10 January 1793. Quoted in Combarieu, vol. II, p. 426.

18. Combarieu, vol. II, p. 433.

19. Combarieu, vol. II, p. 385.

20. *Encyclopédie de la musique et dictionnaire du Conservatoire* (Paris, 1931), Part I, vol. III, pp. 1578-80, 1623-27.

21. Ibid., p. 1622.

22. Ibid., pp. 1587-90.

23. *Allgemeine musikalische Zeitung* II (May 1800), p. 588.

24. *Allgemeine musikalische Zeitung* III (December 1800), pp. 217-18.

25. Castil-Blaze, "Bâton de mesure," *Dictionnaire de musique moderne* (Paris, 1821).

26. Julien Tiersot, *Les fêtes et les chants de la Révolution française* (Paris, 1908), pp. 249-50.

27. *Le Moniteur*, 3 vendémiaire, quoted in F. Lamy, *Le Sueur* (Paris, 1912), p. 66.

28. The rebuilt chapel was inaugurated in 1806.

29. Lesueur, his successor, had a better balanced group: 40 singers and 20 instrumentalists (cf. Lamy, p. 104), which grew to 55 singers and 43 instrumentalists in 1806.

30. Marie et Léon Escudier, *Vies et aventures des cantatrices célèbres* (Paris, 1856), p. 3.

31. Combarieu, vol. II, p. 438.

32. J. F. Reichardt, *Vertraute Briefe aus Paris* (Hamburg, 1804), vol. III, p. 86.

33. *Allgemeine musikalische Zeitung* II (July 1800), p. 711.

34. *Allgemeine musikalische Zeitung* III (January 1801), p. 270.

35. *Allgemeine musikalische Zeitung* IV (October 1801), p. 47.

36. *Allgemeine musikalische Zeitung* VI (February 1804), pp. 312-13.

37. *Allgemeine musikalische Zeitung* V (August 1803), p. 791.

38. *Allgemeine musikalische Zeitung* VII (February 1805), p. 303.

39. Quoted in C. Pierre, *Le Conservatoire nationale de musique et de déclamation* (Paris, 1900), p. 461.
40. Ibid.
41. Quoted in Pierre, *Le Conservatoire*, p. 463.
42. All three reviews in Pierre, pp. 468-69.
43. *Allgemeine musikalische Zeitung* XI (June 1809), p. 604.
44. *Allgemeine musikalische Zeitung* XIII (October 1811), p. 737.
45. *Allgemeine musikalische Zeitung* XI (August 1809), pp. 748-51.
46. *Allgemeine musikalische Zeitung* XIV (November 1812), p. 736.
47. *Allgemeine musikalische Zeitung* XIII (November 1811), p. 761.
48. *Allgemeine musikalische Zeitung* VII (May 1805), p. 528.
49. *Allgemeine musikalische Zeitung* VI (February 1804), p. 313.
50. Quoted in J.-G. Prod'homme, *Les symphonies de Beethoven* (Paris, 1906; reprint ed. New York, 1977), p. 19.
51. *Tablettes de Polymnie* (March 1811), quoted in Prod'homme, p. 61.
52. Ibid, p. 121.
53. Cf. Boris Schwarz, "Beethoven and the French Violin School," *The Musical Quarterly* XLIV (October 1958), pp. 431-47.

Chapter 2

1. Louis Spohr, *Autobiography* (London, 1878; reprint ed. New York, 1969), vol. II, p. 114.
2. Ibid., vol. II, pp. 127-30.
3. Ibid., vol. II, p. 122.
4. Ibid., vol. II, p. 123.
5. Ignaz Moscheles, *Recent Music and Musicians* (New York, 1873; reprint ed. New York, 1970), pp. 26-27.
6. Spohr, vol. II, p. 132.
7. Moscheles, p. 24.
8. Stendhal (Henri Beyle), *Vie de Rossini* (Paris, 1823).
9. Henri-Montan Berton, *De la musique mécanique et de la musique philosophique* (Paris, 1821).
10. Joseph d'Ortigue, *De la guerre des dilettanti* (Paris, 1829).
11. F. Liszt, "De la situation des artistes et de leur condition dans la société," *Revue et Gazette musicale* (May 3, 1835). Reprinted in F. Liszt, *Pages romantiques* (Paris, 1912), pp. 1-83. Incident reported on pp. 38-40.
12. S. Hensel, *Die Familie Mendelssohn* (16th ed., 1918), vol. I, pp. 174-76.
13. Adolphe Jullien, "Weber à Paris en 1826," *Paris dilettante au commencement du siècle* (Paris, 1884), pp. 7-66.
14. Ibid., p. 53.
15. Alfred Loewenberg, *Annals of Opera, 1597-1940* (Cambridge, 1943), p. 337.
16. Hector Berlioz, *Memoirs*, ed. Ernest Newman, trans. R. and E. Holmes (New York, 1932), pp. 58-59.
17. Ibid., p. 63.

18. Méhul, *Eloge* on Gossec, read at the Institute in 1808. Quoted in *Encyclopédie de la Musique*, Part I, vol. III, p. 1639.

19. Berlioz, pp. 40-41.

20. Ibid., p. 31.

21. Victor Hugo, quoted in Raymond Evans, *Les romantiques français et la musique* (Paris, 1934), pp. 94, 144.

22. Curtius, pp. 98-99.

23. Stendhal, *Racine et Shakespeare. Etude sur le Romantisme* (Paris, 1823/ 25), pp. 33-35, 40.

24. Alexandre Dumas père, *Mémoires*, quoted in C. H. C. Wright, *A History of French Literature* (New York, 1912), p. 660.

25. Alfred de Musset, *La confession d'un enfant du siècle* (Paris, 1836), Chapter I, translated in Frederick B. Artz, *France Under the Bourbon Restoration* (Cambridge, 1941), p. 269.

26. Jouffroy, "Comment les dogmes finissent," *Le Globe*, 1824. Quoted in Artz, *Reaction and Revolution* (Cambridge, 1931), p. 203. Cf. also T. R. Davies, *French Romanticism and the Press: The Globe* (Cambridge, 1906).

27. Quoted in Frederick Niecks, "Romanticism in Music," *Musical Times* (1 December 1899), pp. 802-805.

28. E. T. A. Hoffman, *Kreisleriana* (Bamberg, 1816). Reprinted in *Musikalische Novellen* (Regensburg, 1919), pp. 60-61.

29. Cf. A. Schering, "Aus den Jugendjahren der musikalischen Neuromantik," *Jahrbuch Peters* (1917), p. 52.

30. Quoted in Prod'homme, p. 61.

31. Berlioz, p. 49.

32. *Revue musicale* III (1828), p. 145.

33. All documents pertaining to this matter are published in C. Pierre, *Le Conservatoire national*, pp. 180-85.

34. *Encyclopédie de la musique*, Part II, vol. III, p. 1645.

35. "Exposé de moyens que l'on peut prendre pour mettre en évidence les résultats des travaux de l'École royale." Quoted in Pierre, *Le Conservatoire*, pp. 471-72.

36. Cf. A. A. Elwart, p. 61.

37. *Revue musicale* III (1828), pp. 145-49.

38. Berlioz, pp. 76-77.

39. *Revue musicale* III (1828), pp. 199-206.

40. Ibid., pp. 273-76.

41. Berlioz, p. 78.

42. Prunières, "French Chamber Music," *Cobbett's Cyclopedic Survey of Chamber Music* (Oxford, 1929).

43. See Jacques Barzun, *Berlioz and the Romantic Century* (New York, 1950), vol. I, p. 73.

44. *Revue musicale* III (1828), pp. 422-24, quoted in W. J. Turner, *Berlioz: The Man and his Work* (London, 1939; reprint ed. New York, 1974), p. 89.

45. Berlioz, pp. 94-95.

46. Alfred Einstein, "Beethoven's Military Style," in *Essays on Music* (London, 1958), p. 246.

Chapter 3

1. Julien Tiersot, "La symphonie en France," *Zeitschrift der Internationalen Musikgesellschaft* III (July 1902), pp. 391-402.

2. Barry S. Brook's definitive study, *La symphonie française dans la seconde moitié du XVIIIe siècle* (Paris, 1962) has contributed much to a reevaluation of that period.

3. Paul Henry Lang, *Music in Western Civilization* (New York, 1941), p. 791.

4. B. G. E. de Lacépède, *La poétique de la musique* (Paris, 1785).

5. Ernst Bücken, *Handbuch der Musikwissenschaft* (Leipzig, 1928-34), vol. V, p. 235.

6. Lang, p. 791.

7. Cf. Heinrich Strobel, "Die Opern von E. N. Méhul," *Zeitschrift für Musikwissenschaft* VI (April 1924), pp. 362-402.

8. C. M. von Weber, "Joseph in Aegypten," in *Sämtliche Schriften*, ed. Georg Kaiser (Berlin, 1908), pp. 278-79.

9. Grétry, *Mémoires*, vol. II, p. 60, quoted in Henri Lavoix fils, *Histoire de l'instrumentation* (Paris, 1878), p. 339.

10. Quoted in R. Brancour, *Méhul* (Paris, 1913), p. 91.

11. H. Berlioz, *Evenings with the Orchestra*, trans. Jacques Barzun (New York, 1956), p. 355. Berlioz's entire essay on Méhul (pp. 344-55) is enlightening.

12. A. Pougin, *Méhul...* (Paris, 1893).

Brancour, *Méhul.*

H. de Curzon, "Méhul," in *Musiciens du temps passé* (Paris, 1893).

13. H. Kretzschmar, *Geschichte der Oper* (Leipzig, 1919).

H. Botstiber, *Geschichte der Ouvertüre* (Leipzig, 1913).

14. *Mercure*, 12 May 1792, quoted in G. Favre, *Boieldieu* (Paris, 1944), vol. I, p. 85.

15. P. M. Masson (1937), quoted in Favre, ibid.

16. Strobel, pp. 369ff.

17. Strobel, pp. 376-78.

18. Pougin, pp. 145-46.

19. Brancour, p. 104.

20. Lavoix, p. 340. This error found its way into Botstiber's *Geschichte der Ouvertüre*, p. 163.

21. Quoted in Pougin, p. 188.

22. Weber, pp. 279-80.

23. Cf. Botstiber, pp. 154-62.

24. M. and L. Escudier, "Musiciens de l'Empire," *Vie et aventures des cantatrices célèbres* (Paris, 1856), p. 3.

25. *Courrier des Spectacles*, 29 January 1797, quoted in Pougin, pp. 138-39.

26. David Charlton, "Two Lost Symphonies Found," paper presented at the Cambridge Conference on 19th Century Music, 7 July 1980. See also Charlton's preface to the score editions of Méhul's *Symphony No. 1* (Madison, WI: A-R Editions, in preparation), and to *Symphonies Nos. 3 and 4* (New York: Garland Press, 1982). I am grateful to Prof. Charlton for his permission to quote from his as yet unpublished writings. In the Méhul chapter, all comments ascribed to Charlton are taken from one of the above listed sources.

27. Sauvo's review and Méhul's answer are in Pougin, pp. 300-03.

28. Anton Schindler, *Beethoven in Paris* (Münster, 1842), p. 3.

29. *Journal de Paris*, 14 March 1809. Quoted in Alexander Ringer, "A French Symphonist at the Time of Beethoven: E. N. Méhul," *The Musical Quarterly* XXXVII (1951), p. 548.

30. Quoted in Pougin, pp. 302-03.

31. Quoted in Charlton, paper presented at Cambridge Conference.

32. Entire review quoted in Pougin, p. 304.

33. Pougin, "Notice sur Méhul par Cherubini," *Rivista musicale italiana* XVI (1909), p. 750.

34. *Revue musicale* IV (1830), pp. 152-3.

35. E. J. Fétis, *Biographie universelle des musiciens*, 2nd ed., vol. VI, p. 61.

36. Tiersot, "La Symphonie...", p. 391.

37. Brancour, pp. 108-09.

38. Schumann, *Gesammelte Schriften* (Leipzig, 1888), vol. II, p. 169.

39. We are quoting from the analysis of Charlton since the scores of Méhul's Symphonies Nos. 4 and 5 were not yet available at the time of this writing.

40. Hermann Kretzschmar, "Über die Bedeutung von Cherubinis Ouvertüren und Hauptopern für die Gegenwart," *Jahrbuch Peters* XIII (1906), pp. 77-91.

41. Romain Rolland, "Gluck and Alceste," in *Essays on Music* (New York, 1948), p. 208.

42. R. Hohenemser, *Cherubini...* (Leipzig, 1913).

43. L. Schemann, *Cherubini* (Stuttgart, 1925).

44. Quoted in Edward Bellasis, *Cherubini* (London, 1874; reprint ed. New York, 1971), p. 153.

45. Riemann, *Geschichte der Musik seit Beethoven*, p. 144.

46. A. Holzapfel's report, quoted in Walter Dahms, *Schubert* (Berlin, 1914), p. 9.

47. Cf. Otto Erich Deutsch, *The Schubert Reader* (New York, 1947), p. 28.

48. Schemann, p. 345.

49. Alfred Einstein, *Music in the Romantic Era* (New York, 1947), quoted in *The Musical Quarterly* XXXIII (October 1947), p. 574.

50. Review in *Allgemeine musikalische Zeitung* II (1800), p. 733.

51. Weber, *Sämtliche Werke*, p. 65.

52. *Le Censeur*, quoted in Pougin, *Méhul*, p. 138.

53. Ibid., pp. 137-38.

54. Cf. Bellasis, p. 107.

55. Botstiber, *Geschichte der Ouvertüre*, pp. 150-51.

56. Kretzschmar, "Über die Bedeutung...."

57. Cf. Bellasis, pp. 113-15.

58. Schemann, pp. 379-80.

59. Quoted in Bellasis, pp. 120-22.

60. Both quoted in Bellasis, p. 123.

61. Weber, p. 107.

62. Quoted in Bellasis, p. 137.

63. Kretzschmar, "Über die Bedeutung...," p. 82.

64. *Allgemeine musikalische Zeitung* VII (January 1805), p. 245.

65. Kretzschmar, p. 82.

66. Schemann, p. 418.

67. Bellasis, pp. 151-52.

68. Ibid., pp. 153-54.

69. Encyclopédie de la musique et dictionnaire du Conservatoire, Part I, vol. III, p. 1606.

70. Letter to I. Moscheles, 30 November 1839. In F. Mendelssohn, Letters, ed. G. Selden-Goth (New York, 1945), p. 286.

71. Review by F. W. H., quoted in Bellasis, p. 208.

72. Schemann, pp. 629-30.

73. An early "symphony" of Cherubini, performed in 1785 in Paris at the Concert Spirituel, may be identical with a Chaconne for strings, flutes, oboes, bassoons, horns, trumpets, and timpani, which he composed in London in 1785 (cf. Schemann, p. 629).

74. Musikwissenschaftlicher Verlag, Leipzig and Vienna, 1935.

75. R. Schumann, On Music and Musicians, ed. K. Wolff (New York, 1946), p. 240.

76. See Schemann, p. 630.

77. E. Hanslick, Aus dem Concert-Saal (Vienna, 1870), p. 372. The untranslatable original reads "kunstvoll geflochten, sorgfältig gebunden, vornehm getragen — aber doch ein Zopf."

78. Schemann, pp. 630-31.

79. Karl Nef, Geschichte der Sinfonie und Suite (Leipzig, 1921), p. 170.

80. Schemann, p. 630.

81. Bellasis, p. 213.

82. Quoted in Pougin, Herold (Paris, 1906), p. 20.

83. Ibid., p. 22. See also Pougin, "La jeunesse d'Herold," Revue et Gazette musicale XLVII (1880), pp. 169f., 194.

84. J. Tiersot, "La symphonie en France," Sammelbände der Internationalen Musikgesellschaft III, p. 391.

85. Encyclopédie de la musique et dictionnaire du Conservatoire, Part I, vol. III, p. 1669.

86. F. Hellouin and J. Picard, Catel. Un musicien oublié (Paris, 1910).

87. He noted his impression after a performance in 1847 (cf. Schumann, Gesammelte Schriften, vol. III, p. 162).

88. Berlioz, Memoirs, ed. Newman, p. 77.

89. Schemann, p. 31.

90. This is described rather humorously by Adolphe Adam in Derniers souvenirs d'un musicien (Paris, 1859), pp. 290-93.

91. H. Lavoix fils, La musique française (Paris, 1891), p. 140.

92. Kretzschmar, Geschichte der Oper (Leipzig, 1919), p. 250.

93. Ibid.

94. David Cairns, in The Memoirs of Hector Berlioz, ed. Cairns (New York, 1975), pp. 550-51.

95. Ibid., p. 106.

96. Weber, p. 72.

97. Allgemeine musikalische Zeitung XI (August 1809), p. 763.

98. H. Berlioz, Evenings with the Orchestra, trans. Jacques Barzun (New York, 1956), pp. 176-77.

99. Ibid., p. 176.

100. See H. Kretzschmar, "Die musikgeschichtliche Bedeutung Simon Mayrs," *Jahrbuch Peters* XI (1904).

101. H. Berlioz, *Evenings*, p. 177.

102. E. Newman, *Berlioz, Romantic and Classic*, ed. Peter Heyworth (London, 1972), p. 26.

103. Berlioz, *Memoirs*, ed. Newman, p. 46.

104. Quoted in Jacques Barzun, *Berlioz and the Romantic Century* (Boston, 1950), vol. I, p. 152.

105. Berlioz, *Memoirs*, ed. Newman, p. 45.

106. R. Schumann, *On Music and Musicians*, p. 189.

107. Mendelssohn, *Letters*, p. 230.

108. Schumann, *Gesammelte Schriften*, vol. II, p. 107.

109. Schumann, *On Music and Musicians*, p. 189-90.

110. Berlioz, *Memoirs*, ed. Newman, p. 103.

111. Berlioz, *Memoirs*, ed. Cairns, p. 104.

112. Ibid., p. 528.

113. H. Berlioz, *A Selection from His Letters*, ed. H. Searle (New York, 1966), p. 23.

114. Ibid., p. 26.

115. Ibid., p. 29.

116. Berlioz, *Fantastic Symphony*, ed. E. T. Cone (New York: Norton Critical Score, 1971), p. 28.

117. Barzun, *Berlioz and the Romantic Century*, vol. I, p. 156.

118. Ernest Newman, *Berlioz, Romantic and Classic*, ed. P. Heyworth (London, 1972), p. 168. (The essay "Schumann on the *Symphonie fantastique*" was written in 1933).

119. See reference note 116, pp. 249-77.

120. Mendelssohn, Letter to I. Moscheles, 7 February 1834, in *Briefe aus den Jahren 1830-1847* (Leipzig, 1875), pp. 18-19.

121. Berlioz, *Fantastic Symphony*, ed. Cone, p. 13.

122. Berlioz, *Letters*, ed. Searle, p. 33.

123. Berlioz, *Memoirs*, ed. Newman, p. 114.

124. See B. Schwarz, Introduction to *The Symphonies of Herold and Onslow* (New York: Garland Publishing Inc., 1981), p. XXXVIff.

125. Barry S. Brook, "Symphonie concertante," *The New Grove Dictionary* (London, 1980).

126. Brook, "The Symphonie concertante: An Interim Report," *The Musical Quarterly* XLVII (October 1961), pp. 493-516 (quote on p. 503). See also Brook, "The Symphonie concertante: Its Musical and Sociological Bases," *International Review of the Aesthetics and Sociology of Music* VI (1975), pp. 9-28.

Chapter 4

1. Arnold Schering, *Geschichte des Instrumentalkonzerts* (Leipzig, 1905), p. 171.

2. Ibid., p. 169.

3. A. Pougin, *Viotti et l'école moderne du violon* (Paris, 1888), p. 5.

4. *Berliner Musikzeitung* (1794), report from London, quoted in W. J. von Wasielewski, *Die Violine und ihre Meister*, 5th ed. (Leipzig, 1919), p. 170.

5. Pougin, *Viotti*, p. 86.

6. Ibid., p. 22.

7. L. de la Laurencie, *L'école française de violon de Lully à Viotti* (Paris, 1922-24), vol. II, p. 396.

8. Andreas Moser, *Geschichte des Violinspiels* (Berlin, 1923), pp. 389-90.

9. Miel, "Rode," *Dictionnaire historique des musiciens*, ed. Choron and Fayolle (Paris, 1810-11), vol. II, p. 227.

10. Remo Giazotto, *Giovan Battista Viotti* (Milan, 1956), pp. 291-368.

11. G. B. Viotti, *Four Violin Concertos, Vol. I* (Nos. 7 and 13), ed. and with a preface by Chappell White (Madison, WI: A-R Editions, 1976).

12. Archiv Produktion No. 2533-122. Stereo.

13. Baillot, quoted in Pougin, *Viotti*, pp. 122-23.

14. Schering, "Aus den Jugendjahren der musikalischen Neuromantik," *Jahrbuch Peters* (1917), p. 58.

15. Pougin, *Viotti*, p. 149.

16. Giazotto, p. 153.

17. Chappell White, "Toward a More Accurate Chronology of Viotti's Violin Concertos," *Fontes Artis Musicae* III (1973), pp. 11-124, especially p. 124.

18. Andreas Moser, *Joseph Joachim, Ein Lebensbild* (Berlin, 1908-10), vol. II, pp. 241-42.

19. Berthold Litzmann, *Clara Schumann* (Leipzig, 1909), vol. III, p. 375.

20. J. Joachim and A. Moser, *Violinschule* (Berlin, 1905), vol. III, p. 86.

21. Moser, *Joachim*, vol. II, pp. 243-44.

22. Leopold Auer, *Violin Master Works and Their Interpretation* (New York, 1925).

23. Carl Flesch, *Die Kunst des Violinspiels* (Berlin, 1928), vol II, pp. 165-69.

24. Schwarz, "Beethoven and the French Violin School."

25. Joachim and Moser, vol. III, p. 246n.

26. Quoted in Arthur Pougin, *Notice sur Rode* (Paris, 1874), p. 10.

27. Louis Spohr, *Autobiography* (London, 1878; reprint ed., New York, 1969), vol. I, pp. 61-62.

28. J. F. Reichardt, *Vertraute Briefe aus Paris* (Hamburg, 1804), vol. I, p. 403.

29. *Allgemeine musikalische Zeitung* V (February 1803), p. 333.

30. Ibid., quoted in Moser, *Violinspiel*, p. 399.

31. *Allgemeine musikalische Zeitung* IX (June 1809), p. 601.

32. Spohr, vol. I, p. 165.

33. Letter to Archduke Rudolph, 29 December 1812, in *The Letters of Beethoven*, trans. Emily Anderson (London, 1961), vol. I, p. 391. See also Schwarz, note 24.

34. *Glöggl's Musikzeitung*, quoted in Wasielewski, *Beethoven* (Leipzig, 1895), vol. I, p. 330.

35. *Allgemeine musikalische Zeitung* XI (June 1809), p. 601.

36. *Allgemeine musikalische Zeitung* (1800), No. 41.

37. Ernst Ludwig Gerber, "Kreutzer," *Neues historisch-biographisches Lexikon* (1812-14), vol. III, p. 118.

38. Fétis, "Kreutzer," *Biographie universelle des musiciens*, vol. V, pp. 106-09.

39. Henri Expert, Preface to Kreutzer's *42 caprices* (Paris, 1915).

40. Gerber, vol. III, p. 116.

41. Fétis, *Biographie*, 2nd ed., vol. V, pp. 106-107.

42. Gerber, vol. III, p. 116.

43. Expert, Preface.

44. See B. Schwarz, "Beethoven."

45. Joachim and Moser, *Violinschule*, vol. III, p. 104.

46. Dimitris Themelis, *Etude ou Caprice* (Munich, 1967), pp. 101-103.

47. Fétis, "Baillot", *Biographie*, vol. I, p. 219.

48. Thayer-Deiters, *Beethoven*, 3rd ed., vol. III, p. 502.

49. Quoted in Wasielewski, *Die Violine*, p. 389.

50. Cf. *Allgemeine musikalische Zeitung* VI (April 1804), p. 474 and XII (February 1810), p. 331.

51. Cf. Marc Pincherle, *Feuillets d'histoire du violon* (Paris, 1927).

52. H. Prunières, "French Chamber Music," in Cobbett, *Cyclopedic Survey*, vol. I, pp. 430-34.

53. *Wiener Musikzeitung* (1817), quoted in Wasielewski, *Die Violine*, pp. 389-90.

54. *Revue musicale* V (1829), pp. 16-18.

55. *Gazette musicale* I (1834), p. 327.

56. Fétis, "Baillot," *Biographie*, vol. I, p. 222.

57. Spohr, vol. II, p. 130.

58. Wasielewski, *Die Violine*, p. 392.

59. Fétis, *Biographie*, vol. I, p. 220.

60. Fétis, "Lafont," *Biographie*, vol. V, p. 163.

61. Spohr, vol. II, p. 129.

62. Julius M. Schottky, *Paganinis Leben und Treiben als Künstler und als Mensch* (Prague, 1830), pp. 300-301.

63. Ferdinand Hiller, *Ein Künstlerleben* (Cologne, 1880), vol. II, p. 53.

64. *Harmonicon* (London, 1830), p. 177.

65. P. Lichtenthal, quoted in de Courcy, *Paganini the Genoese* (Norman, OK, 1957; reprint ed. New York, 1977), vol. I, p. 150.

66. Schumann, *Gesammelte Schriften*, vol. I, p. 191.

67. Schering, *Instrumentalkonzert*, p. 173.

68. Quoted in Wasielewski, *Die Violine*, p. 592.

Chapter 5

1. *Revue musicale* VI (1830), p. 122.

2. Mendelssohn, *Letters*, ed. G. Selden-Goth (New York, 1945), p. 190.

3. Chopin, *Letters*, trans. E. L. Voynich, ed. H. Opienski (New York, 1931), p. 154.

4. Cf. Einstein, *Mozart*, p. 114.

5. Curtius, p. 69.

6. T. de Wyzewa and G. de Saint-Foix, "Un maître inconnu de Mozart," *Sammelbände der Internationalen Musikgesellschaft* X (November 1908), pp. 35-41.

7. G. de Saint-Foix, "Jean Schobert," *Revue musicale* III (August 1922), p. 122.

8. Quoted in Einstein, *Mozart*, p. 296.

9. G. de Saint-Foix, "Les six sonates de Méhul," *Revue musicale* VII (November 1925), pp. 43-66.

10. Pougin, *Méhul*, pp. 36-37.

11. Cf. G. de Saint-Foix, "J. L. Adam," *Revue musicale* VI (June 1925), pp. 209-15. Also G. Favre, Preface to Boieldieu's *Sonatas* (Paris, 1944).

12. Cf. G. de Saint-Foix, "Les frères Jadin, *Revue musicale* VI (August 1925). Also G. Favre, Preface.

13. H. Riemann, *Geschichte der Musik seit Beethoven*, pp. 312-13.

14. Fétis, "Boieldieu," *Biographie*, vol. II, p. 3.

15. G. de Saint-Foix, "Boieldieu," *Revue musicale* VII (February 1926), p. 107.

16. Fétis, "Boieldieu."

17. Catalogue in G. Favre, *Boieldieu* (Paris, 1944), vol. I, pp. 297-305.

18. Cf. letter of L. Jadin dated 29 October 1834, published in *Le Ménestrel* on 9 November 1834. Quoted in Favre, *Boieldieu*, vol. I, p. 89.

19. Favre, Preface, p. XXVI.

20. *Allgemeine musikalische Zeitung* IV (December 1801), pp. 226-27.

21. Favre, Preface.

22. Ibid.

23. Ibid.

24. Ibid., p. XXIV.

25. G. de Saint-Foix, "Boieldieu," p. 108.

26. Favre, Preface, p. XXXII.

27. Schumann, *Gesammelte Schriften*, vol. III, p. 156.

28. Ibid., vol. I, p. 151.

29. F. Chopin, *Selected Correspondence*, ed. Arthur Hedley (New York, 1963; reprint ed. New York, 1980), p. 93. (Letter to A. Kumelski, 18 November 1831).

30. Schering, *Instrumentalkonzert*, p. 187.

31. Schumann, *Gesammelte Schriften*, vol. I, pp. 174-175.

32. Ibid., vol. I, pp. 171-72.

33. Schering, *Instrumentalkonzert*, p. 188.

Chapter 6

1. Republished by Edition Senart (Paris, 1923), ed. G. de Saint-Foix.

2. Saint-Foix, "Boieldieu," *Revue musicale* VII (February 1926), p. 107.

3. Favre, *Boieldieu*, vol. II, p. 31.

4. Cf. Einstein, *Mozart*, pp. 114-16.

5. Mendelssohn, *Letters*, p. 33.

6. Hugo Riemann, "Paer," *Musik-Lexikon*, 12th ed.

7. Cobbett, "Rode," *Cyclopedic Survey*, vol. II, pp. 298-99.

8. Bellasis, p. 318.

9. Ibid.

10. Schumann, *Gesammelte Schriften*, vol. II, p. 140.

11. Ibid., vol. II, p. 141.

12. Ibid., vol. II, p. 132.

13. Quoted in Schemann, *Cherubini*, p. 637.

14. Schemann, pp. 642-44.

15. Maurice Emmanuel, *Antonin Reicha* (Paris, 1937).

16. *Journal des Débats*, 3 July 1836, quoted in Emmanuel, p. 22.

17. Ernst Bücken, *A. Reicha, sein Leben und seine Kompositionen* (Munich, 1912), p. 37.

18. Quoted in Emmanuel, p. 31.

19. Berlioz, *Memoirs*, ed. Newman, p. 46.

20. Ibid., p. 47.

21. Ibid., p. 46.

22. Spohr, *Autobiography*, vol. II, p. 131.

23. Bücken, *Reicha*, pp. 44-45.

24. Ibid., pp. 11-14.

25. *Allgemeine musikalische Zeitung* XX (1818), pp. 119 and 240-41; XXVII (1825), pp. 198ff. Quoted in Bücken, *Reicha*, pp. 43 and 120.

26. Berlioz, *Memoirs*, ed. Newman, p. 38.

27. Spohr, *Autobiography*, vol. II, p. 131.

28. Bücken, *Reicha*, p. 64.

29. W. H. Riehl, *Musikalische Charakteröpfe*, 4th ed. (Stuttgart, 1868), vol. I, pp. 294-95.

30. Schumann, *Gesammelte Schriften*, vol. II, pp. 131-32.

31. Cobbett, "Onslow," *Cyclopedic Survey*. See also Schwarz, "Onslow," *Die Musik in Geschichte und Gegenwart*.

32. G. Chouquet, "Onslow," *Grove Dictionary*, 3rd ed.

Chapter 7

1. Schemann, p. 31.

2. Ernest Newman, *Berlioz, Romantic and Classic*, ed. Peter Heyworth (London, 1972), p. 26.

Bibliography

Adam, Adolphe. *Derniers souvenirs d'un musicien.* Paris, 1859.

Adler, Guido. *Handbuch der Musikgeschichte.* Frankfurt am Main, 1924; 2nd ed. Berlin, 1930.

Ahlgrimm, Hans. *Pierre Rode. Ein Beitrag zur Geschichte des Violinkonzerts.* Dissertation, University of Vienna, 1929.

Apel, Willi, ed. *Harvard Dictionary of Music.* Cambridge, 1947; 2nd ed. Cambridge, 1969.

Artz, Frederick B. *France under the Bourbon Restoration.* Cambridge, 1931.

——————. *Reaction and Revolution.* Cambridge, 1934.

Babbitt, Irving. *Rousseau and Romanticism.* Boston, 1919.

Baillot, Pierre Marie François. *L'art du violon.* Paris, 1834.

——————. *Notice sur J. B. Viotti.* Paris, 1825.

Baldensperger, Fernand. *Sensibilité musicale et romantisme.* Paris, 1925.

Bartenstein, Hans. *H. Berlioz' Instrumentationkunst und ihre geschichtlichen Grundlagen.* Strassburg, 1939.

Barzun, Jacques. *Berlioz and the Romantic Century.* Boston, 1950; 2nd ed. as *Berlioz and His Century*, New York, 1956; 3rd ed. 1969.

——————. *Romanticism and the Modern Ego.* Boston, 1943.

Beethoven, Ludwig van. *The Letters of Beethoven.* Translated and edited by Emily Anderson. 3 vols. London/New York, 1961.

——————. *Sämtliche Briefe.* Edited by A. C. Kalischer. Berlin, 1907-08.

Bellasis, Edward. *Cherubini: Memorials Illustrative of His Life.* London, 1874.

Berlioz, Hector. *Correspondance générale.* Vol. I: 1803-1832. Paris, 1972.

——————. *Evenings with the Orchestra.* Translated and edited by Jacques Barzun. New York, 1956.

——————. *The Memoirs of Hector Berlioz.* Translated and edited by David Cairns. London 1969; 2nd ed. New York, 1975.

——————. *Memoirs.* Translated by R. and E. Holmes. Edited by Ernest

Newman. New York, 1932.

_____. *A Selection from His Letters.* Edited by Humphrey Searle. New York, 1966.

Berton, Henri Montan. *De la musique mécanique et de la musique philosophique.* Paris, 1826.

Botstiber, Hugo. *Geschichte der Ouvertüre und der freien Orchesterformen.* Leipzig, 1913.

Bouvet, Charles. *Spontini.* Paris, 1930.

Brancour, René. *Méhul.* Paris, 1913.

Brenet, Michel (Bobillier, Marie). *Les concerts en France sous l'ancien régime.* Paris, 1900; reprint ed. New York, 1970.

_____. "La librairie musicale en France de 1653 à 1790, d'après les registres de privilèges." *Sammelbände der Internationalen Musikgesellschaft* VIII (1907), pp. 401-466.

Brook, Barry S. "Symphonie concertante." *The New Grove Dictionary of Music and Musicians.* Edited by Stanley Sadie. London, 1980.

_____. "The Symphonie concertante: An Interim Report." *The Musical Quarterly* XLVII (1961), pp. 493-516.

_____. "The Symphonie concertante: Its Musical and Sociological Bases." *International Review of the Aesthetics and Sociology of Music* VI (1975), pp. 9-28.

_____. *La symphonie française dans la seconde moitié du XVIIIe siecle.* 3 vols. Paris, 1962.

Bücken, Ernst. *Anton Reicha, sein Leben und seine Kompositionen.* Munich, 1912.

_____. *Handbuch der Musikwissenschaft.* Vols. V and VI. Leipzig, 1928-34.

Buschkötter, Wilhelm. "Jean François Le Sueur: Eine Biographie." *Sammelbände der Internationalen Musikgesellschaft* XIV (1912-13), pp. 58-154.

Carse, Adam. *The Orchestra in the 18th Century.* Cambridge, 1940.

_____. *The Orchestra from Beethoven to Berlioz.* Cambridge, 1948.

Castil-Blaze (Blaze, François Henri J.). *L'Académie Imperiale de Musique de 1645 à 1855.* Paris, 1855.

_____. *Chapelle musique des Rois de France.* Paris, 1832.

Chabanon, Michel P. G. de. *Observations sur la musique et principalement sur la métaphysique de l'art.* Paris, 1779.

Charlton, David. "Méhul." *The New Grove Dictionary of Music and Musicians.* Edited by Stanley Sadie. London, 1980.

_____. *Orchestration and Orchestral Practice in Paris, 1789-1810.* Dissertation, University of Cambridge, 1973.

_____. Preface to Méhul's *Symphony No. 1.* Madison, WI, in preparation.

_____. Preface to Méhul's *Symphonies Nos. 3 and 4.* New York, 1982.

_____. "The Symphonies of Méhul." Paper presented at the Second Biennial Conference on 19th Century Music, Cambridge, 7 July 1980.

Chopin, Frederic. *Letters.* Translated by E. L. Voyniche. Edited by H. Opienski. New York, 1931.

_____. *Selected Correspondence.* Edited by Arthur Hedley. New York, 1963; reprint ed. New York, 1980.

Choron, Alexandre E. and Fayolle, F. J. M. *Dictionnaire historique des musiciens, artistes et amateurs.* Paris, 1810-11.

Cobbett, Walter W. *Cyclopedic Survey of Chamber Music.* London, 1929.

Combarieu, Jules. *Histoire de la musique.* Vol. II. Paris, 1935.

Cone, Edward T., ed. *Berlioz' Fantastic Symphony.* New York: Norton, 1971.

Courcy, Geraldine I. C. de. *Paganini the Genoese.* Norman, Oklahoma, 1957; reprint ed. New York, 1977.

Cucuel, Georges. "Quelques documents sur la librairie musicale au XVIIIe siècle." *Sammelbände der Internationalen Musikgesellschaft* XIII (1912), pp. 385-92.

Curtius, Ernst Robert. *The Civilization of France.* Translated by Olive Wyon. New York, 1932.

Curzon, Henri de. "History and Glory of the Concert Hall of the Paris Conservatoire." *The Musical Quarterly* III (1917), pp. 304-18.

_____. *Musiciens du temps passé.* Paris, 1893.

Dahms, Walter. *Schubert.* Berlin, 1914.

Dandelot, Arthur. *La Société des Concerts du Conservatoire de 1828 à 1897.* Paris, 1898.

Dauge, Maurice. "La Révolution francaise et la musique." *Le Ménestrel* XCVI (1934), pp. 169-70 and 177-80.

David, Hans Theodor. *Johann Schobert als Sonatenkomponist.* Kassel, 1928.

Davies, T. R. *French Romanticism and the Press. The Globe.* Cambridge, 1906.

Della Corte, Andrea. *Paesiello.* Turin, 1922.

Deschamps, Emile. *La préface des etudes françaises et étrangères: Un manifeste du romantisme.* Paris, 1923.

Deutsch, Otto Erich. *The Schubert Reader.* New York, 1947.

Dickinson, Alan E. F. *The Music of Berlioz.* New York, 1973.

Dietz, Max. *Geschichte des musikalischen Dramas in Frankreich während der Revolution.* Vienna, 1885-86.

Dufrane, Louis. *Gossec, sa vie, ses oeuvres.* Paris, 1927.

Dumesnil, René. *La musique romantique française.* Paris, 1944.

Eckardt, Hans. *Die Musikanschauung der französischen Romantik.* Kassel, 1935.

Einstein, Alfred. "Beethoven's Military Style." In *Essays on Music,* pp. 243-49. London, 1958.

_____. *Mozart, His Character, His Work.* Translated by Arthur Mendel and Nathan Broder. New York, 1945.

_____. *Music in the Romantic Era.* New York, 1947.

Elwart, Antoine A. *Histoire de la Société des Concerts du Conservatoire impériale de musique.* Paris, 1860.

Emmanuel, Maurice. *Antonin Reicha.* Paris, 1937.

Encyclopédie de la musique et dictionnaire du Conservatoire. Part I, vol. III. Paris, 1931.

Engel, Hans. *Das Instrumentalkonzert.* 2 vols. Wiesbaden, 1971.

Escudier, Léon. *Mes souvenirs. Les virtuoses.* Paris, 1868.

Escudier, Marie et Léon. *Vie et aventures des cantatrices célèbres. Musiciens de l'Empire.* Paris, 1856.

Evans, Raymond L. *Les romantiques français et la musique.* Paris, 1934.

Expert, Henri. Preface to Kreutzer's *42 Caprices.* Paris: Senart, 1915.

Favre, Georges. *Boieldieu: Sa vie, son oeuvre.* Paris, 1944-45.

—————. "Les créateurs de l'école française de piano: Nicolas Séjan." *Revue de musicologie* XVII (May, 1936), pp. 70-78.

—————. "L'école française de Piano-Forte avant Boieldieu." Introduction to Boieldieu *Sonates pour le Piano-Forte.* Paris: Droz, 1944.

Fayolle, François. *Paganini et Beriot.* Paris, 1831.

Fétis, François J. *Biographie universelle des musiciens.* 2nd ed. Paris, 1860-65.

Flesch, Carl. *Die Kunst des Violinspiels.* Berlin, 1928.

Foster, Myles Birket. *History of the Philharmonic Society of London.* London, 1912.

Franks, Richard Nelson. *George Onslow (1784-1853): A Study of His Life, Family, and Works.* Dissertation, University of Texas, Austin, 1981.

Gaudefroy-Demombynes, Jean. *Histoire de la musique française.* Paris, 1946.

Gelrud, Paul Geoffrey. *A Critical Study of the French Violin School (1782-1882).* Dissertation, Cornell University, Ithaca, New York, 1941.

Gerber, Ernst Ludwig. *Neues historisch-biographisches Lexicon der Tonkünstler.* Leipzig, 1812-14.

Giazotto, Remo. *Giovan Battista Viotti.* Milan, 1956.

Grétry, A. E. M. *Mémoires ou Essais sur la musique.* Paris, 1789; reprint ed. New York, 1971.

Hanslick, Eduard. *Aus dem Concert-Saal.* Vienna, 1870.

Hardy, Joseph. *Rodolphe Kreutzer. Sa jeunesse à Versailles, 1766-1789.* Paris, 1910.

Hellouin, Frédéric. *Gossec et la musique française à la fin du 18e siècle.* Paris, 1903.

Hellouin, Frédéric and Picard, Joseph. *Catel. Un musicien oublié.* Paris, 1910.

Hensel, Sebastian. *Die Familie Mendelssohn.* Berlin, 1880.

Hiller, Ferdinand. *Ein Künstlerleben.* Cologne, 1880.

Hoffman, Ernst Theodor Amadeus. *Beethovens Instrumentalmusik (Kreisleriana).* Bamberg, ca. 1816; revised ed. Regensburg, 1919.

Hohenemser, Richard. *Luigi Cherubini: sein Leben und seine Werke.* Leipzig, 1913.

Hopkinson, Cecil. *A Dictionary of Parisian Music Publishers, 1700-1950.* London, 1954; reprint ed. New York, 1979.

Jahn, Otto and Abert, Hermann. *W. A. Mozart.* Leipzig, 1919-21.

Joachim, Joseph and Moser, Andreas. *Violinschule.* Vol. III. Berlin, 1905.

Jullien, Adolphe. *Paris dilettante au commencement du siècle.* Paris, 1884.

Kapp, Julius. *Berlioz.* Berlin, 1917.

—————. *Paganini.* 5th and 6th eds. Berlin, 1920.

Kolneder, Walter. *Das Buch der Violine.* Zurich, 1972.

Kretzschmar, Hermann. *Geschichte der Oper.* Leipzig, 1919.

—————. "Die musikgeschichtliche Bedeutung Simon Mayrs." *Jahrbuch musikbibliothek Peters* XI (1904), pp. 27-41.

—————. "Über die Bedeutung von Cherubinis Ouvertüren und Hauptopern für die Gegenwart." *Jahrbuch der Musikbibliothek Peters* XIII (1906), pp.

77-91.

La Borde, Jean B. de. *Essai sur la musique ancienne et moderne.* Paris, 1780-81.

Lacépède, B. G. E. de. *La poétique de la musique.* Paris, 1785.

Laforêt, Claude. *La vie musicale au temps romantique.* Paris, 1929, reprint ed. New York, 1977.

—————. "La vie musicale au temps romantique." *Revue musicale* X (1929), pp. 16-24 and 218-31.

La Laurencie, Lionel de. "L'apparition des oeuvres d'Haydn à Paris." *Revue de musicologie* XIII (November 1932), pp. 191-205.

La Laurencie, Lionel de. "Les débuts de la musique de chambre en France." *Revue de musicologie* XV (1934), pp. 25-34, 86-96, 159-67, 204-31.

—————. *L'école française de violon de Lully à Viotti.* Paris, 1922-24.

La Laurencie, L. de and Saint-Foix, Georges de. "Contribution à l'histoire de la symphonie en France vers 1750." *Année musicale* (1911), pp. 1-123.

Lamy, F. *Le Sueur: Essai de contribution à l'histoire de la musique française.* Paris, 1912.

Landon, H. C. Robbins. *The Symphonies of Joseph Haydn.* London, 1955.

Lang, Paul Henry. *Music in Western Civilization.* New York, 1941.

Larsen, Jens Peter. *Die Haydn-Überlieferung.* Copenhagen, 1939.

Lassabathie, Theodore. *Histoire du Conservatoire impérial de musique et de déclamation.* Paris, 1860.

Lavoix, Henri, fils. *Histoire de l'instrumentation depuis le XVIe siècle.* Paris, 1878.

—————. *La musique française.* Paris, 1891.

Liszt, Franz, "De la situation des artistes et de leur condition dans la société." In *Pages romantiques,* pp. 1-83. Edited by J. Chantavoine. Paris, 1912.

Litzmann, Berthold. *Clara Schumann.* Leipzig, 1909; English trans. London, 1913; reprint ed. New York, 1980.

Locke, Arthur Ware. *Music and the Romantic Movement in France.* London, 1920.

Loewenberg, Alfred. *Annals of Opera, 1597-1940.* Cambridge, 1943; 2nd ed. Geneva, 1955; 3rd ed. Totowa, New Jersey, 1978.

Lorenz, Alfred. *Musikgeschichte im Rhythmus der Generationen.* Berlin, 1928.

Lucas-Dubreton, Jean. *Restoration and the July Monarchy.* Translated by E. F. Buckley. London, 1929.

Luguet, Henri. *Etude sur G. Onslow.* Clermont-Ferrand, 1889.

Madelin, Louis. *La Révolution.* Paris, 1911.

—————. *L'Empire.* Paris, 1915.

Mason, Daniel Gregory. *The Romantic Composers.* New York, 1940.

Mendelssohn-Bartholdy, Felix. *Briefe aus den Jahren 1830-1847.* Leipzig, 1875.

—————. *Letters.* Edited by G. Selden-Goth. New York, 1945.

—————. *Reisebriefe* (1821-1832). Munich, 1947.

Méreaux, Jean A. L. de. *Les clavecinistes de 1637 à 1790.* Paris, 1867.

Mersmann, Hans. *Die Kammermusik: Führer durch den Konzertsaal.* Leipzig, 1933.

Miel, E. F. A. M. "Notice historique sur Viotti." *Biographie universelle Michaud* XLIX.

Moscheles, Ignaz. *Recent Music and Musicians.* Translated by A. D. Coleridge. New York, 1873; reprint ed. New York, 1970.

Moser, Andreas. *Geschichte des Violinspiels.* Berlin, 1923; 2nd ed., revised H. J. Nösselt, Munich, 1966.

_____. *Joseph Joachim, ein Lebensbild.* 2nd ed. Berlin, 1908-10.

Moser, Friedrich (pseud. F. M.). *Pierre Rode.* Berlin, 1831.

Mozart, W. A. *The Letters of Mozart and His Family.* Translated by Emily Anderson. London, 1938.

Müller, Gottfried. *Daniel Steibelt: Sein Leben und Klavierwerke* (Etüden und Sonaten). Strassburg, 1933.

Nef, Karl. *Geschichte der Sinfonie und der Suite.* Leipzig, 1921.

Newman, Ernest. *Berlioz, Romantic and Classic.* Edited by Peter Heyworth. London, 1972.

_____. "Berlioz, Romantic and Classic." In *Musical Studies*, pp. 3-67. London, 1905; 2nd ed. London, 1910.

Niecks, Frederick. "Romanticism in Music." *Musical Times* XL (1 December 1899), pp. 802-05.

d'Ortigue, Joseph. *De la guerre des dilettanti, ou de la révolution opérée par Rossini dans l'opéra françois.* Paris, 1829.

Pater, Walter. *Appreciations: With an Essay on Style.* London, 1890.

Pierre, Constant. *Le Conservatoire national de musique et de déclamation: Documents historiques et administratifs.* Paris, 1900.

_____. *L'école de chant à l'opéra de 1672 a 1807.* Paris, 1896.

_____. *Les facteurs d'instruments de musique.* Paris, 1893.

_____. *Histoire du Concert spirituel.* Edited by François Lesure. Paris, 1975.

_____. *Les hymnes et chansons de la Révolution: Aperçu général et catalogue.* Paris, 1904.

Pincherle, Marc. *Feuillets d'histoire du violon.* Paris, 1927.

_____. *Les violonistes compositeurs et virtuoses.* Paris, 1922.

Pougin, Arthur. *Boieldieu.* Paris, 1875.

_____. *Herold.* Paris, 1906.

_____. "La jeunesse d'Herold." *Revue et Gazette musicale* XLVII (1880), pp. 138-321 passim.

_____. *Méhul. Sa vie, son génie, son caractère.* Paris, 1893.

_____. *Notice sur Rode.* Paris, 1874.

_____. *Viotti et l'école moderne du violon.* Paris, 1888.

Prod'homme, Jacques Gabriel. *Les symphonies de Beethoven.* Paris, 1906; reprint ed. New York, 1977.

Reichardt, Johann Friedrich. *Vertraute Briefe aus Paris, geschrieben in den Jahren 1802 und 1803.* Hamburg, 1804.

Riehl, Wilhelm Heinrich. "G. Onslow." In *Musikalische Charakteröpfe*, vol. I, pp. 293-306, 4th ed. Stuttgart, 1868.

_____. "Viotti und das Geigenduett." In *Musikalische Charakteröpfe*, vol. III, pp. 51-92.

Riemann, Hugo. *Dictionnaire de musique.* Paris, 1931.

_____. *Geschichte der Musik seit Beethoven (1800-1900).* Berlin, 1901.

——————. *Musiklexikon.* 12th ed. Mainz, 1959.

Ringer, Alexander. "The Chasse as a Musical Topic of the 18th Century." *Journal of the American Musicological Society* VI (1953), pp. 148-54.

——————. "A French Symphonist at the Time of Beethoven: Etienne Nicolas Méhul." *The Musical Quarterly* XXXVII (1951), pp. 543-565.

Rolland, Romain. *Essays on Music.* New York, 1948.

Sachs, Curt. *The Commonwealth of Art.* New York, 1946.

Saint-Foix, Georges de. "Les premiers pianistes Parisiens." *Revue musicale* III (August 1922), pp. 121-36; "Jean Schobert."

Ibid., *Revue musicale* IV (April 1923), pp. 193-205; "N. J. Hüllmandel."

Ibid., *Revue musicale* V (June 1924), pp. 187-97; "Edelmann."

Ibid., pp. 192-98; "Riegel."

Ibid., *Revue musicale* VI (June 1925), pp. 209-15; "J. L. Adam."

Ibid., *Revue musicale* VI (August 1925), pp. 105-09; "Les frères Jadin."

Ibid., *Revue musicale* VII (November 1925), pp. 43-46; "Les six sonates de Méhul."

Ibid., *Revue musicale* VII (February 1926), pp. 102-10; "Boieldieu."

Schemann, Ludwig. *Cherubini.* Stuttgart, 1925.

Schering, Arnold. "Aus den Jugendjahren der musikalischen Neuromantik." *Jahrbuch der Musikbibliothek Peters* XXIV (1917), pp. 45-63.

——————. *Geschichte des Instrumentalkonzerts.* Leipzig, 1905; 2nd ed. Leipzig, 1927; reprint ed. 1965.

——————. "Kritik des romantischen Begriffs." *Jahrbuch der Muskbibliothek Peters* XLIV (1937), pp. 9-28.

Schindler, Anton. *Beethoven in Paris.* Münster, 1842.

Schletterer, H. M. *Studien zur Geschichte der französischen Musik.* Berlin, 1884-1885.

Schottky, Julius M. *Paganinis Leben und Treiben als Künstler und als Mensch.* Prague, 1830.

Schrade, Leo. *Beethoven in France.* New Haven, 1942; reprint ed. 1978.

Schünemann, Georg. *Geschichte des Dirigiens.* Leipzig, 1913; reprint ed. 1978.

Schumann, Robert. *Gesammelte Schriften über Musik und Musiker.* 3 vols. Leipzig: Reclam, 1888; 5th ed. 1914.

——————. *On Music and Musicians.* Edited by Konrad Wolff. Translated by Paul Rosenfeld. New York, 1946.

Schwarz, Boris. "Beethoven and the French Violin School." *The Musical Quarterly* XLIV (1958), pp. 431-47.

——————. *Great Masters of the Violin: From Corelli and Vivaldi to Stern, Zukerman and Perlman.* New York, 1983.

——————. "Problems of Chronology in the Works of G. B. Viotti." In *International Musicological Society, Report of the Eleventh Congress, Copenhagen 1972,* Vol. II, pp. 644-47. Copenhagen, 1974.

Schwarz, Boris, ed. *The Symphonies of Onslow and Herold.* New York, 1981.

Sondheimer, Robert. "Gluck in Paris." *Zeitschrift für Musikwissenschaft* V (1922), pp. 165-75.

Spohr, Louis. *Autobiography.* Translated from the German. London, 1878; reprint ed. 1969.

_____. *Lebenserinnerungen.* Edited by Folker Göthel. Tutzing, 1968.

Stendhal (Beyle, Henri). *Racine et Shakespeare. Etudes sur le romantisme.* Paris, 1823.

_____. *Vie de Rossini.* Paris, 1823; new ed. by Henri Prunières, Paris, 1922.

Striffling, Louis. *Esquisse d'une histoire du goût musical en France au XVIIIe siècle.* Paris, 1912.

Strobel, Heinrich. "Die Opern von E. N. Méhul." *Zeitschrift für Muskwissenschaft* VI (April 1924), pp. 362-402.

Thayer, Alexander W. *The Life of Beethoven.* Edited by Henry Krehbiel. New York, 1921. German translation by Hermann Deiters, last two volumes edited by Hugo Riemann. 5 vols. Berlin and Leipzig, 1866-1908.

_____. *The Life of Beethoven.* Edited by Elliot Forbes. Princeton, New Jersey, 1964; 2nd ed. 1967.

Themelis, Dimitris. *Etude ou Caprice.* Munich, 1967.

Tiersot, Julien. *Les fêtes et les chants de la Révolution française.* Paris, 1908.

_____. *Hector Berlioz et la société de son temps.* Paris, 1904.

_____. *La musique au temps romantique.* Paris, 1930.

_____. "La symphonie en France." *Zeitschrift der Internationalen Musikgesellschaft* III (July 1902), pp. 391-402.

Toye, Francis. *Rossini: A Study in Tragi-Comedy.* New York, 1934.

Turner, W. J. *Berlioz: The Man and His Work.* London, 1939; reprint ed. New York, 1974.

Vallat, Gustave. *Etudes d'histoire, de moeurs et d'art musical sur la fin du XVIIIe siècle et la première moitié du XIXe siècle.* Paris, 1890.

Vernaelde, Albert. "La société des concerts et les grandes associations symphoniques." In *Encyclopédie de la musique et dictionnaire du Conservatoire,* Part II, vol. VI, pp. 3684-3714. Paris, 1931.

Vidal, Antoine. *Les instruments à archet.* Paris, 1876.

Wasielewski, Wilhelm Joseph von. *Ludwig van Beethoven.* 2nd ed. Leipzig, 1895.

_____. *Die Violine und ihre Meister.* 5th ed. Leipzig, 1919.

Weber, Carl Maria von. *Sämtliche Schriften.* Edited by Georg Kaiser. Berlin, 1908.

Williams, Michael Day. *The Violin Concertos of Rodolphe Kreutzer.* Dissertation, Indiana University, Bloomington, 1972.

Wright, C. H. Conrad. *A History of French Literature.* New York, 1912.

Wyzewa, Théodore de. "A propos du centenaire de la mort de Joseph Haydn." *Revue des deux mondes* (15 June 1909), pp. 935-46.

Wyzewa, Théodore de and Saint-Foix, Georges de. "Un maître inconnu de Mozart." *Zeitschrift der Internationalen Musikgesellschaft* X (1908-09), pp. 35-41.

_____. *W. A. Mozart: Sa vie musicale et son oeuvre.* Vol. II, Paris, 1912; Vol. III, Paris, 1936; reprint ed. New York, 1980.

Index

DATE DUE

4-30-87			
ILL: 3052061			
Alma College			
ILL 668105 9-28-95			

DEMCO 38-297